The Samurai

Other works by Julia Kristeva
published by Columbia

Desire in Language: A Semiotic Approach to Literature and Art

Revolution in Poetic Language

Powers of Horror: An Essay on Abjection

The Kristeva Reader

Tales of Love

In the Beginning Was Love: Psychoanalysis and Faith

Language: The Unknown

Black Sun: Depression and Melancholia

Strangers to Ourselves

Nations Without Nationalism

The Samurai

A Novel

Julia Kristeva

Translated by Barbara Bray

Columbia University Press
New York

Columbia University Press wishes to express its appreciation for assistance given by the government of France through Le Ministère de la Culture in the preparation of the translation.

Columbia University Press
New York   Oxford

Library of Congress Cataloging-in-Publication Data

Kristeva, Julia, 1941–
   [Samouraïs. English]
   The samurai :   a novel / Julia Kristeva; translated by Barbara Bray
      p.   cm.
   ISBN 0-231-07542-1
   I. Title.
PQ2671.R547S2513   1992
843'.914—dc20   92–22714
                                                         CIP

Casebound editions of
Columbia University Press books
are Smyth-sewn and printed
on permanent and durable
acid-free paper.

Designed by Teresa Bonner
Printed in the United States of America
c 10 9 8 7 6 5 4 3 2 1

Contents

PART I   *Atlantic*   5

PART II   *Saint-André-des-Arts*   71

PART III   *Chinese*   143

PART IV   *Algonquin*   211

PART V   *Luxembourg*   291

Memory is like
a soldier's
courage: it has
no room
for hypocrisy.
—STENDHAL

The Samurai

June 24, 1989

There are no love stories anymore. And yet women want them, and so do men when they're not ashamed of being tender and sad like women. But men are all in a hurry to make money, and to die. They beget children in order to survive, or else when they forget and talk to themselves as if they weren't talking to themselves, in the midst of pleasure or in its absence. They're always taking planes, high-speed metros, high-speed trains, space shuttles. They don't have time to look at that pink acacia stretching out its branches toward the clouds and the strips of sunlit blue silk in between; the pink acacia with its tiny quivering leaves and the light fragrance that the bees turn into honey.

Olga feels at home now in the scarcely visible, sweet-smelling shade. The tree has been there for more than twenty years, ever since she came to this country, which means in a way that she and the tree are the same age; or, more accurately, that her love is as old as the acacia. Hervé is there too, in the hammock under the umbrella pines. He's listening to Haydn's Quartet No. 50: the triplets, the rapid waltz rhythm, the swiftness as smooth and clear as himself and as the ocean in front of him.

How am I sure they're there, under the acacia by the Atlantic? I scarcely know them, I pass them in the street in Paris, patients who are friends of theirs talk to me about them. . . . So I can visualize the scene. They're together because they're separate. What they call love is this shared fidelity to their individual independence. It keeps them young; they look like teenagers, children almost. What do they want? To be alone together. To play at being alone together, tossing the ball back and forth between them now and again to show there isn't any resentment in their solitudes.

My patients tell me about their emotional troubles, and make sure they suffer from them. But these two just lick their wounds like wild animals and calmly carry on.

Love, while it lasts, reaches right down into our predilections until all our five senses submerge us in pain or delight. Love is said to last when the adventurers involved manage to bind up their wounds, when the skin heals, and they start to look at each other again like Narcissus contemplating himself in the water. It calls for a lot of patience and a great respect for time. Where love's concerned, you have to take good care of time.

Not time in the sense of duration—that's just a spin-off from the art of loving—but time in the sense of the magic that transforms a moment of perception, disquiet, or happiness into a gift. The gift of a word, a gesture, a look. Just a little sound to show you I'm taking you with me, that we like being here together under the acacia and the pine, in this whirl of flowers, waves, quartets, migraine, and backache. That's how the sensation of time is born. And once given, these perceptible moments join up into minute acts. Though they come out of the void, they join together and bear us up. So it's obvious that time can't exist without love. Time is the love of little things, of dreams, of desires. You don't have time because you don't have enough love. You waste your time when you don't love. You forget times past when you haven't anything to say to anyone. Or else you're the prisoner of a false time that doesn't pass.

The love of death, the desire for death, is a secret to which we shut our eyes so that we may look and not see, so that we may sleep and dream.

If we didn't shut our eyes, we'd see only emptiness, black, white, and broken shapes.

So I shut my eyes and imagine the story of Olga, Hervé, Martin, Marie-Paule, Carole, and a few others whom you know or could have known. A story I am involved in myself—but only remotely, very remotely.

I. Atlantic

1

She put down the two worn russet leather cases on the baggage counter, brushed her lips against Mama's and Papa's damp cheeks, gave Dan what was taken to be an amorous wink, climbed the steps to the Tupolev without looking back, spent three and a half hours on the plane without thinking of counting the minutes—her head was empty and there was nothing but the taste of tannin in her mouth—and landed in a gray and muddy Paris. Flakes of snow were endlessly falling and melting. The so-called City of Light didn't exist—the French didn't know how to clear snow away. Her disappointment was complete: she could feel it from the saltiness in her throat. Of course, Boris wasn't waiting for her at Orly, and five dollars was all she had on her. No laughing matter. Disaster.

"May I give you a lift to the embassy? I'm being met by an official car."

The fat woman who'd sat next to her on the plane, obviously the wife of some dignitary, used a smooth voice to conceal her ugliness. (How long had she been doing it? Ever since she was a child, ever since she realized she was unattractive, ever since she realized how humiliating it was to belong to the powers that be . . .)

"May I . . . ?"

Olga, of course, said she might, though it only postponed her problem. The leatherette armchairs were official too, as were the faded paper and the atrocious pictures by young avant-garde painters hanging on the walls—the whole embassy was ugly and official, pointless and cold. Twenty-two years of life back home had crystallized into a few maxims, also official and dull. "If you have a problem, consider the possibilities . . . consider the possibilities . . . consider the possibilities . . ." The phrase irritated her like a series of pinpricks, and the cold of the official drawing room was becoming depressing. "Consider the possibilities . . ." But there was no face, nothing you could come to grips with.

"Albert Lévy!—you here? I thought you were in New York. Just passing through? I don't think you know Olga Morena. Olga, may I introduce . . ."

The smooth voice of the dignitary's wife shook Olga out of the quiet panic that had started to numb her.

"May I . . . ?"

Again Olga of course said she might, all the more willingly because she knew Albert Lévy, or at least had read some of his work.

"Have you really? Well, I never!" said the tough, lean little man standing there like one of those small rock plants that can withstand all weather.

He'd just published a collection of articles on the Thaw—rather mediocre pieces, but passionate and severe. Olga had written a long review naively praising them. And the next day both she and Lévy were slaughtered by the official critic. Her parents began to be frightened again, and to listen anxiously for the sound of the elevator in the small hours. Was it "them," the

officials, coming to haul them off to some interrogation or—
who knows?—some camp? But no, "they" forgot about them this
time.

Albert Lévy didn't need to have things explained to him.
Olga's wide eyes, gazing keenly at him through the yellow half-
light of the embassy, might have seemed to convey some erotic
invitation. But they held only avid interest, mingled with wonder
and fear.

"We'll have dinner first; then, if you have no objections, you
can go and stay with Véra, my Parisian pen pal."

Olga had no objections. She wanted to trust that strange face,
in which mischievous lips contradicted the permanent melancholy of the eyes. She never saw him again. Years later she
heard by chance that he'd died of old age, or boredom, or both.

And so it took her only a dozen or so hours to land on Lévy's
friendly irony and Véra's gruff shyness. Sympathy: the most
insipid of feelings, but as unchanging as a Chinese screen. A
worn-out word that doesn't mean anything anymore. But she
couldn't find a better one: it seemed the most apt for here and
now. One of those colorless words that you finally adopt not
because there's nothing better but because there's nothing simpler, because you're overwhelmed by thwarted tenderness. One
of the words that spring from elementary things, like the quiver
you felt in the pit of your stomach, in Véra's kitchen, at the
smell of toast or hot milk, or the strong, safe taste of stewed tea.
. . . Outside, Paris, the City of Light, went on melting away
under the sloppy snow. The whole place could turn to water—
Olga was in no hurry. She'd stopped being in a hurry, for the
moment.

She'd put him (Dan) in parentheses; she'd separated herself
from them (her parents) as by a cesarean section. She hadn't any
feeling or awareness (of being brutal or grasping). She was free.
Empty. With the detachment of astronauts. Of orphans. Of
foreigners (male and female). Of libertines (male and female)
who indulge in all kinds of games precisely because they feel
themselves to be detached, out of the world, tough and ascetic,
blank pages ready to record every sort of experience (until the
time comes when the very memory of them has faded away).
Her own memory was putting a damper on itself. She was ready

to translate it. To betray it. She was an active body with an active soul, in a state of weightlessness.

Ivan absorbed Parisian slang voraciously, reproducing it in his incorrigible Slav accent. He'd just translated a collection of contemporary poetics for Hervé Sinteuil's celebrated series *Now*, published by the Editions de l'Autre, and regarded himself with some justification as somebody in the swim.

"You were crazy to rely on Boris—he's completely Frenchified. You didn't imagine he was going to lend you any money? Your grant doesn't begin for another two months? You really are nuts, leaping into the void like that! Oh well, you can pay Véra back bit by bit. . . . Come along, help yourself—it's duck with ginger. Terrific, isn't it? Haven't you ever had it before?"

He was generous, Ivan, and hospitable, with his Chinese restaurant, his knowledge, and his information. A little tart perhaps, as if restrained by his own dogged ambition.

"So, as I said, don't waste your time at the Sorbonne—it's square, impossibly square . . . do you know the word? I go to Armand Bréhal's seminars at the Ecole d'Etudes Supérieures—he's the neatest prof there is, an artist in concepts. The other day he got Hervé Sinteuil—haven't you heard of him?—to talk about Mallarmé. Sublime! But as you'll have to go back home one day, and as you are, after all, a Marxist . . . well, more or less . . . I suppose . . . I advise you to go and see Edelman. But do as you like. . . . Have some rice—don't be shy. While you're here, take everything you're offered. And above all, work, and work hard. That's our only advantage—work: the French won't do a hand's turn if they can help it. . . . Yes, Edelman's the chap for you. . . ."

So Edelman it was! Graying, potbellied, smiling, with his shirt open and of course no tie, he addressed everyone by the familiar *tu* and was always ripping up existentialism and lauding dialectical reason (as overhauled by Pascal), alienation, and the New Novel.

"Olga who? From the East? Tomorrow at five o'clock at my place . . ."

The big flakes melted on her cheeks like vanilla ice cream on the tongue. The bare chestnut branches didn't hold the whiteness but shone gray and black like eels just out of a pond. A kind of dirty mush was building up on the sidewalk and sticking to the soles of the handsome boots Véra had bought her, which were more for show than for wear. The boulevard du Montparnasse sloped up toward the Observatory, invisible through the haze; passing cars spattered pedestrians with mud. Women looked in dismay at the marks on their coats; children tried in vain to make snowballs, which melted right away; men (as usual) thought only of their desires. Edelman's apartment building, with its white marble staircase and red carpet, was a comfortable if showy refuge for middle-class citizens even keener than usual to get home and sit by the fire, surrounded by the family heirlooms that seem especially reassuring in such weather.

She met Fabien Edelman on the stairs. He'd forgotten about their appointment. He apologized, but it didn't matter—he had a few minutes to spare, they'd go and have a cup of coffee. He held out a large, warm, limp hand like a shovel a child might make out of modeling clay, then led the way to a nearby tearoom behind a pastry cook's shop.

Edelman talked a lot. Olga didn't understand all of it.

"It's impossible to stop being interested in the world, and at the same time impossible to find peace in it. Man needs some kind of totality—God, the Future, Structure, the Other (call it what you like, it comes to the same thing)—on whose existence he can only wager . . ."

(Yes, it was impossible . . . She herself took an interest in everything, yet she too loved peace. As for "totalities," what were they? She'd have to see . . . And she did need something, certainly—but what?)

"The Jansenists, who reflected the spirituality of the legal aristocracy then excluded from power, understood all this. From the time that Jean Duvergier de Hauranne, abbé of Saint-Cyran, was arrested and Antoine de Maître, the first of the Port-Royal solitaries, went into retreat—from then until the first performance of *Phèdre* the message is clear: it's impossible to lead a good life in the world. . . ."*

("How do people live in Paris?" wrote Mama, suddenly af-

---

* In the seventeenth century, Port-Royal, an ancient Cistercian convent, became a center of Jansenism (an austere theological doctrine based on predestination) and a political bone of contention. Racine was a pupil there. Jansenism was espoused by Pascal and opposed by the Jesuits, who feared it as a rival, especially in the field of education. Louis XIV and the Pope both persecuted the Jansenists, and the convent of Port-Royal was destroyed in 1712. *Tr.*

fecting elegance. They protest. They think things are "'im-possible.'" They speak well and eat well. So much ephemeral beauty disappearing down luxurious lavender-scented toilets. Are they perfumed with lavender in this tearoom? Or with wild pine?)

". . . Admittedly it's only divine judgment that dooms man to tragedy. But although God isn't here anymore, the longing for community and a universe hasn't disappeared. Pascal was the first to experience it. *Deus absconditus. Vere tu es Deus absconditus.* God is hidden. . . . So what does Pascal do? He makes a wager, and so do we, but on a certainty that's uncertain. The future; fame; structure; a game of roulette; chance itself—you can't be sure of any of them, but you take the plunge. Well, it's this paradox that's at the heart of tragedy. Man can neither avoid nor accept it."

The coffee cup tilted awkwardly in Edelman's shovels, threatening to spill at any moment. He automatically gulped down first a salami sandwich and then a cheese one.

"Tragedy actually consists in the paradox. At least that's the way I see it."

(Even when you laugh at clowns, you're laughing at paradox. Nothing like slapstick for ramming paradox down your throat!)

". . . 'Two infinites, one middle.' 'Nothing can define the finite between two infinites.' Is that a call for moderation? No—for the heartbreak of paradox!"

"Isn't that rather depressing?"

She got out her camera. She couldn't bear to think of all that lovely food, so beautifully presented, just disappearing without a trace down the toilet. She couldn't swallow a morsel herself. Photography is a defense against disappearance. A weapon against water-closets. No more waste—everything saved for eternity. But what if the waste mounts up to eternity? Would that be tragic or comic? Photography is paradoxical. Flash. The snap's taken.

"So you film objects, do you? You must be interested in the New Novel." (Edelman was obviously quick on the uptake.) "The New Novel is merely a tragic vision controlled by the commodities that have taken the place of God. Stories about things. God's not just hidden—He's been absorbed into the consumer society, and it's from there that He contemplates us. Life is nothing more now than merchandise being contemplated by the deification of merchandise."

"We can neither know with certainty nor absolutely not know." (Olga at last managed to show how well educated she was, meanwhile taking several snaps of a couple of chocolate éclairs. One was vanilla-flavored and one praline, but they lay there untouched: she still couldn't touch anything to eat.)

"To sum up," the philosopher went on, "I consider you have a future. We'll extend your grant and you'll work under me."

(All she'd done was take some photographs. She hadn't said anything. Was silence always golden?)

"You haven't finished your éclairs. But we mustn't leave anything for the capitalists!" said Edelman, devouring them. "So I'll be waiting to see you with your idea for a thesis. Call me when you're ready, okay?"

(Funny. Pathetic. Sweet.)

"Thank you."

"And don't forget—we've all taken the plunge. Pascal with his probable God, Marx with the Future of the Classless Society, and you with your thesis. Only freethinkers think they can choose not to wager. But we have to wager! It's not a question of wanting or not wanting: we've already taken the plunge!"

It seemed to her the freethinkers got out of it rather well. She must see if there were still any of them around. You couldn't count on it.

Edelman's students, a huge crowd including many foreigners, seemed rather keen on Jansenist solitude. But that didn't stop them from talking. They all talked to themselves, babbling at top speed in a kind of conspiratorial seclusion, each one alone while forming part of the whole. And they all went on talking to themselves out in the little cafés around Saint-Michel, though eager to offer Olga, the newcomer, a drink. Thus Heinz and Roberto:

"No one talks anymore in our country, you know. Edelman says it's because our parents were Nazis. He's right—silence is ideology: it reveals ideology's unspoken essence."

(She was still taking photographs—of bottles of mineral water, pots of tea, and aperitifs.)

"You wouldn't have a bit of Japanese blood, would you—clicking away like that with your camera?"

They made her laugh. Taking snaps of them was her way of withdrawing from, of expressing disagreement with the world. Was it tragic or comic? It was a paradox.

"Tell me, Heinz, do you think an intellectual *has* to withdraw from the world?" (Roberto was still speeding along on his own theme.) "*I* think we're right at the heart of the thinking machine, and we have to challenge it until it either breaks or changes."

Olga put the camera down and looked at them affectionately. These feverish intellectuals were infectious. They were restless. Accelerated particles. They talked about time in terms either of seconds, minutes, and hours or of years, decades, and centuries. As if they were living out of time, for real time is made up of days, nights, months, and seasons. Their time was either minute or infinite, and it was from that position that they rebelled against all the rest, against time as seen by the conformists.

At Bréhal's seminar—she went anyhow, to annoy Ivan—the room was even more crowded, and she had to listen to the master's voice—a slow, lascivious vibrato—from out in the corridor.

"I've never heard anyone so irresistible," whispered a blonde in jeans as she stood on tiptoe trying to catch a glimpse of her idol. "I think I'm in love with him."

"That beats all!" said a pale little youth in glasses, addressing all and sundry. His voice was blasé and sarcastic, as if he knew something no one else knew. "You'd do better to try Strich-Mèyer's conjuring tricks with the senses, my dear, because that's what Bréhal provides at second hand, and what you're getting now if you did but know it!"

"Shut up, Cédric—we can't hear!"

"*You* shut up, Martin! Carole, can I borrow your last week's notes?"

Bréhal was talking about *Sodom and Gomorrah*. He was carving up Proust's text sentence by sentence and word by word, taking pleasure in highlighting and reassessing various components of the well-known passage that describes the Narrator waiting in anguish for the elusive Albertine. "I too was anxious to get away from Monsieur and Madame Guermantes as soon as possible.

Phèdre ended at about half past eleven. Albertine ought to be there by the time I got home." An unexpected meaning was gradually emerging, one that had nothing to do with homosexuality or the duplicities of high society but was related instead to the painful ear of jealousy: "the sound of a call" . . . *"Tristan"* . . . "the purr of the telephone" . . . "the braying of a bicyclist's horn" . . . "a woman's voice singing" . . . "a brass band in the distance" . . .

As it followed the inflections of Proust's words, Bréhal's voice imprinted their beauty on the rapt faces of the listening students, then wove correlations with the help of a scholarly but elegant vocabulary, tracing the amorous anamorphosis of the Narrator into a shallow woman. Finally the aural memory changed into a colored surface—"the pink complexion of a seaside flower"—but it was still a metaphor for the one sensuality, that of the Narrator, iridescent with love.

In this way, Bréhal was saying, love is time made tangible. It is not a matter of organs, or even of minds on fire, but a pact by which words turn into perceptible memories. Words that remember having once been perceptions of sounds, colors, scents. Proust in love invents a story to make the Narrator, enamored of Albertine, relive that transport of the mind and senses that is passion's true element. Is Proust remembering Albertine, or Méséglise, or his childhood, or Baudelaire's correspondences? Rather he is operating a mystical metamorphosis in which all the senses become one. . . .

The crowded rows of students were fascinated.

"He's reinterpreting Aristotle—no, re-creating, reincarnating him!" whispered four-eyed Cédric. "He's doing more than illustrate last year's lectures on the *Poetics*. He's inventing the real poetics of love."

For a moment Olga felt uneasy. This embroidering on the music of Proust seemed rather like the tapestrywork of some learned spinster. But no—in it you could find hitherto missing words for a passion that you'd experienced but been unable to name, or that you'd never even suspected.

At the next seminar she found herself sitting next to a girl dressed in black and pale as a nun doing penance. But her cheeks were flushed and she wrote down Bréhal's every word.

"My name's Carole. Have you only just started? Never mind, you'll soon get the hang of it. Bréhal may sound a bit technical, but he really does deal in literature, and everyone can understand that. Anyway, it makes a change from anthropology—I must admit I find that a bit anonymous."

You felt you were becoming *someone* just by listening to Bréhal. Did the students agree with him? Did she? The question didn't arise: they were all captivated. As by a philosophical conversation, a mistake set right, a courtesy that neither palliates nor betrays. But what was it? It was a weaving together of individual vagaries into a tolerance so perfectly expressed it resembled rhapsody. The lecture was a kind of rhapsody.

But she couldn't take any photographs. Never mind—she'd do it later. Bréhal had a sort of tamed eccentricity. He seemed not to believe in his own existence; he transposed it into other people's writings. Olga felt that a delight shared in this way would never turn into autobiographical confession. And that this abstractedness, this self-effacement, tasted of death. Bréhal, frail and serene, was a master by default.

She was touched as one is whenever some disturbing strangeness turns out to be really just a familiar habit, but one that is childish and unmentionable. The smell of a toy box. Or the brush of hand on breast, flooding deep sleep with sensual light. Bréhal's voice changed words, whether smooth or ornate, into a lover's touch. She wanted to go up and speak to him. But of course, she mustn't, she couldn't.

"No need to stand on ceremony!" (Ivan was acting as steward, if not pilot, of Bréhal's plane.) "Come along—I'll introduce you!"

The streets around Saint-Michel were gray and dull. The lights were few and far between and looked like fireflies frozen in the fog. Cars sped by, the crowds of people swirled and chattered. Suddenly she felt tired and lonely, so lonely she could have cried.

But she wouldn't cry, she'd go and freshen up.

Véra's mirror told her of rings even deeper than usual under her almond-shaped eyes. They slanted upward above her prominent cheekbones. Whenever she lost weight, they changed her oval face into a triangle. Fatigue emphasized the Asian aspect of her appearance: if it hadn't been for her squirrel-colored hair and the pink tints in her complexion, she might have been taken for a Chinese.

She put on her emerald-green suit. The soft wool clung to her breasts and hinted at their hardened curves. She lengthened her eyelashes and applied some dark red lipstick: that would do. Luckily her cossack-style coat happened to be in style in Paris this year. She untied the black ribbon that had been holding her squirrel's tail up on top of her head and tugged her light-colored fur cap over her eyes, letting her tawny hair down over her shoulders, glinting darkly. She looked nice, but definitely off-beat. She resolved to ignore it: she hated weirdos.

"It's Christmas, so we're going to Notre-Dame."

Véra liked rules and regulations.

But it was a silly idea. The cathedral had been taken over by tourists. You could tell the real French people by the restrained smartness of their clothes, which an unsophisticated observer might have taken for poverty. The whole congregation followed the ceremony as if their thoughts were elsewhere. She must preserve those opaque, deserted faces on film. Flash. Snap. Flash. Snap. And they too were parceled up in shiny paper like gift-wrapped packages. That was what she'd seen everywhere—gift-wrapped packages. In Passy, at Denfert-Rochereau, at the Etoile, at Jean-Jaurès. Gift-wrapped packages from Cartier or the super-market. Packages from André, the cheap shoe store, or from Sévigné, the expensive chocolate maker. Upmarket, downmar-ket, all being paraded through the streets, titivated and untouch-able. Presents for whom? Exactly: for no one. No one remem-bered to deliver them. No one wants them and they don't want anyone. They're exhibited because they exist. That's all. For no one. Snap. Flash. What did Edelman say? Alienated? Reified? Gift-wrapped packages politely following automatic trajectories, slumped like shapeless old raincoats.

Tonight's mass was shapeless too—a show that flopped. But foreigners adore tradition: it makes them feel they belong to something that the natives, tied up in their gift wraps, are only too eager to avoid. But amid the hubbub made by the indifferent majority (flash, snap) a few believers solemnly swallowed their consecrated wafers, holding their bellies with the earnest expression worn by expectant mothers. Snap. Flash.

Whether because of fatigue or of dizziness, everything began to go round and round. The nave of the church, the strains of the organ, the faces—all were blurred. Only the panels of stained glass held firm. Olga gazed fixedly at the dazzling kaleidoscope of the rose window to keep herself from fainting. She clung to it with her eyes and, as she often did when her legs began to give way, concentrated on an idea. The thought that this muddy city, inhabited by gift-wrapped packages intended for nobody, also contained tiny islets: rose windows. Careful craftsmen cut out, colored, and assembled surfaces, imparting to all the grayness a multicolored life. The craftsmen's names were Cédric, Heinz, Carole, Roberto, Martin, Edelman, Bréhal . . .

These new acquaintances overflowed with an enthusiasm that was austere but incredibly intense. The passion they put into studying, discussing, delving into words and texts, and comparing subtly different yet basically converging views—this common ardor made them into a strange species of their own. Up till now Olga had never dreamed they could still exist. In the Middle Ages, yes. In totalitarian countries too, of course: under political pressure ideas come to be a kind of religion. But here? Do these people have any idea how strange they seem?

She was struck, bewildered in fact, by the way they immediately admitted her as one of them. It was more than just acceptance, it was a kind of spontaneous kinship. As if they'd all lived together since they were children. And after all, wasn't that true in a way? She was almost ready to think so. They'd read the same books. What she hadn't expected were their open doors—the open doors of their studios, maids' rooms, seminars, laboratories, institutes. Or their curiosity about what was going on back home, though they were less interested in "Stalinist error" than in what they called the "groundswell," the "wind from the East," which they tended to elevate into a myth. Were they dangerously naive? They made idols out of the "origins of the Revolution" and "aesthetic avant-gardes," probably to bring out the contrast with the gift-wrapped packages they saw all around them. Cédric, Heinz, Roberto, Martin, and Carole made her feel they saw in her what they'd have liked to be themselves if their own families hadn't been so reactionary or underprivileged. They seemed to want France to become the most advanced of Eastern countries, whereas she envied them their unlimited access to every memoir, every library, every country and sex and state of consciousness—an inordinate advantage of which they themselves seemed to have no idea.

These bizarre interrelations changed the small triangle that lay between the Ecole d 'Etudes Supérieures, the Institut d'Analyse Culturelle, and Saint-Germain-des-Prés (where *Now* had its headquarters) into a kind of port or haven that was cosmopolitan and yet uniquely French, perhaps even simply Parisian in its liveliness, casualness, and gaiety.

Olga was well aware that this was a clandestine space created by her new friends as a challenge to all norms: a temporary Utopia in the midst of incomprehension, indifference, and hostility, all of which might suddenly explode. As they had in the Bréhal-Jobart affair, when the master of the Moderns had been shot down in flames by the Sorbonne. And as they did in the suspicious, vague, or spiteful looks she met with from people she passed in the streets near where she lived. . . . As for the understanding between the intellectuals themselves, what was it? A brief truce? A short-lived aberration?

She thought about all this, and was transported from seminar to stained-glass window and from rose window back to seminar. Bréhal, Edelman, Cédric, Martin, Carole, Heinz, and Roberto: each had his or her own stained-glass window with which to save the sinking ship. For their elation represented a sleepwalker's consciousness of shipwreck. Rose windows and books against shipwreck and misfortune. What misfortune? Hers?

It was all happening too fast, and there was something artificial about that understanding between minds on the run. Everyone thought he was revealing some unknown part of himself in his work, but everyone forgot himself in it too. A tightrope of intelligence over an abyss of unease and confusion. And solitude. She could touch it, feel it quivering on either side of the perfect beauty of multicolored jigsaws and of texts reread, taken to pieces, and meditated on.

The candlelight and the sleet filled her eyes with little sparks, made them burn with lack of sleep. Tears tried to dim her own secret stained-glass windows. No more snaps or flashes. She'd learned long ago how to weep dry-eyed. All you had to do was concentrate on a shape or a phrase, and your balked strength rose to the surface again. A deliberate mask hid the pain that went on withering away within, invisible and delicious. She fell asleep with it.

At the Rosebud, almost empty at ten o'clock in the evening, the cyclamen light from the central hazelwood lamp wasn't shrouded yet in its usual cloud of smoke. You could smell pine polish from the leather seats, and the spicy perfumes worn by a group of girls sitting at a nearby table—they hated flowery scents, of course, and drenched themselves in Vetiver.

"I'll have a Perrier to start with," said Bréhal. "And you? . . . Two Perriers, please."

He looked at her again with that strange sweetness of his that ended in indolence, as if he were restraining a kind of maternal tenderness for fear of seeming ridiculous.

"You were marvelous. Accurate, of course—that's indispensable—but above all, strong. I mean it—strong. A bulldozer! It's true, Olga, you're a bulldozer. No, I'm not making fun of you, you mustn't think that. Whatever anyone may suppose, in the present context I intend that word as the highest possible compliment."

He was wearing the same kind of pepper-and-salt suit as before; he must have had a dozen of them. His shirt was plain and, according to whether it was white or yellow or blue, either dulled or enhanced the brightness of his pale eyes. His nose was shaped like a can opener and slanted to the left, and this made him look ingenuous or arrogant, depending on circumstance or the play of feature. His eyes and lips freely expressed the pleasure—or, frequently, the boredom—he derived from listening to others.

His body was racked by stifled but irrepressible fits of coughing. It was a body that must have known illness, and that, sagging and slack beneath the well-cut suits, seemed never to have been used except for some undemanding solitary pleasure. He was quite thin, despite his jowls and thickening middle. But he gave off such a reassuring calm, and his gait was so measured and elegant, that everything about him irresistibly inspired affection.

"No doubt about it—this Perrier's too cold. Waiter, will you take the ice away, please? . . . Well, history and the body are texts as well," he went on, after taking a deep breath to suppress a fit of coughing. "We can't leave them to the tender mercies of grammar—we've got to put them under the microscope, as you did in the case of style. It was true, what you said, in the musical sense of the term."

Olga was delighted to hear him apply his favorite expression to her. He used it only when he was particularly pleased with something.

"Yes, it really was true, in the musical sense of the term. You said the novel is descended from carnival. Of course, we suspected as much, because of Rabelais. . . . But you also say dialogue is irony, a sign both of the impossibility of understanding and of the fragmentation of totality—that's very good. What you're really saying is that Plato's irony is novelistic, and that the novel is ironic, indeterminate. As you may imagine, I like that."

"Like conversation between a man and a woman: is *that* mere irony, nothing in common, a novel?"

Why on earth was she being so coquettish? She was the one most embarrassed by it: she loathed women who tried to get off with men who didn't like women. Just the same, she was vaguely disturbed. As for Bréhal, he blushed, confused by a bulldozer that seemed not to know its place.

"Do you think so? How amusing. . . . No doubt you know what you're talking about. For my part, I stick to texts, and I don't mind telling you your lecture this evening was a great hit. Oscar wants to invite you to Boston."

"How could anyone go and teach in the United States while the war's still on in Vietnam?"

"I personally find the United States very tiring. As for political morality, I prefer to believe (like Proust) in the beauty of pleasure—guilty pleasure, I need hardly say. The war's intolerable, and a whole mythology is collapsing: the myth of American infallibility, of the U.S.A. as the guarantor of liberty against totalitarian regimes, and so on. You'll see—their army will be defeated and pull out, and for years they'll have a left that's surly and aggressive but incompetent and marginalized. We'll be called aesthetes, and they'll bring out all the old outmoded ideologies. I say all this, but of course, I may be wrong. Politics give me a pain."

"Edelman thinks we ought to go there and conquer imperialism from within."

"Fabien's always been an optimist, but I'm afraid he overdoes it. He doesn't take care of himself properly. Ah, here's Sinteuil. Hervé, you weren't at Olga's lecture—we'll tell you all about it. . . ."

"I wasn't invited, that's why. A J&B, please, with ice," said Sinteuil, sitting down by Bréhal and examining Olga idly with the eye of a connoisseur.

He was sitting facing her, and smiling with overdone but indifferent politeness. His round face acted as a foil to his Bourbon nose ("No, Sadean," he said, laughing, when they knew one another better)—a sign of controlled sensuality, restrained to the point of coldness sometimes. He was a rather tall, portly young man; his physical appearance gave no hint that he was really an avant-garde intellectual, "the Pope of Saint-Germain," as the papers called him. He looked more like a poised and wily doctor who played tennis and golf in his spare time. Everything struck him as an occasion for irony, if not for laughter—laughter that was loud, aggressive, and arrogant, but never vulgar, even when he was wiping the floor with his opponent.

"It seems you've let a bulldozer loose on the preserves of structuralism?" Loud laughter. "Bréhal's delighted to have a woman by his side when he advances through Strich-Meyer and Lauzun's minefields."

"The funny thing about Sinteuil is that he sees war everywhere." (Bréhal was entering into the spirit of the thing.) "And not only is he right, but his martial view of the world seems to do him good. I might almost say it stimulates you, mightn't I?"

"If you like!"

"We were talking about Vietnam. Do you think someone could 'disengage' himself or herself enough to go and work in the United States?"

"Oh dear, engagement—that old chestnut of Dubreuil's! He

still can't bring himself to drive Billancourt and the unions to despair. But despair got to the poor fellows a long time ago, and to all the salvation armies, including his own. So his friends are bereft of speech, while we and your Olga dig through millimeters of words and phrases to get a bit of pleasure—or, in other words, of meaning—out of the stereotypes we chat about over a drink. In order to reinvent ritual, the ritual of conversation in particular, or to restore what you call the flavor of words. That's the situation, as you well know, Armand. And if this microscopic revolution is only an ant's blind alley, well, speaking for myself, I'm attached to it. It's my thing."

Olga had noticed the interview with him in *Red*, the Communist student review, where Sinteuil expatiated on the same idea. That the transformation of society is only a cheat if it doesn't mean the transformation of individuals. That individuals—he called them "subjects"—are "talking beings," and that you have to begin by changing their ways of speaking. Hence the revolutionary role of literature, and of the avant-garde in particular. It wasn't a matter of esotericism or art for art's sake; it was an incredibly delicate "surgical operation" on the most sensitive tissues of society—the tissues of speech, style, rhetoric, and dreams.

"Sinteuil's flirting with the Communists," observed Cédric, the four-eyed student from the Ecole Normale Supérieure who'd been at Bréhal's seminar.

"No—he's only reviving a Surrealist idea," retorted Heinz.

"Futurist too," added Olga. "At first, in the USSR, the modernist poets thought they were the natural partners of the revolution."

"And they ended up in Stalin's camps!" insisted Cédric. "You have to make more effort than that nowadays."

"But Sinteuil isn't as naive as you think," said Martin. "I suggest you read *Now* a bit more carefully. . . ."

The Rosebud was gradually filling with smoke, and the girls wearing spicy perfume had been replaced by a couple who were kissing one another avidly on the mouth without missing a word of the conversation going on nearby. Bréhal let his own friable discourse be jostled by the bracing draft that accompanied Sinteuil everywhere, sweeping in through the open doors of questions, eddying around casually, but apparently never losing its bearings.

"I've just read your manuscript on Balzac's *Cousin Pons*. A masterpiece!" (Sinteuil had already moved on, and was including Bréhal in his own pleasure as a reader, making him see unsuspected landscapes in his own book.) "First, there's Pons himself, the greedy collector—you know the original was one of the major benefactors of the Louvre?" (The footnote was for Olga's benefit.) "Pons is the humiliated artist—you and me. We adore words and styles in the same way as Pons is fascinated by Madame de Pompadour's fan, allegedly painted by Watteau. We're all scroungers after a free meal, if you don't mind my saying so. People regard us as parasites. Who? Eternal France, the Balzacian France of shopkeepers and money. Also, I may add, publishers, critics, universities, academies, and political parties, who all want everything to be *useful!* They feather their nests out of our little collections of phrases, but never miss an opportunity to show we're a nuisance and would do better to remove ourselves. . . . Second, there's the frigid passion between the two grotesque artists, Pons and Schmucke: that's superb! Your chapter on 'the two nutcrackers': 'the psychical significance to be found in the most trifling of creations'! Is that ultramodern expression really in Balzac? Who'd have thought it? The subtlety of these two, contrasted with the stupidity of the family! 'The poor conductor had greatly extended the meaning of the word *family*': that's right, people are always inclined to overextend the meaning of the word *family*, and take themselves for a 'cousin' instead of sticking to the solitude of a collector. And why collect? In order to oppose the collectivity, the group, of course! 'Collecting beautiful things by way of a contrast with politics, which secretly collects ugly deeds.' But when you say that, you're dabbling in politics! Yes, you are—don't deny it!"

A man at a neighboring table, with dyed fair hair, powdered cheeks, and painted lips, and acting too young for his age, was making desperate efforts to attract Bréhal's attention. He succeeded.

"Wait for me here, I'll join you afterward," the master whispered out of the corner of his mouth.

Sinteuil, pretending not to notice, went on:

"Third, how clever to detect these contrasts—which exist in the social movements of Gaullism as well as of the July Monarchy, hence the topicality of lectures." (This too was directed at Olga.) "How clever to detect them in the very sounds of the words! No one ever thought before of seeing Balzac as a musician. On the one hand, there are the piercing *s* sounds in *house, cousin,* and *parasite*. And on the other hand, the more somber range of *s, sh, k* in *Pons* and *Schmucke:* the lovers and the source of art, the subterranean fire of opposition. And the ambiguity of the two trends united in the two friends' nickname—the *n, k, k* of *nutcrackers*. As a matter of fact, you get the same thing in the title of the book, and if you juggle the consonants a bit, you can make Balzac's name into an anagram of the French for *nutcrackers*. So here we have Balzac the cabalist, the musician of meaning!"

Sinteuil was enjoying himself. With his incomparable memory and practical gift for imitation, he was critic, teacher, student, and writer, one by one and all at once—Bréhal, anti-Bréhal, super-Bréhal, and more-than-Bréhal. Brilliant, trivial, profound, irritating, scintillating—and irresistibly lively.

"It takes you to read a manuscript like that, Hervé! I didn't realize I'd said all those things!" (The affectionate perfidy of his smile.) "The fact of the matter is, a good friend makes a good reader."

He was pleased.

"Have you thought of a title?"

"No, that's the trouble—I'm stumped."

"Why not *Literally Balzac?*"

Sinteuil drew the letters *c, s,* and *z* on a book of matches.

"Too condensed . . . incomprehensible," said Bréhal hesitantly.

"Anyone who reads what you've written will understand it."

"You're right—I must show from the outset that I expect the reader to study the text right down to the music of the letters. Right, I'll adopt your suggestion. You're a genius . . ."

Olga listened, rather stunned, to this minuet of compliments, a strange mixture of dry observation and compliment from which the dancers disengaged themselves with an ironic word or intonation.

"And how's the review going?"

"Not too badly. Everyone does what he can."

Sinteuil suddenly took on the mysterious, absent expression of a paralytic, or of someone who means to keep to himself an idea that has just occurred to him. His face looked as if it had been cut in two. Silence.

"Everyone does what he can," Bréhal repeated, to bridge the gap.

"Yes, Maille's our social representative: he copes with dinner parties, cocktail parties, first nights, and all the other things I loathe; he's even coping with Lenin now! Jean-Claude, our ace Freudian, is up to his neck in psychoanalysis—we go to Lauzun's shows together. Hermine has just settled in Florence. She wants to translate Lucretius and Petrarch, if you don't mind, and that takes time! As for Brunet, he occupies the middle ground, as inflexible as ever."

"And you?"

"Oh, I don't do anything!" (Again laughter wafted him up out of the conversation and himself; then he came down again.) "I write and read and observe. Little things."

"Speaking of which, I was forgetting that Olga wanted to ask you some questions. But it's getting late . . ."

Sinteuil turned to the girl.

"I'm leaving early tomorrow for Venice. But if you'd like to come to my office two weeks from now, at five?"

He smiled at her persuasively and almost ran out of the room, pausing long enough to give Bréhal a couple of friendly pats on the shoulder accompanied by a brilliant smile.

"See you soon. Work well!"

"I'll call you when you get back."

2

He looked right into her (Olga's) large mouth, with its wide, full lips. No, you couldn't say she was stupid. . . . She (Olga) felt her thighs opening and wanted to cuddle up to him. The thing was, would he ever love her?

"Have you ever been really in love? I'm the one asking questions now—kindly put that camera away. I mean *really*?" (Hervé)

"I could tell you anything you'd like to hear." (Olga)

"Go ahead!" (Hervé)

"I'm beginning to find you out . . ." (Olga)

"I'm listening . . ." (Hervé)

"It doesn't take two people to make love. They say it does, but really it's enough if you yourself are very aroused. Then your adversary catches it from you and turns into a partner." (Olga)

He was still exploring her lips.

"And you mustn't stop halfway—you must let things take their course . . ." (Olga)

"Where to?" (Hervé)

"There isn't any boundary. It can always get pleasanter or more painful, more ethereal or more prosaic. But I can always tell when it's over. Not dead, but if it went on, it would mean death." (Olga)

"So that's what you're like, is it?" (Hervé)

"Perhaps even more so. That's what I used to be like, anyhow. Perhaps I want to burn my fingers. After all, I've got nothing to lose. A woman's like the proletariat *back home*—she has nothing to lose but her chains." (Olga)

"Your chains?" (Again the arrogant or sympathetic laugh. Annoying, stimulating.) "Have you read *The Story of O?*" (Hervé)

"The story of what?" (Olga)

"O, as in Olga. You haven't? Sorry, it was a pun. A facile one, I admit." (He was gloating, not apologizing.) "You'll read it one day. Some women experience pleasure only when they're in chains." (Hervé)

"With me it'll be war." (Olga)

"Let it be war then!" (Hervé)

"I've read your books and I find them rather gentle. Erotic, but gentle. Chains? I see: ethical chains, spiritual torture—can one say that? Whether or no, I don't want to kiss a sheet of paper." (Olga)

"Haven't you ever made love to a writer before?" (Hervé)

"Yes—to men I knew who happened to write, too. But you're just a collection of photographs and sheets of paper. Sinteuil's a pseudonym, isn't it? A hideout for Hervé de Montlaur. Sinteuil is a pure, expanding spirit . . ." (Olga)

"You've hit it exactly! I have a bark, like a tree, like the 'laurel' element in 'Montlaur.' And I'm a stone, too, like the 'mountain' element in it." (Hervé)

"But under the carapace there's vulnerable flesh." (Olga)

"Right. And loads of women." (Hervé)

"I don't like women. I adore men." (Olga)

"You don't like women? You may think so. . . . But why not?" (Hervé)

"Probably because I think I'm better than all the rest of them.

And if he, the man, doesn't feel that, and if they, the women, don't see it, then it's war." (Olga)

"Right! War's okay by me!" (Hervé)

"But you'll have to wage it on your own. I'm going home." (Olga)

She was very disarming with her squirrel tail and her nape like that of a well-behaved little girl. He took hold of a tress and planted a swift kiss among the roots of her dark red hair, on skin that smelled like geraniums.

"Rushing things a bit, aren't you? Who do you think you are?"

She tore herself away and caught the last metro from Duroc.

He vanished, she avoided him. Then they met again at the Rosebud and spent the whole night huddled together, kissing each other on the mouth with a Carlsberg and a Perrier standing on the shiny table between them. Then another night kissing some more—hungrily, as if they'd never done it before, and talking . . . talking and kissing. Then another night, and another, kissing still. Then he disappeared again.

After ten days' silence:

"Hello! This is Hervé Sinteuil. I hope I'm not disturbing you?"

She was just listening to the shimmer of his voice: on the telephone it sounded gentle but not weak, though it was capable of suddenly becoming as rough and curt again as raw silk. He told her about life at the magazine—some dispute between Bréhal and Scherner that he himself had got dragged into. It struck her that Sinteuil was all frontiers: on the one hand, his sophisticated social surface; on the other, an almost childlike or even feminine attentiveness, which you could hear in the restrained breathing and the voice so studied as to seem naturally courteous. And on top of all this, drawn shutters, a roadblock, the closed-off area, the hermit's cave where no one was ever admitted. What did he have hidden away there? Affairs, secret liaisons, some unavowable sexual proclivity? Or maybe just the story he was writing; perhaps he had thoughts only for that and nothing else? Perhaps there wasn't anything but the protected area of his writing: nothing outside at all, just the enclosure. Maybe it was this, detached from the rest, that gave him his cheerful but distant manner. Yes, that was the word: detached.

That evening Véra wouldn't be home; she was away working

on a story. If he liked, Olga could invite him over for a cold dinner: she'd always been his guest before, which was rather embarrassing. Till this evening then.

Eleven P.M. Not a soul. Of course he hadn't turned up. That would have been too easy. It was only to be expected: one step forward, two steps back. The contemporary Laclos, stager of seedy modern dangerous liaisons, must have decided it was vulgar to advance so easily over enemy territory. She applied more green to her almond eyes: it would make her look less dreary, more self-assertive.

The rolls of smoked salmon, surrounded by slices of lemon, were wilting on their dish in the middle of the blue tablecloth. The ice was melting in the bucket. But Olga had put the bottle of vodka back in the refrigerator. He wasn't coming. She wouldn't wait any longer. It was quite obvious: she'd spend her life hanging around for him, it would always be the same, he'd always be late, or else he wouldn't put in an appearance all night and she'd be left waiting for him on the other side of the frontier. Right. After all, why not? She'd always liked frontiers; perhaps her own personality had been created out of those mysterious border crossings, those flights from her own country that he would never experience, whose existence he didn't even suspect. Well, they could wait for one another like two strangers; why not? She'd wait. Waiting never hurt anyone. It was called patience, and was an elementary form of culture.

But no, he goes too far, this must stop here and now. A bit of salmon—a taste of seaweed and ozone and a soft-textured mound of pink. Delicious, especially when you're full of iced vodka. Salmon like getting drunk in glaciers . . . She fell asleep on the sofa.

The intercom:

"It's Hervé."

"What time is it?"

"Two o'clock. Sorry."

He kissed her full on the mouth, his tongue licking hers, exploring the insides of her cheeks as far as her throat. He liked the taste of salmon and lemon, the breasts offering themselves up to his lips, the thighs opening to his hands. He drew her over to the table, got his breath back, sucked up and ate a rosette of orange salmon, was reminded of the taste of her mouth, and helped her to some more of the same. They ate the salmon together, ate one another together, rolling about on a dark gray fitted carpet that was rough on their damp, open bodies.

No, not here. What are we doing on this cozy middle-class territory?

"Shall we go out for a breath of air? We could drop in somewhere for a drink."

He led her out into the purple spring night; she couldn't see anything. She clutched the steering wheel of the old Ford with her right hand, while with her left she stroked his thigh, his penis. They stopped and got out, avoiding the pools of light around the streetlamps, and went on breathlessly kissing and caressing. At Montparnasse the Palladium was empty; the prostitutes on duty didn't even glance at them. They sat down, still clasped together, lips joined, fingers laced.

"A Carlsberg and a Perrier."

They drank, they kissed, there was a disc of Duke Ellington and his band ('39 or '40?) on the record player. The trumpets soared, inviting the sumptuous trombones to talk to them; the saxes provided a voluptuous but syncopated background, pierced through by the clarinet. The staccato rhythm blew off the roofs, languished into a tango, stretched out like the cry of a sea gull opening the day, or ending it, or like a bold girl suddenly bursting into tears. . . . Into this sober mood the piano wove a lacework of silken thread, a thoughtful laugh, sparkling and gay, which drew the two lovers' hands and legs into a dizzy but lucid beat that didn't miss a note. Then came the lullaby again, which could go on and on without making you sleepy; you sank into the mingled tones of Rex Stewart and Cootie Williams (a marriage of cornet and trumpet) until Ellington's fingers on the piano jabbed through the thick velvet of brasses, woods, and winds: a dotted line of awakenings. "Downtown in Boston, Massachusetts"—a black voice completed the whole. The barman put the same record on again, and the trumpets soared and swirled once more, harrying the cornet and calling to the sumptuous trombones, while the man and the girl went on kissing, alone on the leather seat in the empty Palladium.

Then they opened their eyes and gazed at each other very

closely, seeing who could hold out longer without blinking. At the first wink they burst out laughing and swooned again on each other's lips.

"There, that's enough. We can't just go on like this. Wait till you see . . ."

The nearby hotel was strange. No reception desk, nobody in sight except a heavily made-up woman who looked at Olga suspiciously.

"How old is the young lady?"

"She thinks you're a minor. A nice compliment, eh? Don't worry, madam, everything's in order . . ."

The room smelled of rose water. The mirror-lined walls showed her burning skin and Hervé's hands loosening her hair and slipping off her black velvet sheath dress. He wanted to see everything—his own stiff penis, the curve of her breasts, the opening of her womb between her thighs, her labia, her long slender legs. To see, to cover with kisses, to enter, see, cover with caresses, enter, see. While he took her slowly, not missing a glimpse of all the images reflected back from every angle, in every position, from the shiny cube of the walls, she let herself be entered, and soared, floated, quivered, eyes shut, seeing nothing, concentrated within, ablaze as never before, anywhere—and all the time there.

It was a dream of blue sea, smooth and shining; she could feel the sunny coolness of the waves on the muscles of her arms and thighs. She thrust back the soft masses caressing her face and hair; she was moving forward; no, she was sinking, the waves were growing heavy, dragging at her. The sea was raging, flecked with foam; the inky-blue water was sweeping him away; his face was far away, too far, she couldn't reach him, he couldn't help her anymore, Hervé . . .

"Did you call me? You must have been dreaming. Go back to sleep—it's too early . . ."

She heard his voice and felt ashamed (as one is ashamed in dreams, violently, confusedly) at having revealed that he was always with her now and always would be. She tried to go back to sleep, close to his big, warm body, clasped between his soccer player's thighs, their legs intertwined. Through half-open lashes she checked that they were in his room. The daylight was already filtering in through the orange blind; the green velvet cushions and bedspread lay strewn on the floor by the bookshelves. The whole attic was bathed in the golden blood of the sunlight: it was like being inside a pomegranate full of shiny pink juice. She put her lips on his neck and inhaled his scent of milk and amber—was it that of man or infant? The night made the question more acute—and plunged back again into sleep.

It had taken him months to open up his sanctuary to her. For a long time she wasn't allowed to enter the "garret." They were almost always together, but always in restaurants or hotels. Then he would vanish for whole nights and days together, abandoning her, absentmindedly or amusedly, after passion.

"The pleasure you give me! I've never known anything like it. I feel it entirely, totally, not just in one organ, not just in a part of my body. The fact is—and don't forget it—I love you."

It was a sign that he wouldn't be with her that night. He marked out his territory, prevented her from invading it, cruelly burning his bridges as soon as he felt exposed. He wasn't going to let her think the battle was over and she'd got the better of him! Far from it: a man had his own resources! Was he sure he loved her, at least? More and more! He dreamed about her and woke up with her name on his lips. "It's as clear as day," Hervé would tell himself, mocking the romantic swain shaving himself in the mirror. "Watch out!"

Then he would suddenly remember the primitive tones that could be heard in her voice sometimes—not exactly an accent, more like one of those tunes from nowhere that split your eardrums and suggest some kind of brutality. Careful! And the way she had of plunging into books and speaking a learned language, her incisors stained with lipstick. Watch out! Yet here was a woman with whom you could both talk and make love, despite the lipstick on her large upper incisor. She thought of everything, but couldn't see herself, with her ridiculous smudged tooth. And then that heady perfume—probably musk, bought in one of those kitschy little Indian shops so popular now: it made you want to fling the window open. . . . Strange, those mystical eyelids, that somewhat severe expression, like a Byzantine icon. Frail as a little girl menaced by some exotic malady, with her lilting French and her misty eyes—yet capable of suddenly revealing, with the candor of a depraved adolescent, a supple gymnast's body, slim yet full of curves. A dual (at least) personality, but unaware of it: at once childlike and disingenuous.

"You're just dazzled by the unknown, old boy. But could you be in love with anything else? Of course not—this only goes to show. Still, imagine *me* getting caught by a 'fair unknown'—that doesn't happen every day of the week!"

Hervé found he was moved—rather inappropriate for a *libertin*,* but it suited him very well for the moment.

"It's an absurd situation." That was his final conclusion. But he knew how to keep mum, and suddenly stopped asking her questions and ceased to pay attention to the questions she asked him. He pretended to ignore her work, whereas before he'd always been very encouraging. Olga felt like a castaway.

"You and Sinteuil seem to be inseparable," Carole remarked at the Institute. "Can you really trust someone so—how shall I put it?—so self-centered, so elusive?"

"But I don't trust him—I love him! If I trusted him, it would be all over for me. . . . Which it is anyway . . . because the fact is, I love him because I've changed. I trust *myself*, I'm learning self-sufficiency—the serene side of loneliness. And when he's there, we share. Intermittent exchange. The intermittences of sex and spirit. And I'd always imagined passion as dependence."

"What else?"

"With him it's independence. Everyone wants it, but when you've got it, you're not so sure . . ."

"Especially when you're a foreigner. You need to be able to count on somebody."

"You're telling me! I have everything to learn: how to speak to the woman in the bakery, how to open a post office account, how to register for Social Security. No use counting on Sinteuil for that sort of thing. I doubt if he knows himself."

"There's always me."

"I know. Thanks. I'll try not to be too much of a nuisance.

---

* *Libertins* were originally (in the seventeenth and early eighteenth centuries) free-thinkers and skeptics, but as a result of much controversy (and some actual laxity of behavior) the word came to mean a debauchee. The ambiguity still exists. *Tr.*

Anyhow, maybe I'm meant to be independent. It does suit me. It makes me work. And cry. And take initiatives. Which Hervé backs up, by the way, when he notices. He's a feminist really, you know. Well, the consequences of his actions are feminist, even if his intentions are not."

"Either you're very strong or you're a complete masochist!"

"Or perhaps the two go together. The thing is, I like to experiment with all the different things that I observe. I try to be a spectator rather than an actor in the plays that are being performed all the time . . . ."

"You sound like Descartes."

"Maybe. I'd rather sound like the marquise de Merteuil. She was a Cartesian too, if you ask me—she liked observing things. For her, sensations of pleasure and pain were just so many facts to be collected and meditated upon. And *she* managed to exercise her talents effectively enough on the stage of the world! All liaisons are dangerous if you only look at them properly."

"Have it your own way. Good luck. Don't forget to call me!"

Distant, secretive, evasive, unpredictable. He advanced, withdrew, withdrew some more, followed his own bent, but yielded—no, clung—to pleasure, which helped his work. So what was natural to him might seem strange to the other person. If you didn't set yourself up as a dam to stem his flow, it could give you a surprise. A pleasant surprise.

"I hear Véra's chucked her job and left Paris. Time you came and stayed with me."

This announcement came between mouthfuls of underdone steak—"Really rare, please!"—as casually as if he were asking the waiter to bring a different kind of mineral water. Olga nearly choked, but answered impassively.

"Do you think so? Perhaps. Rather a good idea really. When?"

"Tonight. Here's the key. See you later. Sort things out for yourself."

He didn't even see that moving was quite a complicated business. Fortunately she had Cédric and Carole to help her.

"Patrician aloofness," Martin grumbled as he carried suitcases upstairs.

Yes, thought Olga: and also the fear that everyday life might destroy the uneasy concordat that united and excited them. But she didn't say anything to Hervé or Martin. There were so many factors involved, and they were all so incompatible. The whole thing was incompatible with itself.

So she went to live inside the pomegranate that filtered the morning sun, the labyrinthine attic, the nest of little rooms; and set up a study for herself under the roof. Again she breathed in the milk and amber, again started dreaming her blue dream. The waves lulled her, then swept her away; the sea was black and raging.

They were still asleep, but their bodies embraced; he could feel her hardened breasts against his chest, he swallowed her lips, felt with his fingers for the way into her womb, opened it, stroked it, and entered, turning gently, deep, very deep; she moaned, he was still asleep, then gradually woke up, panting, and exploded inside the young woman who was now his; by now they were both dazed, bereft of memory, sunk in their sexes.

He delighted in her pretty face, and the peace that made her cheeks smoother, tauter over the cheekbones, after making love. "Let's don't move." Then he went and fetched a tray of croissants and black coffee, together with the tea that she liked to drink with milk in it—slowly, smiling and silent.

"Don't say anything. Stay quiet and rest. I'll get on with my story."

He put the tray to one side, reached out to the bedside table for the notebook crammed with the minute handwriting of his current manuscript, and went without any transition from their embraces to the dense, dreamy text, the prose like carved jade, that was his own kind of sensuality, at once shocking and sober.

As she deciphered the blue characters, her quick brain recognized the music in the phrases, the allusions to ancient myths given new meaning in this bed. She was in the state of "temporary epilepsy" said to be so rare in women—this always surprised her—a state that shies away from words: words, the last refuge of the sacred, but in fact just a "shallow stream" in which only timid souls drown when ejected from the round of words and capering and laughter. . . . That was what Hervé thought: all belief began with belief in the mystery of women, but some people don't give themselves up to it because they are able to express it.

She skipped a few lines where the writing was too small to decipher, then went on reading.

Hey, this sounded familiar. "If there was ever a generation of men in France whose minds were keener than any before them, in France or anywhere else, they would need new words and signs to express their new ideas. The words we have now would not be enough. . . . There might be a greater degree of fury, passion, love, or wickedness than mankind has so far exhibited . . ." Did Hervé really write this, or had he taken it from *The Philosopher's Study?* And what about this worship of form, which the way Hervé expressed it sounded rather like Diderot: "What do I see? Forms. And what else? Forms. I don't know anything about things. We wander among shades, and we ourselves are shades to ourselves and to others. Living people often imagine they're dead, standing beside their own corpses and taking part in their own funeral processions. Like a swimmer looking at the clothes he left on the shore . . ." She felt as if she were reaching right down to the sources of these concentrated lines, recognizing herself as in a mirror.

But her body was still throbbing, and her hand crept under the sheet, found the stiffened penis and began to stroke it. As she did so, he went on writing, until, under the sheet, she took his warm member into her mouth and kept it there, gently, hungrily.

Suddenly he stood up. One o'clock. He absolutely had to make a phone call. She realized he meant to bring the game to an end, point out the funny side of it, and take back his freedom. Very well, she'd take her own back too.

The face that looked back at her from the long mirror in the bathroom was so woebegone she pinched her cheeks, pulled a mocking face, and bolted the door on the inside. The foam bath was nice and hot, and the noise from the crowded street wafted up through the leaves of the chestnut trees. Everything was bright and lucid, and lucidity is never sad.

3

The Institut d'Analyse Culturelle was in an old building painted dark gray and lit by lavender-gray neon. The offices inside had pale lavender-gray wall-to-wall carpets and were crammed with even paler lavender-gray shelves and boxes containing world culture in the form of card indexes. In here you could learn the logic of all a naive and superficial mind might consider illogical: the IAC had reduced to formulas the rules that govern marriage and myth all over the world, not to mention the most sophisticated literature. Olga, who'd been working in the literature department for the last few months, considered the Institute's color scheme very successful: depending on his mood, a researcher could either sink into the gray uniformity promoted by the Institute's view of the world or, disloyally indulging his own taste, dissect the dazzling human exceptions to universal logic that go to prove the rules.

"Have you seen this?" (Martin had rushed into her office brandishing a circular.) "Does he think he's God Almighty or what?"

A notice from Professor Strich-Meyer, director of the IAC, drew the attention of the "staff" to unnecessary expenditure and singled out as a bad example "Mademoiselle Olga Morena, who neglected to switch the lights off last Monday at the end of office hours."

"It's not the stinginess I mind. We all know what he's like and don't give a damn about that," Martin raged on. "What I can't stand is that supercilious tone, that contemptuous reference to the 'staff.' Why doesn't he call us the 'servants' while he's at it? Has he ever written a note about your research, or mine, or Carole's, or anyone else's? Not likely! We're just here to do the dirty work! We're all supposed to know our place, our humble place, in the hierarchy ruled over by His Majesty Strich-Meyer. One day the whole thing will blow up—there's trouble brewing everywhere!"

"You're right." (Olga tried to calm him down, though she did feel rather guilty and embarrassed at being singled out so stupidly and unexpectedly.) "But he's not the worst of them. At least he does try to respect other people in his work. He's the one who rehabilitated the 'savages.'"

"Listen to you! You still defend him even when he attacks you! For one thing, it isn't certain he did rehabilitate the 'savages,' as you call them. He may just have annexed them: they're like us— in other words, *like him*—and he's the one who tells us so with much elegant condescension. But never mind about that. Even if your respect for him was justified, I still think it's outrageous that someone with a mind like his should behave like the worst kind of petty tyrant when it comes to everyday life. It's worse than if he were just an ordinary boss—a write-off. It's unworthy of him and unfair to us."

She agreed with Martin about that. But he had reasons of his own for agitating against Strich-Meyer. He'd been working for years on a thesis called "Work and Death in the Myths of the

Wadani Indians," but no one had ever seen a line of it. Martin, excessively hard on himself and oscillating from one theory to another, from Marx to Hegel, from Freud to Lauzun, and fascinated of course by Strich-Meyer's rabbinical rigor, was discontent personified. But if he took everything to extremes, he was also very clear-sighted; he was critical, alert, abrasive, intransigent; a great dandy and a great egalitarian; both esoteric and populist—in short, an unstable mixture that exploded more and more often against the "bosses." Then the lavender-gray nuances of the IAC became incendiary.

Today's minirevolution was interrupted by the telephone. Dan's voice. He'd written that he might come, but to hear that he was actually in Paris, at the other end of the line! . . . Olga was quite flushed with delight and self-consciousness. Martin stood up.

"Ciao—we'll talk about it again later!"

"Where are you exactly?" (She was trying to talk to Dan, to imagine him, to see the once familiar features. What *did* he look like?)

"At the Pantheon, at the Hôtel des Grands Hommes."

The Great Men's Hotel. That was all she needed! The clumsy humor of foreigners. Their unconscious heavy-handedness. She knew these characteristics in herself and tried to avoid them, humiliated but somehow involved whenever a well-meaning rough diamond from back home confronted her with the familiar image.

"Right. I'm on my way."

She withheld the expected laugh, but immediately forgot the circular and rushed out to meet him.

Dan soon emerged from the limbo to which she'd consigned him since their farewells at the airport, and enfolded her in a homely, animal tenderness reminiscent of the affectionate ways of cats, which can bring tears to the eyes of people who live alone.

Dan. . . . No, she hadn't forgotten the fair, massive body, the straw-colored hair, the eyes—invisible behind their thick glasses—which would have been blue if it hadn't been for all that reading. His stubbly cheeks, girlish hands, sagging but comfortable shoulders. He'd never played any game but chess, and even that bored him: he laughed and overturned the board every time he lost, which was always. On the other hand, he knew practically every language and had read all the important works ever written in English, German, French, Russian, Spanish, and Italian, from the dim distant past up to the present. He was a glutton for culture and had absorbed all the great writers, philosophers, and poets. Like some representative of the Age of Enlightenment strayed into an obscure country and another age, he bestowed his erudition on the ignoramuses around him in the form of skeptical parables. To him Olga owed all she knew about Shakespeare and Cervantes, Browning and Emily Dickinson, Mallarmé and Faulkner. Their love had been one of lips and eyes: they read the same books in the same bed, talked about them, kissed, discussed; and sometimes, almost without noticing, they would go all the way, as the saying goes. Then they'd turn back to their books.

The little room in the Hôtel des Grands Hommes was too small for the tall youth of almost forty whose rough-hewn mountain robustness completely concealed his spiritual delicacy. His physical bulk added to the pair's awkwardness; they found it difficult to get back on their previous footing. Their bodies were tense, their sexes thought they were eager but remained unmoved. He was tender and welcoming, but she realized she couldn't make love to someone who was so much like a kind brother. That full body, those maternal gestures didn't lack force—Dan was very strong. But they did lack distance, and they could never come to seem elusive. Olga realized that her own pleasure henceforth lay elsewhere: in the eroticism of a foreigner who got enjoyment from being on the qui vive. Dan sought in vain the drowsy confidence of the little girl who out of youthful, sisterly innocence once used to allow him the excitement of her womb, her breasts, and her lips. He found Olga's body thinner and lighter than ever, but with an impenetrable lightness; a shell. Oh well, never mind, they could see how things went later on.

"Is your book out yet?"

She was eager to get back onto the easy terms of the past.

"*Hagakuré; or, the Art of War?* Yes, I brought you a copy. It's just been published, I still can't understand how. The censors must have been misled by its appearance and taken it for a popular version of a Japanese romance."

The dust jacket was adorned with one of those innumerable Japanese prints of cherry blossoms that to the initiate symbolize the beauty and precariousness of life, but are so understated they leave the layman cold.

Olga could remember the legend quite clearly; she'd presided over its birth, as she had over the genesis of all Dan's other writings. This book dealt with Jocho Yamamoto, a samurai who became a priest in late seventeenth- or early eighteenth-century Japan. His sayings, recorded by one of his disciples and known by the title of *Hagakuré*, became the moral, military, literary, practical, and of course funerary code for the whole samurai tradition. But Yamamoto, who'd proclaimed, "I have found that the way of the samurai is death," didn't kill himself. Though he'd decapitated his cousin in the course of the latter's ritual suicide (this was one of the duties of a second), he himself accepted the new legislation that forbade suicide in the territory ruled over by his feudal lord, Nabeshima, and withdrew from the world for two decades, dying in 1719 at the age of sixty-one. "Hidden among the leaves," discreet and sensitive, the author of haikus and *wakas*, an expert in the rhetoric he considered just as important as the martial arts, he was a man of honor who had also been a man of action, and who believed it is only death that makes us act. The Japanese revived his kamikaze ethic during the last World War, and the fanatical exploits that resulted threw lasting suspicion upon the ancient master. Dan made the case against Yamamoto worse by linking him to the ethic of violence in *Zarathustra*. But the lesson he drew from this parable—for he transposed the historical facts about the eighteenth-century samurai into the world of imagination—was all his own.

In fact (at least this was how Olga recalled Dan's theory), we are inhabited by an unknown force that causes us to act, but when circumstances thwart us, this energy turns back on us and makes us helpless, effeminate, and decadent. Then men of action must follow this trend to its conclusion, not trying to save their lives but spending them unto death. Voluntary self-destruction doesn't end the life of action of an honorable man, it fulfills and crowns it.

The virtuosity of the philosopher-poet, his skill in the martial arts, his sensitivity in the service of the court and of his lord, even if only at a drinking party, form a whole, a circle completed only in the violence of the supreme act of suicide.

Dan was well aware that this strange ethic might derive from a morbid kind of pleasure: its delight in certain pointless acts was rooted in the pain they could cause. But being devoid of all perversity himself, he abandoned the erotic strand in the Yamamoto texts that Mishima was to reveal to an astonished world a few years later. Instead Dan embarked on his own personal meditation.

His book was like some hybrid flower—inspired but completely lacking in structure and clarity. It was like so many fables generated on Slav soil, which might either inflame or enervate; but, caught between the lucidity of the West and the spirituality of the East, they remain unknown and without effect until one day some foreign expert unearths them as curiosities.

So instead—perhaps for some legitimate reason—of committing suicide, Yamamoto started to speak. Moreover, though he himself was proscribed, his words were written down and published. For Dan, all these transgressions gave rise to a question: What if the samurai had meant to hint that there was no better way of acting—before, in, and after death—than joining together the art of war and the art of writing? "Human life lasts but a moment. So let us spend that moment doing what we like. In a world as fleeting as a dream, it is folly to live wretchedly doing only what we hate." Couldn't this be interpreted as an exhortation to write?

And supposing we agree that writing is the only lasting act of pleasure and war combined? Suicide together with secret self-love; exultation in the pain of silence together with self-assertion through the formulation of one's own caprice? Of course, this doesn't apply to all writing. So to which? That which disobeys, which says "I" against all interdictions while pretending to accept them, which appears polite, civilized, attractive, even self-effacing, but only the better to "hide in the cherry tree" and deal the fatal blow, not once and for all but constantly, in the ritual but always slightly different details of a poem perhaps, or in sword-play or calligraphy. For every art is a martial art where you kill in order to attain a new body, a new form.

"Your interpretation is attractive, but perhaps too Christian. Your Yamamoto dodges the ultimate point and portrays writing as a remedy against suicide: isn't that the same as the Passion conquering the Grave?"

"You seem to have forgotten already that I'm in dispute with the regime back home. We have no absolute answer; we can't reject everything. So intellectuals have to compromise to a certain extent when it comes to action. But Yamamoto's parable reminds us there are some compromises that are not surrenders: one is called writing—the kind where the writer risks his job and his life."

"So you're still a moralist, even if you do look like an aesthete."

"There are two things I can't stand: submission and technique. They're both aspects of laziness. Back home, everyone tends to submit to authority, or to the general opinion, which amounts to the same thing. Here you're all technicians. Even you have taken to cutting Mallarmé up into logical and linguistic formulas. But Mallarmé is a man of faith. Frigid, but of faith."

He never used to criticize her. He must have guessed that she'd escaped, that she was increasingly elsewhere.

"For one thing, it's very good exercise for the mind—it strengthens it. Second, it's quite relevant to Mallarmé, who tries so hard to be clear he becomes obscure. You used to keep quoting Pascal, another invalid—'Atheists must express themselves perfectly clearly'—to prove it's impossible to be an atheist. Well, that's precisely what they do here—they try to be perfectly clear. It's a kind of martial art—for a lot of people, anyway. Third, it annoys the Sorbonne!"

"Just as I thought! That's your problem: you're mere technicians because you haven't a solid enough political or religious power to fight against. So you attack any old target instead—empty forms, the Sorbonne, any Tom, Dick, or Harry—and you dissect Mallarmé!"

He addressed her now with the plural *vous*, as if she stood for all the dull inhabitants of the West, deaf to the word of the samurai. He didn't want to admit how alike their manias were, with their shared Utopia in which writing was a martial art. She didn't much want to either.

"I hardly recognize you! What, you trying to stop people from dissecting Mallarmé? You talk like the people who censor your books! Besides, you know as well as I do that if we don't dissect Mallarmé, we don't dissect anything—we just swallow what you call the discourse of power. If you only knew it, they're more politicized here than they are back home. The 'technicians,' to use your terminology, seize every opportunity to criticize the authorities. I met yet another one this morning. They're furious. And their anger's growing. . . ."

"It's just a game. They protest because they're quite safe. You've lost the sense of death—both as a threat and as a motivating force."

"You speak from the outside. Inside, I assure you, people are passionate—"

"To hell with 'people'! What matters is what's written, and your precious structuralism's completely bloodless."

"It's funny to see you so sure of yourself. It doesn't occur to you for a moment there may be something you don't understand, something you don't know how to interpret. . ."

"It suits you, being angry. You're beautiful. More beautiful even than before. Finer, more elegant. Your mother would say you'd got thin. I love you as much as ever, and no doubt forever."

He stroked her hair, and again there was a frontier between them, a barrier slightly more affectionate after their unaccustomed skirmish, but also more inevitable.

"Come on—let's leave the Great Men. And I'll show you the ordinary people and the streets."

The rue de Richelieu went up from the Palais-Royal toward the sinister Bibliothèque Nationale. The vast belly of the reading room, usually so reassuring, smelled dusty. They left. Molière, surrounded by businessmen on their way to the stock exchange, looked sarcastically down upon the fountain. They went through a shopping arcade, then down a hidden flight of stairs to the rue Montpensier and along by the gardens of the Palais-Royal. No more noise now, only the calm safety of classical architecture and the rare equilibrium that transmutes geometry into happiness. The harmony of gray stones, trimmed branches, fountains. Not one millimeter too many, just the impeccable sense of proportion that makes things both light and final. Parisians knew how to relax: the shiny paper of the gift-wrapped packages opened up to the sun, revealing peaceful or mocking faces, letting out joyful laughter, bold jokes, and animated discussions to mingle with the cries of birds and children.

"Do you know what makes the French different? They don't insist on being miserable. Even the middle classes can be carefree and lighthearted."

"I've met Germans who were serious, Italians who were thoughtless, Slavs who were emotional. The French are—"

"Delightful," said Olga.

"Offhand," said Dan.

.

Two weeks went by. Dan could see she'd merged into her new language, her new dresses, her new city.

"I thought we'd make the journey back together."

She didn't think so; she didn't know.

"Do you suppose you'll go back?"

She couldn't, wouldn't answer.

They were on the metro, going from the Bibliothèque Nationale to Montmartre. The empty train swayed horribly, but they remained standing, holding on to the metal rings. They were moving so fast their voices were carried away, and they gazed at each other, already parted, separate, inaudible to each other. Dan was leaving Paris the next day.

"What are you doing this summer?"

"I'm leaving this evening for the IAC symposium. As you know."

She didn't mention that she was only going to drop in on the symposium and then join Hervé on his island.

"Of course. As you know, I'm sad."

"I'm sure we'll meet again."

"I'm sure too. All the more so now that I'm a disciple of Yamamoto and believe in the eternal way of the samurais. We shall all meet again on that way: if not among the cherry trees, then in death."

The noise of the train took some of the pathos out of this farewell. Olga pretended not to hear, and let Dan put his arms around her, enfolding her for the last time in his strong fair body, his once blue eyes growing more and more empty of color.

4

There's no wind so salty as the wind off the Atlantic. It swelled the sail, beat at jib and temples, plucked at eyes and lips with a sharp tang of iodine. Hervé had met her at the station and they'd gone aboard his comfortable nutshell dinghy with its broad hull, resonant in the gusts of wind and glowing like a mahogany cello in the waning afternoon sun. The pearliness of the waves beneath the orange rays, the foam flecking the surface with silver dust, the metallic reflections of the sky—all made the sea look as if it were solid. Sometimes they sped along at top speed, sometimes they just let themselves glide over the smooth, pearly inner skin of that open oyster, the stretch of water known as the Fier, between the coast and the chain of islands.

"It's the open sea, and yet we're as sheltered as if we were inside a shell."

"I'd never heard of this island before."

"No one knows about it except me. It's the Secret Island. I make you a present of it."

He was extravagant and yet full of reserves, ardent and yet austere as his ocean. She had learned to accept him without words, with just a shy but delighted tension in her eyes and cheeks. She was still disoriented by the wind, and stepped onto the landing stage with the lost expression sailors wear, which landlubbers take for affectation. In fact, it's the natural dizziness of an inland bird that has strayed among the gulls and is drunk with oxygen and light.

"I'll show you the toilet and your room, and you'll meet everybody at dinner. They're very old hat, but there's no harm in them. I can't bear either to see too much of them or to break with them altogether—you'll see why. A different world."

The discreet beauty of the place derived from the flatness of the salt marshes. Newly mown lawns merged imperceptibly into the stronger, shiny green of the vineyards. The landscape was too reminiscent of paddy fields to inspire love at first sight. What it did produce was the kind of slow attachment that clever women create, through time and carefulness.

A large garden occupied the site of the old manor house, of which only a few ruins survived. The Montlaur family, when they came here for vacations and weekends, lived in a sort of farmhouse known as the *mas*. It was built around an old windmill with a pointed slate roof, which had become Hervé's own domain. Some distance away from the main house there was a modern annex where a local couple lived as caretakers. Olga was installed in the west or guest wing of the *mas*. The French windows of her room opened onto the gravel of a dying garden that sloped down toward the water. A low wall of old stones acted as a border between the Montlaur property and the inlet. On the horizon you could see a curve of the island and what was known as the Whales' Lighthouse. Daisies dotted the grass, geraniums in their urns stood out against the gray and pale blue background; an immense sky streaked with scarlet contrasted with the pallor of earth and sea. The sun had started to set, and soon its blaze would make men, houses, and plants all invisible. There was nothing; you were alone on a thin film floating in a dark red, orange, and indigo sky. The island was just an excuse for living in the sky.

"I love this place because when you're here, you're alone with the light."

You were even more alone in the mill tower. Beyond the entrance hall, where the Montlaurs liked to take their aperitifs looking out through a broad window onto the ocean, a spiral staircase led up to Hervé's studio—to the bedroom and the bathroom. Another staircase went up higher still, and there, under the converging beams, Sinteuil had chosen to have his study. There, leaving the Montlaurs behind, he lived alone with the light and his books and his work.

"Did you have a good journey, mademoiselle?"

Jean de Montlaur was tall and thin, very polite but taciturn. He left small talk and literature to his wife, Mathilde (née des Réaux), Hervé's mother, and spent his time running his factory with the help of his younger brother, François. François was the bachelor of the family, and followed Jean around like his shadow. The brothers were so absorbed in their work they were practically never apart. Mathilde seemed absolutely to bloom between these two gallant escorts. She liked to wear dresses and blouses made of spotted fabric, with big bows in front, which gave her an imposing, almost regal appearance.

"Mama, this is my friend Olga Morena."

"Delighted to meet you, mademoiselle."

Olga also met cousin Xavier des Réaux and his wife, Odile, who'd come to spend a few days by the sea. Everyone seemed very attached to the old family house.

"Hervé must have told you about our legend," Mathilde began, a glass of champagne in her hand. "There used to be an old manor house here that was given to our great-great-great-great-uncle des Réaux by Louis Seize in return for some service or other—before the Revolution, of course. He was a sailor, and used to come here to hunt. Shooting, like our family's other predilections, for swordplay and fencing, is a hereditary skill: it can't be taught—it's handed down from generation to generation. So Hervé's naturally a perfect shot, though he isn't in the least interested in it. . . ."

She was an excellent storyteller, voluble yet accurate, enthusiastic yet ironic, and kept her audience spellbound. The story continued up to the Occupation, when the Germans destroyed the manor house, together with other old buildings in the area, to make way for fortifications against an Allied landing on the Atlantic coast.

"The Germans razed everything to the ground. Needless to say, we were against them, and my husband—a very reticent man, as you'll have noticed—did a lot to help the Resistance. Oh no, we didn't get any medals. Unless you count the destruction of the house as a kind of negative tribute awarded by the enemy. To make a long story short, you can imagine what a scene of desolation we found when we came back after the war. We tried to hide the scars with gardens, and we patched up the *mas* and the mill, but it's not the same anymore. I shall always see the island as it was in my father's day. He used to sit on the bench in front of the house just as our ancestor did, and go duck shooting."

"How horrible!" said Hervé.

"Perhaps. We saw things differently in those days."

"I hear you're getting more and more famous," put in Odile des Réaux. She was a woman of the world and knew how to change the subject.

"I don't know about that. But things aren't going too badly . . ."

"And is the young lady in the same line?" asked the cousin.

While Olga wondered what that line might be, Hervé came to the rescue.

"Olga's doing a literary thesis for the CNRS."

"I thought the CNRS was a scientific setup."

"Olga's a kind of literary scientist."

That was sufficient, and sufficiently obscure, to allow the matter to rest for the moment.

"And do you have good news from your parents?"

Mathilde was certainly a perfect hostess.

Olga remembered the last letter she'd received: her grandfather had just died, and she could imagine the cemetery full of flowers, the smell of incense and candles, the mixture of bitterness and happiness the families of the departed feel as they gather together in the graveyard, a place of bustling solitude out of sight both of the regime and of history. She could imagine the harbor town nearby, where she used to spend her holidays at Grandfather's when she was a child; the whole peninsula, with its hundreds of churches built of red brick and white stone; the garlands of fish hung up to dry on the timbered housefronts.

"They're surviving somehow or other, thank you. Dad has his medicine, the church, music."

She stopped. Curiosity is merely politeness. People don't want to hear all the details.

"It seems you've taken to writing for the Communist press? You may even have become a member of the Party!"

Uncle François was using the information at his disposal to attack Hervé on behalf of the family as a whole.

"Not at all! No connection! Just because you're not a conformist, it doesn't mean you're a Communist."

But Hervé was trying to make too subtle a distinction.

"I can understand him, you know. Well, up to a point."

Xavier des Réaux was proving an unexpected ally.

"In my village"—he was referring to the village near his château in the Gironde—"they've been socialists for a couple of generations now, I believe. And do you know, I'm with them— if you hold yourself aloof from them, you're done for. That was the trouble with the people who spent their time at Versailles instead of staying on their estates with their peasants. It was all their fault. We got the guillotine because we weren't socialistic enough, if you see what I mean." He was addressing Hervé, who eyed him mockingly in return. "I know you agree with me, Jean."

Jean always agreed so long as everyone was happy and he didn't have to offer any explanations.

Olga didn't know what "fault" Xavier was talking about. Hervé leaned over to explain that Cousin Xavier was expounding his theories on the causes of the French Revolution.

"You'll frighten our guest with your stories of guillotines and Communists—she's only just escaped from all that!"

Mathilde was feeling her way. She didn't know yet whether Olga was a Communist trying to lead Hervé astray or a refugee deserving of pity.

"I can remember '36," she went on. "I was carrying Hervé at the time. And our workers—for whom we'd made so many sacrifices!—had turned rebellious and called me every name they could think of. It was awful!"

"They may have had their reasons," retorted Hervé. "Didn't you ever wonder about that?"

"So my son's ready to forsake his mother for his ideas, is he! But you know, Olga (I hope you don't mind my calling you by your first name?), whenever I hear Hervé going on like this— and all the rest of it: he hasn't treated us to the whole rigmarole yet—I tell myself there's a remedy for it!"

Mathilde's humor was helping her get her own back.

"Why don't we change the subject?" suggested Jean de Mont- laur soothingly. "Politics isn't the ideal subject for family discus- sion."

"But we'll come back to it," Hervé threatened.

Mathilde led the way in to dinner. Oysters cooked in white wine and bass braised with fennel provided a temporary lull.

("Did you bring your camera? Now's the time to use it!" "Of course I brought it. But some other time . . .")

After dinner they all retired to their rooms. Hervé came and fetched her and they went out on the beach, where they made love at length on still-warm sand alternately illuminated and abandoned by the turning beam of the lighthouse.

They couldn't bring themselves to part, so she slept in the mill. The Montlaurs pretended not to notice. Every morning Germaine or Gérard left her breakfast outside the door of the guest room in the left wing.

For ten days Olga and Mathilde continually observed and grew closer to each other. Meals tended to last a long time, and Hervé, impatient, would soon leave the table. But Olga, think- ing it wouldn't be correct for her always to leave when he did, sometimes waited and kept his mother company. Mathilde was delighted: conversation was a passion with her.

"You know the whole family now, my dear Olga, except my daughter, Isabelle. She doesn't come here very often, I'm sorry to say! It's rather strange, actually—she and Hervé used to be very fond of each other. Isabelle adored her little brother. They used to spend whole days shut up together in his room talking or, more often, listening to the latest records—Gillespie, Ellington . . . I'm sorry, I expect I've mispronounced the names. Jazz, anyway. And then Isabelle met a nice young fellow called Georges Duval—between ourselves, a very undistinguished young man—and eventually married him. I can't think what she sees in him, though I'm told he's a good tennis player. Can you see the point of that—a man being very good at tennis? I can't. And he's got a good job in insurance. But of course, he's not one of us. And apart from tennis, which my daughter seems to set such store by, and insurance—I do hope he doesn't get his sums wrong!—he hasn't got anything to say for himself. And he doesn't make any effort either. With the best will in the world, my dear Olga, I can't say I find a man with nothing to say very entertaining. In short, I feel sorry for Isabelle, and don't see her very often. To my great regret, of course, Olga dear."

When Mathilde felt she'd been too frank, she drew back, but in a way that implied she did so merely out of consideration for the distress Olga must have felt at her indiscretion. Then the girl's eyes stared blankly, from beneath their slanting squirrel eyelids, at her grand and voluble hostess.

Mathilde knew all the tradesmen and storekeepers in the village and all the mayors and members of the local council, past, present, and to come, together with their families, which had of course been "close to ours for generations." They in turn revered her. She offered her opinion on every local problem, and if ever she failed to do so, they would come and ask for it. If she'd been a few years younger and taken a crash course in contemporary terminology, she'd have made a good cabinet minister: her quick wit and ready tongue lent her an efficiency far beyond what was traditional in her class. Hervé secretly admired her, but he found her wearing, and mocked when he wasn't actually quarreling with her.

Surprisingly enough, her son's talent, and even more his success, had rather thrown Mathilde. But she had her own views about him. It was unfortunately clear that he couldn't be counted on to take over the factory, so the family would have to think about selling it, and in the meantime trim their lifestyle. But it was becoming increasingly obvious to all of them that Hervé had a talent for writing, as had been observed from the start by

Vaillac and Valence, "the favorite authors of the Vatican and the Kremlin, to quote the newspapers, though I find it hard to believe, myself. But of course, art is a matter of taste—it's so personal."

Nonetheless Mathilde regarded Hervé as a rebel. No, she wasn't thinking of all the screwing that found its way into his books. ("He'll get over it. After all, libertinism was a noble tradition even if our family's never gone in for that sort of thing: our ancestors tended to find themselves on the battlefield or in the cloister.") She was thinking of the Algerian war.

"It's still too close to us—France is still suffering from the trauma. I don't know if you've noticed, but no one ever talks about it. Hervé was supposed to go into the army: Loïc's father, General Charlier, who has a love-hate passion for him, arranged for his file to come out on top. Hervé was duly called up, but he was ill and managed to get himself declared unfit. Thank God for Pange and Darleaux, who was already minister at the time— if it hadn't been for him, Hervé would have been killed on the Tunisian front. I'm not exaggerating. All his friends who went did get killed. Paul, his best friend, was the first. Hasn't he told you about it? I'm not surprised. Paul was the most brilliant of their group, and Hervé adored him. When we heard of Paul's death, Hervé first shut himself up in his room and then disappeared—we didn't have any news of him for a month. Whenever he gets gloomy and withdraws to his mill tower—the Pythoness's Lair, I call it, trying to make a joke of it—then I know he's thinking about the other world, about Paul, about death. If death really *is* another world for someone who doesn't believe in heaven and hell. What do you think? They used to make plans together: the review, novels, essays, and I don't know what else. It must grieve Hervé to be the survivor; he feels obliged to drive himself to the limit, to carry everything through to the limit, in an attempt to achieve what his dead friend can never achieve. That's how I see it. He became an extremist, or, as they say nowadays, a member of the avant-garde, after Algeria, after Paul's death. He's looking for some meaning in the void. That's what I think. And that pseudonym of his, which of course is a reference to Proust, do you think it's just a declaration of war on the family? Maybe. But I see it as a mask worn over a void. Oh, I may make you laugh, Olga dear, but before I read Vaillac, our regional author, whom I adore, I read my Bossuet, too."

Olga was suddenly listening intently. Did Mathilde possess a piece of the Hervé jigsaw that she herself knew nothing about? He'd never breathed a word to *her* about Paul, or Algeria, or the war. "A massacre—nothing more or less," he would sometimes say before going on to talk about something else. "Some people try to forget it. But they're all survivors—this is a survivor standing in front of you now. I manage as best I can. How? Ask me another!"

"You've met François, my brother-in-law, haven't you?" Mathilde had already strayed from the subject. "A charming young man, isn't he? A bachelor, like Hervé. 'Like Hervé, so far,' as my husband points out. François says he's refrained from marrying so as not to split up the estate. But I don't believe in altruism. I suspect he may have a secret passion—don't you agree, a splendid fellow like that? A hidden passion for some fatal beauty."

Or for his brother? And why not even for Mathilde? Olga felt she was getting submerged in the family saga. Enough! It was time she got herself out of this.

"I'm afraid I must leave you—I've got to correct some proofs."

"You run along, my dear—I know I'm a chatterbox."

"Of course you're not!"

"Of course I am!"

Olga found herself getting to like the magnanimity of the old Montlaurs, the frivolity so easily discerned through their facade of propriety, their determination to adapt themselves to a new world in which they too were mere survivors—survivors who held on firmly to their place but were ready to take on another if the occasion arose.

This was shown by the fact that they weren't too shocked to see their son taking up with a foreigner.

"The girl seems very well mannered," said Mathilde to her husband.

"It looks as if she and Hervé get on well. At least, she calms him down," said Jean de Montlaur.

The Sauternes and the Médocs, together with the bream and the bass, vanished when the older Montlaurs departed. Olga and

Hervé stayed on at the island until the middle of September, smooth and dark from sunbathing, steeped in the mauve and yellow light of the sunsets. Long hours of swimming out of sight of the shoreline stretched their muscles and tautened their skin like raw silk. A few shrimps, grilled sardines, a salad, and some peaches were enough to satisfy their hunger. The local wine, dry and light, imparted the headiness that warms and stimulates limbs, lips, breasts, and sexual organs but leaves the eyes and mind intact. There's nothing like wind and sun and the chill of the open sea to keep you lucid in the middle of summer and in the middle of a dream. Sometimes Hervé would take the boat out on his own and stay away until the next tide, or the one after that.

He liked to be on his own. He liked to be on his own and meet people she would never know. He liked to be on his own with women known and unknown. He liked to be on his own writing letters, making phone calls, and roaring with laughter, writing more letters and receiving them, making still more phone calls, and meeting people who left him stimulated but still completely alone.

Was she being neglected? You had to be very proudly humble—and her humility *was* proud—not to think yourself the cause of his running away, and to draw strength from his absence. Whether you give way to anxiety depends on how well you can hold out in the test of nerve that's known as love. Women tend not to know this, and to think of themselves as victims because they see themselves as mistresses. Olga did know it, because crossing the boundaries of countries and languages matures the mind at the same time as it renews the body. Some injuries help their victim find his true place.

This precocious maturity of hers had taught her not to worry. When Hervé shut himself up from noon till sunset in the study in the mill, she occupied herself learning the code of the gulls—how to get near them without frightening them, either by swimming silently or by diving into the waves and disappearing into the salty foam. Moreover, ozone in the wind and the tang of seaweed are great stimulants to reading. She'd never read so much in her life. *Remembrance of Things Past* and *Inner Experience* went wonderfully well with the white of the dunes. She had a couple of articles to finish and some proofs to correct, and when she felt sleepy, there were ideograms: she would memorize at least ten Chinese characters, outlining them on the palm of her hand or crouching down and drawing them with a gull's feather in the wet sand until the dying waves came and lapped around her calves.

"How's the Chinese coming? Keep at it—the best way to see things is from a distance, from the antipodes! Here's your mail. There are going to be problems at *Now*—I've just had Brunet on the phone."

As Olga opened Carole's letter, Hervé went on.

"Have you ever heard of somebody called Bogdanov?"

"The one who was criticized by Lenin? Vaguely."

"Well, in the present context you're him, and Lenin—you'll never guess—is our friend Maille."

"How's that?"

"Your essay on the logic of carnival and its ambiguities and whatever—you know what you wrote better than I do—together with its links with Lautréamont . . . Well, what all that adds up to, my dear, is a statement that truth doesn't exist, or at any rate, that it's unknowable. And it seems that's exactly what old Bogdanov dreamed up before he got ticked off by Lenin!"

"What a joke!"

"I think it's a nuisance myself. It's all very well for Maille to pursue you with snide remarks, since he can't do it any other way. But what's more serious is that they're trying to link the review to the Communist party. Your stuff about carnival, laughter, death, ambivalence, and so on, not to mention eroticism and other inner experiences, has nothing to do with it. But they want to grab everything in the name of the Revolution! But as long as I have anything to do with it, the review will never be an 'organ' of the Party. As they very well know."

"Who are 'they'?"

"Certain individuals who are going to come unstuck and be shown the door."

"Editions de l'Autre must want to be a responsible magazine, perhaps not exactly CP, but credible and therefore in touch with the 'great problems' of the day."

"I do keep in touch: as you know, we'll be going to the conference organized by *Red*. But that's as far as it goes. We do discuss things, which is complicated and tedious enough, but not in order to serve either the Communists or anybody else. Writing obeys a different kind of logic—it enables people to live and breathe and make love, and to die if you like—but *our* real object is to express the need for fresh air. And as far as literature is concerned, fresh air begins with music. 'Objective' and 'subjective,' 'true' and 'false' belong to the examination hall and the Central Committee!"

"I always wonder whether people like Maille, who're so infatuated with Lenin and October and the rest of the folklore, are merely dangerous innocents, or whether, as you seem to think, French culture is so different from all the rest that it produces a completely different crop when communism or socialism is grafted onto it. You'll probably get me to agree with you in the end."

"You can't expect to shake up an old country without giving it a bit of a fright. That's the height of chic, my dear, only present-day observers don't understand snobbery and take it for terror. Real snobbery calls for suspicion—you need to play the game and sleep with one eye open. Without suspicion a snob degenerates into an ideologist or a party leader. It's childish of Maille to try it on. We've no intention of becoming a puppet manipulated by our own strategies."

"It's hard to draw the dividing line, as you've good reason to know."

"Hard, but not impossible. All you have to do is go on writing, instead of philosophizing or being an activist. Literature is something so individual it can only preserve you from the masses—both from being preached at *by* them and from preaching *to* them. As for literature's ability to change things . . . yes, I believe in it, but only after the manner of dreams—beneath the surface and in the long term. Indefinably, as you put it."

"We're not going back to Paris just because of that . . . ?"

"We'll see. Anything new with you?"

"Everything's fine. Carole's enjoying herself with her Indian myths and organizing another expedition. Apparently the atmosphere at the Institute is getting more and more explosive. Martin has started a Revolutionary Club that solemnly dissects Russian and Chinese texts, and he's calling for a thorough reform of lectures, examinations, and recruitment."

"That could be more fruitful than the activities of our own follow-the-leaders—all they want is an organization that'll help them promote themselves. Why shouldn't Martin start a Revolutionary Club? The academics need to find themselves some scope for action. Even attempting to reform the CP from the inside, or as a fellow traveler, is worth a try. Between you and me, poor old Wurst's got his work cut out for him, and we'd better give him a hand. But hell, we're writers, not Boy Scouts, even if our elderly young men seem to have forgotten it."

Hervé is on the warpath. His eyes fill with rage; the face of a reckless fighter can be seen under the yachtsman's tan; wrath transforms him into a potential killer. The gentle body and boyish laughter are engulfed in the salt marshes of anger. Wait till he surfaces again.

"What else?" He's noticed she's still there, reading her mail. "You get as many letters as a government minister!"

"Ilya Romanski is coming to Paris to help Benserade set up an International Society of Semantics, and he wants me to be general secretary. They've noticed that the meaning of what people say can't be explained wholly in terms of grammar. Phew! If I take the job, I'll be working with Benserade—the expert on Indo-European mentalities, the most profound and cultured linguist there is! It's terrific!"

"You'll have to look into it. What else?"

"Edelman's in Baltimore—apparently the students are restless and revolution's on the way."

"Led by Pascal?"

"Edelman's quite capable of bringing him into it. Lauzun and Saïda have taken part in a symposium on psychoanalysis. They were so obscure no one could understand a word they said. But they're in the process of turning into gurus. Especially Saïda."

"All right, fine—France's influence is spreading through the world and the Great Evening is getting nearer." Hervé was smiling again. "Why don't we swim farther out?"

The tide had swelled the bay with a mass of warm water smelling of kelp. They crossed the great womblike pool and reached the chilly ocean beyond. The westering sun shone straight into their faces, and they had to swim with their eyes shut to avoid the light and the salt. They didn't feel any weariness: the cold water whipped their muscles and stimulated their blood, and they could feel their skin getting darker, warmer, smoother.

"Oh, I forgot to tell you—Hermine's had an operation. You know I'm fond of her." She knew he'd loved her. Olga's long, Mongolian eyes widened and tilted into a fan: the sign, in her, of a question. "Gynecological butchery and a divorce in prospect."

Hervé was talking as he dried himself. Breathless after their two-hour swim, he spoke quickly to avoid sounding too dramatic. "Why didn't you tell me about it?"

"It's just life, my dear. The usual thing. As soon as you get beneath the surface of your—and my—correspondents' lives, that's what you find: a bad novel. Don't worry, she'll manage."

The sun was about to set, and they took refuge by the window in the mill. Nothing like a modest white wine and sulphur-yellow, dark red, and indigo fires on the horizon for taming nagging anxieties and muffling the cries of the gulls.

5

The details of everyday life—insignificant, petty, and horrible . . . I can imagine every point of view and play all the relevant roles: be insignificant, petty, and horrible as the case requires. Actually I can understand what people say to me best (or rather, come nearer the excess or the senselessness of it) when I make up my mind to hear, amid the insignificance of the story they tell, something contemptible crying out for forgiveness. Why? In order to know myself, or maybe in order to draw a bit nearer to another and less tiresome horror, and so on and so forth, until life becomes livable—that is, a matter of supreme indifference which is occasionally amusing.

And so I am deep in horror. I don't complain—it's my job. People pay to be stupid and wicked, even contemptible when they feel like it, in my presence, in the no less abject but touching hope of being reborn, of making a new life for themselves. "Madame Joëlle Cabarus, psychoanalyst—help!" For some, it's a new reli-

gion; for others, the latest fashion in charlatanism. For me, it's the only true way of life. That may sound rather highfalutin.

But really it's more like a surreal encounter, around a couch, between a bullfighter and a verbal alchemist. The two protagonists occupy all possible positions, simultaneously or alternately. I am the bullfighter, aiming at my patient's confused meaning; then suddenly I'm the bull, stung by a banderillo hurled straight at my physical, intellectual, or family weaknesses. I dissect the screen phrases in search of the word or syllable concealing the unsaid; but I can't find it unless the other person's phrases become temporarily my own. I'm desired, I love: no, it's not a game, it's a wild passion! But there are still two of us—I insist on that. It's my job to insist that there really are two of us. Or rather, three. It's a debilitating journey, a round trip between words and the body, with the rare reward of sometimes hitting the spot. What spot? A memory, pleasure, or pain which suddenly makes sense and brings about a change.

I studied psychiatry, like Arnaud, my husband, who's now the great authority, the mandarin. We go on with our hospital work: I put up with the burden, but madness doesn't fascinate me anymore. It still interests me, though, as is shown by the fact that I'm always rubbing shoulders with it: they say that's how psychiatrists escape it. Arnaud's completely wrapped up in the hospital; he believes more and more in the supreme importance of brain chemistry. I understand, but I don't altogether agree. Anyhow, we're growing farther and farther apart. We scarcely speak. One day we won't even notice when we pass each other in the bathroom. But there's still the old genetic complicity between us that nothing can shake. I call it "genetic" because of the accumulation of memories and actions inside us both, made up of all we did and read and felt and lived through together once, in the past, as intensely together as twins: making love, pleasure, forgetting; understanding without words, merging; without need for speeches or comments; close together or apart. Now, two stars launched on parallel orbits, interdependent because of the laws of gravity, but unable ever to meet.

Arnaud never tried to stand in the way, but he thought my analysis with Maurice Lauzun was absurd. Sometimes he'd let fall a scathing remark: "Of course, your nonconformist analyst actually worships the medical and every other kind of establishment. So having a Cabarus on his couch . . ." I know. It's true. So what? No one ever said an analyst had to be a saint. Lauzun at least has the courage—a bit too exhibitionistic, probably—to flaunt the opposite view and even elevate it into a theory.

All those intellectuals and literary people who come to his seminar: I *wonder what they're after. Above all, I wonder how people can write novels, and thus create untruth, a world as they'd like it to be and not as it is, while everyone is sick with lies. They think to cure lies with a lie that is beautiful. A false notion if ever there was one. . . . And yet here am I, writing these notes. Is it a diary? Am I trying to make up for the lack of conversation with Arnaud? Is this the erotomania of a thirty-something woman using writing to express repressed desires? A compensation invented by an unneeded mother? I had Jessica very early, when I was still studying; she passed through my womb like a dream and I handed her over to my parents—"The best present you ever gave us!" my father pronounced. She was a second daughter to them: a precocious reader, brilliant. "Don't worry, Mom, I can manage without you"—that's about all she ever says to me, and it's hard to be proud of it. Is this notebook a substitute for another child? Perhaps it also represents a desire to commune with myself, to draw myself in after all the days spent spreading myself out to fit into the lives and words and weaknesses of others.*

Interpreting is shaping things according to what one decides to eliminate. So it's closer to writing than is generally supposed. The joy of discovery! Isn't that the kind of vanity that afflicts "creative artists," who claim to be so serious and ascetic?

This morning Lauzun's lecture referred to persecution as the artist's friend. What is one to write about? Hatred. A writer persecutes a persecutor. Oedipus doesn't kill Laius—he hates Jocasta because he desires her, and vice versa. So Oedipus isn't Oedipus anymore; he becomes—for example—a painter. Is the war of the sexes the secret subject of the arts? If so, what about the troubadours?

Short of that eternal and universal conflict, there's the night of disgust. The enemy doesn't take on an external form—it invades me, and all I have to fight it with is repulsion, a repulsion in which horror and I are bound together. And what am I expelling, horror or myself? Neither; both at once. Amid this murk one certainty emerges: the certainty, which can turn hostile, that I am someone else.

May 22, 1967

The cocktail party at Editions de l'Autre—a ritual entertainment for the intellectual set. But because they're Arnaud's publishers, we went. The reception room and the caterer's tent weren't big enough to hold so many shams: we didn't just rub shoulders, we were crammed together like sardines. They were all so jealous of and full of hatred for one another that the smiles they exchanged were quite blatantly meaningless. In this interplay of masks, a kind of poor man's Versailles, devoid of elegance, all the men and women were alike. I could see fifty examples of Marie-Paule Longueville's coiffure: bleached yellow hair with a tuft by each ear and slides on either side of a middle parting, the whole thing framing flabby, overred lips frozen into the typical grimace of a charming up-to-the-minute socialite. Fifty Marie-Paule Longue-villes—it was like a picture by Andy Warhol: Ten Jackie Kennedys, Twelve Marilyn Monroes, *a series of flashes not of the same person but of the same fragments of what might have been a person. A sequence of images designed to be consumed, but where were the consumers? Everyone was canceled out by everyone else in sated familiarity. Only a Warhol could make out the minute differences between all these mass-produced products of weary snobbery. But wait—among the almost identical faces, I made out, as with a series of spotlights, the carnivorous jaw of Madame Bigorre; Catherine Maille's hair, standing on end with migraine; Josette Wurst's eyes, pale with repressed age. Then my spotlights started to rove about and became quite entertaining: not very kind, but almost bearable. I followed Warhol's example. I collected details so as not to get caught up in the production line myself.*

The green stripes of the tent, for example, reminded me of shutters by the sea: grass-green paint standing out against sun-steeped mists soon to be swept away by the wind from the incoming tide. I clung to signs and shapes that led me to other signs and shapes. I gazed at the footprints of my memory so as to escape what was around me and without memory. People at the end of the road, sipping champagne to kid themselves they were sparkling.

"Well, Madame Cabarus, the Word has been made flesh, has it? And more and more expensive?"

Sinteuil's line is mockery. He's like a youth challenging the boredom all around him, spraying it with his laughter. To underline his determination not to belong, he was standing a long way away from the tables laden with petits fours, popping open bottles of champagne at frequent intervals.

"You hate artifice, don't you? Well, this is a veritable fireworks display! It may not be visible because these fireworks are of the mind, as befits such an august setting. The mind, the spirit—but spirits, though they may not be seen, can certainly be heard . . . and drunk."

A roar of laughter accompanied the broaching of another bottle.

How do you talk to a man who uses a pseudonym? I'm inclined to think that beneath a mask of laughter he hides someone who's a stranger to himself. But I'm sure he doesn't think so. I've read what he's written, and his psychedelic books suggest that for him, communication is . . . how shall I put it? . . . viral—that's it: perpetually contaminated by viruses which fragment, merge, and destroy things, and sometimes put them together again. But it seems this viral rhythm can produce neither appearance nor essence—no, everything is imagination, metaphor, scintillation. He's a funny chap, Sinteuil. So I didn't answer, just gave him a broad smile. I doubt very much if his logic is therapeutic, but it may correspond more closely than others to the world as it is.

I went back into the reception room, breathed in the fetid air of the cocktail party, and wondered if it was going to make me ill. I caught a glimpse of Sinteuil's girlfriend's high cheekbones and squirrel-tail hair. Olga, I think her name is. They're the season's star attraction, the pair of them: everyone watches them with sham indifference, hoping to detect some pretext for scandal. In this trivial society it takes something really out of the way to produce a lasting liaison. So they're regarded as freaks. And it looks to me as if, exposed to such observation, they're beginning to see themselves as freaks. Maybe that's what they are. Olga went over to the champagne and sank her teeth in an olive-topped canapé.

"I didn't know intellectuals had such voracious appetites," remarked Bigorre, winner of some recent prize or other of which the poor girl seemed unaware.

She almost choked on her olive.

"I suppose they don't get much to eat back home," whispered Catherine Maille, loud enough for her victim to hear.

"Hunger never stopped anyone from spying. On the contrary," Madame Bigorre continued.

They both went on drinking mechanically, not knowing what they drank.

"Do you really think that? She looks so innocent!"

I recognized Marie-Paule Longueville's accents behind me:

"Joëlle, darling, how lovely to see you! You and Arnaud must come to dinner one of these days—you really must! One never sees you at all now, and it's silly to lose touch like that."

"We don't go out much these days. So much work . . ."

"Exactly! I want to see you for professional as well as personal reasons. I'm . . . how shall I put it? . . . Can you guess? I really must talk to you."

"In that case . . ."

I left it to her to clinch the matter.

"May I call you?"

"Of course."

I got off lightly there. Next time I'll pass her on to one of my colleagues.

Marie-Paule and Arnaud used to go sailing together in Brittany when they were in their teens. The Longuevilles and the Cabaruses used to see a lot of one another. But later . . .

It was getting beyond a joke. I was starting to see Marie-Paule Longueville's bleached hair proliferating again: fifty of her curls, fifty of her faded, powdery smiles, a hundred bottles of mineral water, two hundred glasses of Beaujolais-villages, a hundred and fifty pieces of toast spread with foie gras . . . I wanted to throw up.

"Let's leave, shall we?"

Arnaud's firm voice. Once again, without exchanging a word, we were on the same wavelength. Outside in the dark I thought I recognized Ilya Romanski, the elderly linguist, on the arm of some young beauty. Though he's practically blind, he's still attractive. He was preceded by a Zorro-like cape and a fragrant cigar: Lauzun, who couldn't have been flashier if he'd tried.

September 29, 1967

I'm more shocked by sham than by stupidity or illness. There's nothing more cruel, more widespread, or more eternal than duplicity. Those who've mastered it are gamblers who rule the world. But I must admit my moral reservations yield to my fascination with their skill at pretending not to pretend while in fact they never do anything else.

For after all, isn't the art of pretending, or imitating, necessary to a child if he's to become an independent being, that unique individual we all aspire to be? As parents and educators know, pretense is part of "becoming authentic." Error—and horror—creeps in when people get stuck in it: when they are always pretending but are unaware of it (the nitwits), or when they're aware but persist (the cynics). Another alternative is that they know, suffer because of it, and either kill themselves or consult a shrink (the patients). The people at the cocktail party belong mostly to the first two categories; very few of them think they're ill.

Someone once said it took talent to be ill because illness—the stupidity of the body—calls for exceptional brightness to make up for the failure of cellular intelligence. Well, it takes another kind of talent to be a patient—or an "analysand," as Lauzun calls it, to underline the fact that the person on the couch is an active participant.

Talent is a desire to make what we have bear fruit (see the parable in Matthew 25:14, from which the word is borrowed). And what we have is *naturally a weight. Is this weight made of gold? Who can give it, and to whom? And how can it be turned into cash? The lowest form of talent consists in defining stupidities and turning them, without artifice, into cash. Artifice is an addition that makes stupidities look handsome and witty. Without it there is only the dull talent of the plow, a primitive furrow scratched out at ground level. Desire must be of a childlike audacity to succeed carelessly in throwing off care. Such patients produce a literature that's primitive and graceless.*

Then there are the boring ones—the ones I haven't the talent to understand, and whom I refuse. I won't accept them as patients—let them try elsewhere. Those whom I keep, and who decide to stay, try to find speech to fill the silence that's hurting them. They try to fit empty, feeble, wild, and always inadequate words to the sensations and passions they imagine they experience, but that in fact exist only when they are named. By "exist" I mean attain a meaning or direction that promotes life. That's it—speech is an additional immune system: unknown, mysterious, unpredictable.

And what about the inexpressible? Yes, but that grows less and less, comforted by the hope of reaching, briefly, the shore of living words.

Patients are failed or fledgling writers who have no readers—they are unskilled but bold. They're always trying to survey their stupidity; they revel in it so as not to die of it, and by putting it into words they make an obscene kind of map.

A cocktail party is full of unwitting patients. But the people who come and inflict their balderdash on me confront me with a senseless banality that I'm supposed to make sense of. No easy task. I have to start by numbing my faculties, by immersing myself in my own stupidity.

Take Frank, for example. He couldn't be at the Editions de l'Autre's cocktail party, but he'd have made an ideal guest jabbering away at a jamboree thrown by his own high school. But high schools don't give cocktail parties, and Frank doesn't know what to do when there's nothing to be done— it makes him anxious, and with him anxiety is a complaint, a cocktail of complaints.

It's up to me to help him get by. But he gets by on his own, by talking to me: I'm his mother, his sister, and another woman, too—more and more another. I must proceed with tact: touch him, but not too much.

An underground anthill: we dig away, and between the armchair and the couch we weave a labyrinth of little details as insignificant as nail clippings—pathetic if you look at them in terms of happiness or unhappiness. An anthill that rises toward the surface and cracks appearances. Those who worm their way through manage to change their lives—or at least their jobs, their professions, their husbands or wives, their power, or their money. The most committed (the most deeply wounded? the most passionate? the most hysterical?) want everything: they want to blast everything, have everything, use up everything. Frank attacks the Essential, the Ministry, the System, and, to use his own expression, "puts his shoulder to the wheel" by going to seminars in the Latin Quarter with his friend Martin.

One day he'll be able to transform his ideal pattern into a tableau vivant *reflecting his own desires, his fears of being seduced, and his phantoms of a maternal father and flagellant mother who between them ravage and delight him. He talks to me about them four times a week in secret, in the hope of being able to decide to belong to only one sex.*

Is it possible to belong to only one sex? Perhaps, if you don't belong to any sex at all anymore. Like me. Like me? My little anthill flows into the streets of the protesters. That's its weakness. Or its strength.

What on earth am I doing here, with Madame J. Caca and her Russian shopping bag? It's like being in another world, an unknown universe. In Greek "lousy foreigner" is Barbara Kaka—I assure you, I'm not making it up, my dear lady. Aeschylus said it, and Benserade quoted it as recently as yesterday. Perhaps you knew that already, and I'm wasting my time here. Wasting, losing myself. Barbara Kaka.

A certain talent. A baby bombards its mother with its sphincters, the one above and the one below, for fear she might drop or mutilate him. And he gets pleasure from it, he doesn't remain passive. The scourged one scourges. He hits out with what he's got. I survive his attacks. That will be all for today. He goes away relieved.

II. Saint-André-des-Arts

6

The rue de Seine, flooded with sunshine, seems to lead down to the sea. But when the stroller comes out by the broad gray river, its course held back by its banks, he realizes all the wind from the ocean has done is swell the light that hovers over the water—an expanded light that lifts up the sky, dazzles the present, and suspends eternity over a Paris still pursuing its earthly history.

Martin Cazenave has just left the marital apartment over the Longueville Gallery on the corner of the rue des Beaux-Arts, and can't make up his mind whether to make for a café terrace in the rue Callot or for one in the carrefour de Buci, farther on. But instead he turns right, onto the quai Conti, walks past the regular but barren beauty of the Institute, conceived by Le Vau to fulfill Mazarin's bequest, and finds himself on the pont des Arts. The promontory of the Vert-Galant, laden with weeping willows, acacias, and chestnuts, stands out on the right like the innocent camouflage of an aircraft carrier. The île de la Cité. Martin is alone at last.

His marriage to Marie-Paule Longueville three years ago caused a scandal that delighted him. "I don't understand you," his mother had protested. "Marie-Paule is your cousin and much older than you. And to top it off, though it's no use telling you because you don't share our views about morals—she's a divorcée!"

Exactly. To have his mother's sister's daughter in his bed was disturbing, and Martin loved to lose himself in the lips, hair, and ample breasts he'd known before in another life, the life of an infant. And that wasn't all: to the charms of this perfumed paradise Marie-Paule added what a Cazenave mother could never possess—the muscular legs of a horsewoman—plus a sure instinct for provocation which had brought her out of the Ecole du Louvre and into modern art. Like all women who live on unhappiness, Marie-Paule had begun by marrying a man she found she couldn't bear, and then got a divorce. So her father made her the director of the extremely bourgeois Longueville Gallery, which she ran very badly. She proceeded to quarrel with her family and surround herself with young men whose talents lay in the future, and who counted on her to enable them to live from their art. Marie-Paule's attitude was one of unwitting subversion, arising out of anxiety. In 1965 women like her weren't feminists yet, but they were quite prepared to exchange a Balenciaga dress for a pair of jeans, or to marry some mysterious young man, like Martin, who might turn out to be a genius. "Some wear out their prey with persistence," Bréhal used to say. "She hooked him with admiration." And certainly Marie-Paule didn't stint on the compliments, infusing Martin with the enthusiasm necessary to go on reading the philosophers without quite knowing why. Marie-Paule had been raised in a family of wealthy industrialists with a penchant for investing in objets d'art, and she had a collector's eye. But whereas she didn't know what to call this passion for beautiful things, Martin did know. She thought he looked like the young man in *Luncheon in the Artist's Studio*. "There's a certain something . . . It's quite obvious—can't you see it? I can, but I can't describe it."

Was it the fair skin, brought out in the Manet picture by the straw hat and the striped tie? The wide nostrils, which made Martin's nose look like that of a boxer? The slightly asymmetrical pupils, the divergent glance at once distant and intimate? Or the way he seemed to be posing, but with a touch of carelessness suggesting dissent from the world, the aftermath of a quarrel painful at first but dwindled into weariness? Was it the opaque elegance, indifferent as a suit of armor or an oyster?

Martin brought along books on the subject. He explained that Manet had achieved an inner "region of supreme silence," and that rather than depicting a subject, *Luncheon in the Artist's Studio* was a denial of bourgeois convention. No more mythology or theology: instead, Martin parroted, Manet painted the people of the age he lived in, grand and poetic with their ties and their boots. But these heroes were dissociated from their setting and separated from themselves—they were nothing but shapes, colors, and the opposite of well-being. Martin was proud to think that for Marie-Paule he embodied the combination of uncertainty and snobbery, the aloof superiority that was to lead Manet to the sensibility of Impressionism. "Manet shocked people," he explained, "by seeing, and demonstrating, that a man or a woman is like a stick of asparagus or a bunch of violets—neither more nor less. A mass of colors arising out of a trivial theme and soon to become a mere impression. *Olympia* is exciting because of its insignificance; beautiful because it is anonymous; a symphony that instead of being heroic is erotic because of its very ordinariness."

Marie-Paule would listen to him, fascinated. This learned young man brought her what she lacked: the knowledge, and better still, the eccentricities, of an intellectual. He was quick-tempered, timid, incomprehensible. When, the first night, he drank too much and fell asleep at her place, she decided she'd keep him under her roof for good. She could reassure him, look after him, raise him like the child she'd never had, and initiate him into the secrets of art. She often woke up just to watch him sleeping, moved by family features that reminded her of photographs of herself as a rather masculine-looking girl. Martin was Marie-Paule as a boy, her rejuvenated male double. She came to feel sure of herself: they were bound to merge into each other.

Martin liked being a source of scandal, and in the intimacy of their relationship possessed Marie-Paule with angry pleasure. Marriage would allow them to flaunt their defiance openly, but unfortunately the young man's ardor was damped by legality. And once she was Madame Cazenave, Marie-Paule found herself with nothing to do, nothing to plan for. She lived on her nerves, but was never ill. Anxiety acted as a protection in her case: her uncertainties, while wreaking havoc on the people around her, preserved her own athletic body intact, without any need for respite or sexual gratification. It didn't matter too much if her husband didn't make love to her, but she did require him to take an interest in her. And he did so less and less.

Once you're married to a woman, thought Martin, her psychical life is of no further interest. Marie-Paule bores me.

He began to stay late at the Institute library, studying the peculiar customs of the Wadanis. Marie-Paule noticed, was depressed, but found a way of fighting back. She forgot her anxiety attacks and was inspired to invent the Club.

Young men and women meet at her house to make love. They all wear black eye masks. The Club consists of four couples of Regulars who take turns staying away from the meetings and are replaced by a pair of Strangers or Unknowns. Madame Cazenave-Longueville selects the surprise guests. So much for the arrangements. What about the action?

Marie-Paule goes up to the female member of the Unknown couple and kisses, undresses, and caresses her. The others imitate her, touching, caressing, and arousing one another. When the Unknown guest is ready, Marie-Paule selects one of the men, who are in a state of erection, and guides him into the woman. Martin brushes against breasts, lips, penises, and cunts, jerks off, and is jerked off. Marie-Paule brings him gently toward the mouth of the Unknown woman, who is moved by the other man's pleasure. Martin feels the woman Guest's tongue move on his own penis in the same rhythm as she herself is penetrated. He is caught up and starts to groan. Marie-Paule licks his face, his neck, his back, his buttocks. When she feels Martin coming, she avidly disengages his sex from the lips of the female Guest and plunges it into her own vagina. Martin explodes like an animal, like a creature without a brain, inside Marie-Paule. He sees himself as a woman between the two women—an animal obeying their desire. He comes, under the thrusts of the man, though he himself is stronger than any man. Seeing. Seen. Active. Passive. The complete androgyne, pulverized. He comes with such violence that it embarrasses him and surprises the others. He leans back unconscious until they have finished, and leave. When he comes to in the early hours of the morning, he has only a vague memory of resigned and courteous bodies.

No scandal, just the muted game of accepted excess that is known as politeness. A new Olympia every week, several regular Olympias: anonymous and there for the taking. Neither words nor passions, only the impeccable force of an eros passing through them all, men and women, the whole Club, setting Martin on fire and annihilating him. He feels as if his bones had been ground up by a volcano, as if his sex had emitted a flow of lava.

From then on Marie-Paule and Martin lived together only for that weekly celebration. Marie-Paule bought films, magazines, and hashish in Amsterdam, and used all her ingenuity organizing the sessions. In between she collapsed, afraid of being deserted if by some misfortune the pantomime failed. Martin couldn't do without what was now a drug, which drained him at the same time as it saturated him with pleasure. But he spent most of his time trying to curb his violence and maintain some peaceful territory for his body and thoughts to work in. Then the creature without a brain was superseded by a completely different person, who loathed distraction.

Marie-Paule became a mere housekeeper to his new, augmented, geared-down body. Like the masked bodies of the members of the Club, she was no one: her feelings, her moods, her psychology, were of no interest to Martin. But as stage manager of the orgies, she masterminded things (Martin had to grant her that; she saw to everything, he left it all to her). And she provided the once timorous young man with limitless sensuality. Thanks to the complaisant services of Madame Cazenave-Longueville ("She hooked him with admiration," as Bréhal always said), he was now supplied with pleasure by a series of indifferent accomplices who amplified it to infinity. She knew his attachment wasn't love, but feminine pride kept her from complaining of not being chosen for herself. But she also knew he couldn't do without her now; she had him where she wanted him. But for how long? Marie-Paule, at once sure of herself and panic-stricken, lost no time in calling up Joëlle Cabarus.

Martin was spreading himself too thin in the Club; the Club was overwhelming him. It was nothing and everything. Cellular ecstasy and hopeless dependence.

Martin had become the contented slave of games he didn't regard as forbidden but which, though restricted to his orifices, organs, and skin, exercised irresistible power over him. As soon as he realized his total dependency, he was seized with anguish and started to wander around Paris, walking himself into a daze, incapable of either thought or work. He had to get away. He set off for the Wadanis.

So today his legs have carried him across to the Right Bank, and now he's walking along the quai de la Mégisserie, among the crowds of pedestrians and pots of flowers: oleanders, huge houseplants with unknown names, magnificent azaleas, modest pansies, clumps of lavender, lemon-scented geraniums—a great rainbow made up of countless tiny petals. Snatched from their hothouses, the arrays of colors and perfumes lie on the sidewalk, smiling and absurd. The sounds issuing from Vilmorin's, the pet shop, add to the impression of a circus aimed at simpleminded children: making their presence felt are belligerent cockerels, anxious hens, surly dogs, whining ducks, inscrutable guinea pigs, and drooping parrots.

Martin hurries across the pont au Change, then the pont Saint-Michel, and rushes toward Mutualité and the lavender-gray shelter of the Institute.

Olga's in the catalog room.

"So you're back! What a surprise! Strich-Meyer wasn't expecting you till the end of the month. What happened?"

"I managed to get a plane and avoid the rainy season."

He could still see the lofty mountains covered with tropical forests that turned to grassy savannah above two thousand meters. Over ninety-five degrees at midday and no more than forty degrees at night. For six months he had shared the Wadanis' sweet potatoes, manioc, corn, pork, bananas, and game. He'd learned how to make bars of salt by burning cane, filtering it, pouring the resulting solution into molds, then leaving it to evaporate and cook for a week in a clay oven. Like them, he had dressed in a loincloth made of bamboo and a cape made of bark. He hadn't had his nose pierced, but he had worn a red band around his head as a tribute to the Sun and a yellow band as a tribute to the Moon. He'd slept in the Men's House.

"It's a society without a police force—without any state apparatus. But power exists there just the same, and it belongs to the men. . . . You think that must have appealed to me? . . . It's a complicated setup. Imagine every village divided into two: on the one hand, there's the women's quarter with the Women's House, where they take refuge when they're defiled with menstrual blood, which the Wadanis regard as noxious; on the other hand, there's the men's quarter and the Men's House, where the boys go through their initiation ceremonies. Once a year, near the Men's House, they build a Palace of Rites called 'The Member' or 'The Organ.' That tells you something, doesn't it? It's a symbol for the whole community, women included. In the middle of the village is the family quarter. But there, too, every house is divided inside into a female area near the entrance and a male area near the fire."

Martin wasn't allowed to stay anywhere but in the Men's House, on the top of a hill. There the little boys of the community, taken away from their mothers at the age of five, were kept in isolation for ten years to learn about suffering, pleasure, hunting, war, and magic.

"The adult men and youths beat them, rub them with nettles, and make gashes in their backs and thighs, but they show no sign of pain. What looked like horrible torture is experienced by them as no more than a kind of writing or painting on the body. Yes, that's it—art using flesh as its medium; initiation into the power of the group via the body of the individual."

"It doesn't sound very pleasant!"

"Sperm is the supreme force," Martin went on, as if now approaching the agreeable part of the subject. "For months a young husband feeds his wife on sperm, until she's strong enough to be fertilized. Women's milk— another magical substance—is regarded as a mere transformation by the female of the male sperm she has ingested. But sperm circulates in great quantities in the Men's House, too. The younger boys gain strength by drinking the semen of the older ones—though never that of anyone who's had dealings with a woman. Anyone who refuses has his skull broken."

"Doesn't all that encourage homosexuality?"

"The Wadanis have no sense of sin; fellatio's a religion with them. It may reinforce the males' sense of community, but it also makes sex an area of power quite different from that of procreation and production."

"How so?"

"The men's desire creates another kind of power, a power that has nothing to do with the everyday needs of the community. But this power, though it represses women—Carole would have something to say about that!—isn't above or against the group. Because it's rooted from the outset in the body, in desire, because it's incarnated in the flesh, they don't feel it as a constraint."

"But I suppose these people do have leaders?"

"They do have Masters—warriors and shamans—but they're not 'leaders' in our sense of the word. Do you know who's a Master among the Wadanis? Someone who's expert at some technique (the art of fighting, say, or of healing), but primarily someone able to *give* and to *speak*. In short, a Master is a generous poet, capable of persuasion and of bestowing gifts in such a way as to keep the group peaceful. A Master may end up stripped of all his possessions: sometimes he becomes a complete down-and-out."

"No need to preach that gospel in Paris!"

Martin had learned from Papuans, Indians, and other savages that power resided in the penis, and he saw the Wadanis as confirming Lauzun, for whom the unconscious says the same thing. The trouble is, a superchief may arise, a Big Brother who forgets about sex and goes in for trade. He accumulates wealth, outstrips the group, and surrounds himself with henchmen. Finally a State emerges and divests the initiate body of its power. You can go through as many rites as you like, the Wadanis are told, but you'll have to knuckle under to Superman and his gang. In the end you won't bother about initiation anymore. It's not worth the trouble. The One watches over everything, and the State is his servant.

His study of the Wadanis had led Martin to the conclusion that the State was synonymous with Evil. And from this he argued that what was needed was the rediscovery of the body and desire. What was everyone waiting for?

"What I'm going to tell you now will probably strike you as naive, but its implications are enormous. Remember, my dear Olga, the Wadanis don't believe in the Word. That's where the difference lies: they're neither Greeks nor Jews nor Christians. So their prophets resist Big Brother not with some kind of discourse or political system but just by turning bars of salt—I learned how to make them myself!—into sculptures. That's their protest against merchandise, against the surpluses Big Brother would like to introduce in order to amass 'capital.'

"The Wadani prophets vented their fury on the bars of salt: they smashed them, hacked them up, ground them to pieces, daubed them over their bodies and faces, and finally drank and drugged themselves to death with them—the salt's poisonous when ingested in large quantities. It was collective suicide after an artistic performance. And all to prevent the creation of any kind of policing authority; to make sure no other power should supplant that of their own society, with its corporeal complicities . . .

"All that may strike you as anarchic or Utopian. Maybe. But—Wadanis or no Wadanis—isn't our own problem, after thousands of years of history, how to redistribute the power of the State? A State that's indistinguishable from the police because it has set itself above bodies, above what's known as the social body?"

"Sounds as if you'll be writing a political pamphlet instead of a thesis."

"I don't know that I'll be writing anything at all. I've had enough of that. But action, yes. Power—that's what comes first. Class, struggle, economics—they come later. But where does power lie? Who has it? 'That is the question.' You *can* change the seat of power just by withdrawing salt from circulation, making it into sculptures, daubing yourself, and killing yourself with it. But even among the Wadanis that isn't a satisfactory solution.

The most you achieve by letting yourself be rubbed out is to leave behind a legend for the next Big Brother to hand over to the whites. As for changing power by holding meetings at Maubert-Mutualité—no way! And yet that's the only thing worth doing—acting in such a way as to alter the seat of power. Inside us. For our own sakes. Don't you agree?"

All the time he was telling Olga what he'd learned from his visit to the Wadanis, Martin could see in his mind's eye the bodies of the Wadani youths at the various stages of their initiation.

In the six months he'd spent among them he'd come to think he understood them. He put himself in their place, wanted to take part in their rites. But no white man had ever done so. And in the end all he managed to do was help them purchase a pickup truck. . . .

During the twenty-hour northward flight back to Paris, he'd felt an abyss opening up between Martin Crusoe and Martin Cazenave. There was a savage inside him, but there was a dandy, too. He felt a kind of hypertrophy of the brain, in which two different existences conspired to fight and contaminate each other. Marie-Paule had written to him every day, but her letters either went astray or arrived in bunches. She had given the Club a vacation, and was waiting for him to start the meetings up again. Martin couldn't really remember what she'd said in her letters. He'd scarcely glanced at them. They were all about the problems afflicting young painters, the difficulty of selling pictures, her own attacks of love or migraine, the races at Longchamp, or the weather in Paris. He missed the drug the Club had provided; by way of compensation, he gloated over the tortures inflicted on the young Wadani initiates, and their acts of fellatio. One foot among the natives, one foot in the rue de Seine. A hiatus stretched over the whole flight. Could it be contained within one man's heart? It was cosmic expansion on an individual scale: the schizophrenia of the human sciences exacerbated by the habits of the jet set. I have neither hearth nor home, thought Martin. There was no place for him anywhere on earth. Wherever he was, he saw it from somewhere else. He was at once a rebel and a slave. No peace was possible. Any excess, any new savagery awakened an immediate response in him. He could hardly wait. He literally became the men, acts, and thoughts that had attracted him. There was no distance between him and them; instead, a mystical unity. Moderate people made him feel ill. But he hadn't the patience to transpose this dark passion into the light of a disciplined correlative. He did try, as conscience and education required, but succeeded only in borrowing the styles and ideas of the geniuses he took as his models. Martin's own genius was for pastiche; he could have made a stage career out of impersonating famous actors and politicians. He would sometimes entertain friends with a perfect imitation of some author or philosopher.

His escapade among the Wadanis channeled rather than ex- acerbated his fever. He thought that by jumping from the black men's savannah to the lavender-gray files of the Institut d'Analyse Culturelle he would be able to balance with one magnet the two forces that might otherwise have torn him to pieces. Meditating on the savages is my own version of psychoanalysis, he thought to himself. Instead of paying out fees to Lauzun, I treat my strangeness myself with forty hours in a plane and all that that entails.

But was what he felt inside himself a magnet or a blank? He needed air. His lungs were either empty or flooded. He was stifling. His chest felt tight. His heart was thudding. He was sweating. Whatever it was, magnet or blank, he felt awful. "Olga, could you open a window?"

The long hours above the sea and the clouds had made him melancholy. He didn't want to go back to the consumer society, though he knew very well the Wadanis didn't live in any age of gold. There was their exclusion of women, for a start: females were regarded as mere items to be exchanged between families, machines for transforming the elixir of men's sperm. (Though, according to Carole, they managed to create zones of pleasure for themselves: before she nursed her own infant, a mother would let adolescent girls nuzzle at her breasts.) But above all, he could see that the equilibrium of the Wadanis' stateless soci- ety was heading for extinction; Big Brothers were springing up everywhere, if only to trade with the whites. The revolutionary prophets were merely a legend. So then what?

In the beginning was Power, Martin kept telling himself. No,

Power is still here, Power is the beginning. The beginning, which is always a beginning of the end, appears with the power of the One against All. So then what?

Why, that a twenty-hour plane journey demonstrates that melancholy's a bore; with a bit of luck it even comes to seem grotesque. Martin began to laugh to himself as he looked at the flight attendant, who was overwhelmed by the extravagant demands of long-haul passengers. What was he, Martin Crusoe, going to do in the streets of Paris? Club or no Club? Did he have to go around the world and frighten himself with the cries of rutting savages just to find out what everyone else knew already—namely, that it's urgently necessary to bring together authority and the masses, power and popular initiative? But even if the fact was familiar to everyone, who knew what pleasure and torture were involved in the change? Some people argue that if all the lawyers were sacked, France would become a nation of lawyers. But they're wrong. If we destroyed the State, we'd all become Robinson Crusoes, savages, creatures without brains. Martin knew it in his bones. But was that the ideal society? Perhaps not. But . . . Anyhow, it was a necessary phase. And then? We'd see. Who could say? No one. It was still too soon. He laughed to himself, laughed at himself for laughing, laughed at himself for laughing at himself.

"You've got a very funny look on your face."

Good grief—Carole! Had she changed, or was this the first time he'd really looked at her? Her sleek presence reflected a continual desire for precision. As if her body had opted for the essential. Nothing but skin and bones, weightless, no more flesh than a little girl. And yet a strange grace precluding any suggestion of scragginess. The clear lines of the face might have seemed ascetic were it not for a cheerful expression that lent the spareness a surprising mobility. Her eyes, her lips, and the muscles in her cheeks reacted minutely to the slightest variation in light or breath, speech or attitude. With her black hair and her black sweater and pants, she looked like a long stroke of India ink drawn vertically on the air.

"Frank asked me to tell you the Marxist-Leninist League is meeting tonight at my place."

Martin remembered it was a Club day. Carole would have made a marvelous Stranger. So would Olga, for that matter . . .

"So you've joined the League, have you?"

"Looks like it, doesn't it?" said Carole.

"See you at eight o'clock, then?"

"All right." The Club could wait till midnight.

"The students held a meeting at the Sorbonne this afternoon, and the cops have just cleared everyone out."

"Disgusting!"

"They've called a demonstration for tomorrow morning."

"Right! Eight o'clock at your place, then!"

Carole was so fine-spun; her voice was almost a whisper. But the things she suggested all seemed completely rational: at eight o'clock they were to meet at the Café de Cluny; tonight Frank would contact the people who'd been thrown out of the Sorbonne; Cédric would go and test the temperature at the Renault works; Martin would try to get hold of the Communist students and persuade them at least not to block the meetings.

That was all. Apart from that, she said nothing. Martin, Frank, Cédric, and the others commented on the situation, the different forces at work, the likely developments. Carole listened. A calming, levelheaded grace. Her mobile countenance accompanied the speaker, followed and approved. Even if she didn't agree, she encouraged him to go on. Her black clothes and raven hair might have been erotic; but no. In Martin's eyes they barred the things of the body, and Carole herself stood out as an agent of harmony. Of absolute trust. Pure love. The diametrical opposite of the Club. Martin couldn't approach her. He could breathe again. His heart and lungs felt miraculously free, reminding him of the respite that descended on the Wadani village after the initiation ceremonies. Impossible to leave her.

It was after midnight, but Martin didn't want to go to the Club now. Not tonight. "I'm tired out after the journey—I can scarcely move." He lived only a stone's throw away. "May I sleep here?"

It was a huge empty studio, like a New York loft. She was one of those women who are never surprised. He glanced out the window.

The rue Saint-André-des-Arts is too poor and too old, too youthful and too out of the way for respectable families to feel at home there. In this year of 1968 it seemed a setting in doubtful taste, rather grubby and pretentious. Exactly right for the story of Martin and Carole, pathetic and insipid, incredible and sentimental as it was. On top of everything, it was true.

7

"Down with the police state! Ten years is enough!"

A crowd at Denfert-Rochereau. Red and black flags. They were heading for the Etoile. Martin and Carole and lots of students, shoulder to shoulder. A few yards ahead they could see Olga's squirrel's tail; Sinteuil couldn't be far away. Would the police let them past? They crossed the Pont Alexandre-III without any trouble. Where are we, where are we going? What did it matter? Everyone was excited, het up. Some knew the "Internationale," and the others pretended they did and picked up the words as best they could. Olga wondered if they really knew what they were doing. She'd just come away from the "Internationale." Only the evening before, Ivan had been amazed to see all those young innocents repeating the apparatchiks' jargon for hours on end, all night long even, in the overheated lecture rooms of Nanterre and the Sorbonne. And it was indeed disturbing, the faith of these artless youngsters rushing guilelessly toward a world of oppression. But perhaps it wasn't quite the same thing: they were more cheerful, more anarchistic. It was more of a carnival, with teams of stewards pretending at being stewards, efficient, deadpan. And why not? History never repeats itself, as the repeaters of History say.

" 'It's the final struggle!' " sang Olga, who'd known all the words of the song since she was six years old, when the Dominican nuns who ran the kindergarten were expelled and replaced by government-appointed mistresses; when Catholic exhortations to the faithful gave way to slogans about the oppressed.

The procession made its way back toward the Latin Quarter. This time the police were waiting for them in Montparnasse.

It had been going on for four days, and it was heating up. The Quarter was sealed off by the police, the university was shut, some students had been arrested after the scuffles on May 3, six hundred people had been taken in for questioning. . . .

"The CP's trying to pull a fast one! Down with the Stalinists!"

Martin was uncompromising, and Carole thought he was right. There could be no question of replacing the old bureaucrats with new ones: they were all Stalinist bastards! Changing life itself—that was the objective. Changing families, love . . . all that.

"We'll never get anywhere until the workers are with us."

Hervé was emphatic: it was time to break out of mere intellectual circles at last. Students and artists might act as an avant-garde. But the avant-garde of what?

"Tomorrow we're going to the Renault works at Flins. Are you coming?"

Martin didn't know. He didn't trust the Communists.

"You and me both! But we must break free of the Latin Quarter and influence the country as a whole. And the CP has a marvelous communications network—ideal for propaganda. That's where the real battle lies: either they'll annex us, and there's some danger of that, or we'll win *them* over. But anyhow we have to go!"

Maille and Jean-Claude didn't think there was any danger. Everyone was going to Flins and that was that. Without the workers the momentum would soon be lost. Hervé was more dialectical—or more Jesuitical, as Maille put it.

"Sinteuil won't choose between the red flag and the black," said Brunet, summing it up. "For *Now*, that's the correct line at the moment, as Chairman Mao would say."

"It's a red spring, at any rate."

Hervé wouldn't give up on his idea: there was to be no more literary experiment in ivory towers; there had to be links with the masses. *Now* was no longer enough; it had to emerge from the Sorbonne. Intellectuals had always been timid radical-socialists; they had nothing to do with literature. A worker at Citroën was more romantic than a prof. And after all, poverty was an explosive force, and numbers counted. So why shouldn't *Now* go to Flins? Culture knows no class—the world is full of illiterate aristocrats and stupid bourgeois. But above all, Hervé had a flair for the media. And in 1968, for a little while yet, the unions were more powerful than television.

Carole disliked half measures. And ever since the night of May 3, when Martin stayed the night at her place, her life had changed. She'd never meant to become attached to another person—only to get away from her mother and do the opposite of what *she* had done. That curvaceous model had married Benedetti, the famous Turin banker, because he was rich and generous. As for him, he was weak and shy and had never possessed such a beautiful woman: marrying her made him feel more sure of himself. Carole was the link between them. The only one. A compromise between two incompatible worlds. Her mother had had her in order to keep Benedetti; Benedetti had begotten her to keep his model. "A child is death for a woman," Carole's mother used to say. "So is a man," she added, though she made sure to have several. Benedetti turned a blind eye and lived amid his ledgers and airplanes and capital cities. Carole longed to be understood and dreamed of a faithful couple, perfect understanding, indissoluble *yin* and *yang*. She was prickly and suspicious. Inward. Frigid and impassive as cooled lava.

She had seen the shy, intense, almost distraught admiration in Martin's eyes. They understood each other almost without words, without having to spell things out either about the Wadanis or about the objects of the Marxist-Leninist League. Martin didn't speak of himself, and Carole had a horror of confession. Just right. Martin showed her the League pamphlets, and she either suggested corrections or pronounced them perfect. He brought her the student union's publications, and they laughed together over the maneuvers of the old Stalinists. He bought the *Peking Daily News* and read aloud from it: the articles were just as Stalinist as the others, but on that paper, in those tiny characters, the age-old saws seemed strict enough to scourge all bureaucrats and apparatchiks. "One can be divided into two." "Revisionists lose face." "Rely on your own strength." Didn't that mean something? "The lowest form of information: slabs of meaning," joked Bréhal. But they said everything if you were prepared to add in what couldn't be said, what made men's hands tremble and their brows run with sweat.

At first Martin slept on the couch. Then he started kissing Carole, caressing her long and chastely, in bed. He was still just as admiring and trustful. And speechless. When he disappeared one night and came back in the morning wild-eyed, Carole could smell women on his mouth and hands. She became even more reserved. She pursed her lips, and there was no longer any question of letting him kiss her. Marie-Paule Longueville-Cazenave was never mentioned. Did Carole even suspect there was such a thing as the Club? Martin was living with her just in order to forget it. He loved her lanky, bosomless body, her boyishly muscular thighs and buttocks, her cool little-girl cheeks. She aroused him, but with a strange hothouse stimulation that drew back and remained within him; a kind of embryonic masturbation, dispersed without any explosion. Like a chord kept vibrating by what they did together.

The warm spring covered Paris with a pall of smoke: eyes smarted from the aftermath of tear gas bombs. Carole drifted amid the fog. All the time she felt a kind of misty pressure in her chest, an irritation in her eyes that almost made her cry. But it was all too indefinite to be called a feeling—it was more like an uneasy presentiment. Current events, that month of May, relegated everything else to a vague and incomprehensible background. It even seemed quite normal that she and Martin didn't make love, because they loved each other, because everything was so strange, and because events were moving so fast. Since she'd found a man who was different from all those her mother had had . . .

That night, after some time spent stroking her flat chest and full hips, Martin put his hand on her stomach and brought his erect penis close.

"I'm going to make love to you. I'd like to have a child."

She pushed him away, suddenly sober.

"Out of the question."

His anguish always vanished as soon as he entered Carole's place in the rue Saint-André-des-Arts. It was like being reborn, an acceptable kind of initiation. She alone could rid him of his acephalous body. But in order to become another man, he needed this other child—boy or girl, it didn't matter which. To start again from scratch. They'd stay together because of the child. What other reason was there for living together? Except to facilitate their political activity, of course; but that was another matter. The idea of the baby made him happy but at the same time rather foolish. I'm going gaga, but what does it matter? he thought when reason reasserted itself. Then he let himself be carried away again by his frantic dream. Carole was the only one he could share it with. Finally he'd plucked up the courage to talk to her. Why did she refuse?—it was so natural, so obvious. Could he have been mistaken about her; was she less extraordinary than he'd thought; was there something important that he hadn't understood?

"Listen—I only want one! And only with you. It will mean a new life."

"Of course. But my own life is enough for me. And that's complicated enough already."

"You must be the only woman in the world who doesn't want a child. What's the matter with you? You're the only woman I want to have one with."

"You've got it all wrong. Women are interested in other things besides motherhood nowadays—hadn't you noticed?"

"There's more than one kind of mother. I wouldn't mind looking after a child myself."

"There are two Madame Cazenaves already—isn't that enough for you?"

"Marriage is another matter, and one of them is enough for

me. But I love you, and I want you to be the mother of my child."

Carole recalled the smell of other women on his hands, and the long hairs she sometimes saw on his shirt when he came home in the early hours.

"As I told you before, I'm not interested."

Her mother ought to have had an abortion, ought to have killed her when she was a baby. Carole would rather have been dead than act as an artificial link between a birdbrained model and an absentminded banker. She would never have a child. She'd swallow as many pills as it took, she'd have dozens of abortions, and if after all that a child did get itself born, she felt quite capable of drowning it or throwing it off a cliff—anything would be less criminal than what her mother had done, bringing her into the world as coolly as if she were just opening a bank account.

She dressed hurriedly and ran downstairs. There was always something going on, day or night, during this month of "events." She made her way up the boulevard Saint-Michel, avoiding police barriers by taking side streets. In the rue Gay-Lussac, university and high school students were digging up the roadway and making heaps of cobblestones. She ran into Frank.

"Hi!"

"Quick, help me move this car—it'll do as a barricade! The cops are going to charge!"

Cédric was holding a Molotov cocktail and waiting for the chance to use it.

"Do you know what we did this morning? We decided to abolish the Ecole Normale! The vote was unanimous!"

Wow! Carole thought it was rather amusing. But she wasn't thinking at all. The acid from a distant grenade was hurting her eyes; she wished the warm pall hanging over Paris would break up; what was needed was a storm, a downpour.

She'd thought Martin loved her for herself.

She'd imagined theirs was a unique reciprocal love—what a joke! When all he really wanted was a baby machine. Once again she'd have to stifle her affection, numb all tenderness. She'd been naive. Her mother used to tell her she was just an idealist.

Martin was like all men—a swine or a father, or both.

But there must be some mistake. She'd known him a long time. And for the last few weeks she'd been observing him. That beauty spot on the left of his upper lip, which twitched when he slept with his mouth open . . .

"Bréhal was here a little while ago—did you see him? I'd never have thought structuralism would take to the streets!"

"Don't worry, he'll soon see it's not his scene. Look—he's leaving already!"

"Valence got nabbed in the Sorbonne. He's got some nerve! He's still a revisionist, but he still wants people to approve of him."

"I'm not surprised he was arrested. Dubreuil's meeting was reasonably okay, but even he struck people as square. And that won't wash anymore."

The barricade was forming; the cops took no notice. Edelman, his shirt flapping open, unsteady on his feet, couldn't restrain himself from inspecting the troops. *His* troops! Heinz, Roberto, Olga, Frank . . . Not that they applied his teaching literally: dialectic was alien to them, and the present craze for seeking pleasure in destruction was nihilistic rather than tragic. But he had indoctrinated them with a belief in protest, in divine discontent.

"Hey, Fabien! I don't think there are any loners left now, even in Port-Royal—Jansenism's on the decline. Have you noticed how the French have started talking to one another on the metro? And I hear Brichot actually spoke to his concierge for the first time in his life! Don't tell me that's the exception that proves the rule. God's no longer hidden—He's taken to the streets."

Sinteuil was joking as usual, good-naturedly or sardonically— you could never tell which. Edelman was disappointed. They didn't understand one another anymore. The generation gap.

"Down with the police state!"

A sudden hail of stones descended on the cops, who count- ered again with grenades.

"You haven't seen Martin, have you? He hasn't been around for several days."

Marie-Paule Cazenave-Longueville, panic-stricken, was look- ing for her husband.

Carole gazed at her out of brimming eyes, knowing she wouldn't be recognized in the tear gas fumes. Her heart started to rise within her like a startled bird, seemed to stick in her throat, throbbing. She noticed the smoothness of Marie-Paule's complexion, the peachlike skin that clung so tightly to the muscles that her face seemed void of all expression. She may look blank, Carole thought, with such objectivity as she could still muster, but she'll never have lines on her face either: she'll grow old like a terra-cotta statue, without a wrinkle.

But Marie-Paule, wearing earrings on the barricades, was just as appearance-conscious as Carole's mother. Slightly less frivolous, slightly more snobbish, but just as much of a coquette. Carole hated that. She herself had opted for the minimum: a minimum of flesh, a minimum of clothes, no makeup, and no jewelry. She was a cyclotron padlocked on the inside. She felt a sudden impulse to hurl the cobblestone she had in her hand at that cling peach skin, destined to remain forever young, like some ancient statue. Instead she threw it at the cops. They weren't slow to reply. Charge. Nightsticks. Stampede. Some people were knocked down, others taken off in police trucks.

"Down with the police state!"

People were running in all directions, and Carole lost sight of her friends. She kept on running, suddenly feeling light, liberated, airy as a balloon. No weariness or anger—just a great sense of relief, of speed, of wings. The storm of tear gas had passed over her as over a swallow's plumage. She was reborn. Free! But where was she flying to? There was chaos everywhere. Panic-stricken people. Ambulances. And yet still this marvelous sense of freedom. Martin must be somewhere in the streets. Six in the morning. Things seemed to be calming down. She must try to find him. But did she really want to? It would be better to go to Olga's place.

Hervé wasn't there.

"Lots of cars were set on fire. He went out to try to save his, and I haven't seen him since."

Ambulance sirens, fire engines. The radio reported hundreds of casualties among both protestors and the police. Olga was worried. They called up the main trouble spots. The Ecole des

Beaux-Arts, now a "People's Workshop." The Odéon theater, which had been proclaimed "Headquarters of the Creative Revolution." Martin was probably there. They heard Hervé's voice.

"I hid out in the Ecole Normale for a while, but the cops were picking everyone up at the exits. So I started to walk out beside a stretcher party carrying a casualty, and a cop said, 'Watch out, Doctor,' and let me through. It pays to look respectable, you see!"

They were tired but triumphant. Weary and surprised. The radio was still giving out casualty figures and descriptions of the clashes. Churchmen and scientists appealed for calm. Olga made coffee.

"Calm, for God's sake! There'll be a strike before long!"

Sinteuil had learned from his contacts in the trade unions that major activity was imminent from the workers. There'd already been the May Day demo, and the unions were getting together in the west of the country. A general strike would soon paralyze Paris and France as a whole. Unemptied trash cans were piling up everywhere. There was no more gasoline. No more public transport. Two million workers on strike. Six million. "Havoc," as de Gaulle called it, though he expressed himself less politely than that. "We are all German Jews." "No one's completely in control of events," said the prefect of Paris. Perhaps "participation" would calm people down? Too late. "Revolution is the only solution!" "I goofed, didn't I?" (de Gaulle again). Unions and employers met for talks in the rue de Grenelle. Were the unions collaborators? Charléty urged the students not to let themselves be taken over.

"Frank says *Now*'s run by revisionists and social traitors."

It was Olga who reported this. She was only half amused, for she was beginning to realize that in Paris "revisionist" didn't mean liberal—it meant out-and-out collaborationist. Editions de l'Autre's little office was like a clandestine cell. Brunet, with his fin-de-siècle manner and walking stick, maintained that it was more necessary than ever not to seem like a dropout.

"I may belong to the extreme left, but we can only survive if we're protected by the working classes."

"I've been to see Comrade Pousset, of the Central Committee," said Maille.

"Was that really necessary?" said Brunet in his usual languid manner.

"This morning the anarchists wouldn't let Lauzun give his lecture. And do you know what he did? He tried to find Sinteuil, to ask him to get the porters to find him another room. He assumed that they were all union members and therefore manipulated by *Now.*"

Jean-Claude thought this a great joke. Sinteuil was even more amused.

"I fear my influence with the unions is rather limited. Anyhow, I gave Lauzun a miss today. I thought the time would be better spent finishing some translations for the next number. Some of Mao's poems."

"By the way, the Marxist-Leninist League calls itself the Maoist League now."

It was Carole who'd told Olga that.

It was Martin's idea, but the rest had accepted it unanimously. The wind from the East was sweeping away bureaucracy and urging the young to oppose all the ossified old establishments. The whole world was turning in the same direction: the Taoist anarchism now advocated by hundreds of millions of Chinese was being seen by the Paris rebels as an example for the next millennium. Were they rioters? Dogmatists? "The bourgeois and the revisionists are scared witless. The Maoists are spontaneists who want everything—in other words, the impossible. Those are the facts!"

Martin was completely caught up in the League's militant enthusiasm. Since the organization was banned by the Ministry of the Interior, his activities as a member had to be clandestine, and this made him more enigmatic than ever. He would set off for Frankfurt and Milan "to coordinate the action of the comrades" there. He scarcely spoke to Carole, apart from reading "collectivist texts" aloud to her. Was the movement flagging in France? Was it being annexed? The first thing to do was turn to the grass roots and carry on the struggle by other means. He trusted Carole implicitly, though for the moment all he asked her to do was distribute extremely radical revolutionary leaflets. The studio in the rue Saint-André-des-Arts was their political laboratory, the monastic cell of their mutual adoration. He didn't say any more about children. Now was a time for action. Martin worshiped this neat young woman with an idolatry that burned like ice. The tension that accumulated inside him because of her found release in the antics of the Club, but he soon fled from that to escape Marie-Paule's whining. Meanwhile Carole compressed her lips more and more tightly, and her body withered as if from anorexia. But she didn't feel that she was growing weaker: their mystical affair supplied her with nourishment in the form of spiritual exaltation. That was her version of voluptuousness.

Why didn't they become terrorists? Who knows? Perhaps it was because they lived in Paris, where a gleam of eternity steals in from the ocean to hover over the Seine. Or because the gargoyles of Notre-Dame impart an air of carnival to all religions. Or because Carole had learned, trying to cope with the pretty stupidity of her mother and the harsh weakness of her father, to cling to her solitude: she might let others influence her, but she would never let them dominate her.

Martin wanted her all to himself. If she bestowed the slightest word or look on anyone else, or paid them any other attention, he became quite crazy with jealousy, brutal and vulgar. Did she feel flattered? Slightly. But above all, she felt frightened. Her mouth grew more and more pursed; her lips looked welded together.

Martin never held forth about the savages now, but the Wadani prophets, together with the May barricades, had had their effect. Martin had started to paint.

Most members of Marie-Paule's Club, and most of their guests, were painters without any talent. He had no intention of being like them. Carole's loft was transformed into a studio. Just two mattresses for sleeping or sitting on, and lots of cloth and canvases for "dripping." Carole, the unemployed ethnologist, observed as Martin, the action painter, went into a trance between a night at the Club and a clandestine meeting of the League. Her eyes grew darker and darker: they were like two pieces of incandescent charcoal when it still seems intact, just before it bursts into flame and disintegrates.

By some absurd but irresistible magic she remained attached to Martin. He insisted on having his own way without offering any explanations and with a force that brooked no comment. She'd got the point and didn't argue anymore. For her, what other people called his fanaticism was merely a sign of his integrity, his fervent honesty. Strangely enough, she put all her trust in instability. After all, what was more reliable than passion, even if it was inconstant?

This silent loyalty to a man she couldn't talk to but to whom she had to belong generated in Carole a need to surround herself with plants. The large unused balcony of the loft in the rue Saint-André-des-Arts adjoined the roof of the building. The whole formed a kind of huge patio that Carole turned into a garden. While the new artist in perpetual motion crouched, knelt, or went down on all fours, flinging paint over cloths and canvases, Carole slipped away like a cat to the shelter of her plants. She watched over the growth of the buds, the opening of the flowers, the progress of the leaves, the bending of the stems. They were living things that were stable. Only a plant could be faithful. It might be ephemeral, but as long as it lived, it was always dependable. A plant can't move, can't desert us. And because it can't move, it depends on our care. Carole took the place of nature—earth, water, sunshine—because deep down she was consumed with a longing, never confided to anyone, to devote herself to something.

In a way she had devoted herself to Martin, but he hadn't noticed—she was sure of it. He didn't really see her anymore. And his life was becoming so uncertain and vague: a spray of water, a pointillist picture. Could anyone be devoted to an aerosol, whose only response to the pressure of your hands was to escape?

At a meeting of the Revolutionary Feminists—a movement that had split off from the Maoist League, and which Carole joined immediately—she offered to look after Jeanne, an activist who'd been paralyzed in a car crash as she drove back from putting up posters in the suburbs. Jeanne was a queen bee around whom all the other young women revolved, as if her handicap revealed to each of them a secret disability of her own, a permanent hemorrhage. Bernadette, the leader, who called herself a "follower and improver of Lauzun," explained that women didn't suffer from a castration complex—they were threatened by the total liquidation of both their bodies and their personalities.

"We're completely lost, body and soul, when we lose the one we love—in the first instance, our mother. It doesn't matter for men. They never lose their mother: they look for her and find her—alas, it's all too obvious—in their wives or mistresses. So they force us to repress our grief, force us to make ourselves attractive. Some women take their lover or their husband for a mother. And when their Prince Charming abandons them, they wilt away," said Bernadette, stroking the breasts of the girl sitting next to her.

"You may be right," replied Jeanne from her wheelchair. "But I think men took power one day, and from then on the patriarchal society imposed its own image of the female body on us— an image of a body that's so weak, helpless, and handicapped that we have to keep on painting it and dolling it up. Don't you agree, Carole? Tell how the machos seized power over women among the Wadanis."

Carole did agree, but she had no desire to talk anthropology. Somehow she felt rather like a Wadani woman, or like Jeanne: talking would have seemed like a betrayal of something genuine, some suffering. So instead she washed Jeanne, dressed her, and emptied her chamber pot. She even wrote to the Chinese Embassy to find out if acupuncture might help her. Then she listened to the women's grievances against their men, and wrote leaflets. At last there came a respite and she could go back to her plants.

The garden had become her refuge. There was a bed of marigolds the color of the rising sun. Forget-me-nots were shy little girls hiding their blue eyes and budding breasts. Pansies were big-headed women students at the Ecole Normale, short on grace but with plenty of what it takes. Geraniums were chattering seductresses waving their arms about and angling for pickups on café terraces. Damask roses were pretty, blooming mothers carrying sweet-smelling goodies for the baby insects clinging to their skirts. Haughty and elusive intellectuals were represented by creeping conifers and silver pine.

Carole, herself air and earth, silent and supple, aquatic and luminous, felt at home in this vegetable world. Faithful among the faithful. But rather melancholy, rather sardonic: "When I'm not throwing stones at Marie-Paule, I'm cultivating my garden."

The inaccessible Benserade, who knew forty languages, spoke twenty, and because of his intelligence ruled the frisky computer logicians with a rod of iron, invited them and Olga to his place to prepare for the London meeting of the International Semantics Society. The apartment was dimly lit, full of the smell of fusty books, and pervaded by the fastidious bachelor charm of its owner, seventy years old and shy as a schoolboy. Watching him bring in the trolley laden with coffee and cookies, Carole saw him as a medieval monk. But no—he was a faithful subject of the Utopian asterisk prefixed to Indo-European words that are supposed to belong to the premigratory period. He soared so far above human necessity that there was nothing animal left about him. Yes, that was it—Benserade was a plant; he might have had a place in her garden. Or even in the loft itself: a faithful man, the only faithful man. A conifer. A cypress. She'd put him in the sun to fill him with air and chlorophyll.

"You look very pensive, Mademoiselle Benedetti. What are you thinking about?"

"Oh, nothing. I've got some plants . . . they're so faithful . . ."

The words came out in spite of her. She felt embarrassed, she should have kept a better hold on herself. It was the least she could do—Benserade wasn't interested in her plants.

"What's that you say? The word *plant* leads you to the word *faithful*? How extraordinary! You're a natural etymologist! Do you know where *dru* comes from? It's the root of many words that mean 'faithful' in the Indo-European languages, such as 'to trust' in English and *trêve*, meaning 'truce,' in French? (Of yes, *trêve* is linked to fidelity, for if you cease hostilities, it's because there's a certain trust . . .) Well, *dru* means 'tree,' 'wood.' And you talk to me about plants!"

Benserade wasn't an oak. More like an ancient reed, a papyrus. But so charming. She'd have liked to cuddle up to him; to bequeath him the Benedetti fortune, say, if it would make him more comfortable; in short, to adopt him. But no—it was more likely he might dream of adopting her.

Olga didn't dream. She was always consulting an invisible bibliography in her head, and wanted to know everything about everything, and right away.

"Did I imagine it, Monsieur, or did I really see your signature on a Surrealist manifesto?"

"An unfortunate coincidence, Mademoiselle . . . I'm sorry— Madame de Montlaur."

Benserade had gone purple in the face, and Olga wondered what sort of brick she'd dropped. A couple of cookies and a sip of coffee calmed the old linguist down.

"No, you didn't imagine it—of course it was me. But it's better not to mention it now I'm a professor at the Collège de France. Or, as you'd say on the barricades, now that I'm part of the establishment. Whereas then . . . Blood was being spilled at the Closerie des Lilas, Breton was like lightning: either he burned you to bits or you left. I left. I didn't care for fighting. Oh, I know, it's all become a mass movement now. But when I was young, the manifesto you referred to was—how shall I put it?— a sort of written Molotov cocktail."

Carole thought that if she'd been him she'd have let Breton burn her to bits. She didn't know now which she preferred—a silver conifer or perpetual motion. When you came to think of it, you could only have a truce after there'd been some action.

"I love you," Martin would say, and kiss her passionately, look her solemnly in the eye. After which he'd go off to the Club. Carole knew he was going to make love to Marie-Paule and her pals. But she didn't want to think about that life, because he didn't think about it either, didn't really see it. It wasn't that he was lying: more simply and more inexorably, that explosion, that release, was something that had no real place in his consciousness.

"I love you," he'd say again when he came home, with the same solemn eye-to-eye stare that seemed to be seeking oblivion. Carole knew that if she showed the slightest sign of suspicion or mockery, Martin would feel ill—perhaps faint or lose his temper. So she said nothing, and they stayed together. A setup that stood firm because it was empty. Carole's apprehensive affection and longing for vegetable constancy were the diametrical opposite of Martin's troubled violence, of the constant hunger hiding beneath his pose as a well-bred young man. He alternated between desiring to be the flattered lover of a horde of compliant bodies, and wanting to be the father of a dynasty of children who would prolong his own existence into eternity. The feelings of the woman were canceled out by the fantasies of the man: the two had nothing in common. It was a nonexistent relationship. But it lasted because of its circumstances: because of the admiration we feel for what we can never understand. That was what maintained the excitement that served instead of real trust.

Sometimes the circumstances surrounding their empty relationship became a threat. The pill that Carole took every night seemed to erect a barbed-wire fence condemning Martin to impotence and uselessness.

"I've heard it said some women take the pill to conceal the fact that they're barren. Perhaps you don't want a child because you can't have one?"

He said it to hurt her, with the spitefulness characteristic of unconscious murderers. The idea that Carole was protected from his sperm made him lose all desire to touch her. Then he'd rage against his own limp penis, and start to hate her body, too, because its owner preferred solitude or pleasure to motherhood. Because she refused to be invaded. To belong to him.

" 'I exist only imperfectly. And you do not help me to cross the baleful sea.' Do you know what that is? One of the Wadani prophets' chants. If someone's alone—that is, One—the Wadanis regard him as accursed. They're not a bit like the Greeks, the Wadanis! For them, the One isn't the Good—on the contrary: they see Unity as an evil. Can't you understand that? Spreading oneself, breaking out of one's own lousy little autonomy—that's an experiment we don't like to risk because we're afraid of pleasure. A group is a threat to His Majesty the One. So are children . . ."

Carole believed that groups and children all entailed irksome restraints, but she didn't want to argue. She didn't mind acting. "Action abolishes melancholy and upsets the One-plus-One-plus-Ones joined together in disciplined wholes." "You do not help me to cross the baleful sea . . ." How could she possibly have helped him, when she was the one who needed a lifeline? But without knowing it, without acknowledging it to herself. She had just shrunk that much more deeply inside herself after Martin's blow: "Perhaps you can't, perhaps you're barren!" Surprising how the depths inside you can get deeper still, and darker. You think there's no room left, and then you find you can huddle into an even more secret, even more inaccessible corner.

Was it Carole's abstinence from speech and action that made Martin start to hate words? He went on campaigning, but now it was Frank who wrote the leaflets. Martin let himself be taken over more and more by a rage against surfaces, which issued in droplets of paint being sprayed over panes of glass, canvases, and walls.

"Pollock—there's a real prophet for you! He doesn't need to understand—he acts! *Number One:* what a title for a picture! Some unity—it's pulverized! And can the series of numbers ever end? In infinity, yes. And I can include irrational numbers if you like, because Pollock invented 'happenings' before the Japanese *guta* in Osaka and the New Yorkers in '59 . . ."

A rhythmical force, a ritual dance lent order to the chaos Carole saw in his wild and swarthy eye. Martin broke through sight as though it were a membrane or a wall, and on the other side his canvas came to life, haunted by deadly laughter. Like a Zen master piercing a screen with a stick. Like Ping-Pong balls clattering down from the ceiling. Like small but powerful flashlights piercing invisible darkness and restoring its energy. Echoing Pollock, and to help Carole understand what he was doing, Martin bestowed mythical names on the results of this choreography. *Hyena in Moonlight:* a native sorceress, a descendant of de Kooning's monstrous women. *Male and Female Nudes with Knives:* strong brush strokes suggesting Cézanne's bathers high on LSD. *Iphigenia or Eriphilus:* A woman is to be sacrificed. But which woman? A mystery in spattered mauve and ocher. *Daphne:* (This is for me, thought Carole.) The girl changes into a laurel to escape the pursuit of Apollo.

A laurel made of pink and green piled up in an undulating pyramid: the eye felt the breathlessness of the chase; the gold-tinged, shimmering emerald invaded the sense of smell as well as of sight, so that the image became a scent. Daphne was an intangible mist, an entrancing and impalpable female perfume. Carole crossed to the other side of the retina and entered into a Baudelairean world where scents, colors, and sounds paralleled one another. "It's because I love him. Who else could see such magic in these crazy transports?"

Martin took the flat bottle of bourbon out of his pocket. It was becoming more and more useful for his pulverized painting. He told himself that if stupidity was collective, it was also first and foremost unique. Any idiot could win sympathy and love if he didn't imagine he was somebody. But the arrogance of idiots was unbearable. The frozen loaves who imagined they formed a group inside the family bread-box must be broken up. The Indians had crushed their bars of salt, got drunk on the poisonous flour, and rolled in it. Martin preferred communion of tissues via the skin that contained them, an osmosis of pleasure and pain that disregarded the stupid, supervised communication favored by society.

Carole watched him casting red, green, and yellow onto canvas spread on the floor. Using a brush to sketch angry eyes and compressed lips amid those clouds of color, or perhaps only circles, pebbles, or cobblestones. Was he really fondling himself? Striking, slashing, or murdering someone else? Or was he inseminating the canvas as a substitute for impregnating a woman? Was he making love without anyone resisting or protecting herself from him—alone, without anyone else present, a big bang in the void? After all, he had a perfect right. Just as she had a perfect right to be barren. Whether he liked it or not, that's how it was. She wasn't angry, she forgave him. But it was a fragile forgiveness that floated on a pool of anxious and implosive rage. The rage of the humiliated, of nobodies, of unloved little girls and barren women.

Every man to his passion. She went out into the roof garden to see if the buds she'd seen on the Provins rosebush the day before had opened. Yes, three sweet-smelling tea-colored clusters were holding up their voluptuous heads.

The rue Saint-André-des-Arts sloped away thin and gray as a sullied stream. Behind the shutters, Carole imagined indifferent neighbors, people who'd taken part, making the V sign, in the demonstration on May 30 at the Arc de Triomphe. "Clean out the Sorbonne!" They didn't want any trouble: what they were interested in was patching things up and going on ruling the roost. And yet during the nights of the barricades, timorous but supportive hands had been seen sluicing away the tear gas with pails of water. Since then, though, the shutters had been closed again. Carole hid her thin face in the Provins roses, while in the studio Martin went on action-painting.

8

*S*inteuil wasn't afraid of anything except ridicule. French susceptibility to Slav charm was a bore. Madame Hanska and Balzac—yuck! Self-loving Roger Nimier imitating Valmont and dodging the love of a Czech girl, herself enamored of beauty—very nice, but no thanks. Sinteuil wasn't going to lead any guided tours around Saint-Laurent's showrooms or over the Mont-Saint-Michel. "Mental health is maintained by distance, and distance fosters talent." A word to the wise, thought Olga.

The blue Ford had just left Saint-Maixent behind and was approaching Niort. The ancient province of Aunis, now part of the two modern departments of Charente-Maritime and Les Deux-Sèvres, is already a coastal region. The grass grows greener, the trees lean inland against the winds from the sea, the sky grows pale from salt-laden mists.

"As soon as he gets past Niort, a southerner knows he's come home."

Olga was trying to feel like a southerner. She'd tamed the cold water of the Atlantic, the oyster beds now seemed quite ordinary, and the Montlaurs had resigned themselves to looking on her as one of them. Naturally no one had come to their wedding. Anyhow, is a civil ceremony really a wedding? But a few months later, in the aftermath of May, which caused upheavals in the best-regulated families, she'd had a phone call from Mathilde.

"My dear Olga, I heard Professor Bréhal praising you to the skies on the radio! Congratulations, dear! By the way, do you like diamonds? I've just had some mounted, and you'll probably be getting the ring tomorrow or the day after."

What efficiency. Mathilde de Montlaur was as good as a government minister . . . of any department you like—family and social affairs, for instance. Nothing affected about her when it came to serious matters. Olga now belonged to the clan, to the name de Montlaur.

France might have quieted down since the previous spring, but calm was far from being universally restored. Feverish discussions still went on: philosophers, writers, and artists were all supposed to have a "riotous" or at least a "subversive" streak in them.

"Protest will only rebound on the students—the flame must be kept burning outside the university now," Hervé had said again in September.

"All the innovators have been annexed by the CP, or are busy trying to patch up academia," said Brunet. "But what can you do?"

Maillet had decided to break with *Now*: he flirted with the CP, but didn't like the "Maoist line" and held forth interminably about the genius of Lenin as compared with Stalinist bureaucracy.

"It's the Russian avant-garde of the thirties all over again! All right, perfect, nothing wrong with that! But times have changed, we've had enough of social-democrat hangers-on." (Sinteuil was growing impatient.) "The Chinese show what the real problem is: What do you get if you add democracy to national tradition? For the time being, permanent rebellion and a cult not of personality—how archaic!—but of inconsistency."

"Social democracy hasn't said its last word in the East. In Prague they're trying to revive the desire for internal liberty, which is probably an expression of social democracy, though not the kind favored by the kind of radical-socialist worthy you get in France. The Czechs have had enough of Stalinist, Eastern barbarity."

Olga felt a surge of solidarity with the people back home.

"Yes, maybe," said Hervé, "but here all that is being taken over by conservative humanists. 'And why not?' you ask. I'll tell you. My only moral criterion is literary: these people simply don't know how to read. They don't read either your Czech Nezval or our Sade. The supporters of the Prague Spring over here are noble squares of the Paul Bourget school. All that revolution just to land in the same stagnation as before 1914! Personally I prefer to wait and see."

Hervé was an extremist because the rate at which he lived made him eat up stages, gradations, and transitions and go straight on to paroxysm. He foresaw new trends. Or else got it all wrong. An ideologist—him? He was prepared to support advances, yes. But to act as an intermediary, to beaver away as a pedagogue or an activist—never!

"People feel like talking. The 'events' of May opened their lips. But lots of words are still stuck in throats."

"So what do you suggest?"

Olga suggested that *Now* should organize Analysis Groups once a week in the main lecture hall in the rue de Rennes.

People were fighting to get in all winter, and the groups were to continue after Easter and during the next academic year. The first evening, Sinteuil, with Jesuitical subtlety, delivered a commentary on Mao's essay on inconsistency.

"People come to learn about Hegel's dialectical logic, but also to learn how to throw it overboard," said young philosophy lecturers from the Sorbonne, who drank up every word.

Bréhal was there, of course. He took an aloof attitude to the

"vulgarity" of the May "events" ("All they achieved," he told
Olga, "was to make people drop the old formality and call one
another *tu* instead of *vous*"), but he had nevertheless been affected by them. So much so that he reread his Sade and treated
his audience of recent activists to his own interpretation of the
divine marquis: Sadian violence issues in fantasies and monstrous
tales, whereas philosophy, at last transferred from the school-
room to the boudoir, is the most powerful antidote against
revolutionary terror and its sinister patroness, Madame Guillotine. It's better to write down your violence than to tear up the
cobblestones. "Counterrevolutionary talk!" whispered the audience. "He has a point," said the more enlightened.

Saïda took advantage of May to pluck up his courage and
address himself to time. His meditations, inspired by *Finnegans
Wake* and Heidegger, irritated the philosophers and reduced the
literature merchants to silence—both bodies were confronted
with their own transcendental stupidity. Everyone was tight-
lipped, no one was won over. The ceremony used to last nearly
three hours, and sometimes there were even two sessions—six
hours in all. The survivors could be counted up afterward. They
were to be the first fans of the "condestruction" theory: the word
was invented to show that one should never construct without
destroying, too. It wasn't a very elegant expression, it didn't
sound French; in fact, it sounded downright woggish, as Paul
Leroy maliciously pointed out in *Left-Wing Witness*—that beat
everything! What exactly did it mean, "condestruction"? The
formerly timid Saïda broke down every word into its minutest
elements, and from these seeds produced shoots so flexible he
could weave them into his own dreams, his own literature, rather
ponderous but as profound as it was inaccessible. This was how
he started to acquire his reputation as a guru, which was to
overwhelm the United States and the American feminists, who
all became "condestructivists" out of affection for Saïda and
endogenous dissatisfaction.

"Wait a bit—metaphysics has got some use! It makes it possible to assert an ethic, and to fight!" protested Frank, who'd
become an admirer of Schirmer and campaigned against prisons
and the death penalty. "Condestruction is really just nihilism!"

"Every man to his own literature . . ."

Hervé was ready to extend a tolerant blessing to all of them
. . . until condestruction attacked his own writings, and Saïda
went over to the CP, while *Now* became more and more pervaded with Mao-Tao.

Olga wanted to talk about Céline. The outcast from all ideologies. The devotee of rhythm. The spectacle of the Deluge as
against the timidities of the right-thinking. Including the conformists of the left. Until he himself foundered in the destructive
fire of his own anti-Semitism.

"No, the argument's too subtle, no one will understand. They'll
take you for a right-wing anarchist or an aesthete. You can do
that later. Isn't there anything else you want to do now?"

She wrote a commentary on Sinteuil's novel, *Exodus*. Memories
of the Spanish Civil War. The Occupation, the displacement of
populations, the Resistance. The experience of an exile from
self, abandoning a calm account of events for biblical incanta-
tion. Death of the self can be a rebirth when expressed through
an attempt to harmonize beauty and the senses. Olga saw *Exodus*
as a hymn to the divinity that resides in the individual's universal
and infinite ability to use language and adapt it to his or her own
purposes. Sinteuil saw a letter as a plastic image, a syllable as a
symphony, and meaning as a torrent of sexual, political, and
moral allusions.

He'd written down a dream of his own death, and of his
resurrection via the voice and literature. Some Indian texts considered language as a seed, an egg, a taste. These texts provided
a better definition of language than did Western formalists—a
theory of the Word made flesh and similarly unmade. Olga
explained that *Exodus* was an example of the alchemy of word
and body that transforms the esoteric experience of writing into
the real creation of a new person. *Exodus* was the death of an old
gambler and the construction of a new one, who necessarily
demanded and perhaps even caused changes in other people.

"Olga's close to Lauzun and Saïda, but much more moral,
historical, and subjective," said Cédric approvingly.

"She talks like a woman, perpetually concerned with loss and
regeneration." (Carole was trying to bracket Olga with the revolutionary feminists.)

Pange, the great poet, caught up in the same vortex as the

others, and an attentive listener at the Analysis Groups, felt his own writings were rather alien to the enthusiasm of these young people, even if they did go along with the pagan rigor he applied to objects.

"Dear Olga, you'd have been a mystic if you hadn't in the last resort been a bit too emotional—for my own taste, of course."

The ferry. The smell of seaweed. The curves of the island. And now at last the gate and the pines. Lilacs, wallflowers, and irises were the only flowers that bloomed close to the coast at Easter. Germaine and Gérard had got the bedrooms ready. You needed a fire in the evening, and logs cut from the nearby wood in the summer were dry and only waiting for a match. Hervé would see to that. Olga unpacked their bags in a bedroom newly fixed up in the wing of the *mas* used by the Montlaurs. She closed the shutters. Even with them shut, the April squalls in this part of the world were so violent they kept you awake at night. Sleepless, moonlit nights full of a piercing lucidity that wasn't tiring but, whether they started out trying or stimulating (the two are often the same), left you permanently awake. So you could make love all night, like fishes. Nights when you saw each other clearly and loved each other better, with a fondness free of illusion.

Xavier and Odile des Réaux insisted on coming to say hello to Olga. The Montlaur trio—Mathilde, Jean, and François—would of course come with them, "just for coffee."

"No, no—come to lunch!"

Hervé hated being treated, in his role as a husband, as practically indistinguishable from a family heirloom: "We've got a Louis Quinze writing desk, a Louis Seize chest of drawers, a couple of Voltaire chairs, and a young man who found us this charming young woman. A sweet boy, isn't he?" Hervé told himself Olga was too much of an intellectual to bother about this kind of interior decorator's talk—in other words, she was too absentminded to notice it. She did seem like an intellectual. But was she really one?

Cousin Xavier had an intelligent face, like a beagle. He told Olga he'd joined the Socialist party "since the events," for where his château was, in the Verdelais near Saint-Croix-du-Mont, the

local farmers and craftsmen had voted for joint worker-manage-
ment and were becoming a threat to the landowners. And now
that he was a socialist, he was in a way on their side, waiting to
see what would happen. Odile looked at him with the admiration that would have been due Napoleon if he'd foreseen and
avoided the battles of Waterloo and the Beresina. He demon-
strated the application in the laboratory—i.e., in the vineyard—
of the highest form of geopolitics.

"Would you believe it, the people here on the island demanded independence, just like Corsica or Brittany! I wonder
how they think they'd survive on their own, with their potatoes
and their shrimps! But we are and will remain Gaullists. And
proud of it!"

Mathilde de Montlaur wasn't to be impressed. She was dressed
in burgundy-colored silk with white spots—unless it was the
other way around. She always did wear blue or burgundy fabrics
with spots, and the limited but always distinguished variations
these elements allowed enhanced a regal air that she managed to
preserve even while her conversation darted from one subject to
another.

"Do you see this laurel bush, Olga dear? Well, it's all ragged—
you must remember to have it clipped. Politics is a subject about
which I feel more and more indifferent, but what's the use of
being indifferent to everything if you're not indifferent to your
own indifference? I just take an interest in this and that, but it's
not a real interest, more a kind of withdrawal, you understand.
Take the roof of Hervé's tower, for instance: you must send for
the man to come and see to it—lots of tiles were blown off
during the winter, and you'll be inundated one of these days, the
first time it rains heavily. It's up to you to see to this sort of thing
now—I'm getting old. Yes, yes, I know I am—I'm not fishing for
compliments. Have you noticed the little wall by the river? It's
falling to pieces. If I were you, I'd send for the mason right
away—if you put it off, the repairs will cost you a fortune. We
called in at mass on our way here: nothing but old folk! The
young ones are leaving the village, it's true, but religion is losing
its hold as well. Admittedly the priest isn't very inspiring: he
drones out the Gospel as if nothing was going on outside his
little church, and of course, the younger generation chases after

what *is* going on. I don't think you've noticed the dining room chimney isn't drawing properly—a bird must have nested there again. It happened before, a few years ago. You ought to call— who used to cope with that sort of thing, Jean? . . . Young Pelletier, that's right. Call young Pelletier, his family's devoted to us . . ."

It was lucky, thought Olga, that she was too abstracted to take in or remember all these instructions. Otherwise she'd have had her hands full! Mathilde made her dizzy: you needed to counteract her with Zen emptiness and deaf listening.

But her mother-in-law didn't really rely on her. That performance of hers was only rhetorical. Could you see Olga as steward of an estate? The Montlaurs would be ruined! It mustn't be allowed to happen. Mathilde might be in the process of making a kind of premature will, but everyone knew—and she, the queen, knew best of all—that as soon as she finished her coffee, she'd start organizing the necessary army of workmen, experts, maids, and helpers of all kinds.

Hervé noted Olga's flushed cheeks and the childlike laughter in those slanting eyes. Her mouth, on the other hand, was serious, almost ponderous. But the whole effect soon canceled itself, and everything else, out. This made Olga look volatile, distant, as if immune from anything base. Apparently. But he could swear to it. Almost.

"You haven't forgotten Hermine's arriving tomorrow?"

Of course she hadn't forgotten.

"She asked if she could bring Aurélia. I said of course. You don't mind, do you?"

What a surprise . . . They'd met Aurélia the year before at the Odéon theater, before it was evacuated, during the June election campaign. When there was a kind of round-the-clock party. People petted, danced, shouted revolutionary slogans, wrote pamphlets, painted posters; some of them made love. Aurélia adored Hervé's work: she'd taken them back to her apartment one evening, and there were all Sinteuil's books in the place of honor on the shelves. And she thought Olga very sexy. She clung to the Squirrel, wreathing herself around her like a cowboy with a floozy in a saloon: it was a sort of amorous joke. She didn't avoid men, but preferred to make a third. Hervé enjoyed her lighthearted admiration, the poise that seemed not to have a soul but did possess a head of bobbed red hair and an unproblematical sex. In the atmosphere then reigning at the Odéon their threesome was unremarkable; it was the "in" thing.

Olga was surprised she wasn't more surprised by Aurélia's arrival on the island. Was it by any chance because she, Olga, liked women? The idea wasn't unpleasant. But that was as far as it went. What really amused her was the game of chess involved. A game that would be played by three people, or four. Rather more complicated, rather more emotional and exciting than the usual version, but strangely enough, more neutral too. What was it the nun who taught her French as a child used to say? "My child, there's only one way I know of to humble our pride, and that is to rise above it." This precept seemed to her almost as profound as Chairman Mao's "One can be divided into two." With the aid of these axioms you were invulnerable. "Rising above it" and "dividing oneself"—this took you into regions where there was no more psychology, nothing but logic and mathematical permutations. And pure love, if it survived.

Hermine brought a marvelous record player with her. Fantastic!—the Montlaurs' record player was old and damaged the discs. Aurélia came laden with hash, which, according to the latest fashion, you were supposed to take with honey.

The sea was unfriendly at Easter, and Aurélia was the only one who went in: purple with cold but bubbling with pride and laughter. Hermine and Olga basked in the strong sunshine, lying by the lilacs on the grounds of what had once been the manor house. They only dabbled their feet in the water, but the tan they got! Their skin was like olives. Hervé liked cycling best, and the four of them rode all over the island, which was so flat it might have been specially designed for them. They skirted the salt marshes, dotted with gulls and herons. They followed the cycle tracks that linked the villages, stopped in the marketplaces, nibbled a few strawberries. Hermine would buy some old white-embroidered peasant smock to turn into a nightdress; Aurélia filled her basket with bottles of lavender essence; then they would all pedal on to Whale Beach, where horseback riders galloped across sand made smooth by the night waves. Either the wind was against them and made it difficult to advance, or it was behind them and drove them on. Their calves and thighs ached, they began to feel as dizzy as if they were at sea. But the smooth, level landscape was so inviting they forgot about turning for home. When they did get back, the whole gang of four was exhausted, but the local white wine soon revived them. Hash left Olga feeling perfectly serene. Hermine couldn't stop laughing. Hervé pretended to be high, imitating the ghost of a knight who'd been thrown from his horse and couldn't remount the unruly steed, which was also his body. Only Aurélia was really stoned—a latter-day Saint Teresa.

That evening she clasped Olga in a feverish embrace, kissing and caressing her as if in a dream. Hermine joined them, with her permanent half-reluctant, half-sardonic manner. Hervé thought that Slav charm was never better than when it was multiplied, and that the only way to avoid becoming a husband-cum-heirloom was to act the actor. He regarded Don Juan not as a mere seducer but rather as the essential artist, capable of every kind of discourse, every kind of disguise, and every kind of pleasure. The paradox of the actor. *Mille e tre?* Three and a thousand. All women—that is, all roles, every one true. Untruth didn't exist. And truth?

The studio in the mill celebrated the communion that existed between the members of the gang of four. From violence to equilibrium. As far as appearances went, it was all perfectly decent. No one was asking anything of anyone. They would part the next day more neutral than ever. And more conspiratorial than ever. But their complicity was pointless. There was just the satisfaction of having set all limits at naught, of having experienced uttermost pleasure. A fortuitous, short-lived luxury. The extravagance of adults for whom eroticism is neither a good nor an evil but merely a thoughtless agreement, a collusion of rhythms. The only thing was, even the most grown-up of adults still have something of the child in them. Fortunately. Otherwise no one would have any qualms. And they did have qualms. Like anyone else. But in a regular harmony that transformed emotion, hurt, and jealousy into ritual. Like the tea ceremony, in which objects and participants—the bowls, the water, the tea leaves, the bowing of the drinkers—are all bound into a set of relationships flexible in themselves but in tune with time and space and nature itself. And that totality is so perfectly balanced, so deeply felt, that it's swallowed up in an impression of emptiness. What lightness! It's nothing. Or so it seems. Nothing but extreme tension.

Olga was sure that, after the cycling, the white wine, and the hash, Aurélia had taken a baby away with her that night. Heaven knows why she thought that! But no one ever found out. Aurélia disappeared. Someone saw her ten years later in an ashram near New Delhi. But no one ever discovered whether she had a little girl with her.

Hermine's record player was wonderful. Olga wanted to make everyone listen to her favorite disc: the whole experience ought to end beautifully, saluting the dark red sun just appearing behind the pines with Monteverdi's *Madrigals of Love and War.*

"Olga doesn't really care about the music—she just likes the meaning of the words."

Hervé was always teasing her.

"She's like me," said Aurélia. "I don't know anything about music, but I adore words that talk about love."

She lay down beside Olga: guilty, willing, delighted. Hermine wondered if she was going to start getting bored. But no—the sun was already rising, and tomorrow, or rather today, they were going to play tennis. Monteverdi was okay by her.

You could never tell when someone was melancholy, deep down. Especially with a young woman who played chess. The Monteverdi began with a gallop. *Tutti a cavallo.* The rhythm speeded up, got carried away, ran wild. Tancred and Clorinda fought, appealed to one another, hatred and love alternated, a wealth of sentiment and sound issued from a single voice and a few instruments. A Shakespearean kind of story, with a meeting between two characters in disguise. Two masked men about to kill each other. One of the combatants knows the true situation: Clorinda, dressed as a man so as to be near Tancred. Darkness falls on the strains of instruments and voices. Clorinda has been run through and is bleeding to death. Tancred lifts off the helmet of his dying enemy: *"Ahi vista! ahi conoscenza!"* His adversary was a woman—Clorinda! Tremolo was invented by Monteverdi so that a woman disguised as a man might love and die better—the two are practically the same. Tremolo is just right for when a woman agrees to fight like a man, and by losing the battle is loved forever. But was Clorinda really defeated? *"S'apre il ciel, io vado in pace."* She expires on the heights of love, the pinnacle of pleasure. Tancred is left alone, motionless, bereft of words.

Melodrama? Sublimity cleanses sex. Monteverdi showed the gang of four a noble pain they all knew belonged to another age: it was too archaic for the liberated youth of today. The brief but dazzling melody, ranging from gallop through emotion to darkness, turned death into delight. Could the mixing up of the sexes and their subsequent division be a grace? Ecstasy was the light in which solemnity was elevated into equilibrium. Whose? Aurélia's? Olga's? The equilibrium of both, of all four? Which of them was Clorinda?

Good old Claudio Monteverdi! Olga had chosen well, and recaptured everyone through the Venetian's magic. Hervé kissed her, looking straight into her eyes, as always in ineffable moments. Then he put his arm around her waist and led her over to the window. The sun, red now, had just emerged from the sea and was wakening the birds on the marshes. They flew up shrieking with joy, unless it was with fury.

Between the tennis courts and the sea was a dike, acting as a barrier to the waves but not to the wind. The air was so full of oxygen the players were either overcome or almost turned into champions. Hervé and Aurélia were the best at the game, so there was no problem about who played with whom: Hermine and Hervé against Aurélia and Olga.

Hermine: a classic striker, reliable but slow, so casual as to be almost lazy. She'd loiter at the back of the court as if she'd just had a good meal, and yet with her dancer's agility achieved some miraculous returns.

Hervé: amazingly quick on his feet, and with a deadly backhand from which no one was safe. But he was erratic, and some of his drives went astray, like rockets out of orbit.

Aurélia: Olga knew what her more skillful guest would require of her, and usually dealt with the balls Aurélia left to her just well enough to keep the game going. But today it was going to be different: the Squirrel felt like taking the initiative. Like running, hitting, dodging, nonplussing them all, thwarting them, reducing their rackets to teaspoons! Attagirl!

Tennis is a martial art, as the newspapers suggest when they talk of some champion's "killer instinct" at Wimbledon or Forest Hills. Olga had come to understand this during some karate lessons she'd taken with Pierre-Louis, a friend who was an ardent contributor to *Now*, a poet when the fancy took him and karate champion of France. The events of May had put a stop to that experiment, but she might take it up again one day.

For the moment she was amused by the resemblance between a smash in tennis and a barehand attack in *budo*. There was the same alternation of concentration and deliberate relaxation; the same timing; the same assessment of oneself and one's opponent, followed by instinctive but decisive action. Should one aim it to the left, to the right, higher, lower—the physical gesture that would affect and frustrate the strategy of the other? The others? Pierre-Louis was definite: all the best Swedish and American tennis players studied the martial arts as part of their training.

"In my view," he said, "there's a crucial moment. You have to seize your opportunity before your opponent's attack has been clearly formulated, when it's still just an intention in his mind. That's the whole secret—taking advantage of the moment when your enemy's consciousness isn't connected with his movements. In technical terms, you have to take advantage of the temporal *maai*. This allows you to assess, mentally and practically, the real distance between you and your opponent—what's called the spatial *maai*. Make sure you learn how to make that evaluation: it's essential for a woman or an older person—they're both at a disadvantage as regards strength. It makes up for the lack of force. Your energy is transformed into spontaneous calculation—in other words, rhythm, which is what decides who wins."

These fine distinctions struck Olga as typically "structuralist." Talk about splitting hairs, even when it came to war! It was astounding how they tracked down meaning in the smallest fraction of time, space, or action. Admittedly it was an attractive theory. But its adepts seemed rather otherworldly and vague, as if they'd unlearned everything that had ever been known. So did they really need to learn anything anymore?

Olga held her racket in both hands and shifted from one foot to the other, observing the pair opposite and Aurélia to one side of her. She was out of training. All the more reason to enter into a state of suspension, something over and above academic concentration. It wasn't a matter of applying all the lessons of karate—just of going along with the observed rhythm of the others, of seizing the brief empty moments, the time lag between mind and body. *Maai*—that was the word. Bounce. Drive. After a night of *hyoshi*, when the accord between the combatants' minds and lungs had produced perfect equilibrium, they were all playing freely, wildly, with determination and precision.

Olga of course wasn't thinking about anything. She just felt she was living through an amount of time that couldn't be measured: breathless fractions of seconds, full of both rage and restraint. Energy had been transformed into infinitesimal time, time embodied in regular series of strokes. Her muscles carried her to the net and the back of the court. Backhand or drive? No, she left this ball to Aurélia. Here was an empty moment opposite, on Hervé's side: bounce, stroke. Hermine's side: bounce, smash. Aurélia was lurking at the back of the court. Olga went up to the net: pause, volley, smash.

Energy sleeps in the spine. When a dream collapsed and awoke her at night, or in the lazy twilight of siesta, Olga could feel waves rising in her vertebrae, distending her ribs, her pelvis, her shins, pulsating in the tissues of her hips and arms. Tension likes to drowse in closed circuit; you can tame it then, almost talk to it as if to a force that's in but not of you. It can suddenly advance into fervor. Or calmly collapse into fatigue.

But here on the tennis court, whipped by gusts from the incoming tide, it wasn't a question of listening to one's own heartbeat. The foursome quadrupled the Squirrel's energy. All the nodes, joints, and cartilages in her body, all the points at which held-in force accumulated, were awake now and vibrating. Olga, in a kind of hypnotic fury, didn't feel any hatred. She just couldn't bear to be offside, excluded, and if anyone thought for a moment of leaving her out, that person would soon find out his mistake.

Energy is only available when it's directed. Then a racket becomes a weapon, the yellow ball a bullet, as the opponent's arm comes down. Who is the enemy? The people on the other side of the net: Hermine and Hervé. Aurélia too: she liked to reduce the Squirrel to the role of ball girl. O God, save me from my partner—I can save myself from my enemies! Aurélia, Hermine, Hervé. Three against one. If she isn't eliminated, she'll wipe the floor with them. Only impassive anger will produce a hatred that neither explodes nor implodes but strikes straight home. Only a neutral fury can measure its blows.

"You've never played so well!"

Hervé could hardly recognize her. She'd never managed to be a decent partner before: they usually just hit the ball back and forth between them; Hervé's feeblest passing shot knocked the racket out of her hand.

"Forty-thirty. . . . Another game to us!" Aurélia exulted. "We've won!"

The two guests left the next day. Olga came across Aurélia two or three times in Paris, and thought she seemed vague, embarrassed, and in a hurry.

"Are you still playing like a champion? What a game that was!"

Olga did still play sometimes, but that game on the island had been a kind of miracle, a state of grace, the exception proving the rule of her usual mediocrity.

"We must do it again one day, and you can let me into your secret!"

"Of course. But I'm not sure I've got one!"

"I'll call you. Ciao!"

Since when, no news of Aurélia.

"You haven't taken the boat out this time, have you?"

"We'll take it out today. I was waiting for the others to leave. The boat's just for us two."

The damp wind came through their oilskins and soaked their hair, though they were wearing knitted caps. Olga was more intoxicated than ever by the turbulent mix of wind, salt, and ozone. The boat listed to the left and they had to weigh it down on the right to keep it from foundering. Hervé knew what he was doing; Olga obeyed his instructions. There are situations in which that's the best you can do. Follow instructions. Be able to follow instructions.

9

They were waiting for the evening. A time of day that was soothing and filled their bodies with silence, the silence that filled the Fier with pearly light and the beating of wings. Far from the madding crowd and from demonstrations, even pleasure was absorbed into the peace of the lagoon. The still-recent memory of May faded away in the presence of these eternal marshes, leaving behind a memory of slavish agitation—and traces of regret. No real malaise, just an interruption. An interval. Until other agitations started in Paris, other meetings, other speeches. "Listen and hear the gentle darkness advance," as Baudelaire said. Soon the Great Bear would draw the black sky out over the mill.

"Come, my love, come over here. You wonder whether I'm a rebel, inconstant, a sensualist? But you already know—and you're the only one who does—

that I'm one of those who can be trusted. Surprising, isn't it? It might be to some people. Not to you. I was a cheerful child in a paradise of vineyards and châteaux. For a long time I enjoyed the company of sad children, and loved under the sun of Satan. I know the rhetoric of half-solemn, half-decadent lovers. I could produce some for you—women like that sort of thing. Yes, I was a believer, I belonged to a lofty, sly sort of Catholicism, a bullfighting Catholicism if you like—at any rate, it wasn't French. Sin, which is always—as I've discovered—a passion for making love to our mothers, who dream of making love to their own mothers or sisters or the like, was for a long time a blasphemy . . . but it cured me of the dizzy spells little boys suffer from when they've got weak ears and throats. I was loved by women who thought they loved men in order to give pleasure to themselves or one another. One of them told me I was 'beloved of the fairies.' Perhaps. Why not of witches disguised as nymphs too?

"Shall I go on? Are you enjoying this courtly tale of contemporary and therefore cynical adventure? Carmen? She raped me, but I got over it; she left me, but I grew up. Then came Solange, who wrapped me up like a motherly aunt; I was her fetish, a kept man, an infant prodigy. I bowled her over with pleasure, replaced the dominant role she used to play by another she'd never dreamed of, one that was humble and couldn't be thrown off, the role of my perverse governess. And so on. I'll leave it at that for today. You know them all, or will. Women are useful to me and I to them.

"The events of May are proving me right: nowadays a couple is something strange, and it'll go on being so. My solitary ways will be as common as something you buy in a supermarket. But I am and always will be an exception; something out of the way. A whole lot of private peculiarities urge me to go still farther. I'm seeking my own strange, inaccessible paradise—others may enter it, I don't mind, but only in a state of secret, immeasurable happiness. By reading what I write, for example.

"And you, my Squirrel, where do you come in? I went down into hell to find you, and if I haven't succeeded yet, I will. I'll go down under the earth: do you remember when I lay down on the ground on the quai Blériot, rather drunk (you thought)? But I wasn't drunk: when you're in love, you want to break through the earth's crust and turn the globe upside down. You, and I with you, have repeated the migration of the Barbarians—from the frontiers of Asia, or some steppe I don't care to know about, to here, to the Fier with its Romanesque churches. We're in advance of our time—just you wait, twenty years from now they'll all have a lover or a mistress from the East. Europe, from our mill among the marshes to the snows of Moscow and beyond, will be one vast building site run by German foremen. You are my breath, my biography, a hyphen joining me to tomorrow.

"Do you remember the voyager to the end of the night whom everyone execrates nowadays, that incredibly sensitive guttersnipe? He saw us French as the weariest of races, from having made the longest journey: and it might well be exhausting, traveling from the tundra to the Atlantic! Only the most persistent arrive, perhaps the most gifted, but in what a state! Well, you're in very good shape, my Squirrel, and so am I, and there's plenty to do in this land of steeples that's on the way to becoming a museum, prey to collectors and antique dealers. But May interrupted their routine for a moment. As you did mine.

"I love you because you're not fooled. Not too much, anyway. You know you've married someone elusive; permanent revolution, to use the current jargon. Sometimes I feel I belong to the Old School—I'm so fond of Bordeaux, *cèpes*, and entrecotes. But the Montlaurs aren't such fossils that I want to destroy the whole tradition. The old châteaus still contain some baggage we need to take on board with us as we head for other sunsets!

"Do you know what I read in a book about Mao? When he took an American woman's arm to help her across a stream at night, she felt as if she'd been touched by the body of another woman. Then that old tortoise of a Mao, who was a young tortoise then, told her he was incapable of learning foreign languages, he just wasn't interested. 'I'm a poet,' he said, 'and when I write in Chinese, it's as if I were in the tao.' Well, when I write in French, it's as if *I* were in the Tao, and I'll never make you understand, little Squirrel, that your foreignness will always be foreign to me. You can have it. Your mischievous eyes quiz me, but I won't take up their challenge: 'Get on with it, fat Frenchie—try to impress me!'

"My Tartar Ph.D., my Baltic librarian! Hell, it takes some

doing—I can't help laughing to myself under the Great Bear! People think you're a sort of sleeping pill for me, a drug. On the contrary—you keep me awake, you're a night-light, an amphetamine under the pillow.

"I shall only tame you in order to impress you. There are plenty of stones to be shifted in the old houses and churches. You'll be my harbor, Squirrel, my compass, the little white wine that administers a salutary shock to anyone dazed and adrift after a day of sea and wind . . ."

Hervé said all that as he moored the *Violin*—that was the name Olga had given the boat, which she saw as a kind of musical fish. He didn't say any of it aloud. But by the kind of mysterious osmosis you see between couples where through constant sympathy and profound pleasure the man and the woman come to look alike, Olga could hear the whisper of that solemn yet ironic confession. She was quite happy that he should talk like that, to himself. She wouldn't have minded his saying it to her, too. He might well have done so: he could express himself in every possible style, including that of the doleful but flippant lover of the sixties. She'd come to like that kind of language, but she admired it in secret: idyll didn't really go with current events. Nor would Hervé ever have allowed himself to utter such pomposities. He might have thought them, he could have made love to his wife with the naive charm that lay in such words. But say them? He said very little, wrote sometimes, laconic telegrams, nothing superfluous, only the essential words that survived his weeding out of metaphor and psychology:

May 4

A few words just to contain my impatience (you're just due to phone)—how painfully I miss you, every second—the dizzy sensation—as if the world were all muffled and far away (like when I stopped in the street yesterday and leaned against the wall "thinking of you" . . . Does that mean anything? . . . If that's naive, too bad).

DO YOU KNOW YOU'RE MY LIFE?

(Not that I think my life's of crucial importance, but there seems to be a kind of illusory whole, and it's from that that your name rises up, forces itself through my throat and lips—at night.)

H.

August 20

I've already invented a hundred scenes in which you're laughing
and have forgotten me (with a name that ends in *e*, so as to rhyme),
and I don't know how to frame the time that's between us so as to
show you it *as it is*. I've forgotten how to photograph this limited
alphabet.

I LOVE YOU. I NEED YOU. I'M MAD ABOUT YOU.

Insofar as I'm a product of physical chance (a body of chance,
obliged to have a certain number of chance thoughts).

You are the other side, and the night, and I want you as I want
the night and the other side (my vocabulary's in tatters. Loud
laughter).

I NEED YOU. I CAN SEE YOU. (Have a good time, though.)

I love you.

H.

February 15

You can't imagine how tired I am sometimes of having arranged
(it's the only way to keep the wounds open) for everyone, always,
to believe, to be obliged to believe, in my "invulnerability," my
"duality," and so on. I'm waiting for some completely detached
observer who'll see the silent torture I've chosen to come a cropper
in, but won't say anything.

That's enough about that.

I love you.

H.

Perhaps that's what she liked about him best: his skill at master-
ing the whole range of styles, his virtuosity at manipulating them
while never showing anything himself but a classic, an ascetic
restraint. Elliptical treatment of feelings agonizingly concentrated. The conciseness of Chinese calligraphy on a ground of
unbearable passion. Was it fear? Discretion? The exclusive opulence of the great eighteenth-century mansions in Bordeaux. It
was all a riddle still.

She kissed his mouth, his hair, his eyes, his neck—at length.

She didn't have any erotic scenario to offer him. Sometimes
Hervé asked her for a sexy story to fan the flame of their
pleasure, to add spice to the perfectly matched taste of their
kisses. She always produced one, invented from start to finish,

at times rather amusing and at times rather too porno, so that the part she gave herself was completely unconvincing, and instead of arousing Hervé she made him laugh. Any kind of discourse transported her into a lucid world of logical rivalry and competition. It intoxicated her mentally, but too much mind can cancel out sensation. Her erotic fantasies merely passed through words and arrangements of bodies; they were really rooted in her perceptions. Tapestries woven of scents and sounds, of burning skins, ravenous mouths, the flowery inside of the womb. She didn't talk much about love; she made it. If she was an intellectual, she was also a primitive. It was up to Hervé to find the words, the novel.

The fire in the hearth at the mill hadn't caught. They had to re-lay the logs and kindle the embers with the bellows. The sheets on the big bed, damp in this cold spring, grew warm and yielding in the heat of their eager bodies. It wasn't Hervé making love to Olga, or Olga making love to Hervé. They were united as closely as a couple of starfish in the welcoming waves. They clasped each other fast so as to prolong the pleasure in their sexes—they could feel it going on throbbing. Unbearable, never-ending abandon. Pleasure dancing a smiling round, like happy children who've left their cares to their invisible parents. The offenses, challenges, standoffishness, and stress of strangers: all could be banished for a while, sent back to Paris for instance. Here there was just the old *mas* under the parasol pines. The bedroom smelled of the bunches of dried lavender that Olga had picked in the garden last summer; you came on them everywhere—in cupboards and drawers, under mattresses and cushions. The walls were hung with green and pale yellow paper, a foil to the rose-sprigged eighteenth-century curtains, which were a present from Mathilde. . . . There was something normal emanating from it all, something conspiratorial and impossible. It was their family digression.

10

I

can't concentrate, I don't hear what my patients are saying to me. Not that I get things wrong: I don't take a hysterical conversion for a serious anorexia, or vice versa. It's simpler and more fundamental than that: I simply don't listen anymore. Other people's words don't mean anything to me.

Joëlle Cabarus in love? A bad film. With all my experience, at my age! And with whom? With Arnaud's young assistant, of course. Romain Bresson. All the ingredients needed for a farce.

"Bresson seems very aggressive these days—have you any idea why?" Arnaud asked me this morning as we passed each other in the bathroom, definitely the scene of our most important conversations.

Have I any idea? I've got twenty-three! Twenty-three red roses blazing away in the drawing room, and it's never occurred to Arnaud to wonder where they came from. From the florist's, naturally. "Forever. R." In English.

"*They challenge everything nowadays!*" I say, feigning indifference.

"*Yes, but he's overdoing it! I must admit I'm surprised.*"

Arnaud can't bear the smooth running of his department to be disturbed.

I've known about Romain's feelings for a long time. But "forever"? He thinks so. And it's enough for one of a pair to be convinced for the other one to lose his or her head. The other one, in this case, is me. I don't have ears anymore. Just eyes for Romain's eyes, for his desire misted with tenderness when he thinks no one's looking at us. Personally, I couldn't care less whether anyone's looking at me. If you think of it dispassionately, there's nothing more ordinary than those well-behaved, warm brown eyes, like those of a diligent schoolboy. Romain Bresson must have won prizes in every subject; except French, no doubt—he never says anything that hasn't to do with science, and his writings are full of sketches and diagrams, with comments couched in the technical jargon of brain chemistry. But, for me, he has the eyes of a lover "forever": I can see them there above the couch as my patients tell me things I don't hear anymore, because there are those eyes, those hands, that body; because there's Romain. Ever since last year, when we came back together from Brittany.

Arnaud and Jessica wanted to stay on, but I had to come back to Paris: Dad had had a heart attack and needed his daughter. Romain comes down every year to spend the mid-August holiday with us, and he couldn't do otherwise than drive me back to Paris. Nothing could be more innocuous. I suspected something, of course—women suspect everything in novels—but our relationship is so undefined, and the medical hierarchy so full of taboos about such matters, that we were stuck in the awkward politeness that's supposed to last "forever." And then all of a sudden his hand is on mine; the weather's very sultry and I feel like going to sleep or having a drink. I'm not sure what I do want really. His lips, his broad lips, warm as his eyes, the mouth of a woman. "*Don't tell me you're surprised, Joëlle—don't tell me that. You know I want you.*"

I'm beginning to have a body again. My back is straighter, my breasts filling out. I've only to imagine Romain, to think of him, or even not to think anything, just tell myself he's somewhere in this city, that he's breathing and certainly thinking of me, for what remains of my mind to be utterly confused by desire. Like an adolescent girl. This ought to be happening to Jessica—it's more appropriate to her age than to mine. How long ago is it since I forgot I had a body? When my daughter was born?

Soon afterward, during my analysis, I spent five years talking about Arnaud's body, about the pleasure I experienced with him, and how it scared me to see him so quickly satisfied: the slightest thing was enough. While I *went on lying there in bed longing for more caresses, for an infinite kiss; to reach the climax of pleasure just from the contact of bodies and lips. I remember telling Lauzun, "My sex is my whole body; I'm one continuous erogenous zone." I didn't understand how a woman (if all women were like me) could live with a man who was satisfied with the brief pleasure of his member, then walled himself up in his cocoon of sheets, blankets, and serious professional obligations (if all men were like Cabarus). Naturally, Lauzun didn't listen to me. When he was in good form, he just repeated his all-purpose phrases: "You want to be everything, a woman who's everything, but nothing is everything." In the end I exhausted all my complaints and discovered that strange erotic prosthesis—memory.*

That's really the miracle of analysis, though no one ever talks about it. You learn to inhabit your past so intensely that it isn't separated from your present body anymore, and every scrap of memory is transformed into a real hallucination, a direct perception, here and now. The surprising thing is that this almost mystical metamorphosis continues later with the patients—only in the most inspired moments of an analysis, of course, when I follow them so closely that through my words I give them back my own memory and thus my own body, so that they both become theirs. Thus I've been living for years with a multiple body that isn't really mine, but that survives and even changes in time with the others. Joëlle the octopus, the protean jellyfish, the woman without qualities of her own, who takes her pleasures with the tongs of words, via people who think they're living a real life, while hers is mere imagination embodied in moods.

Romain and his clichés in English: "See you tomorrow." "My heart is with you." "Honey." "Love." The language of someone shy: avoiding his mother tongue, which is always too easily available—the smallest syllable of passion can make it obscene. English is another technical language for him: a foreign phrase can put things in a nutshell, cover embarrassment, camouflage someone who feels vulnerable. Romain is rather dull when he speaks French. But his passion manages to skirt around words; he loves with his skin, his muscles, his lips, his sex, his hands, his arms, his thighs. I never imagined a man's body could be so multiple and fluid.

But I don't imagine it, I experience it, it gives me back my own body, just as differentiated and just as sensual as his. A delicacy expressed in nothing but gestures, caresses, attitudes. The soul reduced to tender actions: that's Romain.

I'd like to make myself more beautiful, buy dresses, extravagant lipsticks, new shoes.

I'm going over to the other side, arising from the grave, becoming amiable again. Even Arnaud has noticed I'm wearing a new perfume. If only I could make him want me! Arnaud, I mean. I say as much to him, laughing this time, so as to observe his reaction. He laughs too, and tells me I did so long ago and must be sure of it. But certainty has nothing to do with desire. As a matter of fact, it's the death of it.

Having become a girl again because of Romain, I deliberately flirt with danger. Surprise bordering on shock—why not? And the ridiculous pleasure, expected but always strange, of little presents. Arnaud never gives presents: "Don't you think it's unnecessary between us? After all, we buy everything together, and what else do we need?" Nothing, of course—"we" don't need anything, anything at all. How tedious. "We" is all very well—but what about "I"? Arnaud thinks the Ego is childish, not to say pathological.

Romain doesn't like orchids: "An orchid lasts too long—it stops being a surprise and becomes a marriage," he jests. Could this Dr. Bresson be some sort of pervert beneath his airs of top boy in the class and his talk of nothing but artificial languages? An innocent seducer: the dream of married women who want to stay faithful, but with all the advantages of an inventive clandestine lover. Less and less clandestine, actually. At the hospital Romain's turning into a leftist and is on the warpath against the chief mandarins. In other words, against Arnaud. Who'll eventually wake up. And require Madame Cabarus, in her bathroom, to explain to Monsieur Cabarus why he's being attacked in season and out of season by Dr. Bresson, a nice lad who used to be so fond of all the family. I ask you! . . .

I can't do without Romain—the fact that I can't do my job properly proves it. But Arnaud mustn't notice and be hurt by it. And yet I'd be so glad if he did notice!

Joëlle Cabarus, you're not a special person anymore—you're just a common or garden narcissist, a woman who's got a boyfriend and has lost all sense of truth.

May 15, 1968

How do revolutions affect the psychoanalyst's consulting room? At first there's a fall in attendance: the stiffs arise and go to demos and meetings instead of keeping their appointments with their shrinks. You might suppose they'd been held up by the police or the barricades, or perhaps a transport strike—i.e., some objective obstacle. Nonsense! Revolution is a strike on the part of the "inner consciousness," which is replaced by mass declarations, psychodrama, acting out, or—quite frankly—love. But after a few days' absenteeism Frank and some of the other active militants reappeared. They needed to talk about it all in private. They wanted to be back in the dark room again. To get a better fix on the enemy—and on my supposed complicity with the forces of repression. To refuel the imagination they want to see in power.

Of course, I went on the demos with Romain and the interns on duty. I shouted, "Down with the police state!"—laughing, observing, but also being part of it all. Naturally, Arnaud didn't come. "It's quite appealing," he said. "But so childish!" For once, he agrees with my shrinks, for "it" is very much frowned on by the Psychoanalytical Friendly Society. I know they regard me as an anarchist: can an analysis with Lauzun really be called an analysis? I think they accepted me because of Arnaud, and because, as I don't really take part in the life of the Friendly Society, I'm not a nuisance to them.

Does my affair with Romain mean I need another analysis? Instead of that, I spend a few hours a week at the Bibliothèque Nationale. I look for myself in books—rare books. In manuscripts, archives, forbidden documents regarded as a danger to morals. I'm looking for evidence about Thérésa Cabarrus: a relative? a namesake? another coquette? It's an excuse for living through 1789 over again, a time much murkier than today, and one beside which the present skirmishes are as nothing. Still, if you look closely at the men and women then, you do see connections and similarities. I can be back there indirectly by identifying in my imagination with a woman of easy virtue I think of as related to me . . . Joëlle Cabarus, or the confusion of a "liberated" woman. It's a way of coping with the pain of a love that can only be expressed indirectly because when they're "live," words fail it.

I don't care if I'm laughed at for writing about pain. After all, psychoanalysis is a discourse on pain, arising out of romantic pathos and disciplined by analytical philosophy. Freud applies reason to pain and helps it to transform itself into something else. Has Lauzun forgotten suffering in his eagerness to formulate it? The sunny side of pain is enthusiasm. There was no enthusiasm left, and pain had become something to be ashamed of.

And now enthusiasm has blown up in the faces of the dullards. The power of desire brings people out on the streets, and I wonder how the rebels will react when they wake up to the fact that they, too, want power. They seek an asocial happiness, they prepare microspaces for it, they take pleasure in being free of all law. The most clear-sighted of them see it all as only a transitional phase in the process of creating a new world, vaguer and more flexible—a socius de flux, as Decèze calls it. But for the time being, all we see is excited protesters for whom the sky's the limit. They chop off reactionaries' heads. Only verbally, of course.

I was with Romain in the boulevard Saint-Germain, opposite the Danton statue, when the police charged. We took shelter in the cour du Commerce-Saint-André. It seems this is where Dr. Guillotin tried out—on sheep—his famous and aptly named "philanthropic beheading machine." In an attic. I didn't see any memorial plaque. I suppose they felt awkward about putting one up. But Arnaud says there is one. I must go back and look. Marat used to print L'Ami du peuple *nearby.*

The name Cabarus makes me think of Madame Tallien, who was Thérésa Cabarrus before she was married. Arnaud says it's just a coincidence: "Her name was spelled with two r's." My in-laws are more evasive, embarrassed even. After all, an absentminded clerk can easily leave out an r, *transferring a person's records from one local register to another. "That's your problem," says Arnaud. So be it.*

I'm rather fond of Thérésa. "Another Antoinette," they called her in the Assembly, meaning that like the queen, she was a foreigner, extravagant and not at all backward in coming forward. Jewels, gowns, shawls, perfumes, bare shoulders, wasp waists: the banker's daughter used them all to advantage. Above all, she used them to save her own head. Our Lady of Thermidor, or Sex Against the Terror. A seductress versus Robespierre.

Leftist publications of today are regarded as "daring," "surrealistic," "fanatical." Their authors are all "obsessed by the anal penis," says a female colleague at the Psychoanalytical Friendly Society; no doubt she's an expert on the subject. And yet how tame they are compared with those of Thérésa's day! I was interested enough to read up on the revolutionary press in the enfer—*the "inferno" or forbidden-books department—at the Bibliothèque Nationale, and the license our predecessors allowed themselves just leaves us standing! Whether they supported the royalist or the popular cause, there were no holds barred when it came to denouncing the "female members of the 1789 Club," the alleged adventuresses and shameless intriguers whose only idea was to get between the sheets with members of the party the writer of the pamphlet in question happened to oppose. To pursue my fantasy about the link between Thérésa and the Cabarus family—Arnaud won't know—our ancestress was accused by the* Chronicle of Scandal, *in 1791, of having cuckolded de Fontenay, her first husband, with all the "patriots" in the Assembly. And there were plenty of them in those days.*

Nowadays respectable citizens are shocked by the "goings-on at the Odéon." If they only knew! In 1793 the Théâtre de la Montagne in Bordeaux put on shows that, in addition to "a few dashes of patriotism," exhibited "scandalous and immoral scenes fit only for places of prostitution," and all this under the title of The Temptation of Saint Anthony. *The army board was ordered to clean up public morals and put a stop to such "orgies of debauchery." The eighty-six members of the theater company were arrested. Liberty was not to be confused with license.*

The libertins *were people of taste and tolerance: unconstrained sex softens the manners of those who practice it and keeps them from shedding blood. Sade was revolted by the guillotine; its brisk and direct brutality struck him as barbaric.*

But with the exception of Sade, the world of pleasure and license that was Thérésa's didn't know that passion devoid of inhibition is a passion of death. The libertins *went on enjoying their erotic inventions until their erstwhile slaves revealed that the unwitting object of the whole flighty charade was to die of pleasure. You want pleasure? Here it is—enjoy it to the death! The terrorists of the French Revolution were a fearful species of analyst: totally lacking in benevolence, but with a slave's unrivaled skill at divining his master's deepest thoughts. They held up the glittering blade of the guillotine, and in it their victims saw as in a mirror that the ultimate end of unbridled pleasure—which either usurped the place of God or was surreptitiously reconciled with Him—was suffering, physical pain, moral humiliation, and finally death.*

May 22

I come back to the subject of the press, the popular press of the left as well as of the right, which talks about nothing but sex. Sade must have glanced through the lampoons and pamphlets that found their way into the drawing rooms at Versailles, though the people there failed to see their fatal import. For either the aristocracy didn't deign to read such productions, or else the outrageousness of their language, their crazy scurrility, seemed to have nothing in common with the nobility's own refined elegance. Such publications were contemptible, insignificant, irrelevant. As for Sade—a Freudian before Freud, a natural researcher in the laboratory of eroticism—he was well aware of both the pleasures of evil and the perversions of murder. I can just see him with an obscene pamphlet in his hand, at once disgusted and intrigued. Juliette shows the influence of the sort of lampoons and gossip sheets I looked up in the enfer *at the library. (By the way, Scherner was sitting opposite me—I must come back to him another time.) But there's a difference: the mob that shrieked when Madame du Barry's head fell into the basket, and gloated over the "Austrian woman's" orgies with the women at her court—the mob didn't understand. They were fascinated, their tongues were hanging out for more. But all they saw were "trollops, tramps, streetwalkers, scrubbers, and harlots of no fixed abode, ready to do it at the nearest crossroad." For them, the queen was indistinguishable from the envied image of the prostitute: she had "uterine frenzies," she was deflowered by a German soldier, if not by her own brother.*

Such scenes must have lingered in some people's minds, to unfold again as they crowded to witness public executions, cheering the sound of the lethal blade as it fell. Others tried to imitate the "whore of Versailles," exaggerating her imagined excesses—for there was little to choose between the popular imagination and the perverse inventions of the ruling classes. Only a populist will try to tell you different.

God was already dead, but a new absolute had taken His place. His name was "Fuck," and Monseigneur Duchesne, the ecclesiastical historian, was soon to invest him with political "dignity."

But was "Fuck" the guillotine's enemy or its colleague? Its enemy, you say, thinking of Sade. I think you're wrong: "Fuck" was inside the heads of those who watched other people's heads fall, imagining the guilty pleasure of the courtiers as they did so, vicariously sharing those pleasures.

Just as I think about Thérésa Cabarrus to stop myself thinking about Romain? Or, to be honest, to give me an excuse for thinking about him.

"Run away," a friend advised her. It was good advice: Thérésa had connections in Spain and with the aristocracy. But she was arrested and sent to an annex of the Force prison in Paris. Her supporters tried to move the tyrant to pity by describing the lamentable state she'd been reduced to: "Let them give her a mirror once a day!" said Robespierre. He was tolerant in his own way, and rather pitiful himself.

I try to imagine the night of the 7th Thermidor*—two days before the Revolution of the 9th, which overthrew that of July 14. After five years of revolts, changes, liberations, and terrors, people wanted a rest. They were beginning to appreciate the virtues of indifference.

Thérésa is supposed to have sent Tallien a note, at once plaintive and provocative: "The chief of police has just left. He came to inform me that I'm to appear in the dock—i.e., on the scaffold—tomorrow. Very different from the dream I had last night . . ."

I'd love to know what Thérésa Cabarrus dreamed about. But do people really dream in times of revolution? My own patients don't dream anymore.

* July 25, 1794. Tr.

They act and argue on the barricades, in factories and "Analysis Groups" and debates—but dreams are few and far between. I don't dream now either; my love for Romain is a waking dream. Thérésa might have dreamed the 9th Thermidor, too; might she have programmed it as she dreamed?

There is an even more romantic version of the story. Thérésa, ill, close to death, obtained permission to take a walk in the prison yard. Someone threw her a lettuce, and when she picked it up, she found a letter inside offering to convey messages for her. But there wasn't any ink! Never mind—she would write in her own blood, and then with paints smuggled in for her by the jailer. That was how she managed to send Tallien the note.

The reason I'm fond of Thérésa is that though she's rather repellent, she's also fascinating. "You can be in love with Madame Tallien for a whole day," sneered some. *"She deals only in sensual pleasures,"* added others. *"Her arms, her graceful ways, her broad shoulders, her fine eyes, her Irish nose, her necklace of diamonds and gold beads"—all are cataloged. Even Madame Récamier admired her charms. We're in the world of show business now: discretion is flung to the winds. Thérésa wanted to be seen and adored, so she actually promoted gossip. (And what about me?) But at the same time, she organized some favorable publicity. Her lovers and friends began to fashion the flattering legend of Thermidor—flattering as regards Thérésa, the opposite as regards Tallien: "Madame Tallien, as compassionate as her husband was bloodthirsty . . ."*

My Thérésa dodged as nimbly as a she-wolf between sex and the guillotine, but who won? She wasn't the only person who wished for Robespierre's death, but she certainly played her part in it. Her own idea was dying of pleasure, enjoying to the death, but enjoying with dash and determination. Thérésa Cabarrus stood for the power of a pleasant life as against that of heroism to the death.

She defied the ideals of the purists and cut them down to size, at the same time revealing their underlying terrorism and savagery. I've got too many scruples, myself, to accept without reservation such unrelenting pursuit of personal happiness. But perhaps, if I'd been in her shoes, and possessed of her charms, I might have tried to use them in the same way. Is this an example of typical feminine egoism? Narcissus in a shawl at the theater, being admired (like me at the hospital, and with my patients or "analysands"), incapable of taking part in history? She certainly was no democrat, my Thérésa.

But are our own barricades really being put up for the sake of an ideal? What if the Revolution of 1789 finished only yesterday, at the end of May 1968? Young rioters are breaking up the last remains of the terror of ideologies and parties. They claim the right to pleasure, desire, imagination. But these self-proclaimed "German Jews" are in fact modern representatives of the very French phenomenon of "libertinism." Looked at from the point of view of my own profession, which listens to such wretched woes, don't human rights really consist in just the right to experience pleasure without killing anyone else? And so, after the explosion of the last few days, will there be a new Directory, another Empire? The tepid waters of comfortable belles époques *inevitably spawn new mysticisms. We must wait and see. For the moment His Majesty the Ego reigns supreme, and demands his due of pleasure. Like* Thérésa Cabarrus.

No date

I'm not the only one who amid all the present upheavals looks for a meaning—my meaning?—in the vestiges of the past. When you see people tearing up the cobblestones, it looks as if archaeology's in fashion. And whom did I see sitting opposite me in the enfer *at the Bibliothèque Nationale but Scherner himself!*

It's obvious he doesn't like me, though I couldn't say why. He consulted my husband a lot when he was writing his History of Psychiatry. *Did he like Arnaud any better than he liked me? I'm not sure, and I can't get anything out of Arnaud on the subject. He seems to regard Scherner as a patient. Protected by professional secrecy. But a philosopher's bound to look down on those who in his view have turned mental illness into an object, a business, a worry: so Scherner can't be other than contemptuous of doctors, shrinks included. He's sure medicine hasn't helped the human race by abolishing God's authority over the patient's body and, even more, over mania itself: it has merely shut men up in hospitals and asylums. In his view, if I understand him rightly, the Devil, master of madness among the Ancients, may not be actually preferable to the therapy of the Moderns, but medicine and psychiatry have introduced new forms of satanism which, though more refined, are even more crushing. For nurses and psychiatrists do away with the singularity of bodies and words that's so dear to Scherner, depriving them of their inspiration and their strange techniques of expression by transforming what used to be evil into mere disease. With their straitjackets and neuroleptics, they distort the nature of free will, and may end up by destroying it altogether. Psychoanalysis, according to Scherner, is part of this would-be humanitarian dead end, which is really authoritarian and mutilating.*

But he's wrong. Because since Freud there hasn't been any such thing as madness. Only idiolects. *I like that word; Freud had the courage to make contact with endemic idiocy—he even rehabilitated it: it's what's called the "unconscious." So for me there is nothing but singular states of discourse that I can adjust to fit in with somebody else. Refashioning a body and soul (his, mine) just as you create a work of art or make a violin, a table, a cart. But Scherner doesn't want to understand. He's suspicious. Why? I suppose he has his reasons.*

Some people think that when they read, they're hiding, shielding themselves from the world in a space suit of print. They're deceiving themselves. Nothing is more revealing than a reader who thinks he's unobserved. His masturbating shows in his face.

Scherner looks up from his book, pushes his chair away from the table, and leans back with his head on one side, his mouth half open, and his eyes on the ceiling. This movement makes the whole room turn around on an oblique axis, then come to a halt in an absurd and unstable equilibrium. Scherner continues his meditations in this position, which could be that of an acrobat. Uneasily I observe his expression—the beginning of a strained laugh, as if he'd just been struck by some as yet unidentified cruelty or horror. If you could hear this laugh, still buried in some unspeakable wickedness, it would sound sardonic. But as I look at him there, petrified by the realization of what he's just read, thought, or felt, he is taken over by it. The laugh becomes absurd, corrupting, idiotic.

I'm ashamed to have such thoughts about a man who's unwittingly stripped himself bare in my presence, and who is generally considered a genius. A crabbed mind perhaps, but also wide-ranging, abrasive, and uncompromising. Vicious too: Scherner slaughters anyone who dares to displease him—in other words, everyone, except (I suppose) a few intimates. And even those . . . He's probably like some pitiless hawk, pecking away with his irony at the dead flesh of those who had the cheek to think they loved him.

Genius is almost as rare as a real woman: an error of nature. A genius doesn't have much choice. Either he's morbidly cautious and doesn't reveal himself: this alternative gives rise to inaccessible mystics. Or else he erupts, like some Dionysus discovering a bacchanalian eroticism in himself; mad to abolish the conventions; ready to kill himself to assuage his immortal desire to dominate others. Scherner's mind quiets down only in order to enter the darkness of insanity. It must love only crude, aphasic bodies. The grimace he makes when he laughs is aphasic.

There aren't any "real" women because of the fear that dilutes their words and decoys their passions. So "real" women degenerate into witches or vamps, *unless they go soft and turn into good mothers. But geniuses, who are just as insufferable, seek out crises to show themselves off and institutions that will help them find recognition. And now they've come unstuck. What room is there for geniuses between the barricades in the rue Gay-Lussac and the good form of the university? So they implode, displaying the idiot laughter that's the invisible counterpoint of genius.*

"A cigarette, Joëlle?"

He makes an effort to be polite, but his eyes crucify me. Then he decides it's best not to bother with me.

"I agree the rich shouldn't have vacations. But why shouldn't professors?"

It's very hot, the end of July, so I tried a little joke. Not very bright. Didn't work.

"I'm punishing myself by tackling prisons, which naturally punish the infamous—you know how I love them. You've no idea how horrible the penal system is—I'm not just talking about its history but about what it's still like now. An absolute disgrace! Yet no one bats an eye. And they call this civilization."

Just like Scherner. After psychiatric imprisonment he goes on to the criminal version. He denounces all forms of power; he follows the leftists, and they follow him. He shows first and foremost that knowledge, supposedly so noble, is really a power: the power of the word, which has its own genealogy and its own decadence. It can be seized, and it can be destroyed. Everyone is subject to Power! But is it inevitable? All antagonists are taken over and absorbed by the omnipresence of Power. So what? Forget antagonism. Be an "agonist," an agent, a permanent provocateur. A wild singularity that doesn't want to seize anything, especially not power, but which tends outward, neither relating to nor belonging to anything else. Be an exception.

"Now we're going to try to see all this in concrete form. Not in the 'utterances' of knowledge but in physical bodies, the bodies of prisoners confronted with prohibitions and harassments. The resistance put up by the infamous, the outcasts, is an exceptional test of the self. Whether they talk, like the scoundrels who left memoirs behind them in the past, or are speechless, like most prisoners, for me they are all exceptions. In other words, free men."

He has his great rogues, but he likes to protect poor wretches as well. I think of my Thérésa in her prison, and the revolutionary Terror. Scherner, together with Decèze, is the most Nietzschean of Frenchmen. He's at war with Christianity; he sees its verbalism as ascetic, its search for truth as hypocritical and servile.

I don't know where it comes from, my silent disagreement with an ardor I can't help finding attractive. Perhaps it's because Scherner's anti-Christianity leads him into another religion: death worship, arising from the vehement denial of the soul. I know that all of them, Brichot first and foremost, are monks of the void, members of that freemasonry that's supposed to bring salvation because it "makes the speaking subject disappear." But I listen to subjects who suffer, and before I can destroy the suffering, I have to deal with the soul it inhabits. Scherner dreams of a human race without a soul. His is a radical remedy: destroy the organ of suffering—the psyche—and suffering disappears! And what takes its place? A lovely form which acts but does not speak. The body of the Greek kouros, *as against the animist Christian body that dissolves into the farce of the bourgeois body.*

Romain, with his speechless love, isn't far away from this Utopia, but he has a surprising soul, displayed in a whole range of considerate gestures. Let's wait and see. I've nothing against it, in principle. I'm just afraid there may be too many people dead of pleasure before "fine form" replaces "virtuous soul."

But Scherner can love the music of words. "Before language, or rather inside it, the limit imposed by death opens up an infinite space." Literature. Was he referring to Roussel when he spoke of anguish?—the anguish of transforming oneself into a text too subtle and too polyphonic to be translated into common language, or even suggested by it.

"We've spent too much time on language! Make way for bodies and pleasures!"

I nod. But bodies and pleasures stripped of words are dead bodies, nonexistent pleasures. I must be too Christian, if I can think that. It's been said that "the truth of language is Christian." Scherner probably thinks there are other things besides language. As for Romain, he doesn't say much, but his whole body speaks to me. I don't say anything.

If Scherner thinks that, it's because he tries to think on the basis of his own sexuality—his own homosexuality. He's the only one risking the experiment: his genius is his danger. He'll be recognized for that, and he's ready to pay the price.

Baron Charlus didn't rule out the possibility of being offered a chair of homosexuality at the Sorbonne! Given the "events," the Sorbonne won't be enough for Scherner. I bet he'll go farther than that.

March 20, 1970

This warm, damp spring the little square in front of the church of Saint-Germain-des-Prés is like a great otter to which Paris has just given birth. The barricades are a thing of the past, but people's minds are still in ferment. The Grenelle agreement with the unions has ended the unrest. Wurst has pointed out that the student movement served only to bring about the general strike— "the most important proletarian action in the history of the working classes." People are puzzled: they know that the romanticism of one side and the pragmatism of the other very rarely meet. The Trotskyites fulminate. The Maoists are edgy, but don't desert Wurst. Frank keeps me posted about it all, and yesterday his friend Cédric came to see me, wondering if he shouldn't "try the couch." Stress, he said.

I've just emerged from the crowd that flocks to the Analysis Groups organized by Now. I find them refreshing, a change, I learn something from them. Sinteuil gave us a description of Mao the calligrapher and Taoist. I've written down a poem of Mao's that he's translated: I like it—it has the delicate intensity of a screen of painted silk. Should the credit go to Mao or to Sinteuil? Perfection wrought out of white bone.

> *Winds and thunders rising over the great earth*
> *Then ghosts born out of heaps of white bones*
> *The bonze is idiotic but educable*
> *Disasters come from evil geniuses.*

I feel like an idiotic bonze, so I must be educable. Politics, you say? The people who go and listen to Sinteuil are just looking for a style, and I have a feeling their "historic struggles" take place out of time.

How many deaths have been caused by the Cultural Revolution? We don't know yet. In Paris, people don't even ask the question. The question they do ask is: How can one become unique, an exception? Mao is regarded as an exception who has carried a nation with him. A billion Chinese may be a uniform and manageable mass, but in comparison with our Western tradition, what an exception he is, how unique, with that lunar linguistic elegance combined with acts, with strokes, with pictures! A living invitation to decipher our dreams as if they were ideograms in a sea of jade. To trim and cut and polish ourselves until we strike others as "Chinese."

The Analysis Groups are working toward a theory of exceptions; Sinteuil seems to be their leader. Olga watches him admiringly. When an intelligent woman's in love, she either loses her philosophical veneer altogether or else becomes twice as lucid as before. But is Olga intelligent?

Intelligence is the art our unconscious sometimes possesses of making others intelligent. I watch her face while Hervé's talking to us about Mao's poems. Her Asiatic features are inscrutable—she certainly looks Chinese. But it's quite clear she's passionately involved. She agrees with him, that's it, she's fascinated, the female philosopher mesmerized by her teacher! No, she's frowning now—she wouldn't have put it like that! But now she's with it again, with him, the downcast eyes light up. He's caught her eye, has he? Yes! Go to it! Funny creatures. I don't know if they've got a soul. I hope so, for their sake. Anyhow, they don't show it much. Psychology's not in fashion; people claim they shun it like the plague, and say they experience pleasure only when everything has been explained, structured, and analyzed.

Romain comes with me sometimes, when the subject isn't too literary. The Analysis Groups have already started a science series, with lectures by a mathematician and a physicist. New faces have appeared in the audience, and the old ones look more serious and concentrated. The changes taking place in science—no one can possibly miss that! There's talk of Romain addressing a meeting soon on his favorite subject—the emotions and the brain. I knew he'd played on the same football team as Hervé in high school, but I was sure only Romain remembered. But strangely enough, Sinteuil hadn't forgotten. He's a nice-looking chap, by the way, with brown eyes, like Romain's, that can go warm and shy. And the same body, I suppose. I suppose too much. If I weren't in love with Romain . . . It's well known that Sinteuil doesn't turn up his nose at a pretty woman. And as I've become a pretty woman again, I'm ready for anything.

So it seems that Mao and the barricades have led to incompatible differences and exceptional situations. Everyone's a provocateur, a bit of a situationist, with a taste for excess, challenge, the incommensurable, and—why not?—the absurd. The attack on the power of the One is transformed into a demand for uncompromising singularity. Down with the One because we are all unique!

I wonder if things are being formulated like this anywhere else but in Paris. That way of putting things is very French, and very irritating. I can understand the American psychiatrists whom Arnaud asked to dinner: they thought the cult of pleasure "dangerously ludic and fetishist." I looked as serious as I could and said that if human rights didn't include the right to be an exception, a unique individual, they'd be in danger of collapsing into Terror or Empire. Of course, no one understood what I was talking about. Except Arnaud, who naturally saw it as an expression of my idée fixe.

There, I can't get away from Madame Tallien. I'm becoming obsessed by my Thérésa Cabarrus again. I really do have problems with my name. A fine thing for an analyst to have to say!

III. Chinese

id they have a feeling—even a vague, unconscious feeling, or an unconsciously guilty and therefore
dismissible one—that they were rushing to China to
escape some personal impasse? People often go to the
Balearics, Israel, India, California, and so on—there are
so many blessed places in the world, all more or less
sanctified or sanctifiable—in order to get away from
their own obscure disasters. Which, of course, they
find facing them again a few months or a few years
later. But at least they've gained, or lost, some time,
and that's what matters.

Olga and Hervé didn't exactly feel this, though the
question was one that might arise. But only later. In
Chinese style (especially in the old style, but sometimes
in the modern style, too, if you took the trouble to
concentrate and look beyond appearances) Sinteuil saw

a confirmation of his own predilection for elegant classical el-
lipse. But even so rich and enigmatic a national culture—including Lao-tse and Confucius, not to mention the Taipings, the
Boxers, and other anarchists—was bound, grappling with Marxist universalism, to emerge in a modified form. And this was a
hint of what that same allegedly universal socialism might itself
become, someday, if brought into contact with the cellars of
Bordeaux, Montaigne's tower, Sade's boudoir, and the archives
of the Borgias. To tell the truth, Hervé's ideas weren't then so
explicitly nationalistic: it seemed to him that that kind of thing
must be out of date, and he confined himself (in his lectures) to
postulates that were entirely rational and abstract. But because
he's a timid person as well as a wily one, it may be surmised that
China was a necessary detour for him if he was to return to his
origins without an inferiority complex. In short, let us render to
the Chinese the things that are Chinese, and allow the French
whatever is Catholic and of Bordeaux—in other words, a great
advantage when it comes to taste or casuistry.

What could be more "Chinese"—in the French sense of strange,
absurd, quirky—than China? Through the Chinese you could
free yourself of yourself. Break the mask of conformity. Delve
down not merely to your roots (though, as we've said before, it's
not a bad thing to look into your own heritage) but deeper
still—to the level where there are no roots left, where everything
is eradicated. You could find a counteridentity for yourself and
realize how utterly strange it was by contemplating the country:
a giant at once civilized and backward, a demographic atom
bomb, the genetic Hiroshima of the twenty-first century. And
you could adopt that counteridentity, the better to reveal and
conceal yourself simultaneously.

Olga could see the underlying reason for everything Hervé
thought and did, but that didn't make her forget her own reasons. For a long time France had been a China to her, and she
knew exile could be liberation. She hadn't become really inte-
grated, though, and she knew she never would be, even if she
became the mother of a dozen little Frenchmen. But the events
of May had revived her liking for the incongruous. And the
incongruous, for Olga, was first and foremost Olga herself. Her
suppressed homesickness had hitherto assumed the chilly form

of occasional low spirits, which she was able to convert into a hunger for reading, learning, and writing. But now this hunger was changing into self-questioning. Not "Who am I?" but more meditatively, more intellectually, "What are the extravagances, the oddities, the chinoiseries, I feel within myself but cannot formulate? How is it you can write things you can't say? How is it a woman may be invisible, ignored and repressed (by Confucius), and yet essential and even all-powerful (in the Tao)? Isn't a mother always a kind of China—eternal and unknowable? Could mothers all be Chinese, for us?"

In short, Olga's ultraphilosophical education seemed to have taught her that origins, roots, are a kind of inevitable atavism, and that a person is civilized to the extent that he can do away with them. This being so, her experience as a foreigner was an opportunity to cast off her origins, or even to forget them. What did they amount to, anyhow? A few quite sunny dreams about her mother and father, innocent dreams of vacations—meaningless idylls, for to her only nightmares seemed really interesting and significant. So China became a kind of antiorigin: the most profound and ancestral one possible with its slant-eyed forebears, but also utterly strange, and therefore painless, impersonal, uncolored by childhood memories; just a jigsaw made up of mirages. Or a theater of identities, where people wore masks to convey what was essential, though masks serve only to confuse what is supposed to be so. Olga found she was a true actress: nothing was true but the play. Thus a Chinese peasant woman who took Olga for another Chinese woman *might* be making a mistake, but you couldn't, all things considered, be sure.

Lack of definition is a paradise for delicate spirits. A palette of iridescent pastels and gray, merging into mother-of-pearl. There's nothing to "see" in a Chinese landscape or painted silk. Or rather, the eye must get used to the harmony of nuance, to infinitesimal meaning. Bréhal saw China through the microscope of his own research on language. The leftist chatter of the Latin Quarter had soon lapsed into stereotype. If you were tactful, you could detach yourself from it and return to more forceful kinds of discourse: Loyola, Sade, even photography, which tests words through its sheer self-evidence. Was Hervé in love with Chinese calligraphy? Why not? China was calm, and its engraved tortoise shells were infinitely more attractive to Bréhal than garish posters displayed at public meetings or the incredible *Pi Lin, Pi Kong* campaign. Deep down, Bréhal hoped he'd be able to restrict himself to the pleasure of signs: that was something bound by definition to last, even under the Cultural Revolution. But he went out of his way to insist that he was fascinated by contemporary events in China too, to show he was still young and of the left.

"It might be nice to go to Tibet, don't you think, Stanislas?"

Bréhal, contemplating a complex spiritual rest cure in the monasteries to make up in advance for the ideological chores he'd have to put up with in Peking, was trying to persuade Stanislas Weil to go with him. Weil was the editor in charge of the philosophy list at Editions de l'Autre.

But Stanislas was keen on going to India. Though mistrustful by nature, and by training addicted to rigorous argument, he had suddenly succumbed to the lure of a religion of multiplicity, of a beyond full of infinite color, infinite sound. Buddhism and its ramifications seemed to challenge the plainness of Jewish and Christian monotheism. He belonged to the species, rapidly becoming extinct, of publishers who actually read books; indeed, he was one of the last survivors. But to someone of Bréhal's keen and independent intelligence, this was coming to seem something of a defect. The apparent change was due to the genuinely deplorable fact that Weil, having had the intellectual courage—you couldn't deny him that—to publish Lauzun's work, had since come to regard himself as his guardian, or even a duplicate more authentic than the original, and kept insisting, without a trace of humor, that the wretched Bréhal should conform to the master's doctrine.

"What about the One, Armand? Did you think about that, in Lauzun's sense of the term, of course, when you wrote your article on the subject?—I admit it's very good, but it puzzles me too. To tell you the honest truth, your position on the One doesn't strike me as very clear, and neither does your relationship to the Other!"

"What a pain in the neck!" Bréhal would whisper to Olga and Hervé, who tried to conceal their mirth.

But when Stanislas criticized him, he only stood there like a schoolboy being scolded by his teacher, merely rolling his eyes at any sympathizers who happened to be present. However, Stanislas might well act as a shield against all the political meetings he expected to have to cope with in China.

"But of course, Armand," said Hervé, not waiting for Stanislas's blessing. "It goes without saying I'll put the trip to Tibet in the suggestion book our Chinese comrades have asked us for. I'll put down a visit to a mental hospital, too."

"That's not funny!" snapped Stanislas, though tempted to laugh at Hervé's for once unintentional joke.

But there hadn't been any ulterior motive in Sinteuil's "suggestions": he was just as interested in Tibetan mysticism as he was in the reputedly excellent achievements of Chinese antipsychiatry. Mightn't a treatment for schizophrenia based on Mao's "One can be divided into two" produce hitherto unsuspected results? They'd certainly be even more mysterious than those of acupuncture, which was part of the official program for visitors and didn't need to be put down in the suggestion book.

"I'm afraid you're being too optimistic," said the ever realistic Brunet, secretary to *Now*. "The Chinese comrades have invited us, it's true, but they're still Chinese, and Marxists, and all that follows. They'll show us what they want us to see. The suggestion book is just polite form—it doesn't have any practical application."

"Sylvain understands the Eastern mentality better than you do. I agree with him," said Olga, always ready to share Brunet's pragmatism.

"I can't claim any credit," he said. "It's just that I'm the only one of you who comes from the people, and there's plenty of peasant logic among those despots—sorry, I meant Eastern revolutionaries."

He had resumed his fin-de-siècle tone.

In reality Brunet was a tortured aesthete whose only religion was Cézanne and Matisse. He knew their every brushstroke by heart. "A turning in a picture by Cézanne—do you think it's a

bend in the road? Nothing of the sort! It's the brink of the void—the whole landscape vanishes into infinity. But Chinese painters start off in infinity. Their problem is to set it down. How can you make visible that which by definition is invisible? A row of ideograms here, a flight of ducks there, a few slivers of amethyst (apparently they represent men)—and there's infinity, set down so you can see it. I wonder what's left of all that among the children of Mao. Say what you like, he's a marvelous calligrapher himself!"

Sinteuil insisted on looking on the bright side. Karachi, where they stopped over, was like a dank furnace, but they were all glad of the chance to stretch their legs and guess at the placid mysteries of the Orient, which lay, waiting to be deciphered, beyond the motley crowd in the airless airport lounge.

In the end Lauzun didn't go with them.

It was a strange affair, and no one wanted to hark back to it, but Olga couldn't help thinking about it, huddled up in her seat, over Tibet, on the interminable flight to Peking. Like everyone else, she had gone to Lauzun's seminars, and lately she'd thought she was beginning to understand him. But after this business she really wasn't sure anymore. . . .

Whenever anyone mentioned China, Lauzun forgot to draw on his bent cigar and would look up at the ceiling over his half-glasses. That was always a sign that he was interested.

"You're learning Chinese? Sinteuil too? Dabbling? I learned some at the School of Oriental Languages in Paris during the war, but that was very much in earnest. Right. . . . What can I tell you? The English can't be analyzed because of their language—a fluid gibberish that's very good for making puns (hence British snobs, the best of the lot of them). Or else it degenerates into jokes (though the Yanks beat them for vulgarity). But there's no room there for truth: the One is still cooped up in the vicarage. The true word rolls off an Englishman's tongue like water off a duck's back. Only Joyce can cope with it, but he was a saint and a Catholic, and there's nobody else like him.

"The Japanese? They're unanalyzable too. Repression? Death? They're meat and drink to them. The mother? They've never emerged from her, and sometimes they eat her. They're dissociated kamikazes, brilliant enough insofar as the dull can be brilliant, but how can discourse possibly reach such divided beings, such nonbeings rather, when they don't lack anything? For when everything is forbidden, nothing is, and we all know inhibition is to Japan what *sepuku* is to a samurai. . . .

"Catholics are another matter. They can't be analyzed because theology has spirited everything away. It has analyzed everything already, so a true Catholic has no use for Freud.

"However, as there aren't any Catholics anymore, there's still plenty of work for us here in Paris. Of course, I'm not talking about women—if I don't say that, no one else will. And why? Because they don't give a shit about truth. What do they want? Poor old Freud—what they want is to please, of course. To be attractive. Mirror, mirror . . . Anyhow, we have to go on as if this weren't the case, because if the idiots in my gang heard me, they'd be quite capable of banning women from their couches!

"As for the Chinese, of course they have an unconscious, but it's structured differently. Not like language, but like writing, and the difference is fundamental. And the Chinese are quite another kettle of fish from the Japanese. Because of the Tao. I'd like to hear them from close up! . . ."

For once, Lauzun was being quite straightforward, almost militant: Were we going to introduce the plague into China, or vice versa? Were the Chinese going to wipe out Freud?

"It's plain Lauzun has to head the delegation," said Sinteuil.

"Does that mean Dr. Maurice Lauzun will want to take his colleague Madame Séverine Tissot with him? We have got it right?—she *is* his colleague?"

The Chinese comrades were visibly shocked. In other words, quietly angry.

"Yes, that's it." Hervé hadn't batted an eye. "Dr. Lauzun is a leading intellectual, and can't let his work be interrupted. So his colleague—his right-hand woman, if you like—has to travel with him. She's a great friend of China, by the way."

They got the message. Séverine Tissot was accepted. And Lauzun triumphantly entered his "suggestions" in the famous book: a visit to a mental hospital, naturally; perhaps—by way of provocation—a trip to a rehabilitation camp for recalcitrant intellectuals; attendance at some Taoist ceremonies, of course, and at some Catholic ones, too, if the authorities agreed. Hervé was glad to see some vestiges of Surrealism still lurking behind the deadpan expression of the Tout-Paris's great guru.

A last meeting before setting off for dinner at the Cheval Blanc, with Olga and Séverine in attendance, of course: the usual pink champagne, and everyone will go off to bed at about ten o'clock. The height of both chic and realism.

But surprise, surprise—Séverine's late. "She called me just now to say she might be delayed and we weren't to wait for her." (Lauzun) The caviar is done justice to; also the quail in Périgourdine sauce. Still no Séverine. "I'll give her a call." (Lauzun) "No answer." (Lauzun) Dessert. Coffee. "Perhaps we ought to go around." (Lauzun) "We'll come with you." (Hervé)

Séverine lives only a few blocks away from the restaurant, but it'll be easier to take the car. Ring the bell. No answer. "She's probably left already for the Cheval Blanc—we must have passed each other on the way." (Lauzun) "I'll drop you there." (Sinteuil) No one at the restaurant. "Better go back to her place." (Lauzun) He realizes he's got the key to her apartment: he bought it for her. They try to open the door. They can't: there's another key on the inside. Hervé and Olga exchange embarrassed glances. Lauzun pretends not to understand. "There must be something wrong with the lock—no, it's the wrong key. She must be at the Cheval Blanc. Shall we try it again?" "Of course." (Sinteuil) No one at the Cheval Blanc. "We'll go back to her place." (Lauzun) "She must have been mugged by some loony." (Lauzun) To the concierge: "Have you seen Madame Tissot since this afternoon?" (Lauzun) "I took her mail up at five o'clock." (the concierge) "The mugger must have broken in after that." (Lauzun) "Maybe. . . . Lauzun was attacked recently by one of his patients—he tried to take his money and his checkbook." (Sinteuil, in a whisper, to Olga) Everyone hangs about in the yard outside.

"Perhaps we should call the police," Hervé suggests. Loudly, so that the "murderer" will hear.

"There's a man in his shirtsleeves—there, behind the curtain," says Olga innocently.

"The murderer!" hopes Lauzun.

"Let's leave!" says Sinteuil, realizing what's up. He's an expert at this sort of thing.

"Certainly not! I'm going up there! Come up with me!" (Lauzun)

A frightful scene. Séverine, with one of Lauzun's most faithful disciples! There was a strike, the disciple's train wasn't running, they were together in the apartment, they hadn't heard anything . . . anything at all—are you sure you rang? called? . . . but you couldn't have, we didn't hear a thing, did we?

"I was worried about you—someone might have broken in and attacked you—"(Lauzun)

"Maurice, are you insane? How can you? Do you realize what you're saying? Do you *want* me to be attacked? It's incredible! Try to control yourself!"

Spectacular turnaround in the farce. And Lauzun lets himself be told off, humiliated, ridden over roughshod. Without hitting back. Stunned. Is he overwhelmed by her determination to belittle him? Fascinated by such female effrontery? What a nerve! Apoplectic. Speechless. Purple in the face. Olga feels like kissing the little boy who's being bullied, and trying to comfort him. Hervé is ashamed for the fallen idol.

"Sorry—we have to go."

"That's all right, dear boy. Do."

Lauzun lets his arms drop to his sides, his usual sign of weariness at mankind's murderous stupidity, and just sits in his chair waiting for the onslaught to continue.

"He won't come to China," says Sinteuil. "Séverine means to stop him from compromising himself any more than he has already. This time it would be with the leftists."

"You're right. But I think it's more serious than that: he's never been loved, and he think's that's normal. Fancy letting himself be Sadized like that! I'm not a shrink, but don't you think it's incredible? So passive, so forlorn . . ."

"He's probably just resigned to female paranoia. Nothing to be done about it."

"Don't make excuses for him. There's collusion in his resignation—blind collusion, but with an element of pleasure in it."

"Still, a paranoid woman, even if—or maybe especially if!—she's a psychoanalyst, is a paranoid in a class of her own!"

"Well, of course, if you're off on your favorite hobby-horse . . ."

"We shall shortly be landing in Peking. The outside temperature is sixty-eight degrees. Kindly fasten your seatbelts and extinguish all cigarettes."

They were there. Without Lauzun.

12

The crowds on bicycles, which made the streets of the capital look like a Tour de France with millions of listless competitors, indifferent because they had nothing to gain, weren't allowed into Tiananmen Square. The square itself, the image of a strong though invisible power, was silent and deserted apart from a few groups of pioneers in white shirts and red ties, there to perform the usual rites. They reminded Olga of her childhood, when she was dragooned into the same kind of ceremony: designed to produce collective hallucinations in the young, the rituals were accompanied by so many restrictions they ultimately reduced the Latin prayers to nonsense (apart from their musical beauty). The absence of meaning was fatal: the hallucinations faded, withered into blankness.

But the white flocks did nothing to people the square.

The great space obliterated human beings; it just let itself be flecked with their tiny movements. The classical Chinese painters were realistic visionaries when they showed how spaces can vibrate like this, how the light that fills them can be both empty and majestic. One should let oneself be borne along by their vision. See the present in their terms.

Once the agreeable and inescapable courtesies of green tea, hot towels, and cigarettes had been gone through, the Chinese comrades, who'd just been admitted to the UN, said how happy they were to welcome their comrades from the French revolutionary review. To the great satisfaction of Sinteuil, and under Bréhal's unwaveringly serious gaze, they then unfurled a banner bearing the words "Welcome to our friends from *Now*" in both French and Chinese. Had they ever read the magazine? Who could say? They'd certainly picked out the headlines and the names. A secretary at the embassy in Paris (an academic straight from the seething campus in Peking), as well as another diplomat in Shanghai, had shown they knew the names of all the contributors by heart. They could also tell you who the review's financial backers were. Perhaps they applied the same method to other groups of Paris intellectuals. But no question of entering into debate. Were they afraid of departing from Maoist thought? Or was it too hard for them to bridge the cultural gap? Both explanations were true, probably; concealed by the most Chinese and inscrutable of smiles.

Then came the main preoccupation: an attack on Soviet revisionism. At last! Down with the party apparatus, Stalinism, and ossification. But the attackers looked like the doubles of the attacked. The same speeches, the same clichés: modern China was a Soviet China trying to break with that resemblance without knowing the elementary laws of physics that would enable them to do so. Archimedes and Newton were neglected in favor of political voluntarism. And there was no other model to imitate, either in China's past or in contemporary world history. Perhaps one day it would be found in one or the other of them: it was on the way, but they were still scared, there was no hurry, steady as you go! The Chinese comrades seemed to be stuck, and meanwhile they were exterminating one another. No one spoke openly of the massacres. They weren't going to confide in the *da bize*—the "long noses"! But rumors circulated about ill treatment in the camps and in the rehabilitation "schools" for intellectuals. The rumors even filtered through the official interpreters.

Zhao spoke French like a Parisian undergraduate.

"You haven't got a copy of the latest *Nouvel Obs*, have you? No? What a pity!"

He came out with that right away in Tiananmen Square, the first time they went out, after a night in a luxury hotel (à la Stalinist fortress) and breakfast (à la Stalinist pauper). Zhao was learning French out of the *Nouvel Observateur*, and quite right too. What luck! With someone so bright and unconventional they were bound to find out everything and get whatever they wanted! Just take it easy.

"We wanted to go and see a School of the Seventh of May— isn't that what they call the rehabilitation camps for intellectuals?" said Sinteuil, determined to stick to his guns. "But there's no mention of a visit to the camps in the program we were given, even though we put it down in the suggestion book. Can I rely on you to arrange it?"

"No problem. Easy."

But after two weeks, nothing. Easy, eh . . .

They realized that the request, already mentioned in Paris, hadn't been pressed. It would have been all the same if it had, thought Olga. But we must try to find out the details. In politics and in travel, as in dreams, it's the details that count.

The Chinese comrades did things properly—they wouldn't entrust a delegation to just one interpreter, especially a delegation as important and as unpredictable as the group from *Now*. Anyone can manipulate a single interpreter, but two . . . just let them try! Wherever you saw one, you saw the other. And of course, the second was called Zhao too. We might not be in wonderland, thought Olga, but at least we're in looking-glass land. But what was Zhao No. 2 really for?

"So you want to see some intellectuals undergoing rehabilitation?" (He laughed.) "But you've seen one of them already—you don't need any School of the Seventh of May!"

It finally emerged (through Zhao No. 2) that Zhao No. 1 was a Stendhal fan, and his love of French had made him imagine he was Julien Sorel. So sometimes he used to sport a black cape and recite the speech Julien made at his trial. The comrades from *Now* regarded the content of this speech as fairly revolutionary, though the form wasn't exactly Joycean. . . . Unfortunately Zhao No. 1's compatriots didn't understand him. Or else they understood him all too well. "Individualistic petit bourgeois anarchism"—that's what he was accused of, and he was sent to a School of the Seventh of May. He'd just been released to look after the delegation from Paris. Naturally he wasn't going to utter the name of the horrible place to anyone.

Zhao No. 2 told this amusing story without animosity: he'd have liked to be an eccentric too. . . . Well, he was tempted, but all things considered, no, it was best to stick to the rules and have a quiet life.

Was that the "situation," then? A few rebels, a lot of repression, and even more of the kind of trimming that shows how much people fear the system. And above all, the panic at the thought of abandoning it. Dictatorship protects people like a harsh and fanatical mother: they complain, but they like it. The two Zhaos together showed something of the deceitful face despotic democracy wears among the poor, the peasants, the underdeveloped. Olga, who'd half hoped—you never can tell—that China was going to be something new, felt she had been here before.

"I'd like to film you together, Zhao One and Zhao Two—do you mind? I think it's funny, don't you? You look like twins, but really you've got different genes!"

Bréhal looked as if he was tired of taking notes about the prodigious output of tractor factories in Peking, cooperative farms in Nanking, and naval dockyards in Shanghai. But he went on writing, while a Chinese comrade expounded the results of Maoist thought in terms of kilotons and kilowatts. The apathetic voice of the translator canceled out the speaker's attempt at enthusiasm, placing Armand at a kind of Brechtian distance that allowed him, before the next bout of green tea and hot towels, to set down some of his own dream thoughts and associations.

"Olga, what do you think of the girls in the Peking Opera and in all those pantomimes they take us to—yesterday in that village, and today at the art school in Nanking?"

"Self-assured, brave, more assertive than the boys."

"Exactly. I'd say they really were boys. They've got plenty of feminine grace, but what about those masculine movements, those angry eyebrows, the acting hidden under all that tragic or comic makeup? It makes you wonder. . . . Could they be transvestites?"

At yet another ballet depicting the downfall of a "bad element" through the efforts of a girl inspired by the thoughts of Chairman Mao, Armand managed to get in first, make his way through the rows of chairs, and sit beside a shy young Chinese only too delighted to find himself close to the delegation. Hesitant, confused, but spurred on by desire, Armand took his courage in both hands ("That's exactly what I thought—in difficult situations we always fall back on clichés," he confessed after the performance): he moved closer to the young man, brushing first his elbow, then his thigh, then his knee. No response. "Has he noticed? Shall I be arrested? They wouldn't do that to a guest! I'll have another try." He met with no result at all, but at least he'd tried. He was upset about it all evening. But it was better than being bored.

There was one undeniable pleasure: the cooking. True, they didn't serve up bear's paws or even shark's fins anymore. But the *structure!* First of all, you eat with the palate—that goes without saying. Then with the nose and the eyes: taste, smell, and sight all enter into every dish. In China a gastronomist is a painter and sculptor too. Then there's the balance between the various ingredients, and the different methods of cooking: crispy things, rolled-up things, strips, pieces, little balls (not the same as large ones), peeled things, fritters (made with eggs, in segments, caramelized . . .).

"How can you expect them to believe in one God, Hervé, when they've got such a vast range of tastes, with every one canceled out by its opposite? I'm convinced paganism is a matter of taste: the more refined a person's palate is, the less likely he is to assume the crouch of prayer—always an attitude of anguish. Don't you agree, Olga? The worse you eat, the more frenzied is your religion. Lauzun might say a believer is someone who was weaned too soon, or with difficulty. . . . Look at the Italians. Are they really Christians? Not at all! They're so capricious, so fond of food, such gamblers . . . And why? Because, for them, pleasure begins with the mouth. A good meal in an Italian restaurant might make you think of the papacy in its libertine phase (I say that to please you, my dear Hervé), or some baroque orality, or a hysterical mass—but contrition? Never! On a completely different planet from corn flakes and processed cheese—believe me, and I'm a Protestant!"

Stanislas smiled indulgently. It wasn't worth pointing out Armand's howlers in the matter of psychoanalysis; he didn't know anything about it. All he produced were pointless improvisations that yet again overlooked the impact of the One on every speaking, or even eating, individual.

Despite the foretaste he'd had, like every Occidental, from countless Chinese restaurants in the West, ranging from the modest to the very expensive, Bréhal's revelation of China came to him through its foods. These were quite unpredictable from one region to another. The spices of Szechuan? Armand quite liked them: all Europeans found them very tasty. The only thing was, you could disguise anything with a dash of pimento. The specialties of Peking and Shantung were classic: stews and Peking duck, as delicious here as in Paris. But no, to be quite honest the skin of the duck was crisper here, and the smoky tang of the meat fresher, with a hint of seaweed and violets and a suggestion of pleasure in junks. But there was nothing to compare with the subtleties of Canton: filleted fish, sugared cutlets, turtle, fried snake, beef in oyster sauce—the South offered a whole panoply of faint but subtle tastes that Bréhal had come there specially to collect, regarding such things as synonymous with civilization. No one used to satisfying his appetite with steak and French fries was capable of appreciating the delicate little morsels, some soft, some hard, a whole rainbow of subtly shaded pastels. Never a note too loud, never a garish color; everything was in shades and pale gradations, even to the brink of insipidity. But once the tongue was used to this almost musical scale, it could distinguish the smooth note of a cucumber from that of a sea slug, velvety as an oboe, and appreciate the small bell-like twang of a well-sugared cutlet.

Through the everyday enchantment of food, Armand was able to savor the Chinese body. Barriers imposed by traditional modesty and reinforced by distrust of foreigners disappeared as if by magic at the touch of plastic or bamboo chopsticks. He handled them clumsily, but they still conveyed to his mouth some finally permitted pleasures.

But China didn't have to appeal to authority to defend itself against the "long noses."

"Go on," said Zhao No. 2 mischievously, "walk about wherever you like without us. Here, for example"—pointing to a map of Peking—"it's a working-class district not far from the hotel."

But once they were out in the street they met only averted faces and fleeing backs. Olga made a brave attempt to exploit her degree in Chinese, but it didn't make much of a showing. Half the time, as she expected, she got the tone wrong. Then she'd get out a piece of paper and write down the character that corresponded to the uncomprehended word: written Chinese, though complex, is more accessible than the tonal spoken language. In the end she'd manage to make herself understood. But the reply would only be an amused smile or a rapid monologue: their interlocutors didn't want to bring the Great Wall down on their heads, and you never knew when someone would report you for talking to foreigners.

The result was that the visitors couldn't do without the two Zhaos, and the delegation had to go about enclosed in an invisible space suit.

"Visible, you mean! The space suit is our own faces. They take one look at our 'big fat mugs' and run," said Sinteuil, slipping in a reference to Lautréamont.

So they had to rely on the magic chopsticks and dream of imaginary encounters; they had to interpret and even overinterpret the little that was said, the vast amount that was not. They were restricted to chinoiserie and what they said themselves; they were wandering around a scarcely living museum full of secret signs. Never before had Armand felt so strongly the gulf that existed between the enthusiasm and vitality of words and slogans on the one hand, and on the other the lifelessness of the passions—tense with unbearable hope, obstinately withdrawn from communication, perhaps waiting desperately for some inspired decoder. The separation couldn't just be a device to keep the truth from visiting strangers—foreigners were now slightly more welcome than before. No, it was integral to the regime itself, grotesquely exaggerating a set of immemorial contrasts, in which the sober mandarin world of bureaucrats and scribes was in opposition to the arts of the bedroom and the exaltation of Tao sages.

"Do you know why it's so impossible to analyze the Chinese, Stanislas? That's Lauzun's theory, isn't it? . . . What, he's not sure? Well, I'll tell you anyway: it's because their civilization sanctifies the splitting of things in two—psychosis. The Chinese are socially psychotic, or, if you prefer—for society's natural to man—natural schizos. I take back what I've just said, of course: psychiatric terminology is always pejorative, and I don't at all mean to criticize. I feel put out because I want to understand. Probably a mistake. Like someone wanting to get hold of a secret message so as to have something to tell his students or write about in Zhao One's *Nouvel Obs*—it's awaiting our revelations. So what do the Chinese tell us, exactly? That everything is in appearances, and that there's another world elsewhere that's impenetrable. It's simple enough: One is divided into two, and the two don't communicate with each other. If you've understood that, you needn't feel put out, for that other, separate world can give you peace. Listen to what you're told and think of something else. Or rather, don't think at all—just stay quiet and let yourself soak in the void!"

As the trip went on, Bréhal gradually lost his ambitions as a progressive semiologist and mythologist. He spent his time in dreamy observation scarcely connected at all with the people he observed (even things left him unmoved). Just the rhythm of fingers lifting the lids off porcelain teacups, little pots with wisps of steam coming out of holes the size of a pinhead . . . The pleasure of alighting on relations between the elements, amid mere articulation . . . The logic of the senses. Eternity itself.

Happiness has no history.

A Valley of the Dead, overlooked by the Great Wall, leads to the tombs of the Ming emperors. The Chinese call it the Way of the Spirit or Sacred Way. First, a portico built of white stones; a kilometer farther on, the Great Gate, which is red; then the House of the Stele; and finally the famous Statues.

There all the visitors got off their buses, exclaimed, took photographs (Olga started filming). All the visitors except Bréhal.

"I'd rather stay on the bus. You can see better."

He went on writing in his notebook, his eyes shut to the outside world, journeying through the world inside his head. What more could those dazzling stones offer?

Yes, death is white in China, and its inexorable yet comical presence was more evident here in this valley than anywhere else. After the two columns, one on either side of the path, came a monumental bestiary: a crouching lion, a lion standing up; a unicorn with a cat's face and a mane—a *xie chi*—crouching, a *xie chi* standing up; a camel crouching and a camel standing up; an elephant crouching and an elephant standing up; a *qi lin*—a scaly mythical beast with a bull's horns and tail and hooves—crouching and, of course, a *qi lin* standing up; a horse crouching and a horse standing up.

No one could have said where these animals came from—they'd never been known in China. Whiter even than usual in the May light, they made death seem part of some timeless Disneyland. Not tragic: just a monstrous yet kindly fact. No nightmare: only an exaggerated story told by a supernanny to impress a child without frightening him, so that he'll have a nice long, peaceful sleep. Crouch, stand up, crouch, stand up; that's life. Does death exist? Who knows? Let's dream of horns, of unicorns, of beasts unknown in these parts; there is no death, nothing but a quiet metamorphosis into weird stones. The white immobility of the statues is only a sign that life stops. A certain kind of life. But we mustn't forget the life of the fauns and camels of our dreams, which dream they were once Ming emperors or French tourists. We're left with avenues of mythical beasts, stony mothers who'll cradle us in the fluid of fairy stories. The cosmos doesn't die; a Ming will one day be reborn as an elephant or a horse or a *xie chi*, or perhaps a comrade from *Now*.

While Bréhal pondered on the impossibility of death (Was it really a relief? Didn't the eternal happiness of those Chinese statues, which knew nothing of the hiatus of hell, also exclude the comfort of the Passion? And so on . . .), the others wandered around the elephants, lions, and camels, distraught and detached. A group is never a strong unit. Least of all a group of intellectuals. But there, infiltrated by the bright death of that unmoving Disneyland, they were dead both to their assumed togetherness and to themselves.

Their desire to fit in with the customs of the country, combined with the waning influence of the unity ascribed to their group by the myth-making rumor machine of Paris, threw each of them back on his own solitude. The sculptured beasts, of unimaginable whiteness, were as absurd as monsters made for kindergartens. Never had death seemed so domesticated and, as a result, never had their own identities—which death in the West invests with importance and sanctity—seemed so insignificant. They didn't see one another anymore: Stanislas didn't see Armand, nor Armand Hervé, nor Hervé Brunet, nor Brunet Olga, nor Olga Hervé, and vice versa. They'd become like Chinese to one another—indifferent, cut off from themselves as well as from their group. They were no longer part of a whole; they were blank. But they went on speaking the language of the country and of the day. *Pi Lin, Pi Kong*—fight Lin Piao, overthrow Confucius. Battles, conquests, victories. It wasn't that they didn't believe in them anymore: they went on trying to understand, that's what they were there for, but they'd lost interest. The petrified hinterland of dreams had moved into the foreground, and their political odyssey was becoming more and more what they'd suspected it would be, though they didn't dream of admitting it to one another: a descent into their own secret gardens, where the Valley of the Dead adjoins the Way of the Spirit.

Armand saw himself sitting beside a fragile young man—they all looked as if they were made of porcelain under their blue or gray military-style Mao tunics—as a rehearsal of the Peking Opera took place on the stage at the University of Shanghai: manly girls with smooth calves, low-slung buttocks, and no breasts, whose arms swished through the air like swords. They never danced on their toes. Just a few bold leaps on feet that looked as versatile as hands.

The professor leaned against the porcelain young man's elbow, placed his own leg against his thigh, and reached between the other's knees. The porcelain was frail and trembling; a known familiarity was being refused. The lad was a victim of oppression; he certainly had need of love, but would he dare acknowledge it? Suddenly the youth started up and yelled a few syllables in Chinese. Two fellows just as puny as Bréhal's young man and hitherto quite nonchalant (they'd melted into the crowd, but were part of the formidable but necessarily secret surveillance) threw themselves on Bréhal, pulled him from his seat, and dragged him backstage. Meanwhile the young transvestites went on cleaving the air with their arms and their simian feet. Zhao No. 1 and Zhao No. 2, who of course were there, explained to the discomfited suitor that he'd offended against traditional decorum and Communist morality alike, and would be judged before the people for his crime.

"Will they strip him?" someone asked.

"No, comrade. In China we don't search for bad influences—that's what the KGB and the CIA do. The philosophy of Chairman Mao rejected that sort of thing long ago. But the court insists that he speak. For us, the accused consists in what the accused says."

"Let him admit to his bad character and explain to the angry people his corrupt revisionist aims!" shouted the young female lead from the evening's show. She clung like grim death to the arm of the porcelain youth (but was it the same one?) and claimed to be his fiancée (at least on the plane of ideology).

Armand, scared stiff, thought of sending for the delegation, of appealing to the embassy for help, of making a dash for it.

"The comrades in the delegation disapprove unanimously of your behavior. And anyway, they're not here—they've gone to see the Great Wall," said Zhao No. 2. Zhao No. 1, the "rebel," saw the trial as a chance to put himself forward.

"You've lost face, Comrade Bréhal," he said. "You're on your own now, and all you can do is try to defend yourself. What have you got to say?"

(He's out to get me, thought Armand sadly. He's only too glad to send me to the electric chair in his place.)

"There isn't any electric chair in China." (Zhao No. 1 must be reading his victim's thoughts.) "It's been replaced by the people's court. You can speak, can't you?—you occupy a university chair on the subject. . . . Texts are what you take pleasure in, aren't they, Professor Bréhal?"

Zhao No. 1 was overdoing it. He must be hoping to make up for former offenses with this excess of revolutionary zeal.

Bréhal cudgeled his brains for an attempt at pathos. He was quite incapable of it, but it seemed to him the only way to save himself from the revolutionary tribunal already gathered around him and preparing to write down his confession. . . . But what was he to say? It occurred to him that nothing was more likely to appeal to these shocked moral consciences than Julien Sorel's monologue. Zhao had already made use of it himself, and the French rebels were the ancestors of Mao's thought. He seemed to remember someone had said as much at the kindergarten the day before.

"Gentlemen . . . *sorry, ladies and gentlemen . . . or should I say* comrades *of the jury . . .*

"I have a horror of condescension, but I think I may overcome that aversion in the face of death. Gentlemen . . . Ladies . . . Comrades . . . I haven't the honor to belong to the same class as you. You see in me a member of the bourgeoisie who has rebelled against the vileness of his circumstances.

"I'm not asking you for clemency. . . ." Bréhal put more force into the voice that had fascinated generations of the most distinguished French students. "I'm not deceiving myself. . . . Death . . ." (Hell, he said to himself, I mustn't put ideas into their heads! . . . I'd better adapt Stendhal a bit. . . . Rather sacrilegious, but it can't be helped!) I am to be punished. But . . . But no, it is only right. I have offended against the modesty of the most worthy of men. Monsieur Liu could have been like a brother to me. My crime is a heinous one, and it was premeditated. *I deserve to be put to d— . . . I mean, to be punished, ladies of the jury. But even if I were less guilty than I am, I know some people deny that my susceptibility may be deserving of pity. They wish my punishment to act as a permanent deterrent to inquiring minds, born into the middle classes and oppressed by boredom, but fortunate enough to be well educated and bold enough to become involved with what envious upstarts call aestheticism.*

"That is my crime, ladies, comrades, and it will be punished all the more severely because as it happens I am not being judged by my peers. I cannot see a single desperate intellectual in the ranks of the jury—only furious nobodies—I mean, angry peasants. If only you could remember the God of Fénelon! He might tell you: 'He who has loved much will be forgiven much. . . .' "

Armand carried on in this vein for about twenty minutes, pouring his heart out. Zhao No. 1, though still (secretly) hoping to ingratiate himself with the foreigners, could hardly sit still. But the abstract turn Bréhal had given the debate didn't draw a single tear from the female jurors. This was fatal. Before concluding his defense he returned to the themes of premeditation, repentance, respect, and the power of love which would one day unite young and old the world over and perhaps do away with war. It would be a happier age, in which revolution would triumph and bring pleasure to all men . . .

"No! We can't accept that! Down with Bréhal! Where's his black cloak? Julien Sorel wore a black cloak, and so did I!" yelled Zhao No. 1.

"Put him to death!" bawled the prima donna of the show.

"No, comrade—don't forget socialist humanism. We must give him the chance to come round to the philosophy of Chairman Mao. What he needs is a spell in a School of the Seventh of May. For a start . . ." said a thug belonging to the secret police, clearly better than the others at dialectics.

They tied Bréhal's hands behind his back and bundled him—he was a French guest, after all—into a big Soviet limousine.

"You can't take me away like this! I'm entitled to contact my embassy! I'm very well known in France, my books prove I'm respectable, and free love is the logical consequence of human rights!"

"You're corrupt! You came here to debauch our young men!"

The young dancer and activist couldn't contain herself. Zhao No. 1 backed her up in accents of hatred.

"You and your Julien Sorel! Who do you think you're kidding? I tried that once, and where did it get me? He was just a peasant's son with a petit bourgeois consciousness, who fell in love with the rich and thought he could better himself! And where did he get his consciousness from? First from the seminary, from religion; and then it was perverted by hedonism—Sorel was a fool, a slave to his pleasures! All that is of no use to the people! And you— you're a high priest of pleasure! The body, the body—that's all you think about! You deserve to be stripped naked, you and your cult of the body! Thank your lucky stars for Chinese modesty! But a year in a School of the Seventh of May will do you a world of good!"

"A year? But I'm in the middle of writing a book . . ."

"It'll wait. If all goes well, you'll learn Maoist philosophy fast, and in a year you'll be just like me. And by the way, why do you keep harping on Stendhal? Do you think he's a good thing? I don't! Not anymore! What the Chinese people like is the French Revolution and the Paris Commune. You'd have done better to talk about Robespierre or Jules Vallès. I'm reading Vallès myself just now. He's better than Stendhal. In a way. I recommend him to you."

Bréhal was in a state of collapse. The Zil they'd put him in, his hands still bound behind his back, was approaching a people's commune. Peasants in overalls and straw hats were picking cotton. Two files of men with long *poles were carrying a coffin: the cemetery was on the other side of the commune. But here was the reeducation center, with its concrete pillboxes and blockhouses. He was going to spend a year here, perhaps more, perhaps he'd even die here. One day he might be carried off like the man in the coffin, in the sweltering sun, between two files of peasants with poles. What a business! Was Stendhal to blame? Or Saint-Just? Or pleasure?*

"Look, Hervé!" Olga whispered as they got back on the bus. "Armand looks as if he's dreaming! Perhaps he's had a better walk than we have in the Way of the Spirit."

"Professor Bréhal is tired? He's getting old, eh?"

Zhao No. 1's Chinese politeness had been affected by his reading of the *Nouvel Obs*: he no longer had any respect for the aged.

"Dreaming is the royal road to truth. And a special way to death. Why? Because death cannot be represented, except in the form of a denial, like the giant camels we've just seen. Or you can sleep it, like a baby after it's fed. And that's what Armand's doing."

Stanislas had claimed the last word.

As the minibus entered Peking, pedestrians made way, children waved flags, political activists held up banners saying "Welcome to the comrades from *Now*"—and Armand continued his descent into the purgatory of the School of the Seventh of May, where they were going to try to reeducate him.

In Shanghai, Zhongshan Lu Avenue, formerly the Bund, started from the confluence of the rivers Huangpu and Wusong. The countless people strolling along it that evening had a magnificent view of the liners and junks floating sleepily on the river. If it hadn't been for those great brown autumn leaves, the junks' sails, you might have thought you were in Bordeaux or Amsterdam. The most industrialized of Chinese cities was on its way home or out to take the air. Girls in groups of three or four, with arms linked or around one another's waists, giggled and pretended to ignore the boys, but threw coy glances at them. Youths on bicycles had black-clad grandmothers with bound feet clinging on behind them. A few impassive old men and some young ones too moved away from the water. Equally indifferent to the river, to the skyscrapers where the banks and clubs and offices used to be, to the big modern shops, to their compatriots, and to the delegation just emerged from the Grand Hôtel de la Paix, they began a kind of tortoiselike eurythmics.

"Look, *tai qi chuan*—we saw the hotel staff doing it on the roof this morning."

Hervé went over to an elderly worker who was dancing and, keeping a respectful distance so as not to embarrass him, started to dance too, at first imitating the old tortoise but then moving more and more to his own rhythm. The other Chinese people drew aside, leaving a small invisible arena: they were half amused at the stranger's daring and incompetence, half moved by his eagerness and skill.

"You dance with your arteries and veins, you know—it's not a matter of arms and legs. Your blood surges forward, draws back, and then the time comes when your body's transformed. It doesn't disappear, but the rhythm of your blood is in harmony with the shapes you imagine in space—your body itself is all space, what's inside and what's outside are brought together and redistributed, magnified almost to infinity, anatomized almost to infinity."

"And have you reached that stage?" asked Olga sarcastically.

"Of course not—I've only read about it, you little devil! But this avenue here, the river, and the group of tortoises, old and young, with their impassive ecstasy, all show me something I'd never learn in a gym in Paris or New York: that inside and outside can be abolished; there can be a peaceful osmosis between my body and the world, transforming the world into the body and the body into limitless space.

"You know, Armand," Sinteuil went on, "it's little things like this that make me less of a pessimist than you. True, if the third millennium belongs to these people we're as good as dead! But I'm ready to die to acquire a body like that, and I really think I could. I've got enough energy in reserve—still my usual modest self, you notice! Will they be swifter in war, more original in thought, more at ease in their carcasses because they think the circulation of the blood reflects the magnetism of the planets and recreates the earthly meridians? I couldn't care less. If they can live like that, I'll do the same. But they'll learn something from us too—freedom, and its most elementary form: democracy. They have an almost conscious need for it—isn't that why they invite us here? The comrades from *Now*? Don't make me laugh! Have they ever read it? No, for them we represent Paris itself: liberty, equality, fraternity. If not today then tomorrow, they'll accept the message, shape it to their own requirements, and leave us to tell the world the good news. Because a message that doesn't pass through Paris isn't a real message yet—that's what they think, and that's what I think too."

"I'm quite prepared to believe you, my friend—as a matter of fact that's why I'm here. But at the moment there are more signs of ossification than of *tai qi chuan*. As far as social organization goes, I mean."

"Yes—that's obvious. They seem to cling to Confucian pride as naturally as to Soviet-Marxist rigidity. It's probably a recipe for producing good bureaucrats. For generating oppression too, no doubt—perhaps we'll know the actual figures one day. But when it comes to politics I do the same as Edelman and his friend Pascal: I wager, and I'm prepared to accept tragedy.

"Look at those girls cuddling one another and giggling, and those impromptu Taoists of all ages: don't tell me bureaucracy has crushed the liberty out of the Chinese people! Liberty—pleasure, if you like—will spring up all the stronger in them soon. That's why I like to study them—I'd rather be mistaken with them than ostracize them for fear of being wrong.

"But what about the massacres, what about the murders, you say? I know you think about them all the time we're being shown those puerile operas. So do I. They certainly do take place. All those officials are there to conceal the fact.

"Death . . . It's death, Armand, that makes civilizations. As we ourselves have more reason to know than others, death is at the heart of all the civilizations that have left written records: look at Egypt, the Mayas, China. But our own world, which is Greek, biblical, and evangelical, has come to worship the miracle of living man. It's very difficult to maintain, as we've seen. And it makes us too ready to treat those who are different from us as barbarians. But barbarism, which we identify with killing, isn't the opposite of civilization—it's a part of it, don't you agree?

Society is criminal; it's based on a crime committed in common, as dear old Freud said—he didn't blush and cover his eyes against either sex *or* death."

"Don't tell me you're excusing the massacres and the camps!"

"That's not what I'm saying at all! I simply mean that civilizations differ from one another in their degrees of barbarism. And if China ever comes to allow freedom to individuals and exceptions (if you don't mind my using my own vocabulary), it won't have arrived at that position by the same route as us. You say we should be careful. Of course. I do the same as you—I try to be vigilant. But from within—within *their* civilization and *our* barbarism."

Olga admiringly agreed. Her skepticism waned as she observed how rational Hervé's ardor was, and at the same time how natural. Beneath his pose as a skillful dialectician and erudite scholar, Sinteuil's nature was, as she had reason to know, an intuitive one, based on physical experience. Sight, hearing, or sex; strategy; military or religious adventure—any of these might enthuse or repel him, triggering intellectual imaginings, for or against, which *Now* would disseminate and Paris would read with a mixture of fascination and loathing. But Olga knew that, although future political developments might make his enthusiasm wax or wane, China would remain one of his main preoccupations. And she went on writing her ideograms.

"Take that young man in Luoyang who let me beat him at table tennis," Hervé went on. "Was he fifteen, twenty, or only twelve? Who can say? Anyway, he was stronger than I was, faster, more accurate; he had more concentration, more of the 'killer instinct.' I had to make a terrific effort to equalize. And then he looked at me, and my poor performance, which only let me draw level temporarily (don't forget he was the best player in his factory!), called forth a poised politeness in him: and he let me win by just enough to save face while allowing me to go on my way as an honored guest. Not a major incident, perhaps—but in fifteen minutes an unknown youth gave me a crash course in speed, wisdom, and courtesy. That sort of thing will tell when China becomes a democracy!"

But Sinteuil's argument obviously left Bréhal cold.

Zhao was right, Herve thought. Armand's old hat. And he's always been excessively cautious. What's more, do he and I see bodies in the same light?

The five delegates were taken to see the village of Huxian, county town of an agricultural region. It was fifty kilometers from Xian, the ancient capital of China when it was unified by Qinshi Huangdi in the second century A.D., and great capital of the Tangs from 618 to 906.

There was a heat wave when they visited Huxian. June is very hot in that part of the country, and the fields of cotton, covered with tiny white clouds, reinforced the feeling of stifling drought. The place looked deserted. Where were all the peasants? They must be asleep in the shade. Meanwhile the intrepid delegates prepared to visit an exhibition of local paintings. Sylvain, who knew all there was to know about Cézanne and Matisse, got out his pens and his knowing smile. This was going to be something! Tractors and peasants, especially female ones of course, striking heroic attitudes like those that Russian actors, following Stanislavsky, had been overdoing for a hundred years. . . . Don't say I didn't warn you!

Then, suddenly, there were the people from outer space. The missing peasants were huddled—sitting or squatting—in the village square. In a lunar silence . . . The five visitors got out of their Zils and made for the door into the exhibition, addressing faint smiles at the crouching Chinese comrades. Incredible! The eyes that looked back at them were expressionless, flat, dazed. Not curious or admiring, questioning or suspicious—not even malevolent: such looks might be directed at other human beings— other Chinese. But these were "long noses," who'd just got out of strange motorcars, wearing peculiar clothes: the peasants of Huxian had never seen anything like it. Were they animals, another species, visitors from another planet? The whites aroused a blind, almost atavistic fear in the villagers, eclipsing their own humanity as well as that of their visitors. They were all Martians in one another's eyes.

"Do you see? They think we're men from outer space! To them, *we* are Chinese!"

Olga was staggered.

"No, they just take us for foreigners," said Sylvain. "But there may be something in what you say. People don't look at foreigners like that in Morocco or Saigon."

"The comrades of Huxian are seeing foreign friends for the first time!"

Zhao No. 1 was trying to smooth things over.

"They can't see us because they don't believe we're human beings like them. They think we might be a different species." (Olga)

"This is the real China. The Middle Kingdom has never heard of the Other." (Hervé)

"The real Great Wall of China is here in this little square." (Bréhal was delighted to have this opportunity to express his alienation: it had been increasing in him as the trip went on.) "Racism comes from the land. Racism is a peasant phenomenon."

"Would you really call this racism? It might become that. But I fear it goes much deeper. The Other is invisible. The individual has eyes only for himself or someone like him. But eyes mean thought, mind, love, ethics. These people are trying to exclude us from their field of vision, whereas we're trying to include them in our thoughts. Is that as different as it seems? Or are both attitudes ways of canceling out the Unknown?"

Hervé embarked on a tortuous philosophical exposition. To see things through different eyes. Stop being blind. Is it possible? Everyone is a Martian to other people.

13

*L*ots of tractors and combine harvesters, and the same over-made-up Stanislavsky heroines, in the same attitudes, as in the Peking Opera. Olga moved past the peasant comrades' works of art without seeing them: socialist realism, just like back home. You didn't have to be Chinese to paint like that, unfortunately! No surprises anywhere.

Unless . . . Hey! Where did that one come from? A pastiche of Van Gogh? A Taoist painter who dreamed he was Van Gogh and then woke up in the people's commune of the Bronze Well in Huxian?

The sunflowers, as big as a large Buddha, were painted in a challenging yellow and occupied the whole canvas. No perspective. No human figures. Just, in the pale green foliage under the incandescent suns of the flowers, a few thick ink strokes, two or three tiny spots that might, under a microscope, resemble human beings.

Next to the unwitting Van Gogh, almost swallowed up by an azure ground, were two little doll-like figures lost amid a brood of giant hens, a mass of Impressionist blobs covering the whole range of whites and grays.

Further on, brown ears of wheat combined in geometric shapes; granular Mondrian squares swamped atomlike harvesters; pitchforks punctuated the austere equilibrium of a structure that bore an odd resemblance to a masonic temple.

Further on still a Cézanne-like eruption of reddish trees invaded the whole picture, sweeping with them masses of green, ocher, and brown fields to form a moving pyramid in which you could just see a few shapes—playing or drowned?—perched on the branches.

Zhao No. 1 noticed Olga's astonishment.

"The painter of those pictures is Comrade Li Xulan—she's Party secretary to a brigade of seven hundred people, half of them women, in this village. She's here now. You can meet her if you like."

This *was* a day of surprises! Olga couldn't get over it. And on top of it all the artist was a woman.

The seamed, smiling, chubby little face was there in front of her. The woman was in her forties, with cropped black hair and a squat heavy body. Her hands were rough from some thirty years of heavy work in all kinds of weather: the Comrade Party Secretary was a cotton farmer by profession. She didn't seem any different from the women squatting outside, their eyes full of panic because of the extraterrestrial strangers. Precisely. Her eyes. They swept the room keenly, piercing through all they saw before withdrawing into themselves again. They were anxious as they gazed at you, smiling, but they really didn't aspire to anything outside: they found their own repose by plunging back within, inside a strange being from whose features and attitude, Olga now perceived, there emanated a kind of harmonious calm. Like that of a bronze statue.

"Did you paint these marvelous pictures? I think they're wonderful!"

Olga's enthusiasm embarrassed Li Xulan. She started to laugh—the forced laughter that the Chinese use to conceal everything. Questions. How do you paint? How long have you been doing it? What are they, exactly?—landscapes and things you've seen or experienced . . . or dreams, visions?

"Maybe that's it. I don't paint what I see—I paint after I've been sleeping. When I get back from the fields I'm tired and I dream a lot—always in color—and when I wake up I paint what I've seen in my dreams. Well, not quite: I can't reproduce a dream exactly—my paintings show something that doesn't exist, something that's in between my dreams and my working life. But I've still got a lot to learn before I can produce paintings that are like real fields. Like photographs."

"But I like your paintings as they are! How did you hit on the idea of painting after you've been sleeping? Did you learn about it at night school?"

Li Xulan looked uneasy and started talking to Zhao. She spoke so fast Olga couldn't follow.

"Comrade Li Xulan only learned to read and write two years ago. She isn't properly educated yet, and she asks me to forgive her—she's still a very simple person . . ."

(And a good thing too, thought Olga. Otherwise how would she avoid being indoctrinated?)

"But I do know the speech Chairman Mao made about art and literature at Yanan. That's my inspiration," said Li Xulan, remembering she was a Party secretary.

"Do you really think so?"

Olga had decided to drive her into a corner. Quite kindly, of course.

"What about your children? Haven't you ever felt like painting them?"

What an idea! said Li Xulan's frightened look. She'd had four sons, the oldest now nearly twenty-five—but no, it had never occurred to her to paint them.

"That's because you know they wouldn't be the right subject for you. Your genius is that of a good unsophisticated country-woman."

This was Sylvain, who'd been following the conversation with amusement, declining to be impressed. A gallery of modern art for backward female peasants!

"But that's exactly what makes her work so interesting. Aren't you amazed to find an uneducated peasant woman discovering modern painting all on her own? She's a genius! Yes, Madame Li, you're a genius. Will you allow me to photograph your paintings?"

"Don't let's exaggerate," said Sylvain, jocular as before. "Is it this lady you're so keen on, or your own point of view?"

Li's eyes swiveled rapidly from Olga to her own pictures: perhaps they really were masterpieces if the foreign comrade, who was an expert, said so? Then the stealthy gaze withdrew again, indifferent, back to its roots in some inner field.

Flash. Photo. Flash. Another photo. Olga might have illusions but the camera didn't. The matter could be reviewed back in Paris. . . . But no, she couldn't be so wrong—this woman was an extraordinary phenomenon.

Li didn't know what she was doing, but she knew how to do it. Could Lao-tse or Chuang-tse, or at least one of their talented disciples, have been reincarnated in this woman?—this party secretary and cotton farmer who dreamed of being Van Gogh, Mondrian, and Cézanne, and woke to modify their vision with an inhuman calm? Was Li a true Taoist, unaware of her own identity?

Outside, the crowd waited for the Martian strangers with the same impenetrable gaze as before. Olga could scarcely contain her delight at having found a real person at last! And what talent! Li Xulan breathed retrospective life into the string of stereotyped heroines to whom the visitors had been introduced before: mothers, factory managers, kindergarten teachers, record-breaking workers, students reciting official diatribes against the old revisionist science.

"Do you remember the picture called *Autumn*, Sylvain? The one with red branches turning into a pyramid of abstract forms? . . . Well, didn't it remind you of Cézanne's *Montagne Sainte-Victoire*—the one that's in Bâle? It was painted in 1904 or 1905 and resumes all the previous geometrical ones. Remember touches of green and blue, ocher and black and brick-red. . . ."

"You're very generous! But say we stretch our imaginations a bit and accept the comparison. . . . Your friend Li is certainly sensitive to the vibrations of light. And I grant you a certain rhythm in the reds and yellows, but there's not enough blue there to lighten them. However, don't let's quibble. But where are *The Skull and the Candlestick, The Black Clock, The Temptation of Saint Anthony,* and the grace of *The Boy in the Red Waistcoat*—the one with the long arms, do you remember it? Let me tell you something: your Madame Li only gets by through avoiding portraits, faces, bodies. She's more gifted than her colleagues, more of a dreamer perhaps. She might become quite a decent abstract painter if I had time to do something for her. But is the human face—of which there are plenty of examples in Cézanne and Matisse—is it really finished, as our out-and-out avant-gardists think, who can't even draw a teapot? Of course not! So when your female Taoists reincarnated as Mondrian can produce abstracts containing as much passion as there is in a body or a face, then we'll discuss the matter again! I wish them the best of luck! But they'll have to overcome the superficial posturings of socialist realism and the rest of it. And that's likely to take some time!"

Sylvain was always hard to please. But he wasn't laughing now; he was laying down the law. There was something in what he said. But what use was that if he couldn't enjoy work that broke none of the usual rules but was also inspired by the laws of dreams?

"You're going to China? Write a book about Chinese women then, and we'll publish it. I'll pay your fare—I don't want you to go offering it to Editions de l'Autre."

Bernadette had been both farsighted and efficient, and now Olga, thanks to Li Xulan and some others, knew what the book was going to be. She'd give the Militant Feminists a series of portraits—descriptions of the extraordinary women who in one generation had transformed the bound feet and dreary lives of their mothers into nimble bodies, bold minds, and even distinguished art. Perhaps only now was there a real equilibrium between *yin* and *yang*.

Olga had read that Chinese civilization was the greatest of all matrilinear and matrilocal societies. They'd had lots of discussions at the Institute for Cultural Analysis about the matrilinear family, the primitive commune, and matriarchy.

"Pure hypothesis," said Strich-Meyer. "Just a naive revival of Engels's 'matriarchy.' On the other hand, we do know about 'restricted exchange' and bilateral filiation, where each individual has two references, one paternal and one maternal. From this, if you like, we can deduce the famous dynamic symmetry of *yin-yang*, but we can't, scientifically, go any further. Of course, if you want to embark on fiction . . ."

Carole, who took an interest in Martin's research on Wadanis, despaired of finding that women enjoyed any advantages among them. A Wadani man could marry only the daughter of his maternal uncle. This might be seen as a late development of a hypothetical matrilinear family, but the customs of the Wadani tribe were diametrically opposite to *yin-yang*. It was a real male chauvinist society, exhibiting a sad decline in female dignity!

"You are lucky, going to China. Try to find out if they have any new archaeological evidence about matriarchy."

Olga had promised to make inquiries. Myths reflect customs, and there was one myth she particularly liked precisely because it restored women to their rightful place. And the previous day, in an antique shop in Xian, Hervé had found a print of a first-century B.C. stele engraved with the same myth; everyone had bought a copy. The queen-goddess Nùgua, unlike Yahweh, didn't create the Universe, but she did save it from collapse, and with her brother and husband, the legendary King Fuxi, she created man and invented writing. Hervé's engraving showed the pair of them with human heads and the bodies of serpents, with dragon's tails intertwined; they are equal and interchangeable, *yin* and *yang*, neither dominating the other.

"You don't realize how lucky you are—knowing or at least learning Chinese," Carole had said. "Chinese civilization looks as if it might be very favorable to women . . . free of male prejudice . . ."

Olga was intrigued.

"Keep your eyes open anyway, and make inquiries!" Carole had insisted.

Bernadette had been determined too:

"What we want is a feminist book—a hymn to women liberated at last, rejecting male domination and returning to the origins of the human race, the happy era that male scholars try to hide from us!"

At this point Zhao No. 1 and Zhao No. 2 both announced that "for Comrade Olga" they'd arranged for the group to visit the museum of prehistory at Panpo.

"Our archaeologists began excavating in 1953, and they've found a primitive matriarchal commune, dating from before the age of patriarchy, private property, and class."

"Hegel's tall story again!" said Hervé.

"The leaflet's enough for me," said Bréhal. "It's very well done. I don't need to go and see the excavations."

"One can always learn something, especially *a contrario*," said Weil and Brunet philosophically.

And so the whole group embarked on matriarchy.

No doubt about it. Olga had her book.

A few months later, when she'd finished her account, with considerable effort and haste as well as pleasure, she called Bernadette and told her the manuscript was ready.

"Terrific—leave it at the reception desk and I'll get back to you right away."

Two weeks, a month, went by. No phone call. At last Paule, Bernadette's assistant, rang.

"We're discussing your piece tonight at the office. It's taken time because all the girls had to read it. Democracy! . . . Okay then? Ten o'clock tonight at the office!"

As usual, lots of girls had turned up at the office to complain to Bernadette about their marital, professional, and maternal woes. But it was getting late. Couldn't they get on to the book?

"What book?"

The girls were taken aback. No one had read any book. Olga turned to Bernadette.

"I've read it. Interesting—on the whole. But you seem rather skeptical about matriarchy. . . ."

"I put in different points of view on the subject. I'm not competent to give a final opinion."

"That's what I mean—you don't commit yourself!"

Olga was surprised. What about intellectual integrity . . .

"That's got nothing to do with it. It's a matter of yes or no. It's quite simple: if you're a woman you feel these things inside you." (The spotty little blonde in big glasses was categorical.)

"Is that so?" (Olga thought it wisest to bide her time.)

But Bernadette still hadn't finished.

"And you give women a bad image whenever you deal with the past: they're all depressed or commit suicide, and if they do manage to make their mark it's only because they ape men."

"Those are the facts. What else could women do under Confucianism?"

"Who gives a shit about Confucianism? It's a bad image. You'd have done better to stick to the Taoist mothers—there are loads of them, and *they* are much more relevant." (Bernadette had got the bit between her teeth.) "The fact is, you don't really like women—your book suggests love between women makes them boring, if not suicidal!"

"You put it more strongly than I do, but that can happen."

"Male propaganda! You've been contaminated with patriarchy!" (Spotty was a real militant.)

"Right!" (Olga was beginning to get the message.) "You don't like it? Every woman to her taste. Just hand the typescript back to me—Editions de l'Autre has been asking me for it—and I'll give you your money back."

"That's not the point!" (Paule, the assistant, was trying to get everyone back on the rails.) "All we mean is, you ought to add a foreword saying what you owe to Bernadette and the movement."

That was too much. They didn't know their Olga! She'd had enough of this kind of harassment to last her a lifetime. In the komsomol, for instance. Except that back home it was serious— it was your freedom that was at stake, not your vanity over a stupid little book.

There were lots of peonies in Nanking and Luoyang. Great purple or scarlet, pink or maroon or white heads, incredibly massive and fragrant. Whole streets and gardens full of bloody suns. They rotted on the stem. And that highly colored death was obscene, like some stupid, insolent female sex organ. How fragile beauty was, and how suddenly it could turn into its opposite, into coarse and obtuse horror! The excited faces of Bernadette and her pals, red and white with sick ambition, were rotting peonies.

"Have you gone crazy, girl?" cried Olga, reverting to the belligerence of her militant youth. "Who do you think Bernadette is—Chairman Mao? And even if she was, I didn't go to China to bow down to any Chairman, male or female! If you're trying to set up a feminist dictatorship, you've come to the wrong address as far as I'm concerned! Give me back my manuscript, and goodbye!"

General uproar. Most of those present sided with Bernadette. Others thought there was some sense in what Olga said.

"I go along with Bernadette because she lets me live rent-free in one of her apartments . . . But if it weren't for that . . ." (Olga thought she recognized the voice of one of her students.)

"No need to lose your temper, Olga—we're only offering some friendly advice. Apart from those few points your book's wonderful—it goes without saying we're going to publish it. Oh, I nearly forgot. . . . Just one last thing. . . . You can't call yourself 'de Montlaur' on the title page. That's your husband's name—it would look terrible in a book published by the Militant Feminists." (Bernadette would keep on; she obviously didn't realize how furious the Squirrel was.)

"She could go back to 'Olga Morena'—that's how she signed her articles before she was married," Paule suggested.

"No!" (No concessions from Bernadette.) "The father's name is just as macho as the husband's."

"Are you all completely mad? Give me the manuscript back right away and leave me alone! If you want to change patrilinear society overnight, that's fine, but you'll have to do it without me! Where's that manuscript?"

The Squirrel was stamping with rage.

"It's already at the printer's."

"Is that so? You allow only one opinion, is that it? Everything that doesn't agree with your theory is phallic, a lousy penis that makes you throw up, eh? Well, you can throw *me* up too! There are other feminists besides you!"

"No, there aren't!"

Perhaps not! thought the Squirrel, more soberly, as she slammed the door.

That was the end of her activism in favor of feminism, the Chinese or any other variety. No more politics. Instead, solitude and the little happinesses and unhappinesses of life. The body could meditate on the spirit; the spirit would have no more to do with groups; out of disappointment might come lucidity.

The book on China *was* published by the Militant Feminists in the end—they'd more or less impounded it. Olga let them go on with it, and took no further interest.

But there on the Panpo excavation site she listened carefully. Matriarchy spread out over fifty thousand square meters—though "only" one thousand had so far been actually cleared—you don't see that every day of the week. A village dating back about eight thousand years: six thousand years B.C.!

A young woman of thirty—Chang Chudang, a self-taught historian—quoted Engels's *Origins of the Family, Property, and the State.*

"Our ancestors used to eat millet, rape, and wild plants. The women did the then crucial work of growing the crops, and this gave them a dominant role in political life."

"What about the men?"

Hervé couldn't keep quiet any longer.

"They spent their time hunting and fishing. Later on they raised cattle."

"I can see little penises engraved on the pottery. Was the god Phallus worshiped under matriarchy?"

Neither of the Zhaos dared translate what Hervé had just said.

"The river Zhanhe runs by the village," Madame Chang went on imperturbably. "The shape you see on the pottery is the village totem. A fish."

"That's a very simplistic explanation."

Stanislas now joined Hervé in the debate. But it wasn't to last long.

There were black fish, red ones, brown ones; fish joined together in pairs; human faces sandwiched between two fish.

Then the fish became abstract: squares, triangles, circles. After that they started to go wild and change into giraffes, elephants, and wild birds.

"Anyhow, the marks of women's fingernails are found on all these artifacts. This proves the women were potters as well as farmers, and also, no doubt, in charge of the sacred function of cooking."

Comrade Chang seemed just the sort of feminist Bernadette was after. She continued, with what was meant to be impeccable logic:

"The women collected water in jars, so it's plain they had an empirical knowledge of the laws of gravity"—("Like children in our part of the world today," put in Sylvain)—and the fact that the cooking was done in closed vessels demonstrates that they knew all about steam"—("So Chinese women discovered thermodynamics!" . . . Sylvain was having a wonderful time.)—"All this is proof that women in the primitive matriarchal commune attained a very high level of technology."

"*Na!*" cried Olga.

The four men had to admit defeat. But their guide had kept her strongest argument till last.

"We are now in the middle of the village. You are standing on the site of the great-grandmother's house. It was surrounded by the dwellings where the men and women, hunters and farmers, respectively, joined one another at night."

"What for?"

Hervé was determined to be disruptive, but the two Zhaos remained silent.

"We shall now leave the village itself, and then you'll see two areas separated by a ditch: one contains the burial places and the other the potteries. The best proof of matriarchy is to be found in the burial grounds."

"The mother equals death." (Hervé, of course)

"The women's graves contain more funerary objects than the others: large quantities of pottery, bracelets, bone hairpins, whistles. . . ."

"Sluts' bazaar!" (Hervé)

"What were the whistles for?" (Sylvain)

"The children, silly!" (Stanislas)

"The children were buried with the women. Babies didn't receive formal burial—their bodies were just put in the ground near their houses, in separate urns."

"I think I might have preferred to die in infancy." (Hervé)

"Be quiet!" (Olga)

"On this site the men and women are buried together, but on another site not far away from here there's a necropolis where the Mother is always buried in the middle, with the skeletons of the other members of the family arranged around her. The funeral rites probably took place in two separate stages: first there were separate graves for individuals of both sexes, and then, when a whole family was dead, all its members were arranged around the grandmother. There weren't any sacrifices: none of the skeletons shows any signs of violence. No private property. No patriarchal power. Policy was decided collectively in the house of the great Ancestress. The Mother at the center of things, and a peaceful society. That's what the primitive matriarchal commune was like."

"It sounds plausible." (Olga)

"Too harmonious to be true." (Sylvain was still skeptical.)

"You call that harmonious, having a Mother in the center of things? I wouldn't be so sure!" (Hervé was beginning his counter-propaganda.) "A question, Madame Chang: Where did the family of one Mother end and that of another begin? Could there be two Mothers at the center, and if so, how did they manage? What do *you* say? Chairman Mao seems to agree with me: he's not so sure as Comrade Chang about the power of women at that period. And above all he wisely sticks to the essential truth that the One always devours the Other, and vice versa."

Hervé then produced from his pocket a text by Mao, from which he proceeded to quote.

" 'At first men were subject to women, and then the situation was reversed and women became subject to men. This stage of history has not yet been entirely elucidated, though it lasted more than a million years.' But what's a million years between comrades? 'In this world, everyone devours everyone else, everyone overthrows one another. . . .' You see, the Chairman doesn't take sides: he's neither macho nor a feminist. He believes in *yin* and *yang*—like me. . . . Isn't that so, comrade wife?"

" 'In this world everyone devours everyone else, everyone overthrows one another. . . .' " repeated Comrade Chang, as if in a dream.

14

Was it because of the enigma of China itself, this vapid vastness pretending to unburden itself in borrowed ideas while all the time retreating deeper behind its own bastions? Or was it to do with their own group, with its three crusty old bachelors and Hervé turning everything into a joke? Whatever the reason, Olga was starting to feel baffled. Perhaps it was only to be expected when you were living in a different environment—not hostile, no, not at all, but mysterious, strange. . . . There'd been a story lately about the survivors of a plane crash trying to survive on a glacier; when their supplies were exhausted they'd taken to eating one another. But cannibalism had started long before, with words and deeds of hatred, contempt, humiliation. The human race still practices psychological cannibalism. Civilization may not allow human bodies to be sacrificed, but spiritual wounds, murders of the soul, are to be seen wherever you look. . . . Assuming you believe there is such a thing as the soul, which not everyone does. And perhaps it's in the rejection of the soul that psychological cannibalism begins. . . .

Olga was hunting for souvenirs and trying to speak Chinese. She climbed up the huge Buddhist sculptures in the cave at Longmen, near Luoyang, and deciphered ancient inscriptions telling how to cure mental illness. Another visitor, a peasant woman from Hunan, spoke to her.

"Because of my pilgrimage to the Buddha my rheumatism will be cured—but shall I become immortal? What do you think, comrade?"

Taoist China firmly believed in immortality, no doubt about it. Chinese Buddhism was pervaded by the hope of eternal life, whereas in India they didn't believe in survival after death. But after all, hadn't Lao-tse ridden westward on his ox to preach his own doctrine, and weren't the Buddhas he brought back a simple and rather barbaric version of Taoist eternity?

"I think we all die, but that souls who believe in Buddha are reincarnated somewhere else. . . ."

Olga had launched into a long explanation as pointless as it was incomprensible.

"Wai guo ren, Wai guo ren!—a foreigner, a foreigner!" cried the old peasant woman. She'd soon got the drift of Olga's rigmarole and taken to her heels.

But Olga was delighted. "She took me for a Chinese at first!" She just had time to film the poor old dame as she ran away, throwing a terrified glance over her shoulder.

She took a snap of the dancing Buddha too. Another of the one carved in profile. And one of the mythical beast below, half-woman half-tortoise.

One of Armand sitting on a dwarf Buddha but with his eyes fixed on his notebook. One of Stanislas, who never showed Olga his face: all her photographs were of his back view. One of Sylvain and Hervé together—you could never take them apart: a couple of inseparable pranksters who understood each other without words, always poking each other in the ribs and laughing. She *could* have snapped them separately, but that would have meant leaving the group and finding the right angle. But she felt sufficiently cut off from the group already. If there was such a thing as a group. A group was held together by an obsession, an enthusiasm. But here the frenzied and factitious enthusiasm of the Chinese was undermining the visitors' own obsession. *Now* might survive their return from China, but the spirit of *Now* certainly wouldn't. Their obsession was turning into skepticism, and the group was breaking up.

Flash. A photograph taken in the cave: Hervé whispering something amusing in Sylvain's ear. Flash: Stanislas pretending to look at a stele but really looking daggers at the other two. Flash: Bréhal writing, and yawning over his pen.

At night the three bachelors all went back to their own rooms, which they found "very Spartan." Hervé and Olga had been given a comfortable bed in one of the luxury bedrooms provided for distinguished guests or eminent Chinese officials traveling with their wives.

"Sleep well—we're too tired to make love after such a long day, aren't we?"

Hervé obligingly turned his back, ready to fall asleep right away.

"I suppose you think it wouldn't be fair to the others?"

"In a way. Don't you agree?"

"I couldn't care less about the others."

"Quite right. Sleep well!"

Silence.

Strangely, fortunately, you can communicate with photographs, and even better with film. Both are silent, seeming not to answer. But they register your interest and your point of view, and give your images back to you clearer, more positive or more negative than you expected. Above all, photographs are discerning. And discernment is very necessary when you're overwhelmed by so much immensity: innumerable heads, masses of bronzes and statues, endless slogans and bits of calligraphy, reducing you to a grain of rice in a vast heap sweltering in the sun. Sorting out the faces is the most difficult thing. The faces of children, for instance: a solar charm, love only a lens away.

Olga thought she didn't like children. She didn't hate them, no. She was just indifferent. For example, she'd never played with dolls, or so seldom that Aurora, the only one she'd ever had as a child, had had no difficulty in surviving, and still sat on her parents' divan in honor of their roving offspring. And she hadn't replaced Aurora with miniature cars or trains or airplanes. Simply and directly by books. And by swimming and tennis. All very serious and efficient. She hated anything mawkish and when she was twelve had even quarreled with Hélène, her best friend, because she would keep hanging around mothers pushing baby carriages. Olga's little brother was quite enough for her. She was fed up with his whims and tears and bowls of mush, though they did have the advantage of keeping her mother occupied and leaving her father at loose ends. And one day she and her father decided to escape from the boredom and spend their spare time together at soccer games or, in the evening, at concerts or the theater. In short, she was sure she didn't like children.

But Chinese children were another matter. They were so beautiful, with their perfect oval faces, mimosalike cheeks, slanting slits for eyes, and little mouths full of songs and laughter. So well behaved too. At any public occasion in Luoyang or Shanghai there was always some diplomat's kid, American, English, or French, fooling around on the terraces while his parents yelled at him to come and sit down. Was it only to be expected, at that age? No—Chinese children didn't utter a sound: they just gazed at the universe in ecstasy, or occasionally in dismay. They were polite and didn't disturb other people, and although they were very appealing they never wheedled or mauled you. How charming they were when they pretended to write characters with one tiny finger in the palm of your hand. The saucy little look they gave you before they ran away, scared by their own forwardness. The little boys were more serious; their eyes were sad already, like their fathers': as a matter of fact, Olga had never met with such an expression except in Mediterranean women and Chinese men. The little girls, smarter and more agile than awkward little boys of the same age, dominated all the games in every kindergarten. And it was the same girls who, beneath the fierce and immemorial makeup of the Peking Opera and despite the wildness of their dance, struck the comrades from *Now* with a kind of innocence.

"I adore these kids," said Olga, who now took photographs of nothing but astounded little faces, little hands wielding brushes, little dancing feet, and ecstatic little bellies.

"I have to admit they're delightful," said Hervé, greatly astonishing his wife, who'd witnessed his rages every time there was an ad for diapers on TV.

Anyhow, there was no getting away from them. There were at least three kindergartens or crèches to be visited in every commune, district, village, and town. And despite the contraception campaign—the delegation had to stop and admire the posters on family planning plastered over every pharmacy—the Chinese comrades apparently continued to increase and multiply. They certainly took more pride in showing off their children to the visitors than in exhibiting their pharmacies.

The gynecological department of the hospital in Shanghai. Three newly delivered mothers, tired but radiant; motherhood effacing ugliness. Flash. Photo.

"What's her name?"

"Little Arrow."

"... ?"

Flash. Photo.

"It's from a poem by Chairman Mao: 'Quivering arrows flying/ how many things forever to be done/ heaven and earth in revolution—time so short/ too long ten thousand years/ act now ...'"

Would the child accept the crushing invitation to react against ten thousand years?

"You translated that poem, Hervé—do you remember?"

"Of course! Hi, Little Arrow!"

Jade Knife, Little Arrow's big sister, had just come in. They wouldn't try to trace her name to its poetic source. Photo. Flash. Six years old, would she be? Perhaps. She acted more like twelve.

"These children are surprisingly mature, aren't they? Especially the girls."

Bréhal was awake now. He'd always been interested in intelligent bodies.

"I've got a theory about it," said Olga. "You know Chinese is a tonal language? Well, the babies here can distinguish tones from the age of six or seven months—they can do that all over the world, as a matter of fact—before they can recognize phonemes, or of course words or phrases. Now in our own languages we don't make much use of tones: you can say *chair* in a rising tone or a falling one and it still denotes a chair. But in Chinese *ma* can have five different meanings, according to whether the tone in which you say it is high, low, flat, neutral, or dual."

"What are you driving at?"

The linguistic platitudes were making Hervé impatient.

"Keep calm—I'm coming to it! If a child can distinguish, reproduce, and get some sort of meaning out of tones at the age of six months, that means—this at least is clear—that it enters into a fundamental relation with language at the age of six months instead of two years . . . the age when French and English and Russian children do so."

"And so?"

"And so a Chinese infant is involved very early on in the speech system; he's being formed and influenced by symbols as he drinks his mother's milk. He can speak and sing his intimate bodily battle with his mother—he doesn't have to bury it and wait until he's two years old to express it. Hervé likes quoting 'I alone am fed by the mother.' I maintain that every Chinese infant is virtually a disciple of the *Tao-tö king:* he is fed both by his mother and by the singing of words; music links milk to language. Thank you for listening. That's the end of today's lecture."

"But what you say is marvelous! And very relevant, it seems to me. Tell me what your sources are, will you, Olga?—I suppose there've been some articles on the subject?"

The whole kindergarten at the Shanghai maternity hospital was milling around Olga. With her long full denim skirt, yellow cotton blouse, short brown velvet jacket, and Chinese umbrella made of orange oilcloth, she looked at once exotic and simple, eccentric and dowdy, attracting surreptitious attention on the part of the women, and from the children the kind of warm caresses usually forbidden outside the home. She was beyond taking any more photos. She stroked the little cheeks, planted some kisses in the children's hair and behind their ears. Tinkles of excited laughter from the teachers.

"You shouldn't be doing this. You know that in China you're not supposed to kiss children except when they're asleep." (Hervé)

"But is there anything more irresistible than a Chinese child?" (Olga)

"Yes—two!" (Hervé)

"I want one." (Olga)

". . ." (Hervé)

"Really!" (Olga)

"You?" (Hervé)

"Me." (Olga)

". . ." (Hervé)

"What about you?" (Olga)

"The idea may be aesthetically interesting. From a distance." (Hervé)

"I'd like to examine it closely." (Olga)

"Give me a kiss!" (Hervé)

"I'm serious. Very serious." (Olga)

"We've got plenty of time." (Hervé)

You may think you're going away, but a journey is always an eternal return. And while certain brief hallucinations make us think the place we're in isn't new but the recurrence of a landscape familiar to us from another life—an impossible life, delightful, stormy, and forgotten—with the exception of such experiences the eternal return operates in the dimension of time, not space. Thus, when a journey reaches a peak of pleasure or disgust, the time in which it operates becomes circular and turns you in upon yourself.

The wheel of time—how many writers have tried their hand at it! But the most succinct of them—the most circular, and thus the one most imbued with the strength, the hopeless yet supremely tranquil strength that experience of the eternal return conveys—is Borges. He has read everything, reoriented everything, rewritten everything.

Borges has understood that Plato was inspired by the astrological cycles. But it seems to have been algebra that led to the best-known and most dramatic eternal return—Nietzsche's. In reality a limited number of particles cannot produce an unlimited number of combinations. But in eternity every possible order and combination will be produced an infinite number of times. Borges's favorite hypothesis—"the least terrifying, the least melodramatic, but the only one possible"—is that the cycles are similar but not identical. Anyone who has seen the present has seen everything: "The destinies of Edgar Allan Poe, of the Vikings, of Judas Iscariot, and of my reader are secretly one and the same." The "one destiny possible." "The history of the universe is the history of one man."

But Borges forgot Heraclitus. Why? Heraclitus wasn't quite Greek, or sufficiently infamous, or strictly eternal. He was just incantatory and adroit, dark, disappointed, and rhythmic. Was he Chinese? The wheel-shaped destiny of this country, with its memory half asleep, might be called Heraclitean. An eternal return that transforms the abjectness of hope and the pathos of despair into the brief equilibrium of childhood. And into adults' ordinary yet mysterious power to engender a child. What does that mean?

"Aion pais esti paizon, pesseuon."

Heraclitus encumbered posterity—and eternity—with thousands of translations of the same sentence, all of them possible and all unsatisfactory.

"Time is a child who behaves like a child and plays."

Child's play is wayward and insouciant, and cyclical time is like it: it crushes us as it amuses us. But it's a loop that has no end, for all games survive the players and choose new ones. Games structure the world, and it's only naive or megalomaniac players who think they're in control.

So time behaves like a child. And like a child it may throw away the dice, the pawns, the balls, the kites, the computers. And start all over again.

But what else? Time literally makes children.* Time begets. And here a caesura nicks the wheel though it doesn't stop it: the dead accompany the generations and urge them on. But in the supreme game where we play at being parents though deep down we're still children, we don't mention death even though it's

* In French the verb *faire* can mean "make" or "play, act, behave like," so *Le temps fait l'enfant* means both "Time makes a child" and "Time behaves like a child." *Tr.*

implicitly in charge. For what matters is that the game should go on, and that it should include death.

No, the life of man is not a constant quantity. If you've ever looked at a child; if you know what childish things are, and childbirth; then you know every generation is one more trick played on death, a step toward perfection or debasement, a resurrection for better or worse.

The eternal return that matters with a child, and that it is his right to repeat, is the idea of an eternity that's inconstant. Insouciant. An immortality that's unstable. Changeable. A baroque eternity. These Chinese with their fluid laughter were placidly, because unconsciously, baroque. Even European baroque would be Heraclitean if it wasn't so Christianly tortured at having killed a child called Jesus. In China, which swarms with children and childish things, eternity minimizes death and reduces it to a game. What frightful frivolity. Jesus is nowhere to be seen. So Chinese eternity deals in *little* likenesses and *little* differences: don't worry, nothing is either tragic or triumphant— it's only a matter of rhythm. But the rhythm also comprises *great* likenesses and differences: they're known as revolutions, and history is punctuated by them. Lethally. But peace is restored by the laughter of children. The eternal return of children is a maternal idea. Was Hercalitus haunted by matriarchy?

But the idea of the eternal return as child's play engendering children removes the tragic aspect of procreation and, without either degrading or glorifying it, gives it the serious insignificance of all children's games.

So, whether in a period of growth or a period of decline, Heraclitus the Chinese causes neither sadness nor impatience. With Borges, he persuades us that "in a period of decadence such as the one we are living in now," his *aion*, his eternal return, "is a guarantee that no disgrace, no calamity, and no dictator can have power over us."

So why did Borges forget Heraclitus? Was it because children got on his nerves? Wasn't he a man who liked children? Or was he something of a child himself?

Olga, her heart full of these faces, her heart heavy and yet fired with her thoughts about her own eternal return, dipped her foot in concubine Yang Guifei's warm bath. Babes and sucklings had rescued her at last from the race against time in which she was always straining after knowledge, acquisition, being: all those words became mere numbers, mere quantitative strivings, set against the dimension of time. And the children had wafted her—partly anxious and partly elated—out of time and into a sphere where she didn't yet know what she would find. Perhaps it was just the moment? The endless loop of the moment?

The hot spring—109 degrees, said Zhao No. 1 and Zhao No. 2—flowed from Black Horse Mountain, which overlooked Xian. The emperors came to bathe there from the first century B.C., from the days of the Han dynasty. Fabulous palaces were built there to house the emperors' concubines and pleasures: the Palace of the Warm Spring, the Palace of Glorious Purity.

"Comrade Sinteuil and his wife are invited to visit the bath of the beautiful Yang Guifei. It's a special gesture—the Palace of Glorious Purity is hardly ever opened."

Zhao No. 1 or Zhao No. 2—they couldn't remember which—had announced the news as if it were a geopolitical triumph.

"Unfortunately, the other comrades are invited to the public baths only. But I oughtn't to say unfortunately—they'll be able to see how the Chinese people now enjoy what used to be a privilege of the rich."

"I have no intention of taking a bath." (Bréhal was digging in his toes again.)

"Why not?" (Sylvain and Stanislas had accepted the invitation.)

The concubine's bath was full of the smell of incense, and her canopied bed was hung with ancient restored silk draperies—Olga and Hervé couldn't tell where they came from—in sumptuous blue-gray hues. The pool of warm water was shaped like a butterfly with outspread wings. The mere idea of bathing in it was refreshing.

"It's not the Tao, though." (Hervé)

"Luxurious as it is, they're proud of having preserved it. Just wait—they'll soon exhume the whole of their ancient history, and that'll be the end of dogmatism." (Olga)

"Stop arguing and enjoy yourself!"

"Isn't the water here supposed to be aphrodisiac?"

"Just a minute. . . . Yes! . . . The comrades are right!" (Hervé)
They floated on their backs, forgetting everything.
"We'd better go now—the others will be waiting for us."

Who loves whom, nowadays? One's neighbor as oneself? But there is no neighbor, because there is no self. The "self" comes from a concentrated and agile intelligence capable of inhabiting an inner space, a room of its own. Where does that capacity come from? When you get right down to it, it can't be very common. On the contrary, it's a sort of first wonder of the world, infinitely older than and superior to the pyramids of Egypt, the hanging gardens of Semiramis, Phidias's statue of Zeus, the Colossus of Rhodes, the Temple of Artemis at Ephesus, the mausoleum at Halicarnassus, or the lighthouse at Alexandria. A kind of heroism. Does the ability to love come, as Goethe seemed to think, from the certainty that our mothers loved us? Still the Mother there at the center of things? But it's not enough that they love us; we must also be *sure* of it, and that isn't only up to them. Certainty of the self is outside the power of the central Mother, together with something else.

Olga remembered how as a child by the sea, her feet burned by the black sand, she used to see gaps between the shining pebbles, vibrant spaces in which invisible words seemed to jostle one another, trying to take the place of the stones and make themselves heard. They were like fireflies appearing and disappearing amid the blinding brightness of the beach. But where exactly were those spaces? Between her toes, stubbed by the pebbles, and the hitherto undefined words soon to emerge? Or in her mind? Her head? Her heart? She didn't know, but she was sure that the wonder that was about to appear in the form of a phrase—"The siren has left her pearly tunic on the black sand," for instance; or "The winkle whitened by the waves will not vanish like the sugar in my milk; another child will find it tomorrow on the other side of the sea"; and so on—she was sure the journey from pebbles to words had happened before. That she herself had made it. In the past. In a life without memory. A life forgotten forever. It was pleasant to reawaken all that sometimes, but not too often. That gleam of light could upset every delicate balance; wasn't it like a microbe that could cause illness, loss of self-control, madness? Olga would rub the mysterious space out with her foot and rush into the chill water to forget.

Perhaps it was a buried memory, reviving. Which?

Mother is going away: no more milk, no more breast, nothing to drink, nothing to see. I cry, no one has ever cried so much, all babies cry, the distress of some is devastating, best not to hear them, not to bother. The space starts when the tears dry and mourning has become established: the baby samurai is sad but doesn't admit defeat; its sad eyes seek an image. The image of the taste of milk. The image of a skin touched by Mother. The image of her scent. The image displaces Mother from the center; it's a firefly preparing me a way, a space, toward others. My sorrow is my salvation: I've lost my mother; no, I imagine her; no, I represent her in images, in flashes, in words. Because she loves me; and if *you* love me.

Hail therefore to the "self," which can now love and hate its neighbor as itself!

Hail, fragile self, who'll dissolve with delight if covered in kisses in the fragrant bath of concubine ′Yang Guifei. Who'll collapse bereft of words and images if someone turns his back on you, drops you. Do you know the dreadful surprise a baby feels when it falls out of seemingly safe arms? Like the horror of a mountaineer falling into the void.

But just a minute. . . . If all "selfs" are so feeble, so unsubstantial, so weak, how can they unite with others?

There's a new happiness in Europe. A Chinese happiness. The happiness of the space. Neither One nor All, but immersed, dispersed, unbound. I'm lost: I'm becoming someone again. I love you: neither do I. You hate me: neither do I. Don't think yourself Everything. Don't think. The mirror of your eyes, in which I try to put myself together again, is in pieces. You give me back the image of a kaleidoscope, some horrible, sublime woman by Picasso. The link between us is absurd, and warm, and scented like that concubine's bath from twelve centuries ago which maybe never existed except in Zhao No. 1's overheated imagination or Zhao No. 2's overzealous hospitality. What does it matter, it makes me laugh, you make me laugh. Is laughter a debased form of eroticism? But no, there is nothing evil in the eternal return of children. Laughter is a disrespectful grace:

religion gasping out its last breath at the foot of eroticism. Don't feel guilty—I'm not looking for a man to blame.

You're right, I hanker after complete happiness. I'd rather have that than the innocent exaltation of the Chinese girls making love in the cool moonlit wheatfields. Yet the earth, lately flooded by the spring rains, surrounded them with perfume; and the land, where plants, men, and animals all mingled beneath flights of swallows, was a place of magic to them.

The Temple of Heaven rose up through the mists of Peking, periwinkle-gray enlivened with red and yellow. The gilding pierced the murky air of May like shining dragons in a storm that would not take place. The crowd was faceless as ever, its dull or apprehensive tranquillity just a foil for the fabulous sights. The workers came to pay tribute to History, but it seemed to leave them as it found them. They'd seen so much of it! What was the current campaign? Mao was sacking his aide? Lin Piao was a traitor? Who'd be the next? Did the future belong to the young? Did hope lie in the women? Of course. Let's go home.

The cherry trees were laden with flowers shining white and pink in the rain. The wind showered rainproof passersby with confetti from some dead blossoms; others rotted on the bough. But the sun, emerging from the clouds, shone on sharp little knobs that would soon be round juicy fruit.

"The Temple of Heaven is what I like best about Peking. It's totally lacking in tact. But my austere alter ego is still in love with the Pagoda of the Little Goose in Xian—I think he will stay there forever. But what I'll take away with me is the Palace of Glorious Purity, with or without a concubine." (Hervé)

"If only I could take a cherry tree home with me, and a child!" (Olga)

"Plenty of them in Paris." (Sylvain)

"I've never seen any." (Olga)

"There's lots of mail for all of you at the hotel." (Zhao)

"About time. We're leaving tomorrow." (Stanislas)

"It'll be something to read on the plane." (Armand)

15

May 1, 1974

Dear Olga,

I like to think of you in Peking on the 1st of May, when everyone here is beginning to get bored, though I know you're not really a "political woman." Nor am I, but I let myself be carried along by the waves, and when they ebb away I feel like a little fish, not even a goldfish,* just a sad little gray fish thrown up on the sand. You'll be looking at processions and shows that are probably too noisy, too colorful, too artificial, but have a good look just the same, because happiness (what does it matter if it *is* artificial?) is becoming so rare. I really envy you, being able to share in the people's hope, even if it's doomed not to be fulfilled. Whatever happens, they will take over our destiny: I rather wickedly imagine the not far distant day when Chartres will be a town belonging to the continent of Eurasia, and busloads of little Chinese will come to attend courses on democracy in the place de la Bastille. Make notes of your conversations with the women: when

* In French a goldfish is a *poisson rouge*, or red fish, which allows the author a little joke here that is lost in translation. *Tr.*

you get back everyone will want news of the feminist movement that Mao launched against the Party bureaucracy after the Cultural Revolution. All the more so because, as you know, and whatever you may think about it, the feminist groups are all that survive of Paris '68. Take notes too on the excavations—Chinese archaeology has still hardly got started. You ought to drop literature and concentrate on sinology! If I knew the language I wouldn't hesitate.

As for me, I expect you've guessed I'm not sure I'll be going on with my work on Wadani women. Perhaps I've been infected by Martin's skepticism. I don't know. You probably noticed he gave up ethnology some years ago, and hasn't done anything but paint ever since. I feel tired and at loose ends; I don't know what I'm waiting for. Today I'm alone in the rue Saint-André-des-Arts; I don't even know if there's a demo on; everyone's getting worked up about the presidential election campaign! Imagine! And Martin's not here. I've seen to my plants in the patio, but I don't know how it is—I don't see them anymore. I'm in a daze. My eyes, my lips, my nose, my fingers—they're all without feeling. It's as if I were somewhere else. But where?

I think of China as a country of yellow clay, sometimes quite flat and sometimes ridged, sloping, cracked all over with drought or washed away by heavy brown rain. Where do I get all that from? A sort of desert, heroic Fiesole.

Do you remember my grandparents' huge house in the hills around Florence, where we stayed together last year?

I spent eighteen years in that green sea. One can't imagine anywhere more fresh, more civilized, and I'm afraid that for me the whole world will always be reduced to that. That family stopping-off point. When I shut my eyes I can only imagine Fiesoles everywhere, even in China (though it's yellower there). Reality escapes me. I say, "I'm afraid," and I'm afraid of my fear. It's as if I were still tied to my grandmother's energetic care, her despotic love. Her name was Rosalba Benedetti; as I told you, she died just before we went there. You only met my grandfather Guido—white as a distinguished ghost, you said—in his black suit in the middle of summer. He was the terrifying image of my father.

The garden used to be full of lilac, and I would stand among scented bunches of blossom so thick they lulled me to sleep, imagining I'd become invisible. And so I had. "Carolina-a-a? . . . Where's my Carole? . . . Has anyone seen my Carolina?" Rosalba searched through the bushes, unable to find or pretending not to see me, and I curled up like a rabbit between the warm grass and the lilacs. Or was it the lavender? I don't remember. I also remember the heavy rose scents you find only in Florence, steeped in the burning but ever noble sun that warms up the sap like a skillful perfumer. Rosalba would pick huge bunches of roses, sometimes creamy white, sometimes crimson or scarlet, and we'd go and place them before the Virgin Mary. You must know about that—the magic of icons, the blissful little girl lighting her candle and waiting for the Madonna's eyelids to open and the Mother of God to look at her. But perhaps not—you've probably always been superrational.

Fiesole was always another world, light-years away from the cold cynicism of my mother and my father's vampire pallor. I remember that by the time I was about fifteen I was sure of one thing: theirs was a world I couldn't live in; I was physically incapable of standing all that noise. The roses laid before the Virgin Mary—so diaphanous, so sad, so regal too—were my resurrection. But only a temporary one. For I always aspired to lowliness. "Be careful, my dear," Rosalba would say. "You want to be a martyr, but it's really only pride." Italians act even on their deathbed. She wanted to teach me that, and to root out the self-contempt that leads to melancholy.

How lovely Assisi is! And how my childish heart was filled by the Giotto frescoes there, by the peasant grace of Christ and the Virgin. Or were the frescoes only of the school of Giotto? I forget. Anyhow, looking at them I felt as unsteady as the walls of those cubist palaces. I was rendered speechless in both Italian and French by the villagers' round faces (don't you think they look rather Chinese?), lit up by their faith. I couldn't stop crying. . . . "But how beautiful life is, my little one! Smell the roses, smell them, and see how elegant the Madonna is!" With the aid of Our Lady, Rosalba tried to draw me toward life, but I was becoming more and more of a mystic, a fervent admirer of Saint Teresa, no less. I wanted to follow Jesus in the ignominy of the Passion—wasn't I born for shame? I had even chosen a hymn that put me entirely at the Almighty's disposal. A potential Carmelite! I threw myself into it, I wept buckets—no one could be more familiar than I am with the pleasure of tears and tearful orisons. At the end of the summer my father would come and take me back to Paris and the dissolute creature who claimed to be my mother: I was inconsolable at having to leave my Fiesole heaven of frescoes and roses.

Forgive me for chattering on like this. I've strayed a long way from the 1st of May and Tiananmen Square! As I said before, I'm still being crucified at the intersection of childhood, the Madonna, Rosalba, and Giotto—and I fear I shall stay that way.

Cédric has converted to Islam, you know, and is learning Arabic so that he can read the mystics in the original. But he's still pursuing his career as a high-flyer. What energy!

I haven't gone back to the church. Not yet. But I have looked through the *Sermons* of Saint Bernard, and in them I seemed to find my Fiesole again, my Rosalba, and the delicious faintness that used to overtake me when I imagined myself suffering the Passion in my own flesh—I hadn't got an ounce of humility in my whole body! Anyhow, theology still strikes me as the only thing worth reading.

Make the most of your luck in being able to visit that other world. Does the word *believe* exist in Chinese? I suppose it does, but how do they say it, how is it written, and what exactly does it mean? Benserade said in his seminar, years ago, that ever since the dim distant past, *credo* in Sanskrit means "give one's strength," and also "give gifts or offerings" in the hope of a return. In short, "to believe" is to give credit, in both the spiritual and the economic sense. The Indo-Europeans knew a thing or two. That argument applies to everyone. At any rate, it applies to me and everyone I know in Paris. Rosalba is immortal, and so are the Fiesole roses, and Giotto's Christ and Virgin, and my own shame at being born and having this body with its need to eat and love.

Don't trouble to answer this—I know you haven't got time. But do keep your eyes open, and take notes. You can tell me everything later. I'll go on writing to you, though, because I'm bored and I miss you very much.

Much love.
Carole

May 13

I feel very low today, my dear, because Martin's back. I'm glad about that in itself, because as you know I'm very much in love with him, but he's in terribly bad shape, and it makes me desperate to think I can't do much for him.

His painting fascinates me. It's simultaneously destructive and generous, and I really do believe that kind of beauty is unique in contemporary art. He believes in it too, but not all the time. Drink acts less and less as a stimulant, and only leaves him exhausted, hopeless and helpless for days on end. He was never one to talk much, but in the last year he's become completely mute. I'm regarded as being pretty taciturn myself, so you can imagine the effort I have to make to try to put some life back in him, and if possible some hope as well. But whatever I do it's no good.

His show wasn't a success. The more intense members of the public liked it, and a few young people were enthusiastic, but the critics were very cool and often completely negative. You were getting ready to go away, so you probably didn't read the most recent articles. Martin only laughed at first. "What do you expect? These middle-class conformists don't know how to look! They haven't even got bodies, so how could they understand anything to do with action? As for vision . . . don't even speak of it—to be rejected by them is the highest possible compliment!" To start with, you see, he didn't let it get to him.

What really hurt him was being called a pale imitation of Pollock. There obviously is a connection, but in my opinion Martin is quite original.

When he came in yesterday he looked shocked, distraught. (I hadn't seen him for two weeks—he has new friends these days. . . . Unless he went back to his wife . . . but it's of no importance.)

"Read this shit!" he said.

The article he handed me suggested its author didn't much care for Martin's work: "Martin Cazenave aims at depicting the artist's struggle against nature. He makes a violent bid to give body to his painting and a new form to life. Unfortunately he loses the battle with truth. Calm down, Monsieur Cazenave, show some self-control! Do you think you're a genius? Maybe. But at best you're an incomplete one, either not up to genuine creation or way out beyond it. . . ."

"Disgusting!" I said. "Some idiot eaten up with jealousy."

"Yes, but doesn't the style remind you of someone?"

I admitted it didn't (I've copied a few sentences out for you— you're more well read than I am and have probably identified the author already.)

"People are complete ignoramuses these days! You too! Think, think!"

It was no good. I was stumped.

"I'm ashamed of you!" (Martin was starting to shout.) "Don't you see the bastard's plagiarizing Zola?—the passage in *The Work of Art* where he attacks Cézanne as a failure under the name of Claude Lantier! Haven't you read it? And do you know the fate he metes out to his friend—because Zola and Cézanne *were* friends, believe it or not! Well, he has him commit suicide because he can't carry out a great project."

My heart missed a beat at the word *suicide*, but I tried not to show it.

"I see," I said. "The only thing to do is take no notice."

"Take no notice, take no notice! Is that all you can say? Have you got the faintest idea what a picture is—do you know what it is we're talking about? Does the name Cézanne mean anything to you? Or Zola? Oh, forget it! You'd all like to see the back of me—yes, you too! *I'm* the one who's a Taoist now—yes, write and tell Olga that!—me and no one else! The trouble is, nobody can see it, neither the papers nor of course you. . . . Oh well, it's only natural—a Taoist's bound to be doomed in a show-biz society!"

And he flung out, slamming the door. I couldn't even cry. He came back last night, but I'm afraid for him. For his life. He wants to come to London with me. Says he can't be without me. I think he was stoned, and I think Marie-Paule's opening a new gallery in London. He made love to me passionately, but it wasn't really him, it was less him than ever. I felt terrible this morning; I've been trying to write to you since midday. I try to piece it all together for you, so that you can be a kind of witness.

Have a good time and think of me.

All my love.

Carole

P.S. I got your card of the Summer Palace. It's super. Thank Hervé for his greeting. Love to you both.

The Russell Hotel
Russell Square
London WC1

June 5

Dear Olga,

You didn't miss much by skipping the conference. It was rather dull and very technical. Gildas's pupils impressed one another with tedious mathematical formulas. A female logician from Poland flaunting a big gold cross went to great lengths to show that the Carnap tradition is still alive and well in Warsaw. Roberto and some other Italians you don't know tried to make her laugh by asking if the Pope was in favor of classical Aristotelian logic or a logic of n values—but she thought this very vulgar. Benserade, who always behaves himself, was as bored as a schoolboy in an algebra lesson, but surreptitiously read Artaud's *Letters from Rodez* while the others were droning out their papers. Then during the coffee break he said to me, "There are two great French linguists, Mademoiselle Benedetti." And while I was racking my brain to think how he could have found two (an astronomical number for that subject!), he went on: "I'm thinking of Mallarmé and Artaud, of course. You can write that from me to your friend Olga, and tell her we miss her very much." So there you are.

So much for the pleasantries. Now I turn to the psychodrama. I'm sorry to bother you again with my troubles, but you really are the only person I can share them with.

I was with Ilya Romanski in Trafalgar Square—we'd just come out of the Museum and were standing there with pigeons on our shoulders like a couple of harmless tourists. No photographers though. Just a moment of relaxation after we'd missed a session at the conference. Then all of a sudden Martin appeared, completely crazy, and started to yell and shove me around. He called me everything he could think of: I was a slut; I slept with Romanski and all the rest of the people at the conference; the Russell Hotel, where we were all staying, was a brothel, I'd gone mad, become a nymphomaniac, I ought to consult Lauzun; no, Lauzun was too distinguished for me, Joëlle Cabarus would do. . . . And so on. It was frightful. He wasn't on his own. There was another chap with him, a sort of English hippy wearing Indian clothes and lots of makeup—I don't know if Marie-Paule was around too. I couldn't speak. Romanski was taken aback.

"Do you know this man, Mademoiselle Benedetti?"

"He's the man I live with."

"Both of them?"

Between St. Petersburg and Boston, Ilya has seen everything, but he was so stunned he was trying to appear modern.

"No. But the one I do live with is very complex."

"I can well believe it. He must love you very much to be so jealous."

"Do you think so? I'll try to remember that and forget all the rest."

The hippy dragged Martin away. I can still see him now, his face all drawn and white as a sheet. I was filled with a new kind of disgust that was both welcome and unwelcome. I admit jealousy may be very violent, and I'm not entirely against that. But my main feeling is exhaustion. A love that humiliates is death. Passion like that may have a certain attraction, but the scene I'd just gone through had been a turning point for me. The core of the plant has been frozen, and soon there'll be no plant left, only a heap of frost. I'm completely numb. A black hole. I don't even feel any pain— pain is a sign of life. This must be what they call a breakdown.

Do you know Rothko's pictures? Cubes full of blood or wine, gradually decanted so that the red is brightened and purified. But finally there's no blood left. Nothing but black cubes. The blacks can be incredibly different, but the alchemist's mortar will produce no more transmutations. Rothko died in that black rainbow.

All this will be a change for you after your Temples of Buddhist Peace, not to mention the tractor drivers, the crèches, the production records broken through the enthusiasm of the workers, and the thousand and one campaigns for a better future. I'm counting on you.

Love
Carole

Paris, June 15

How stupid my wretched affairs must seem, Olga, seen from Peking! I feel quite embarrassed, boring you to death with my novelettish doings when you have so many new things to explore. But don't imagine I don't think about you—you personally. I often wonder how you'd have reacted in a situation like mine. But probably you wouldn't have needed to react, because you'd never have got yourself into such a mess. I know Hervé isn't easy—he's so elusive and unpredictable. In short, incomprehensible as far as I'm concerned. But despite his hedonistic airs I'm sure he never takes his eye off his goal, and is always ready to advance on it. And that must make life clear and, paradoxically enough, restful. Whereas Martin's always changing and imploding. But the main thing is that I'm not you. You can be strong. Whereas I'm always despising and humiliating myself; I lack the equilibrium that's probably a rudimentary form of modesty; I meet despair halfway. But what can I do? I made a mess of being born.

My mother, the soul of tactlessness, heaps falsely maternal and genuinely vulgar solicitude on me. "I can tell you're upset, Caroline darling. Men are the end, I agree, but no man at all is hell, don't forget. I hand that truth down to you as a family heirloom! Am I wrong in thinking I haven't seen much of Martin lately?"

Frank asks to be remembered to you. We had a drink together. As you know, he's finished his analysis with Cabarus; and now he's seeing patients under "supervision," preparatory to becoming a psychoanalyst himself. He used to be Martin's best friend, but they've hardly seen each other for a year or so. I tried to tell him, discreetly, how worried I was. And then he made some revelations to me. It appears Martin spends a lot of time with Scherner's friends— we used to campaign for prison reform with Scherner, you may remember. They're a special kind of friend: very "hard," and they go in for the cult of the body, leather trousers and jackets, chains, bondage, S.M., and so on. Martin's supposed to be going to California with them, Frank didn't know when—after the summer vacation perhaps. Old Mother Longueville went to see Scherner of course and threw a fit. Frank could just see him carving the poor woman up with his sarcasms. "I'm telling you all this," he said, "because you're an intelligent woman, and free, and strong." In a way. But I feel anaesthetized. Boxers must feel like this before they keel over.

I should have had that child. It might have calmed Martin down. But Frank's not sure it would have made any difference. He thinks Martin's narcissism is too weak, and that he doesn't know his own desire (Frank's already adopted the professional jargon, you see). He ought to have been analyzed, and because he hasn't he'll always be tossed from one passion to another, one death to another. And so on. I pointed out that Martin had become a very good painter. Frank thinks that's just a good "happening," an expensive and suicidal indulgence, but that Martin hasn't got what it takes for sustained creation—self-discipline and the ability to make use of tradition and the work of other people. By this time I'd stopped listening. I don't think anything myself. I'm empty. A plant killed off by the frost.

What am I to believe? Martin is running about heaven knows where, and because he's going away from me I tend to think he's heading for death. But I'm sure he'll always come back to me every so often, to be with me on the mattress in the loft. Even so, I sometimes find myself thinking, "Martin is dead." No more Rosalba, no more Martin, no more Fiesole. I can no longer dispose of myself, and no one will do it for me.

I ought not to post these letters of mine really. You must think, "What a regression, what a psychological mess!" Anyway, I hope you haven't had time to read all the details, and that I haven't taken up time that ought to have been spent satisfying the lively curiosity I so much admire, or making the observations I look forward so eagerly to hearing about. I shan't write any more after this, as I expect to see you two weeks from now.

Much love.
Carole

Peking, July 1, 1974

My dear Carole,

I'll be seeing you before you get these cards, for we're just about to fly off. But I absolutely must tell you one thing: the imaginings that come from too much self-love cause a lot of unnecessary trouble.

"To believe" is *xinfu* in spoken Chinese; in written form: 信月殳. It is made up of "a man of his word" and "to marry" (or "to abandon oneself to"). No giving is involved, only a linking to the word. Begin rather by creating an empty space: *qixu* or 気虚, and don't forget that emptiness isn't nothing—it's a tiger on a mound, the breath of the *yang* ready to leap on the *yin*.

Look for that primitive emptiness inside yourself; we'll try to find it together.

I'll phone as soon as I get in. I think of you all the time.

Love*
Olga

* In English in the original. *Tr.*

IV. *Algonquin*

16

*I*t can happen when you're in a state either of great concentration or of complete abstraction (and you don't need to go to China for it): you suddenly have a fleeting but indestructible conviction that the people around you, including those you thought you loved, belong to another species.

One faintly painful part of the character known as Olga—a part as diaphanous and dim as a misty sunrise over shifting marshes—was still attached to a vision she'd had in the village square in Huxian, where a crowd of prehistoric peasants watched a group of extra-terrestrial scarecrows. As she confronted a loneliness at once imposed and chosen, an amber-colored wave had frozen and clung to her, and she felt moved to reject every contact and bond she had ever had in the past or might have in the future.

Martinis and champagne can transform the vision of your own irreducible strangeness into a confused and universal truth, which then pervades all human bodies but effaces any proclivity they may have toward drama or tragedy, mixing them all up in a flippant sense of impossibility. When you reach this point (and some get there easily, others with difficulty), you have a choice:

Either you retreat into a solitary and cynical contemplation of the world in which you yourself are a pleasing character, able, with the help of champagne, martinis, or the like, to whip your own bitterness into ironic sympathy.

Or you go on journeying toward other Huxians, to show all the extraterrestrials around you what you already know and they seem not to: that like Huxian the whole world is made up of unfathomable solitudes.

Olga chose the second alternative, for she had a tendency (as you must have noticed) to organize her life in the pattern of a star. Battalions of brave little soldiers set out from a certain point and made for the Atlantic and beyond; they walked, ran, paced, learned, confronted one another, never suffered, suffered from everything, sparkled, rose or fell, but never withdrew. They were champagnized, or under the warm influence of martinis, or of the laser mood of gin; of Hegel's bayonet, Freud's computer, or Joyce's software. And because of these attacks in all directions, the point of departure fanned out in clouds of light that didn't weigh things down but rather relieved and lightened them, breaking up anxious time into soothing space.

The advantage of a life (or a story) in the shape of a star—in which things may move without necessarily intersecting and advance without necessarily meeting, and where every day (or chapter) is a different world pretending to forget the one before—is that it corresponds to what seems to be an essential tendency in the world itself: its tendency to expand, to dilate. The big bang, which has made us as we are and will destroy us in order to write a new chapter, remembering very little of *our* own, is never seen more clearly than in the countless rays spreading outward in a biography full of new departures. The same movement is reflected in a story that keeps making new starts, leaving the reader half disappointed, half eager: he may never find what he's looking for, but as long as progress is being made . . .

So the life of Olga and her friends can only be recounted in a novel shaped like a star; too bad about the people who prefer the wheel to come full circle. Escape is the strong point of the weak: so long as fear doesn't actually paralyze itself, it wins the relay race and starts off all over again. And the rest of us are impressed by the intrepid winners shooting out to the four corners of the world—for which of us has not known fear?

So for now the Huxian effect reigned supreme, and her third dry martini only expanded still further the sense the Squirrel with a Chinese face had of a void growing up between her and the other guests, looking at the pictures in the Sylvers' drawing rooms overlooking the East River.

All she saw were the two big gray eyes that dominated the man's whole face and even his body. He was dressed with quiet, rather British elegance in classic tweeds. The general effect—reinforced by the gray light of one of those summer storms that never burst, lending the late August heat an air of mystery—was that life is extremely complicated, but that one must go through with it anyway. Also that though the man in question was very fashionable as well as very handsome, all this was of no consequence.

The most beautiful eyes in the world, thought Olga, now, as the reader will recall, on her third dry martini. They were moist eyes, reserved, mocking, and absolutely clear. They seemed to reflect acquaintance with another world, proud disillusion, the humor of sea captains who've known shipwreck but will never talk about it. Who was he? A Protestant minister fallen among intellectuals? Or an English reincarnation of Emma Bovary, whom God had taken every opportunity to thwart and injure, but who in spite of a ruined and frustrated life bore herself like a great lady?

"Olga, I'd like to introduce Edward Dalloway. Ed, this is Olga de Montlaur."

Either out of modesty or as a sort of challenge, Olga preferred to drop the "de" and be called Olga Montlaur. But Diana liked to restore the particle of her friend's married name, as if it would remind her other guests of the distinction, and above all the contemporary relevance, of her own alleged researches on the troubadours—labors as mysterious as they were said to be unremitting.

"Dalloway? Haven't I heard. . . ?"

"I expect I know what you mean. Sorry, no connection. I was born in Boston."

Diana liked to invite "unusual and varied" people to her house, elegantly situated on the Upper East Side: it diluted the stress of New York life with a little dash of Europe. A wealthy heiress who owned an unknown number of oil wells in Texas, she had studied French at Harvard and become one of the world's top experts on the literature of courtly love. Guillaume of Aquitaine, Jauffré Rudel, and Bernard de Ventadour held no secrets for her, though her favorite was the more hermetic Arnauld de Ribérac, poet of the *trobar clus*. She was familiar with all the manuscripts: who'd have thought Texas oil would generate a bookworm? She'd worked in all the libraries: the Bibliothèque Nationale in Paris, the British Museum in London, the Bodleian at Oxford, the Biblioteca Vaticana in Rome, San Marco in Venice, the archives in Vienna, Brussels, Leningrad, Chartres, Chantilly, Copenhagen, Berne, Amsterdam, Florence, Geneva, Rouen, Tours, Turenne . . . that will do for the moment. She deciphered the songs, reconstructed the dances, and in obedience to the spirit of the age—the present age—rehabilitated the rare female troubadours. Everyone has heard of the comtesse de Die; but what about Mesdames Tibors, Almucs de Castelnau, Iseu de Capio, Maria de Ventadora, Azalais de Porcairages, Bieris de Romans, and Guillema de Rosers? Do you know anything about *them?* Diana did!

As a well-known academic, Diana had met Olga on her first visit to New York a few years before, when she got back from China. They'd soon struck up one those intellectual friendships, punctuated with professional encounters, which are really kept going by the secret complicity that exists between women who enjoy making the effort to think. In spite of Arnauld de Ribérac, Diana had been loyal to her family's Texas pragmatism and married Hugh Sylvers, "our left-wing millionaire," as her university colleagues called him. He had investments everywhere:

in electronics, real estate, automobiles, television companies, and so on. He was also a "big boss" in IBM, while at the same time, as a self-taught man who wanted to live up to and even impress his wife, he attended lectures on Heidegger at the university.

"With all that wealth Diana ought to be satisfied with running a literary salon, and leave her job as a prof free for someone who needs it. Don't you think so, Olga?"

She'd been asked her opinion on that as soon as she arrived in New York.

"We're appointed because of our work, not our bank balance," said Olga. "I'd rather talk about Diana's research."

The matter was closed and their friendship sealed.

But today, this evening, no one felt like gossiping, nor had such blasé guests any time to spare for the superb view over the East River. They went on debating the merits of the De Koonings, the Braques, and even the few Picassos on the walls of the vast salon. Have you ever noticed how art makes people refine their ideas and elevate their feelings? So as to try to approach—from a great distance, of course—the supreme sensibility that is so far beyond us that, if we lack the courage to join in its mirth, it might crush us completely and reduce us to heaps of exhausted rubble, like visitors to major exhibitions.

The Sylvers had been following the art market for years ("We bought De Kooning when very few people were interested: we couldn't begin to afford him now"), and were regarded as outstanding patrons of contemporary German painting ("Look at this little Kripke—those blacks and those bits of straw are bringing about a reevaluation of German philosophy, not to mention the Holocaust"). Once you start talking about art you soon get on to ideas. And money.

"Do you know why the art market is taking off like this?" said Hugh. "It's quite simple: our contemporaries haven't got time to dream, so they buy other people's dreams instead. 'What about TV?' you ask. Yes, but that's as fleeting as water—the images disappear, and no one's got time to look at them again on video. But a picture fixes something permanently. Painting dreams and fixes the dream permanently. Don't you agree, Olga? . . . I'm so glad to see you back—tell me more about China!"

Hugh was eager to hear not only about Olga's trip, but also about books on the subject of China.

"It so happens I'm trying to do business with the Chinese for IBM. It's not easy with all these political ups and downs—Mao's death, the arrest of Jiang Qing. But that's obviously where the future of the market lies. We're planning a trip there, Diana and I. I'm preparing the ground, and as soon as the deal's ready we're off!"

Olga wasn't sure Hugh was talking about the same China as the one she inhabited. The Huxian syndrome was threatening to reappear. . . . But keep calm. . . . After all, the spin-off from feeling that we're all extraterrestrials to one another is comic boredom that's quite relaxing. Then there was the soporific effect of the temperature (eighty-six degrees). And of the gin. It was like being in a swimming pool full of warm water.

"I'm sure Hervé's fine—I don't even ask. He was born to be on top of the world," said Diana, smiling; polite but critical too. She regarded Sinteuil as an irritating example of the recurrent reincarnations through the ages of Arnauld de Ribérac. "He's so French, such a dandy—I'm talking of course of the mystical dandyism that runs from the cultivated elite of the seventeenth century down to Baudelaire. It's easy enough to concentrate on Sinteuil in a library, but in real life it's a different matter! I don't know how you do it. . . . I need to be made a great fuss of, myself. . . ."

Now that she felt so well understood, so surrounded by kindness, Olga withdrew into the strongest part of herself and closed her space suit against the tactlessness of "real friends." That was her own special technique, and now the Huxian syndrome was no longer a threat. It was actually there in that salon overlooking the East River.

As she had expected, Diana put her between Hugh and Edward Dalloway at dinner. Ed was rather quiet, keeping a correct and ironic distance.

"Is this your first visit to New York?"

"I've been here before for some lectures. I even spent a semester at the American Research Center last year. This time I've got a year's contract."

"Do you teach? That makes us colleagues."

" . . . ?"

"Edward's an international lawyer," Diana explained. "He works in Washington, but he often comes to New York for the United Nations. And he's still got a job in the law department at that American Research Center of yours."

"I spent fifteen years giving lectures and writing books before I realized I was on the wrong track. But I can't really drop it altogether, because meanwhile I got too well known and my colleagues made me visiting professor."

"What of?"

"Government. . . . I know that sounds odd. I suppose in France it might be called political science or political history. But really I just teach what interests me. What about you?"

"I do the same."

"And what does interest you?"

"At the moment, Céline."

"No!"

"Yes. Don't tell me you know him?"

"I've made up my mind to surprise you."

"I'd like that very much."

The clergyman with contemplative eyes was certainly a Bovary with spirit.

Before dinner Diana had told Olga she'd known the Dalloways since they were all students at Harvard. Rosalind, Edward's wife, was a good friend of hers in those days, but since Rosalind left ("a crazy business—I'll tell you about it later on, if you like"), Edward ("after having all the girls in the law school, not to mention those I don't know about—men have a funny way of mourning the love of their life") had been living alone and dividing his time between Washington and New York.

" 'Women's whole nobility is in their legs . . . Beautiful, lovely Molly, if she can still read what I'm saying wherever she is, I want her to know my feelings for her haven't changed, that I love her still and forever, in my own way, and that she can come here whenever she likes, to share my bread and my secret destiny . . .' "

He recited the passage with feeling, an initial touch of irony suddenly vanishing to leave a sincerity unalloyed. He spoke

French with a Boston accent, pitching Céline's melancholy monologue gracefully, somewhere between laughter and tears.

" 'If she isn't beautiful anymore, never mind, we'll manage! I've kept so much of her beauty inside me, and so warm, that there's enough for both of us for at least another twenty years, long enough to outlast us . . .' "

What a very strange fellow, the Reverend Mr. Bovary! Don't say he'd learned the whole of the *Journey to the End of Night* by heart just for this dinner party!

"Would you like some more? Listen: 'I am the damned soul of literature, I am the organ of the Universe. I am composing the Opera of the Deluge. The aural gates of Hell . . .' "

"Do you like it?"

Olga didn't know what else to say. She must keep calm! She was stunned. Dry martinis, wine, Céline . . .

"That's putting it mildly," said Dalloway. "Has anyone written better about the Second World War?"

"No. I agree. Still, isn't it rather surprising to hear that from the lips of a professor of government?"

"The paths that lead to the State Department sometimes pass understanding."

"Did you know that Ed's brother, John Dalloway, is the most left-wing Democrat you can imagine?"

(Hugh always had an explanation for the inexplicable.)

"I can't imagine it." (Olga being coquettish!) "Tell me more about those paths that pass understanding."

"Charles Street, Boston, a big Victorian house by the harbor, the view over the water, wooden steeples in the distance, solitary masts, factory chimneys. And of course I mustn't forget Swiss governesses, French lessons, lawns, gravel paths, the hooves of galloping ponies, drawing rooms crammed with knickknacks and books. A proud family that expected its good works to be noticed and acknowledged in the proper manner—with a tug of the forelock! Typical Bostonians, in short! A little boy who read *Uncle Tom's Cabin* for the twentieth time hoping that the next time the old Negro wouldn't be beaten to death by horrible Simon Legree. And who reread Jack London's *Call of the Wild* for the twenty-first time, imagining Buck wasn't a dog but for a poor little rich boy who if he found himself in the Frozen North would first turn into a husky, and then join his wild brothers as a real wolf."

Dalloway recounted this upper-class comic strip in a barely audible baritone that tried to sound caustically neutral. But can a baritone voice sound neutral and caustic? Strange, emotional, attractive—yes. The inexpressiveness of the voice couldn't disguise the charm, the appeal, of a lonely person who knows it's no use sending out signals to others but can't help doing so. There wasn't any actual warmth, but there was a subdued sweetness that enveloped the other person and asked for a matching reserve. He'd obviously made up this tale of black slaves and wolf-hounds especially for Olga's benefit, to mock what he imagined to be her literary imagination.

"Very charming. But perhaps rather a short path to lead to the upper reaches of politics."

"I haven't finished yet. Next come Harvard, Brandeis, trips to New York, friends in the Village, Bleecker Street, the San Remo, the beats. Do you know them—the elder brothers of May '68?"

"I lived on Bleecker Street last year. But '68 was different from the beat generation: more ludic, with free thinking instead of resentment, and plans for the future in spite of some damaged bodies. Very French, I think."

"I expect you're right—you're younger than I am and you were closer to it." (How old was he? Forty-five, fifty? Perhaps he was past tennis tournaments. . . . Although . . . Anyway, he was still a long way away from being reduced to golf.) "But I think there was a kind of continuity there. Do you know *Huckleberry Fin?* Everyone quotes it nostalgically nowadays. At the end of the book he leaves the town to 'light out for the territory.' He thinks there's another territory. And so do I, when I'm being a professor of government, which strikes you as so amusing. . . . But since the beats, and perhaps since May '68, the Territory doesn't exist anymore. Unless it's inside ourselves."

"A journey to the end of night . . ."

"Exactly. There were precursors."

"So we're back to Céline. You've led me to the heart of your paradox, but you haven't explained it."

"I should think not! What would be left of me if I did? May I drive you home?"

Again that voice which aimed at indifference but was so caressing. Could a modern man be a romantic character? Logically, no. Especially not a professor of government. But there was something indefinable about Ed Dalloway.

"With pleasure. But I live on Morningside Drive. Isn't that rather far?"

The metaphysical gray twinkled.

"Take care," said Diana, smiling.

"Don't forget we're lunching together on Thursday!"

(Francine O'Brian was doing her best to make Olga feel at home.)

"I hadn't forgotten."

Outside, the night sky was high and alive.

"We could drive through the Village and have one for the road, couldn't we?

Mocking but not unduly so. Nice.

"So we could."

" 'Follow your desire'—do what you want to do—it's the only way. 'Follow your desire,' " Hervé had told her on the eve of her departure. "But I think a year's too long to be away, myself. You were in New York for a couple of months last year, and you often go there for conferences. But a whole year . . . I shall miss you too much, even if you come back for the vacations. I'll be lonely, and so will you, you wait and see! And Carole will probably get on even worse without you. No, I shan't forget about her, I'll get in touch when I think of it. . . . But there's nothing for me to do in New York at the moment: no work, no conspiracy, no translation. Next year perhaps. . . . Oh well, do what you want, follow your desire. . . ."

Naturally, Sinteuil maintained that men and women were different: "A man can easily do things a woman can't do at all. And vice versa, if you like." He firmly believed a woman's desire was nothing like that of a man. No danger! But she must let herself go; take advantage of any interest, admiration even, on the part of the male students; rest; follow her desire.

Olga liked the campus on the other side of town, full of imposing buildings, with squirrels on the grass and students who really seemed to think. That's to say they asked a lot of naive questions.

"In France they don't condescend to ask questions," Olga had said. "The only way you can measure how far you've interested your audience is by how aggressive they are. If they attack you it's proof you haven't bored them. Instead of asking questions after a lecture they're more likely to tell you how you could have done it better. But American students can reduce the most abstract discussion to the level of their own experience, and it always ends up with discussions about happiness and unhappiness. Personally I find they bring me down to earth, and I find them very engaging."

"So much the better, my dear—go to it! They think you're the quintessence of France, so go to it! But be careful not to disillusion them!" (Hervé)

"Not the quintessence of France. Of Paris." (Olga)

"So much the better. Follow your desire. . . ." (Hervé)

It had all started with the symposium on "Literature and Evil." Symposia in French châteaus have a great appeal for Americans, and the Château de Marigny had everything going for it, quite apart from the whiff of brimstone emanating from the theme of the debates (organized by *Now*). Professor Peter O'Brian had been very impressed: Olga's treatment of Bataille and Céline seemed to him to strike just the right note between subversion and reason, and he lost no time in inviting her to lecture at the famous American Center—next fall, as often as she could, whatever she could manage. Hervé was both flattered and irritated by all this eagerness, but after all, wasn't Olga our ambassador, our foreign minister? Of course these heavy, slow Americans needed someone from Eastern Europe to spoon-feed them what remained of European culture. What remained, that is, in terms of American taste, which hankered chiefly after the shadow of philosophy—by definition a German discipline. On this subject, Olga and a few others could not be bettered. As for the refinement of French culture, that obviously was and would always remain a closed book to these Algonquins crossed with Protestants. *"Follow your desire!"*

Edward Dalloway's Opel drove along Bleecker Street, then he did his duty as a guide, listing the Figaro, the San Remo, the Kettle of Fish, Minetta's, the Rienzi, the Open Door a bit farther away, even the Waldorf Cafeteria.

"We'll have a drink here on the corner of MacDougal, at the Figaro—it doesn't seem as noisy as the others this evening. But the real Figaro used to be a few doors away from the San Remo, on Bleecker Street."

Edward had first come there in his twenties, fresh from his native straitlaced Boston. Kerouac, Ginsberg, Burroughs, and of course Dylan Thomas then reigned at the Remo and elsewhere. It was said that since the Holocaust no one dared pose as a victim. Everything and everyone was for Success! Achievement was our god! And then all of a sudden these people showed that failure existed and one had a right to fail if one wanted to. A Revolution! But without a Cause.

In due course Ginsberg and Burroughs made it to Saint-Germain and even Meudon. They saw the awfulness of suburban Paris, rather like the outskirts of Los Angeles. They heard big dogs barking. That must be Céline. The poor old quack was very glad to see them: by then no one would have anything to do with him. "Some coffee?" His wife the dancer. His dark suit, his wraps, his scarves, and all the time the howling of the dogs. They'd brought him *Howl* and *Junky*, and other poems popular in Bleecker Street. He hadn't got time for them. What was the point? Who were the present luminaries of French literature? "Fish in a pool." "It's nothing, nothing," he growled. He was still obsessed by the Jews: the dogs were to protect him from them.

. . . Céline's rhetoric, his sentences . . . The recent translation of *Guignol's Band!* The beats were dazzled. As they were by Genet, and also by Henry Miller, Blake, Walt Whitman . . . They kept repeating to anyone who'd listen, "Such Spenglerian melancholy!" "the way those three dots facilitate transition and contrast!" his "oral language"; "his diatribes against the folly of society obviously apply to the United States."

And so, in 1958, when Ginsberg and Burroughs returned from Europe, the Remo discovered Céline . . . the prewar American translation of the *Journey to the End of Night*, before falling in love with the original.

"But I'd rather that journey remained in the night. The night of dreams or the night of books—they're not all that different. I didn't care for the 'underground' style: gunshots and knives, playing at William Tell and shooting one's wife in the head, or being a samurai and merely stabbing her. I was too well brought up for all that, probably too repressed, too puritanical. If you're not Céline, how are you supposed to face up to barbarism?—the barbarism inside us of course, since we've got the beats' message. I had no hesitation: the law was the answer. Especially international law. Everyone can see that the streets of New York are full of horrors—it's impossible *not* to see it. You don't need to go to Harlem, it hits you in the eye a couple of blocks from Diana's place. But horror prevails in the Third World too, in the 'civilized' world's absurd relations with it; in underdevelopment, famine, fanaticism. And let me tell you, we haven't seen anything yet. The real horror is still to come. . . . Excuse the long speech. . . . I felt I owed it to you."

The mocking gray was metaphysical again. Better still, it was intimate, detached from the official words. Naked, thought Olga.

"Why should you owe me anything? You've talked quite a lot. You've been very cautious, but I have enough material to make you out. . . ."

"I already knew you—from a distance, of course. I read *Now* sometimes. A very 'snob' thing to do, as you know, but inevitable if one's interested in what goes on in people's heads in Paris nowadays. . . . But *I'm* a stranger to *you.* . . . Another martini?"

"No thanks. . . . No more now. Less would be better. . . ."

"Don't worry—I don't understand everything you write, and I don't really agree with what I do understand. You split hairs, you chase after mirages. I'm very down to earth myself. I try to find practical solutions. Though often that's just as impossible a task. . . . But still, it's very interesting. . . ."

"What is?"

"You, to start with."

She put her head on his shoulder and let herself be kissed. A man who says he's down to earth and finds practical solutions, but doesn't look like that at all, not in the least, with his distant eyes and sure lips. . . . You do so long to let yourself be taken care of, stop thinking, leave someone else in charge of everything, including you. The whole load of bitterness, tenderness, carelessness—all locked away. The whole unimaginable burden a little girl can amass when she acts the intellectual but still wants to remain a little girl. . . . So she kisses someone else and leaves them to find the practical solutions. . . .

"Here we are. You're home."

"Good night."

"May I call for you on Saturday and take you to dinner?"

She kissed him again. The fresh taste of cigar in his mouth, his strong fingers in her hair—why was it so difficult to part from him?

French people who stayed at the Algonquin Hotel tended to be of the arty kind, looking for real Indians or hankering after the witty New Yorkers of the twenties. Unfortunately the Round Table, the Vicious Circle, and the Thanatopsis Club were all things of the past. And the witticisms (not all that clever) of the famous pre-Depression literati had been replaced by the labored distinction of businessmen from the World Trade Center, and the pretentiousness of intellectuals who would rather be loyal to yesterday's fashion than be seen reading today's *Village Voice*. It wasn't lost on Edward Dalloway—the dubious mixture now lording it shamefully within the Algonquin's honored portals. But he still liked the place. To begin with, no one could deny it was centrally placed there on Forty-fourth Street between Fifth and Sixth avenues—visitors to New York had easy access to both up- and downtown. Nor did Ed dislike the oak paneling, the pink drawing room, the greenish light, the apartments furnished in old-fashioned English style. The Algonquin was a touch of old Boston amid the noise and dirt of New York, a haven of peace amid the motley and violent crowd: it was restful, capable of evoking latent longings without stirring them up unduly. This equilibrium was essential to a loner like him, who didn't deny himself the good things of life but was increasingly conscious of the satisfactions of meditation and work well done. This had been especially true after Rosalind left, when Edward felt physically a young man again, the young man who had painted the Village red in Dylan Thomas's day. But times had changed since then. Edward had vaguely liked the guitars of Cambridge, Joan Baez, Bob Dylan, white rock. But now the punks and the Mud Club were all the rage, and this he couldn't take. Fortunately his women students kept up with it without getting too involved, and he kept up with them in the same manner. Of course, sex, though deep, can give a merely surface satisfaction. But Dalloway's natural distance from himself and other people was making his habitual expression more ironical and aloof.

And now here was Olga. He had indeed said too much the other evening, though it had been an artificial confession, more like an additional disguise. But he'd wanted to make her like him, to undermine a little her Parisian bluestocking's self-assurance. Perhaps too he'd felt a need to open up the Dalloway secret chamber, the inner self that lay behind the facade of the cynical man-about-town, to the wondering little girl whom Madame Montlaur couldn't entirely conceal. Anyhow, he didn't need any more conversations. He'd detected the wordless trust of that body fleeing the storm and taking refuge in a deserted hayloft. The real Edward Dalloway was a boy who lived on a level deeper than words. Strange, that, when he spent most of his time arguing, pleading a case, proving. But behind the speaker there was a another, a false self, an "as-if" personality, as Rosalind had called it. She was probably right. And the underground Dalloway had been waiting for an underground message to summon him forth alive. The message had just come: Olga. And Dalloway was revealing himself. To sum it up, on the one side there was his head (the professor of government, the Third World mediator, and so on), and on the other side there was his sex and its demands (as the priestesses of fellatio at the law school knew). And between the two, perhaps overlapping on both sides, was the deserted hayloft, perhaps not as old as all that after all, full of warm grass and waiting for the visitor.

It hadn't been a bad idea, dinner at his hotel. Olga was outflanked by Dalloway's metmorphoses. The Reverend Mr. Bovary had revealed himself as an ex-beatnik transformed into a legal conscience. She'd been dreading a lecture on the history of the "underground," followed by a sermon on the Third World: instead he was easy, attentive, friendly, almost familiar. The tenderness of the other night seemed to be an accepted thing, intermingled with their comments on the events of the day, the Pomerol they were drinking, the light at East Hampton, the casual ways of the profs at the University College of New York. By way of contrast they talked of how the extreme old-fashioned strictness of the American Research Center, trying too hastily to put the revolts of '68 behind it, was causing it to lose its best staff. Before long no one would be bothering about research anymore; they'd just repeat the old courses. . . . But not while *they* were both there. . . . Both? This steak is very well cooked—

very little cooked, I mean, just how I like it. Why don't we speak English, and avoid the impossible, or rash, choice between *tu* and *vous?* Do you find the nuance erotic? But it's so difficult to understand the exact implications, after a certain point. . . . Yes, we *could* speak English, but I don't speak it as well as I do French, I don't use it so often. . . . It would be like changing my clothes. . . . Or undressing altogether. . . . Don't say I didn't warn you!

"By the way, would you say 'Beautiful, lovely Molly' again? . . . 'I've kept so much of her beauty inside me . . . there's enough for both of us . . .' Please do—I'd love to hear it again!"

"We've got plenty of time. I'll say it whenever you like. We *have* got plenty of time, haven't we?"

She was surprised she loved his body so much. He made love to her at length, patiently, all over. Her mouth, her breasts. Every millimeter of her skin. Her sex grew exhausted under his tongue, with moisture and tension. How many times did he make her come before he possessed her and was assuaged in her? Both together, one last time for tonight. For the moment. They slept awhile. But very lightly. Then found one another again. Isn't it strange? As if we'd been together always. Careful, habit kills magic. Really? I've nothing against good habits.

"I'd have liked to be your wife if I wasn't permanently someone else's."

Why had she said that? She scarcely knew him. He loved her body, she loved his. Did she feel guilty about Hervé? Was it the old, old need to feel right? Or was it just to point out the distance between them?—"Abandon hope! Thus far and no further!" Anyhow, it was uncalled for. A sign that she was completely helpless. Unconditional surrender. Poor woman. She liked it.

"Don't say anything."

She couldn't have said another word. He was still making love to her.

They stayed together till Monday.

"I have to go to Boston, and in theory I'm not expected in New York again for a fortnight. But I'll be back on Friday. Of course."

"Call me."

"I'll come to your place."

After that Edward was never out of New York for more than one or two days a week. They made love to each other, silently, with delight, devoid of memory, in the grip of pleasure. They merged together in the communion of honeymooners: admiring, weary and hollow-eyed, the same landscapes, the same pictures and statues, but seeing only their own exaltation.

"I have some work to do in Ithaca, at Cornell. Shall we both go?"

Two weeks of really living together.

Everyone tells you about the autumn leaves, the superb yellows and reds and browns. Olga looked at them without even seeing them.

Edward's arms carrying her under the powerful spray of Niagara: a terrifying deluge, but she was safe, what could happen to her? Nothing, except that she laughed at the antics of the engaged couples around them.

Then there was the American football game, where she couldn't understand a thing but enjoyed herself hugely. She enjoyed her own enjoyment so much she almost began to understand the game. Almost.

The wary smile of Vernon Witford, Edward's childhood friend: What's my chum doing with this esoteric militant? (They know everything at Cornell, and the dubious celebrity of *Now* and of Sinteuil had naturally reached them before Olga did.) But let's take a closer look. . . . Well, she's a bit better dressed than the other girls on the campus (that's not difficult!). She's clean, and natural, and best of all she talks just like everyone else—you wouldn't guess it from reading her books. Okay, she'll pass.

"Why don't you both come and stay with me for a few days?"

"No thanks—Olga likes us to be alone."

Can a woman be in love with two men at once? But who talks about love nowadays? It's stupid. But Edward talks about it. What does he want? "And what do *I* want?"

"What are we going to do when we get back?"

"You'll come and live with me."

"How long for?"

"Until you make up your mind."

"But you know already."

"I don't know anything, and neither do you."

"Even so."

"Just love me and take things as they come."

It seemed sensible. It was impossible. But inevitable. After all, she wasn't answerable to anyone. Everyone "followed their desire." But it isn't easy to be simple. You know some pleasures are not just physical. Edward's considerateness. His silences, which nipped pain in the bud. The way he applied a caress, like balm, to any word of Olga's that was slightly harsh or unnatural. The way he smiled just with his eyes when she told him how safe she felt with him, and how much pleasure he gave her. And the shadow that passed over the gray of his eyes sometimes, suggesting not even a wound, merely that something would always be impossible. But what? Did he know himself?

The Reverend Mr. Bovary turned out to be an athletic and affectionate lover. Ideal for a young woman on her travels. But she couldn't laugh at it anymore. Well, yes she did sometimes, at night, if she happened to be alone in her apartment. But that was rare. One thing was sure: she didn't want to do without Edward Dalloway now. She must get used to that. Everyone must.

New York was only an interlude: Olga's life was on the other side of the Atlantic. Exactly: this interlude was her own special thing, her secret toy. She was exploring it alone, feeling rather at a loss. But Edward was attached to this particular woman, and that was probably why *she* was attached to *him*. For years she had been constructing a character for herself, as they say. Not an image—the character really was hers: it would be impossible for her to part from it, a kind of death. And Ed had met that "character," had even loved her a little before they discovered together that there was another woman inside the one that you could see.

Perhaps that other woman only seemed so important because she was secret? What if Olga tried to define or understand her? Then the fair unknown would probably disappear like Mélusine, the mermaid wife who vanished when she was seen. Probably the harmony between them, and that harmony's shadowy pleasures, would wither into wretched insignificance if exposed to the light, like starfish in the sun. Not probably; certainly.

It had taken all Hervé's energy and nerve for them to maintain the same ardent desire for each other, exposed to the inquisitive glance of all Saint-Germain. It was from this effort, this exposure, that Olga had needed a rest. Had yearned to live a life that was hidden, invisible, ordinary. To do foolish things. To do nothing, let other people decide things. The sleepy pleasure of a pebble borne back and forth by the sea.

She saw the implications of her image. There was something maternal in the Reverend Mr. Bovary's indulgent laughter—she'd noticed it at once, and that was probably one of the things she loved him for. He gave her back the dark continent of the women back home in the East, who sacrifice themselves so generously for their children; the knowledge that happiness may be passive; dreams lost long ago together with the language of childhood. Ed was an ever-fascinating companion, interested in what was going on in the world, but also concerned about little things. "This pink scarf will go with your gray leather jacket. . . . Look at the ice cubes in your gin—they're making a rainbow! . . . I've brought you some raspberries, and the book just out on Emily Dickinson—you can tell me what you think of it when I get back from Washington tomorrow evening. . . . I'll be away less than forty-eight hours. . . ." He thought of everything. Kept her quite safe.

Maybe Diana was right. "The American climate doesn't often produce a real man these days," she said. "But when it does, he completely eclipses the famous Latin lover—who, by the way, no longer lives up to his reputation." (Diana was an expert on the subject, though since her second marriage, to Hugh, her knowledge had remained chiefly theoretical.) "And do you want to know why? It's because this rare American phenomenon conceals, within the sensual body of a lifeguard, the tiny heart of his poor depressed mother. And the result is, the pleasure of the woman he loves is his religion, and the social success of their marriage is his duty. And when you realize that these two aims taken separately, let alone together, can't possibly be achieved, you see why the American man—when there *is* one—is doomed to failure."

There was something in what the troubadour expert said.

To be fair, Diana considered the world to be inhabited by

women, children, adolescents, and a few American men. For it was American men who came closest—though very rarely—to the missing category of Men. You could put it another way. There were four kinds of men: men-women, men-children, men-adolescents, and American men.

Well, really! Ed might be a Dalloway, but he was certainly not one of those rare specimens Diana classified as American men. And there was nothing to suggest that their affair was going to end in failure, as in Diana's scenario. And whose failure, by the way? All they needed was to cultivate their affair and keep it secret. That was all. It had nothing to do with deception, guilt, and the farcical shifts of underhand adultery. . . . The sort of tricks that people regard as sophisticated but that in fact are merely equivocal, accommodating mutually exclusive opposites as easily as the binary system of a computer . . . The real secret was a kind of alchemy that allowed them to be together without hurting anyone else: the serene tact that ennobles and moderates the will to power. Secrecy gave a woman real fulfillment, whereas man spoiled secrets by trying to collect them. A woman without a secret was a night without a moon: calm, but dangerous; boring. Olga wanted neither the light of day, which creates colleagues but not lovers; nor the eventless darkness preferred by those only interested in sleep. What she wanted was the strange surprise of finding that you're a secret to yourself.

What are you when you're no longer a stranger to yourself? A sage? Not necessarily. More likely you are sick, or almost dead.

Christmas in New York is infantile and aggressive, and forces everyone in on their family. The trouble begins when you haven't got a family, or when you're torn between two or more of them. It was understood that Olga would be going back to Paris for the vacation. Ed flew off rather sadly to Jerusalem, using the break to see his children, who'd been living in Israel with their mother since their parents separated. No problem. Olga and Ed would meet again in January.

After all, her life was in Paris. Ed or no Ed, she was caught up in the events that Hervé told her about regularly over the phone. But they only really dawned on her fully when she got off the plane.

"So here you are! Don't tell me you haven't missed me, because *you're* irreplaceable!" (Hervé always told the truth, even if he told it in the form of a caricature.)

Benserade had had a stroke, as Olga already knew. It had happened in the street: he couldn't speak and had no papers on him, so they carted him around from one hospital to another for two days before he was identified. A nightmare. Now he was being properly looked after, but apparently there was no hope. He'd indicated that he'd like to have visitors. Carole had begun to list the names of the people he knew: X, Y . . . No . . . Olga Montlaur? Yes. The patient seemed excited, tried to smile.

"You must go and see him—tomorrow. Carole? Not too well, but bearing up. Martin's vanished to California with Scherner's gang."

"And how's Armand?"

Olga still liked and respected Bréhal, though they'd seen less of each other since they got back from China.

Hervé shrugged. Armand was tired: still very subtle, of course, that went without saying, but more wrapped up than ever in his own pleasures and his mother's ill health. "I've swallowed the anchor, old boy," he said, and Sinteuil didn't press him: Bréhal couldn't be called on to fight future battles. But nothing could stop them being companions in hedonism, and they still enjoyed meeting at the Rosebud to comment on each other's latest writings with a mutual admiration which if slightly overdone was still as lively as ever.

Sinteuil could transform a literary disagreement into an overall attack on society, and he could do it with or without Bréhal's help. It was the Voltaire side of him: he was prepared to echo the Callas affair—and the La Barre, Sirvin, and Lally Tollendal affairs—in aid of Sade, Ducasse, Joyce, Bataille, or some contemporary writer who was unappreciated and rejected by publishers and the press for being too "obscure" or too "obsessed with sex"—and who became uncomfortably famous as soon as Sinteuil took up with him. At first Sinteuil's friends listened to him, incredulous. Then some of them would start to repeat what he'd said. Then there'd be something about it in the papers. And then it would suddenly become the topic of the day. The media then took it up, and the "new journalists" entered the fray.

Meanwhile Sinteuil, while continuing to follow the matter out of the corner of his eye and from the tip of his pen, was really plunging into the paradise of his own writing, which was sometimes hermetic, sometimes classically clear. But whether it was lyrical, realistic, or erotic, it was always irritating and complex. Was Marxism discredited? Can God alone sanction ethics? The God of the Bible? Of course! But a living, speaking God stimulates inner experience, promotes frescoes and fugues, Venice and Bach . . . The flamboyant aspect of Christianity is erotic; Sade the atheist is the accomplice of Teresa of Avila; theology and the Inquisition are Christian; but the human comedy is a Catholic vision of the world. N.B.: reread Balzac. . . . Not for a second could you ever fall asleep over anything Sinteuil wrote; even his enemies knew they could count on the next row with him to stir intellectual life into action again.

Olga liked his rebellious spirit, recoiled from the controversy that often surrounded him, mistrusted his acts of provocation, laughed, rejected, accepted—in short, she was completely involved.

"And how are you?"

"Me? I'm fine, as always."

Mysterious as ever. He'd never tell you anything. You had to be patient and work it out for yourself from little signs. He'd be more forthcoming about his work.

"And how's *Now?*"

"*Now?* That's a thing of the past. Now it's *Aleph.*"

"Well, well. So you were keeping it as a surprise, were you?"

"What do you think of the new name?"

"Is it meant to suggest the Bible? The infinite? Borges? Not a bad idea."

"I got fed up with all those lower-middle-class types at Editions de l'Autre, them and their religion. And anyway, they don't like what I write."

"That's absolutely basic."

"Everything is basic when you're a writer. And because you're reinventing what people in general are going to regard as basic, it's up to publishers to know their own minds and not dither about."

"Exactly." (Hervé was good at putting things in a nutshell.

Olga listened, intrigued and confident. It was clear her life was here, with this young man, so bold and in such a hurry.) "So who's your publisher now, instead of the Editions de l'Autre?"

" 'Le Différent.' "

"Didn't they approach you when you first started? I didn't know they were interested in the avant-garde."

"Who said anything about the avant-garde?"

"No one. But an avant-garde is an avant-garde because it anticipates a movement, and—you're right—this time the movement has anticipated the avant-garde."

"Precisely. You should see the novel I'm going to present them with next! Stanislas can't possibly like it, so the matter's settled—I have to leave both Stanislas and Editions de l'Autre."

"In New York everyone's talking about Postmodernism."

"Academic jargon. Wait till you hear my ideas!"

Fernand Benserade was in a Health Service hospital, sharing a room with a couple of immigrant workers. They were Algerians, and like him they'd lost the power of speech, though their large families, who often came to see them, were far from dumb. The famous linguist ought to have been in more comfortable surroundings and enjoying absolute quiet, but, having declined to be part of the salaried academic world, he had never paid any health insurance contributions. So it was impossible to get him into a decent private clinic. Wasn't that disgraceful? Couldn't all his admirers get together and pay the necessary sum? Olga was going to look into this horrible business right away. She was sad to discover that the only person who was doing all he could for the old man was a foreigner—good heavens, Ivan again! Apart from him, everyone had left Benserade all alone in that squalid hospital room.

He seemed delighted to see her. Smiling. Aware of what had happened. Not even trying to speak. Afraid of seeming ridiculous. He wrote a few letters with one finger on Olga's chest. How odd it would have looked if a nurse had come in! She got a notebook and a pen out of her bag. And Benserade, looking into her eyes, wrote with a shaking left hand: Theo.

Now it was her turn to be speechless. Was he thinking of God? Which one? Or was it just a scribble? A chance scrawl?

Something quite meaningless? Or a way of getting near the mother's breast? Her breast?

"You've written 'Theo.' Do you mean God?"

Benserade wasn't a believer, but you could never tell. Everyone in Paris was in the process of becoming more or less a believer.

Carole was more depressed than ever when she heard about Olga's visit to the hospital. Olga herself was shattered: she felt as if she were bound to all these serious people, each of them in some kind of impasse. Perhaps because they were looking for words for everything. Even Benserade; especially Benserade. Whereas Dalloway could live without words, satisfied just with loving.

Hervé heard about Benserade and his Theo: he was worried but cool. Unhelping hands. She could have wept. But no need. It was more serious than that. In bed they came together with the same keen pleasure as at the beginning. Hervé was both familiar and strange. The sober warmth of his mahogany eyes; that eager, impatient mouth. Caresses that mocked at the same time as they charmed. Broad shoulders offering rest but provoking challenge. The way his words flew; words that soothed, bothered, excited you; words that shattered you but also lifted you up. "It's not possible to love two men at once. There's madness in the air. It's not Carole who ought to go and lie on Joëlle Cabarus's couch. It's me."

17

*I*t's hard to find a place more kitsch than the Top of the Sixes in New York.

It's on the highest floor of 666 Fifth Avenue. Thick wall-to-wall carpets lead to the windows: through them at nightfall you can see the surrounding skyscrapers light up, and the tiny cars weaving far below around the black blot of Central Park. Men from the provinces and women from the middle classes come here at six o'clock for free cocktails. You can sit here with a glass of whisky or champagne or a Bloody Mary in your hand, and with no danger of running into anyone you know; sit here and meditate on the proud solitude of steel and neon Gothic, the unused freedom of beautiful women in modern metropolises, and the comparative virtues of an aperitif and a tedious conversation with a woman friend or a possible lover.

Diana was only two minutes late, but she was out of breath: ever since she'd been analyzed she'd been ferociously punctual.

"I didn't know you liked this sort of place. Isn't it rather—?"

"Rather what?"

"Well . . . rather modern?"

"It's like feeling above a film. As you do in a plane, or if you go to the toilet."

Edward was still not back from Israel, Diana had a sabbatical semester and was often holed up in her house on Long Island, and Olga needed to take a lofty view of things. From here, on the thirty-ninth floor, New York looked entirely beautiful and theatrical. Poverty is a question of distance. You only had to go down into the streets to see junkies sleeping in their rags around Rockefeller Center, and down-and-outs of all kinds rubbing shoulders with smartly dressed ladies coming out of Cartier's or Bergdorf Goodman's. The middle-class dames of Fifth Avenue, decked out in silk and leather, with their much-bleached hair, their garish foundation creams, and inevitable powder compacts, looked as if they were going to a party in honor of the latest issue of *Vogue*. It was better to see them from on high, i.e., not at all. Better not to remember anything of that appalling consumer society but shining glass and metal cubes reflecting other shining glass and metal cubes. Seen from here, the theater was empty. Not devastated, for there hadn't been a nuclear disaster (not yet), and the scenery was still intact; but the scenery was all that was left, and it was only a complex system of mirrors, a realm of reflections. The fortunate Narcissi were busy shopping; the sick Narcissi were sleeping off drugs or hatching crimes. But this civilization's most characteristic product, the "look," no longer needed either creators or victims. It had stopped being anthropomorphic and become superhuman. Transcendental. Seen from here.

From the Top of the Sixes the reflections dazzled the country cousins and made them think they were citizens of the world. This fireworks display was unlikely to suggest to any idle onlooker that all these lights, instead of glittering away into infinity, might turn inward and hollow out what used to be called an inner space. For every customer at the Top had abandoned his or her inner space. They couldn't go on, they'd had enough of it, their inner space was now only a soap opera, a more and more debased *"Dallas."* . . . *"*Two martinis, please. . . .*"* They were going to give up poring over their psyches, there were plenty of shrinks to take care of that—all quite useless, by the way—so why not feast their eyes on the lights? "Look at that view! Isn't it marvelous!" Let's melt into the landscape!

It occurred to Olga that Rosalind must have felt something like what she was now feeling, up here. And in the end she quit.

According to Diana, Rosalind Dalloway had been a sensitive and intelligent woman. She'd studied modern linguistics at Harvard and specialized in computer-assisted translation. The secret lay in the programming, and no one could come near Rosalind for that.

But Rosalind Bergman hadn't attended the modernist, anti-authoritarian lectures at Brandeis University in Waltham, half an hour away from Cambridge. Diana and Edward had gone to them out of intellectual curiosity and, to tell the truth, out of snobbishness as well. But Rosalind was too positive—"too much of a positivist, even," said Diana—to waste her time in that temple of the Jewish intellectual establishment. It was necessarily progressive and therefore left-wing; implicitly European and therefore philosophical and literary; and explicitly dissident and therefore Yiddish-speaking. Rosalind came from an old family of German Jews who'd lived in Boston for two generations (Rosy represented the third), and who were assimilated and not religious. Her father, Dr. Bergman, respected by the most exclusive Boston society, was more familiar with Goethe than with the Bible. Only a few culinary survivals dear to Grandmother Ida, Mrs. Bergman's mother, suggested that their ancestors spoke Yiddish too.

Of course they were all alert to the slightest hint of anti-Semitism, and regarded themselves as profoundly loyal members of the Jewish community as a whole. But theirs was a simple solidarity, normal and reasonable. They wanted it to be practical ("What can we do for so-and-so? for the local community? for Israel?") and completely devoid of the archaic religious acrimony some people indulged in. A person ought to keep a clear mind and assess every situation lucidly and without dogma or prejudice, even if he is a Jew. Dr. Bergman was a man of the Enlightenment, and everyone knows the Enlightenment respects the universal rights of the Jews as of all men, the Holocaust being just a terrible accident on the way to the inevitable victory of Reason.

So Rosy didn't go to Brandeis, and while she was still very young became a distinguished expert who was soon snapped up by MIT. She was bound to fall in love with a gentle and refined young man like Edward Dalloway, who impressed all the girls at Harvard but preferred Rosy's serious charm to their attractions. The Bergmans had no objection to being connected with the Dalloways; on the contrary. The Dalloways' attitude was not so unequivocal, but Edward had made up his mind, and no one cared to disagree with him. Except Grandmother Ida, but no one asked her opinion.

A happy marriage. Rosalind the talented computer expert was also a wonderful mother. Jason and Patricia were born two years apart, and the Dalloway family was held up as an example by all its Boston neighbors: what manners! what simplicity! Even the feminist movement couldn't create discord between those two impeccable intellectuals, whatever the war of the sexes might do to other advanced couples. Rosy inevitably shared other women's legitimate desire for recognition, but she believed that, all things considered, her own claims were already met: she had an important job, the men at MIT acknowledged her professional skills, and at home Edward helped with the children, the house, and the shopping. The Dalloways already lived in the postfeminist age.

This lasted until Rosalind Bergman was asked to work out a high-power computer program for translating English into Hebrew and vice versa. She didn't know any Hebrew. So she had to learn, and this she did with the aid of another computer expert called Isaac Chemtov, specially brought over from Tel Aviv for the purpose. But the resources of Brandeis were not enough, and it was soon clear that some linguistic training "in the field" was called for. She made several trips to Jerusalem. It was a revelation, and the beginning of a new life.

The previous life of Mrs. Dalloway seemed suddenly insignificant, not to say nonexistent, when she viewed it from this new world of hitherto unsuspected power. The people of Jerusalem were neither tragic nor even dramatic (though with their safety constantly threatened they might well have been): quite simply, they were real. And they made the rest of the world seem unreal. They reduced all the Bostons, Dalloways, and Fifth Avenue looks to triviality. At first Rosalind didn't know why.

There was, of course, the Jerusalem landscape, like the result of some geological catastrophe. That tortured land of hills and dry plains, barren rifts and dead seas, had engendered no luxury or opulence. You could survive there only through a rugged sense of repose joined to perpetual effort: a sense of the sacred.

There was also the tradition of the Book, the ciphered language that Rosalind was now discovering and that gave her back a religion she'd never even imagined before. Everyone knew it was solemn, exclusive, and severe. That it was also complex, ambivalent, combinative—you had to know Hebrew to know that. And to study the infinite mass of interpretations that had accumulated through the ages, awaiting Rosalind not to impart some new inner life but to lighten the existing one by expanding the import of psychology and making feeling consubstantial with intelligence.

Then there was the Wailing Wall: that quintessence of anguish that foresaw the Shoah but proved incapable of preventing it. This was the hardest thing for Rosalind to take. She was somewhat reassured when she came upon Jerry Saltzman in a state similar to her own. The celebrated New York novelist, author of the best-seller *Professor of Disaster,* visibly embarrassed at the sight of so much religious wallowing in sorrow, and even more upset by his own reaction, was wearing a skullcap to try to persuade himself he belonged to a race that made his hair stand on end. For once Rosalind shared his views. She sought information about the history of the Wall, and came back several times to observe the people praying and their various degrees of fervor. In the end she was ashamed at having been spared unhappiness so utterly herself. And while she couldn't cast off all Dalloway restraint, she felt poor and narrow at being unable to lament.

Although all this took a certain amount of time to happen, when it did happen it was a shock. It struck everyone like a bolt from the blue, and not least Rosalind, though deep down she pondered for months and years about the true reasons for her sudden metamorphosis. It struck her as blindingly and as self-evidently as the sun shining down on Jerusalem: Mrs. Dalloway had never existed, Rosalind Bergman had scarcely lived, there was only Ruth Goldenberg. And she belonged to this people, this land, this Book, this Wall. She owed it to herself to adopt the name of her ancestors, Goldenberg, abandoned when they fled from Germany and became assimilated in America—the promised land, it seemed to them, for all free and equal men, including Jews, especially Jews. And so it proved, and so it still was really, despite the false notes and latent animosities that were obvious to everyone but seemed much smaller there than elsewhere. There was no real menace. But now Rosalind discovered that this security was purchased with a kind of sleep, an oblivion, which neutralized you and reduced you to a mere image. Or worse still to a number in some universal calculator that made a clean sweep of passions, conflicts, despairs—all the things without which you don't really love life, you don't really think your loves and hates, you half live, you reflect. Whereas here, after the Six-Day War, some Jews from the Diaspora came back and, while still working at something connected with their previous professions, first and foremost tried to make themselves useful—in the army, in the kibbutzim, in the schools. And Rosalind . . . no, Ruth, also needed to be useful, to do something concrete. Such as what? To strengthen a frontier, build a house, teach a language to people just arrived from poor African countries—elementary things which made you exist, which brought you out of fog and anesthesia, which is what your former, preshock life suddenly seemed to have been. And Ruth regained the calm of a people from whom she now saw she had never been separated, save by two generations of false ambitions.

"It's quite simple. I'm Ruth Goldenberg, and I live in Jerusalem with my children."

But there was still the question of Edward. When he heard the verdict over the phone he thought the lines must have got crossed and he was hearing part of someone else's conversation. Not at all: Rosalind-Ruth had decided to make a quick, clean break. It was the only way to avoid getting bogged down in complications. Practical arrangements could be made as the need arose.

"Are you tired? You're probably overworked, and what with that and the heat . . . How do you feel?" (Edward)

"If you mean I'm sick, you're wrong. I've never felt so well in my life." (Ruth)

"You haven't gone religious, have you?" (Dalloway)

"I didn't have to 'go'—I always have been religious. Without knowing it perhaps. But I've found it out again." (Goldenberg)

"Do you eat kosher?" (Dalloway)

"Of course." (Goldenberg)

"After all, why not? But, listen, there's a whole range of different kinds of Judaism—don't say you're Orthodox?" (Dalloway)

"I don't know. Isaac is, and his friends are probably the best guarantee of Israel's existence." (Goldenberg)

"You amaze me. But we'll talk about it when you get back. It's not the sort of thing I can find out from the State Department. Are you in love with this Isaac?" (Dalloway)

"That's not the problem at all." (Goldenberg)

"Well, you've always been unpredictable, Rosy—that's why I love you. You can explain it when you get home. We're all waiting for you—Jason and Patricia are spending Sunday with your parents. You get in next Saturday at two, is that right?" (Dalloway)

"Saturday's the Sabbath—I'll come back on Monday." (Goldenberg)

"Phew! This is really something. . . . Still, I love you all the same." (Dalloway)

"I'm not saying I don't love you. It's something else. And you're right—it's serious." (Goldenberg)

"I don't think we can talk much further over the phone." (Dalloway)

"I'm sure of it. I've made my decision." (Goldenberg)

"Lots of love, then. We're all looking forward to seeing you." (Dalloway)

"Till Monday." (Goldenberg)

Edward was stunned, but his sense of humor rarely allowed

him to despair: an escapade with Isaac Chemtov was something that might happen to the most reasonable of women—especially to them. Dr. Bergman thought it was all due to a manic phase of the chronic depression his daughter concealed so well, but which a father couldn't fail to see: perhaps it would respond to treatment. Mrs. Bergman was the one who was the most upset and also the most skeptical: since the death of her mother, Ida, who had till then assumed the custody of tradition, she herself had turned increasingly toward the Bible, and political events since the Six-Day War had made her more active than ever in good works for the community. Not to mention her visit to Jerusalem: "The most important time in my life," she said meaningfully, and Dr. Bergman nodded gravely, realizing at once, though not very clearly, the sort of importance she was talking about. In short, Rosy's mother was afraid she understood her daughter all too well, though she thought her decision was crazy, or at least due to a misunderstanding. And had the Dalloways' marriage been going as well as it seemed? This aspect of the matter mustn't be underestimated. As for the Dalloway grandparents, they said nothing, but their silence was accompanied by significant looks: you knew this would happen all along, but well-bred people don't make personal remarks.

Edward had always regarded religion as a survival, and had never come into contact with madness. That Rosy might suddenly become a cool and determined fanatic, though without the external signs of fanaticism, struck him as an aberration inaccessible to reason. But he made several attempts to explain it to himself.

1. Male responsibility, inadequate virility. "There's no escaping it: a man deserted is a man castrated. Am I really a poor lover, an insensitive husband, a man unworthy to be a father?"

However lengthily he considered each of these theories, none of them held water. He had loved her completely—without reserve, with all the ardor he thought a man should be capable of—his dark, buxom Rosalind, who had returned his love with docile pleasure. But who knows? Habit is easily undermined by the attraction of some novelty—any mysterious and dramatic dandy, any desert hero or holy activist was enough to ensnare the most intelligent woman. No point in looking for any way out of it—this flight into Israel was nothing else but a disavowal of Edward himself, a snub to the Dalloway myth.

Ruth . . . (how ridiculous! Edward couldn't get used to the name. Not to mention the surname—a negation of fifteen years of exemplary existence) . . . Ruth didn't ask for an immediate divorce, saying her decision was metaphysical rather than physical. But you'd have to be crazy to shut your eyes to the facts, and anyway the inevitable legal pantomime could not be too far off. For what was to be done about the children? Jason and Patricia were used to shuttling between the two sets of grandparents while Rosalind programmed her computers at MIT and Edward divided his energies between Harvard and Washington: they didn't realize the consequences of the catastrophe, at first. But Ruth Goldenberg was a mother, and a Jewess, and no Jewish mother can do without her children. The two teenagers were rather intrigued, on the face of it: Jerusalem, a kibbutz—it all sounded wonderful compared with boring old Boston! We'll be going away . . . Fantastic! Patricia wasn't altogether sure: she liked going to museums with Father on the weekends. But Jason set the tone, and she wasn't going to look like a timid little Wasp. Anyway, all the psychologists will tell you children ought to be with their mother.

2. He wasn't a failure as a man—far from it. Perhaps, on the contrary, he'd been a bit too zealous. He'd given satisfaction on all fronts, from bed to kitchen to garden, not to mention his restraint over politics: it was bound to confuse a woman. Women like to be frustrated, they're all masochists hankering after deprivation. He'd been a naive idiot not to realize as much. Things were going to change. Edward was going to enter his Casanova period. The Don Juan of the campus. Just wait and see! But his heart wasn't in it. What a chore! It really wasn't in his nature.

3. Ruth Goldenberg's half-political, half-religious fervor was neither here nor there. What Israel needed (in addition, of course, to economic aid) was diplomatic support, and he, Edward Dalloway, was in a position to know the efforts Washington was making in this direction. All false modesty aside, he could claim to be involved. An active Diaspora was absolutely necessary if the political tightrope was to be walked successfully, and if Rosy was so keen on finding a Jewish mystic inside her

pretty little head, she could find plenty with which to keep herself occupied in Boston. Edward was ready to offer some suggestions himself. As for the Orthodox Jews settling in the occupied territories to satisfy their frustration at not having been persecuted enough in Brooklyn or New York, and who rose up with God, guns, and inflammatory speeches against the "Arab hordes," they were dangerous customers, capable of scuttling any attempt at negotiation, which was difficult enough already. And to top it off, this bloke of Rosy's, this Chemtov, this so-called computer expert, seemed to be some frightful extremist. Women were always impressed by the gift of the gab. But surely not Rosy! Yes, Rosy too. From now on, nothing would surprise him.

4. Ruth . . . (she'd always be Rosy to Edward, but since Ruth claimed that Rosy no longer existed, that Rosy was dead, he wasn't going to try to speak to a corpse) . . . Ruth could have suggested he come to live with her in Israel. No, that was ridiculous: Edward Dalloway couldn't possibly go and settle in Tel Aviv, Bursheba, Nazareth, or some other such place. Apparently very few genuine atheists were left in the world now—but what did it matter? If there was only one, Dalloway would be he. Just the same, Rosy ought to have suggested it, out of loyalty to their life together, in memory of their love—that is, if she remembered it. Apparently not, though. She said she did, but that their love ought to remain where it was, in its proper place in the past; and now she, Ruth, was living another truth, her own truth, which didn't admit of compromise.

5. You had to admit that Rosalind Dalloway, or Ruth Golden-berg—hell, what did it matter!—was some woman. What a character! There weren't many wives like that. Maybe he, Edward Dalloway, was a victim, but he'd had fifteen years of happiness with an exceptional woman—though maybe without always realizing it—and you can't expect the exceptional to be permanent. Even now Rosy was set at a distance by the business of the divorce, which instead of obliterating her altogether seemed to place her on an inaccessible height, in a lofty Jerusalem. This forced Edward in turn into a pointless strictness with himself and others that made him pleasantly bitter.

Everyone gets excited when a Jewish man loves or marries a

shiksa. The opposite case isn't provided for. Edward had never felt he was perpetrating some religious or economic crime by marrying Rosalind Bergman. For both him and her (at least while she was still Rosy Dalloway-Bergman), their marriage was just a union between two free and equal individuals. Neither of them concealed Rosy's Jewish origins, from others or from him- or herself. For both of them she was Jewish in the same way as she was dark, intelligent, a computer expert, the mother of two children, and his, Edward Dalloway's, wife. Nobody in their circle knew anyone who was anti-Semitic, though they were as one in combating such of these atavistic brutes as still survived elsewhere. There was no difference between the two Dalloways on that score (or indeed on any other). But since becoming Ruth Goldenberg's ex-husband, (a false description: only Rosy Bergman had had a husband, but since she no longer existed, could you really talk about her ex-husband? What a puzzle!), Edward had felt he was (or had been—another puzzle!) a kind of shiksa. But what did that really mean? For Edward, professor of government and international lawyer in Washington, it meant that he wasn't up to scratch, that there'd always be something he didn't know, that he'd been used for some obscure and impenetrable purposes, divine or sexual—probably the two were often the same. But to his great surprise, his position as an inverted shiksa (the puzzle still wasn't solved!), which should have distressed him—and he had seen it as a kind of affliction for some three years now—this awkward position actually seemed to him inevitable, necessary. No, Dalloway didn't think himself doomed to humiliation by way of divine punishment or some other such foolery. But his melancholy nature, so clearly reflected in the transcendental gray of his eyes (or so it was that Olga described them), felt right in his new position as a rejected husband: as if it was necessary for the reality of his married life to demonstrate an impossibility already evident in his whole being, despite all his culture and his reason.

As in those strange dreams where the dreamer is both arrow and target, Dalloway occupied the entire trajectory of this confused and violent situation, and it made his wounded tenderness even more an integral part of him. Without ever admitting it to himself, he accepted it as if it were an approach to some ineffable truth. But what truth? The link between the Jews and the rest of the world, between Israel and America, between Ruth and him? He didn't want to go into the question. What mattered to him was finding a legal solution to the paradox of the identity between the bow and the target, already glimpsed by Heraclitus.

Women who love completely can perceive the movements of atoms. Olga agreed with Ed, who agreed with Ruth, who had killed Rosalind and ejected Dalloway, who was the weapon aiming at the target and the target too. And who was taken up by Olga. . . .

She went with him through every stage, past all the obstacles with which the affair was strewn, that family or religious or political affair in which chance had involved him. And she saw him at the end of the journey, defenseless. Like her: an animal in pain, proud to be so, and of no importance whatsoever. All you need, in fact, to create eternal friendships, if not eternal loves.

The frost over Morningside Park darkened the blue of the sky, a precious stone hanging over Harlem. Snow muffled sound and blurred contrast in these remote parts of the city, shunned by pedestrians. It made all space seem stellar and translucent. Only the frosty branches were reminiscent of man's fragility: Olga saw herself again in the long winters back home, when blizzards stopped the children from going to school. The hot chestnut and pretzel sellers were never more appealing; white steam from the New York streets seemed to lend darkness a soul and deceitfully suggested a thaw.

The green lights of the Algonquin went well with Edward's quizzical expression: he never showed the darker side of things.

"Are the children well?"

"Fine. Patricia's having some trouble with her work at school, though. Jason's in the army, but that hasn't stopped him from joining a left-wing pacifist movement in order to thumb his nose at his stepfather. As you know, Ruth's married her famous Chemtov."

"No, I didn't know."

"Oh! . . . Well, it doesn't matter. He's a funny guy. He's let his beard grow since he was over at MIT, and at the same time as he updates the army computers he goes around with a gun (I doubt if he knows how to use it) to protect himself against possible stonethrowers. He fulminates against the selfishness of the free world, especially the United States, which he says is leaving Israel in the lurch. I've done all I can to explain to him that negotiation isn't desertion, and that our diplomatic relations with the Arabs don't imply any acceptance of their policies. But it's no good—he thinks I'm incapable of grasping the seriousness of the things, both earthly and divine, that he's prepared to defend. I can understand a mechanic from Texas arriving in Tel Aviv, discovering he's an Orthodox Jew, and joining some tiny right-wing religious party to give his life a moral and psychological dimension it never had before. But that this man, a world authority on computerized translation, should not only be completely devoted to God and his rituals but also ready to rub out some Arabs—that's utterly beyond me."

"He may be right to be careful. You're jealous."

"Mind you, that nut took me to a kibbutz that had been the object of several terrorist attacks, and I must say the people there, who don't pretend to be militant intellectuals but really risk their lives and firmly believe in their Bible, well . . ."

"Well what?"

"Well, in the end I began to think I understood Ruth."

"You love her."

"I'm impressed by her. Everything's serious for her now. No lightness. She doesn't play anymore, or laugh. Except when she does especially well at her military training, or when her students make progress on the computers—she teaches computer science in the army too. Of course, lightheartedness is a privilege you can only enjoy when you're safe."

"Or else it's the acme of woe, the aspect of lamentation that can be shown."

"They treated me as a stranger—they didn't show me that aspect. What's new with you?"

"I've had my fanatics too. You don't need to go and see Isaac Chemtov to find dogmatism—talk to any American Marxist."

"They're getting rare!"

"Not really. I met Tom Moore, a leading historian from Yale— perhaps you know him . . . everyone does. I don't know how we got on to Soviet dissidents. My friend Podolski, the Russian poet, was there—a great writer harassed like a delinquent, driven out of his own country and so on, and relieved to be able to live in freedom at last in the West. 'You're not going to tell me there's more freedom in capitalist countries than in the East,' Moore suddenly said to me, a glass of champagne in his hand, admired by a bevy of beautiful girls whom he instructs in Marxism—for more than a hundred and fifty thousand dollars a year, I hear. I snapped back: 'Yes, of course—didn't you know?' He nearly had a fit. I called him a cynic, a profiteer, a criminal, and I don't know what else . . . the rest of the party was highly amused. He's a typically American phenomenon—there haven't been any dinosaurs like that in France since '68."

"Yes, I know the type. But they're an endangered species."

"Don't you believe it. There are departments at the university that exist for the sole purpose of producing them. And it's not just in order to keep them under control—they still produce plenty of propaganda."

"My dear Olga, you don't know all the tricks 'Algonquin' federalism has up its sleeve. . . . You do call the Americans Algonquins, don't you? . . . Well, they don't eliminate people who are a problem, they marginalize and in so doing neutralize them. And what better margin could you find than the university? It's comfortable (so there won't be any complaints), and it's insignificant (so no one takes any notice of what they say there)."

"Disgusting. And yet you go on teaching there?"

"Among other places. And less and less. But it does act as an antidote to people like Moore."

"May I use the phone?"

"Make yourself at home."

He hadn't asked her anything about Paris. She clearly didn't want to talk about it, and it would have been uncouth to press her.

"I've got a message for Jerry Saltzman."

"Do you like his work?"

" 'Professor of Disaster'? A rather amazing mixture of Henry Miller and Kafka . . . Don't *you* like it?"

"I haven't read it. Ruth's allergic to him. Apparently he's a 'traitor.' "

"You did say she's forgotten how to laugh?"

"Absolutely. With me, anyway."

"There you are then! You ought to read it. . . ." (Very quietly into the telephone:) "Hello? Jerry Saltzman? Olga Montlaur speaking. I'm calling on behalf of a friend of ours—Zoltan Panzera. . . . Yes, yes, he's very well, I assure you—I saw him a couple of days ago in Paris. . . . No, they've never really put out the red carpet for him, he's too talented, and he lives very quietly. . . . Yes, people try all sorts of things. . . . But he prefers to stay out of the limelight. Yes, Sinteuil would like to publish your essay on Kafka in the first issue of *Aleph* . . . *Aleph* is the successor to *Now* . . . No, Le Différent is the publisher . . . How did we come to think of you? Partly because of Zoltan, partly because you're the most amusing of the melancholy authors. . . . Of course that's a compliment! . . . Why not? I adore Château-Pétrus. . . . With pleasure. . . . See you tomorrow then. . . . And thanks about the Kafka. . . . See you tomorrow. . . ."

"Sorry, I couldn't help hearing. Don't you think you were a little bit . . . well . . . eager to please?" (Edward had lost his sense of humor too!)

"How do you mean?"

"I just thought so."

"That doesn't sound like you. You're quoting someone else. It wouldn't be Ruth, would it?"

"Of course not!"

"Then you're just jealous."

She lifted her lips until her heavy dark red hair reached down to her waist, put her arms around him, and held him close. Spontaneous gestures seem theatrical only to an outside observer.

The walls of Jerry Saltzman's study were covered with the same prints of Nùgua and Fuxi, the incestuous royal couple, that Olga and Hervé had bought in Xian. Like all self-respecting "Algonquins," Saltzman had excellent taste in wines from Bordeaux but showed no interest whatever in the French language. On the other hand, every gifted dissident in Eastern Europe had been translated into American through the good offices of the "professor of disaster." But who would have recognized the severe, tortured thinker, capable of pulverizing with blasphemies anyone who stood in his way, in this elegant host, pouring out glasses of Château-Pétrus and laughing at himself for not being able to read Kafka more easily?

"How can you expect a baseball player from Newark like me to understand anything about the law? How could he treat it with the same mixture of mischief and respect as a young man from Prague who's fed up both with his beloved father and with women?"

Saltzman liked to pass himself off as a naive observer of society—"unlike the French, who think of nothing but culture just because they've got some"—whereas, in fact, though he went to great lengths to conceal it, he was extremely learned. The device was a good way of showing politely how disgusted he was with people who clung to tradition (the Jews and the French, for instance), whom one had to watch and love in order eventually to make fun of them. Were the Parisians starting to read his work? Good: that was all he had to say to them. But he had a great regard for Olga, and he hoped the opposite was the case too. They understood each other. Two acerbic individuals who didn't expect anything from anybody, but would always keep in touch with each other, even through the Apocalypse. See you soon.

Carnegie Hall obliterates the inevitable false notes that occur in human relations and hollows out, at least for an evening, a well of harmony amid the harshness of New York, creating the illusion that civilization is universal and might even have managed to flower in the chaos of this city. No easy task.

Edward liked going there. And this evening some famous women singers were singing lieder, a feast for the ear and a celebration of love not to be missed. The music called for the utmost precision, yet offered rest from sorrow. There's nothing like a woman's voice to proclaim that the body may be a permanent joy. Sopranos are rose petals caressed by the dawn. Altos: fleshy cannas bathed in dew. Blue-glinting mystical mezzos: plumbagos tended by Virginia Woolf. The singers' mouths disproved the dogma of female frigidity; their vocal cords glorified a worship of angels far above adoration, which is possible and sometimes necessary, but always rather squalid; a worship of mute madonnas. Olga thought she and Edward shared the same delights; this fount of ecstatic sound was their common ground, the only publicly avowable link between their two eccentricities.

Ruth Goldenberg had nothing to do with the marvelous priestesses of the body now on the stage at Carnegie Hall. Yet Olga could not help imagining a secret connection between the strange Rosalind, who fled habit for a lofty passion, and the subtle elevation of these female bodies, fat or slim or nondescript, in a state of celestial vibration. It was as if a woman's ecstasy were seeking ordeals and obstacles in order to rid itself of a sloth that might lull and extinguish pleasure. At this rate, she might still, in a universe of rules, rites, and artifice, hope for the satisfaction of an infinite inwardness.

The beauty went on, yet the singers still reached after it. But they did so with a tenacity that was painless for, at its zenith, courage, like labor, disintegrates and envelops you in golden dust.

So that night God was a woman transformed into music.

Even the most sensual man is filled with cold fear by such radiant pleasure. Edward, carried away by the skill of his favorite singers, became the unconscious but obedient priest of a cult, a cult like that which terrified the initiates of ancient mysteries by showing them that love, like death, can only be plunged into, not imagined.

The pagan osmosis that took place between the two lovers through the medium of the jubilation issuing from those female throats revealed something very strange: the fact that they shared a common feminine sensuality, like two girl twins clinging to their invisible, melodious mother.

But by transposing them to the level of the vibrant voices, the music brought their ambiguous desires into a sphere of purity and uprightness, a heavenly Jerusalem that Ruth too might have inhabited if she'd allowed herself any imagination. The lieder took them away from Ruth forever, yet at the same time brought them closer than ever to her nomadic adventure, her flight from them to the Law.

The songs showed Olga that Edward had become indispensable to her: a soothing worry, an intimacy of the bone.

She saw again scenes from her Chinese journey; it kept coming back to her, besieging her. The music had the same grace beyond tension as Li Xulan had managed to capture, the woman who could extract Van Goghs and Mondrians from a cotton plantation: assonances, rhythms, and tones beyond images.

Of course Olga knew that no one was farther away than Dalloway from the "mother cults" of ancient China, the prefeminist religions that Bernadette said she hadn't stressed sufficiently. Like Hervé, Edward would probably make fun of the idea that Primitive Woman was omnipotent. But he was so spontaneously and deeply aware of the difficulty of being in the world that a woman was bound to accept him as a natural accomplice. For even the most strong-minded girls experience the stoic helplessness, the frustrated triumph that Dalloway knew so well.

From a certain point of view, he was the victim of a woman, his wife, who had ended up rejecting him in favor of a search for her own identity. The odyssey of Rosy Bergman revealed a free woman, even though Ruth Goldenberg didn't at all identify with the feminist cause. But there again Edward understood, through an immediate intuition, that he had nothing to forgive Ruth. Dalloway's own sensibility—proud yet suicidal, authoritarian yet tormented, distinguished yet withdrawn—had anticipated her. He could have made up all sorts of reasons for her actions. Not rational reasons to do with his own Protestant origins and education, or his professional background of secular jurists tolerant of every nation's rights and suspicious of religious fundamentalism: in relation to the logic of all these, Ruth's decision seemed completely insane. But he had preceded her by himself somehow espousing the kind of passionate reason that leads a woman to sacrifice the status quo in order to fulfill, to give pleasure to . . . what? Not her body (what woman isn't ready to offer that up, at least on certain conditions?), but that taut fiber made up of absolute ambition, immemorial vulnerability, and exquisite dispersal of the self; and in the name of a beloved authority called "my own identity." "My feminine identity," some women say. "My identity as a Jewess," Ruth said.

Dalloway said nothing. That fiber was his own "inner China": his male secret, which could reach out to the utmost strangeness of others, to the kind of "Central Mother" who inhabits us all for better or worse but whom we usually choose to ignore. Or to a "promised land": it seemed to him that even the most abstract monotheism could only exercise a real fascination if it could convey a warm, nonutilitarian, inconsolable feminine dignity. Clearly there was nothing earthy, rustic, or matriarchal in Ruth's flight: she had really gone in search of an invisible Rigor. "That's what she must have missed in the overcozy family life of the Dalloways," Olga would tell herself when she was trying to be objective about it all. But Dalloway himself translated his wife's escapade into the language of his own sensibility. And who knows whether, though he was far away from Ruth's religious experience, his error didn't bring him nearer to those sensitive, maternal, and grandmaternal motivations that had fundamentally reconciled Rosalind with the Unnamable.

Actually, it didn't matter much to Dalloway what name was to be applied to all that, as long as it was a journey and made dissatisfaction echo like one of these lieder. The same dissatisfaction that he unconsciously cultivated inside himself, deriving certain dubious pleasures from it and knowing in a puzzled way that this was what made him Edward Dalloway.

The Algonquin welcomed them back once again, eager and understanding each other's eagerness. The nights of the secret lovers were so short, they were so afraid this night might be the last, that their mouths kissed even as they slept, and their sexes kept seeking each other in the depths of a sleep that was one long embrace, watched over by spirits of song.

18

Carole was definite about it: Paris was deathly now. Her mood was obviously affected by Martin's departure: he had rushed off in search of death, she knew, but he was still alive—at least she hoped so— whereas here people were pining away and dying like flies. Benserade, paralyzed and speechless, was as good as dead. Carole went to see him from time to time, but he was very weak and didn't seem to recognize her. Wurst, after murdering his wife, was just a walking corpse. Bréhal's mother had just died, and Armand was so shattered he talked to everyone about it; imagine spreading your grief about like that! The latest news was that Edelman, whom Carole had long lost sight of, had also just succumbed: according to the papers it was a sudden death.

"If she's got the heart to write she can't be feeling so

bad": Olga was trying to improve her own morale by reading her friend's morose letters. But three things at least were clear.

First, Carole had drawn Paris as permanently enveloped in a shroud. A shroud that smothered everything, including Carole's own Noah's Ark in the rue Saint-André-des-Arts, with its flowers that seemed to have escaped the Flood, and her memories of Rosalba, Fiesole, and the Virgin with her fragile little face sketched in India ink. All this was meaningless now; only antidepressants kept her from actually dying. Pleasure had never been her strong suit, but in the past she had sometimes approached it, as when you hear a sound at night like cicadas or a cat or even a muffled siren far away over the water, and it fades away before you're sure whether you heard it or only dreamed it. Martin produced that impression on her, and so did Bréhal's voice. It's wonderful how a voice can summon up a caress, or the velvety feel of the lilacs at Fiesole. But no, Carole was stone deaf now: an inconsolable widow. Did she want something from someone? You couldn't be sure. But Carole's unhappiness filled Olga with a guilt she couldn't shake off.

Second, enthusiasm had completely collapsed among the comrades, and the only people who kept going were those who had a real passion, preferably professional—for math, say, or linguistics or biology. The list could be extended indefinitely, and included all eggheads. Or else you had at all costs to find yourself a religion. Either that of your parents or even that of your erstwhile enemies—no matter, you must get one without delay. Even Hervé, above all Hervé, had replaced Mao with the Bible, and *Aleph* was managing to persuade the materialistic readers of *Now* that Duns Scotus was the prime defender of individual liberty. The argument was sound enough, given the Subtle Doctor's apologia for singularity. But the less subtle disciples with whom Hervé dubiously surrounded himself extended the verdict on Duns Scotus to the Church as a whole, and Hervé, poker-faced as ever, said they were probably right. Why? To begin with, because it irritated the narrow, rationalistic bourgeoisie. Moreover, Sinteuil was prepared to abolish all religions as long as Catholicism was abolished last, for he maintained that the fanatics it now produced were less dangerous than those produced by other faiths. Of course, by putting it like this he made his argument unassailable. Meanwhile misunderstandings multiplied. Some complained of obscurantism ("Sinteuil's a turncoat: first Peking and then the Vatican!"). Others of blasphemy ("Sinteuil is making a mockery of true religion—he has no sense of the holy"). Even Olga had trouble keeping track, through tricks and stratagems and a quest for truth in mythology. Try to be a bit more serious, please! But she still managed to keep a cool head: don't count on her to support the present fashion!

Lastly, Edelman's death made her realize her own lack of feeling. After all, he'd been the first to welcome and help her— before Bréhal, before Strich-Meyer, before Sinteuil—when no one knew the little foreigner who was to turn out so intelligent or such a pain in the neck, take your choice, but who then was nobody. Except to Edelman. Whom she hadn't stuck with. Who'd relied on her to add a linguistic dimension to his own dialectic and tragic paradox. But she'd been arrogant, insolent, and they'd parted. Edelman overtaxed himself, as Armand had pointed out. But they hadn't loved him enough, Olga included. And yet she had sensed the essential timidity of that tired body, and been attracted by the sallies of his untidy mind. But no, she'd preferred to be a bustling, intelligent young woman, in the swim with *Now:* Marx was dead and Edelman was a square. The cruelty of children who are supposed to be gifted! Some gift! The gift of being able to wound! You see it everywhere, including the universities. Impossible to count the intellectual murders. Thought has no blood, you can't see it die; professors die of cancer of the liver but are killed by bitterness.

It was high time to go back. This craze for deserting her friends must be her own special perversion. And now she was going to desert Dalloway—another burden to bear, she didn't know how. She'd better have a good cry before she left—once she was back in Paris it would be too late. Paris is a city where no one interesting ever cries.

God, like chance, manages things well, and the Secret Island existed, as did Mathilde de Montlaur, who—whether she meant to or not—could cheer up even the most melancholy spirit. The Fier was an emerald casting blue reflections on the undersides of the swallows that dipped their thirsty wings in the water, only to start up again, probably startled by its salty taste. Pyramids of white crystals outlined with alchemical precision the rectangles of the marshes, proof of the dryness of the summer, which nevertheless produced masses of color in flowers that liked arid soil. Jean de Montlaur loved gardening after Gérard had done the heavy work: trimming the drooping rose bushes; watering the earth around the daisies in order to inhale the spicy scent they gave off when their thirst was slaked; cutting stems of mallows and hollyhocks for Olga to remove the blossoms and float them—like fishes suddenly set free—in the large porcelain bowls in the drawing room. Meanwhile Mathilde indulged in her favorite pastime, conversation, which she was skilled at concluding in a dazzling monologue.

"The Pope's overdoing it—you never see anyone but him on television these days. What do you think, Olga my dear?"

Olga didn't think anything, and didn't have any inclination to think—she was waiting for letters from Edward, due to arrive by the three o'clock mail. Hervé came to her rescue.

"The Pope's only doing his job. He has to talk to the people, and the people look at the TV. He's a missionary who moves with the times."

"More of a pop star than a missionary, if you ask me."

"He's a very good theologian. He's written some fine things about the Virgin Mary."

"Since when have you been interested in theology?"

"I've always been interested in it."

"Last year you were criticizing us—to put it mildly!—for sending Isabelle's children to a Catholic school."

"I was speaking from bitter experience, as you very well know. Besides, Catholic schools don't even have a spirit of charity anymore—they're only places to cram for the sons of the bourgeoisie, or nurseries for stultifying their daughters. But I'm talking about theology now, not schools."

"Do you mean theology is too difficult for me? You're probably right. . . . You used to read Montherlant when you were quite small. . . ."

"But Mother, that's got nothing to do with it! Think of Saint Bonaventure, or Saint Thomas if you prefer, or Master Eckehart. There were books by all of them in the library of our uncle the archbishop, who went to India as a missionary and of whom you seem to be so proud. . . . Well, this Pope, by making a stir in the media, draws people's attention to that sort of thing, and it makes a nice change from the things one usually has to read. I assure you. You ought to try it."

"He sees things from the Polish point of view—sorry, Olga dear, but it's not the same as ours. A worker kneeling down in front of a statue of the Virgin, the ban on contraception . . . No, no! . . . You say he moves with the times. Well, all I can say is, they're not *our* times!"

"The worker, as you call him, kneeling down before the Virgin is free from doubt, and that gives him strength to fight against oppression. I've just written a little piece about it, as a matter of fact."

"About the Poles?"

"I *have* written one about them. But I was thinking of another one you'd probably be more interested in—about the Virgin Mary."

"Really? Have you recovered your faith? I'd love to read it. What's the title?"

"*The Hole of the Virgin.*"

"Hervé! Don't be indecent! Anyhow, it's impossible."

"What is?"

"The Virgin can't have a . . . what you said. And that'll be enough obscenity, if you don't mind."

"It's your mind that's obscene. I was thinking about something quite different. Shall I explain? Precisely because she hasn't got a hole, except for her ear to let in the Holy Ghost, the Virgin is an axial vacuum. Now please make an effort to imagine the geometry here. Around this axial vacuum is arranged the relationship between the Father, the Son, and the Holy Ghost. So the Virgin is an absence of body, a hole (in a different sense from the one you referred to), but one that is also a medium. And it's precisely as this body, which is also a hole, that she's destined to free the human race from its erotic obsession. Unless, on the contrary, she arouses an excess of imagination to fill the vacuum. That's what the painters, whose favorite subject and often patron saint she is, are trying to show. In short, the Virgin is a brilliant invention."

"You're blaspheming and misapplying your talent!"

"I see I've made *you* recover your faith!"

"I've got more faith than you think, and I don't need you to tell me about it! By the way, a lady came up to me in the supermarket and said: 'Excuse me, I don't know you'—she was very polite—'but I'm sorry to have to tell you your son's a misogynist.' That was all I needed! I just stood there dumbfounded."

"A madwoman. Yet another who can't read but is full of opinions. You ought to tell women like her to read *The Hole of the Virgin* to learn some humility."

"I'm sorry—I find your sense of humor quite abominable. You haven't even made Olga laugh. He's not funny, is he, my dear? You see, she's looking quite bored."

"No, no, I'm not bored, I assure you! Whenever Hervé's provoking there's always some meaning behind it."

"Well, I don't see it. A woman of my age . . . . Of course, I'm not so highly educated as you two. . . ."

They had reached that point in the skirmish when Mathilde owed it to herself to raise her handicap before showing she had a world of her own and was in full control of it.

"I was just saying to Jean . . . Are you listening, Jean? He loves flowers, Olga dear, and I notice he's always giving you pretty bouquets. . . . No, no, it's not just out of politeness, he's very fond of you, perhaps even more than of his flowers, and that's a rare thing, let me tell you. . . . Well, as I was saying, I've just heard from my old friend Madeleine—Hervé, do you remember Madeleine Olibet? We don't see each other since we've retired to the country. You must have heard of the Olibets, Olga?—the cookies? Well, my dear, would you believe it, the Olibet girl is engaged to the Japy boy—the Japys are the machinery people, old friends of ours, Madame Japy's a very elegant woman. Their eldest son is married to a Moulinex. As you know, my dear"—of course Olga didn't know, and Mathilde knew she didn't know, and it was for this very reason that she was flaunting her social expertise—"the Moulinexes are connected through their wives to the marquise de Sévigné—the chocolates, you know. And *they're* cousins of the Krups, the domestic appliances people. . . . Well, Madeleine believes one of the Krups granddaughters is going to get engaged to the Château Cheval Blanc boy—the wine has a world reputation—and the engagement party's to be held next month on their estate, which is just near us. You know their château very well, Hervé—you were always going there to play with the Cheval Blanc boy. . . . What was his name, now?"

"Yes, Mother, but the Cheval Blanc boy is also being thought of for the Nestlé girl. . . . *She's* a Palmolive on her mother's side. But the Palmolive boy has divorced the Pampers girl in order to marry a Bic, one of the disposable pens. . . ."

"I'm talking about facts—I don't know why you have to make a joke of everything!"

"But don't you realize that when you think you're talking about people you're really talking about products!"

"What does it matter? They have a family product in the same way as we have a family name! The only difference is that they're much better off these days!"

"Of course. But that's not all: the Bic granddaughter is getting married again to the Volvo boy, and the eldest Volvo girl has divorced the Conforama boy to marry whom do you think? The son of United Assurance—'Insure with us and never say die!' "

"Don't be absurd, you're talking about limited companies!"

"So it's no more marriages? What could I have been thinking of?"

"I do admire you, being able to make the ladies laugh in this heat!" Jean de Montlaur, never ruffled, was pouring oil on troubled waters. Mathilde's laughter was rather strained.

As for Olga, she thought the Montlaurs were charming, jewels reflecting true French vivaciousness; and that Hervé was the most amusing of men.

"And here is Madame's mail, bulging with letters from New York!"

Edward wrote that he couldn't get used to the separation, he was trying to get Olga's next trip brought forward, or he might pop over to Paris himself. She suddenly felt worried, and the effort she made to hide it resulted in a twisted smile. She didn't need to make any comment; it was her own private life. But Hervé noticed her reserve and was growing impatient.

"This Jerry Saltzman's beginning to get on my nerves. Why is he always writing to you? Maybe I should challenge him to a duel."

What a good idea—diverting his jealousy (true or feigned?) on Saltzman!

"He's coming to Paris in the fall. We must ask him over."

"Yes! Show him a really good time!"

Hervé was laughing at himself, since he couldn't laugh at Olga. Olga wasn't laughing at anything.

"I believe you like Bordeaux wines?"

"Yes, but I'm not a connoisseur."

"What do you think of this Haut-Brion 1967?"

Hervé was using the old family ewer to decant the bottle by candlelight: this let the wine breathe, and the slight warmth from the flame helped it get back its body. Hervé clearly enjoyed the old-fashioned ritual.

"It's only in France they take such care with wine."

"Only in my house! . . . It's a beautiful country, France, isn't it, Saltzman? Perfect for tourists. Like Italy, Egypt . . . Don't you agree?"

"Never been to Egypt. Not sure I'd like it."

"But you do like France, don't you? Americans all like the foie gras, the cheese. And the Bordeaux, when the books they write sell more than a hundred thousand copies, as yours do. Otherwise they swill Burgundy."

"I get the impression you don't like the uncouth Americans." (Jerry fielded the ball neatly; he was delighted to see the dinner was to be on a war footing.)

"Who, me? Where could you have got that idea? You don't speak French, by any chance? No, I thought not. Why bother? We're not living in the eighteenth century, Versailles's a museum, all you need do is hire a Walkman and a cassette—everything's recorded in English, Japanese, or Russian. I expect you do speak Russian?"

"Not yet."

"You will. The Americans are rich Russians without knowing it, and the Russians are poor Americans who dream of becoming really American. It *is* you who arranged for almost all the dissidents to be translated? Congratulations!"

"Don't mention it—it was a pleasure. I was really looking for Kafka, but he hasn't been reincarnated yet. As far as I know."

"And you don't see anything resembling a dissident or two in Paris?"

"Where's that?"

"I see. Viewed from the top of the World Trade Center, Paris is swallowed up in the French and Italian Department. Cute, isn't it? Olga represents France in some little pigeonhole that isn't even called French, but 'French and Italian'! I suppose they bracket the smaller civilizations together to save money. Let's see, how long has it lasted?—three or four centuries, if you leave out the Romans. But of course nobody's heard of the Latins in New York. What's that in comparison with China, the Bible, or IBM? Nothing! '*French and Italian*'!"

"Maybe. But you ought to see how enthusiastic they are about Olga! Didn't she tell you? A woman as intelligent as she is beautiful! My students talk to me about her, they're mad about her. I wish I could be a student in 'French and Italian.' "

"Try, my friend, try. And don't forget to write a novel about it. Hey, I've just thought of a title for it! *The French Complex.* Pretty good, eh?"

"You *are* in good form, Hervé! There's a humorist of genius in France, and it's you. It had to be me who discovered you!"

"And if I understand you correctly you'll arrange to have me translated? Or at least this interview? Just a small, really funny sample to start with? The American public doesn't like tiring itself. All it reads are best-sellers about melancholy characters exchanging jokes."

"I myself couldn't get any further than *Now*—it got too difficult for someone like me, who came from Newark and whose grandmother didn't even have a cleaning lady to scrub her floor. But I've had girls—and what girls! the prettiest in the whole faculty!—who knew your articles in *Now* by heart, and recited them to me. And they'll go on reading *Aleph*, I promise you."

"I doubt it very much. There's too much sex and religion in it."

"Still, some people are holding up: Saïda and Lauzun, up to a point."

"Imposters! Adulterated goods for export! They're sold, at very

high prices, in America, Japan, and Africa, and they'll soon be
flogging them in Russia too. The French universities will colo-
nize the people of the underdeveloped countries, who still think
they ought to learn something."

"Don't the French? But they read your work, don't they?
You're even a best-seller yourself now. . . ."

"Only in France itself, old boy, only in France. What's more
it's all based on a misunderstanding: the women readers thought
I was talking about them. As you know, it's women who make
best-sellers. And they scented out sex in me. Fell on it like a dog
on a bone. Very bad, that. More and more frowned upon. Right-
thinking people have never had it so good. Say, have you ever
heard of the marquis de Sade, even though you are an American?"

"What on earth did they do to this guy in America? You're
paranoid, Sinteuil! Why, the marquis de Sade was my cousin!"

"Bravo! Old boy, you're a Nazi!"

"There's no stopping him! Olga, help!"

"Don't pretend you don't know: what Sade described in the
One Hundred and Twenty Days the Nazis actually did to their
victims in the camps."

"Now you're going too far! Let's cool it, shall we?"

"A typical nice American! What it is to live in a country where
they never mention Sade on television!"

"What do you expect? I'm just a primitive writer who thinks
the imagination is the imagination and is lost in reality—as I
should have admitted at the outset, and would have done if you
hadn't been so childish and aggressive! Where was I? Oh yes—
I'm all at sea in reality; I live on fantasy. People buy my books
because they need fantasy—just the way they need salt or deter-
gent. And I spend my time fabricating fantasies, just as you
spend your time maundering about between quotation marks."

"How feeble! Never mind about quotation marks—your fantasies could be translated into facts by the next Nazi to show up."

"On the contrary, fantasies purge the death wish, provided
they're related with talent and humor."

"So you agree with me?"

"He's got it at last! Rather slow on the uptake for a Frenchman,
isn't he, Olga? But seriously—is that true about Sade and the

Nazis? Where does it come from? Anne Dubreuil? The French Academy? Who? After all that's been written by Brichot, Bréhal, and you yourself? Because I do sometimes read your stuff, you scoundrel!"

"Ah, this old country's not what you think, my dear Saltzman! You see before you the best specimens, but as for the rest . . . But I'd like you to try this Château-Margaux 1964—it's excellent with sweetbreads. We're both people of the Book, you and I— the Book that is the Law—because it calls for an infinite number of interpretations, a profusion of what you call 'quotation marks.' But I don't have to warn you about all the solid citizens there are about, people rooted in their reason, their institutions, and their interests. They don't see anything anywhere but reality, that's what they want, it reassures them, lends power to their stupidity. You mustn't fantasize, Saltzman: fantasy's infinite, an abomination. Whereas men and women, real men and women, are . . . well, one mustn't be ashamed to say they're finite. Real people are narrow-minded and are always yelling, 'In the name of Reason, arrest these madmen, these writers, these Jews—no, these Nazis!' They'll use whatever word happens to inspire the most fear and horror at the moment, but their purpose is timeless and always the same: 'Death to imagination!' "

"And to think I was going to try to find a pied-à-terre in Paris! My dear Olga, your husband is one of the most charming and reasonable paranoids I've ever met. I wonder how you put up with him!"

"To your health, Saltzman!"

"Next year in Jerusalem, Sinteuil!"

"But where will Jerusalem be next year?" (Olga)

"I'm afraid that yet again we'll have to be satisfied with what's been written. The promised land of the imagination." (Hervé)

"Okay, marquis! (Saltzman)

"Why am I always the one who's deserted?" wrote Edward, half comically, half tragically. But Olga wasn't deserting him. It was just that Sinteuil's intellectual vitality, provocativeness, and perpetual readiness for a fight provided her with a supply of oxygen that made the flame of her life burn brightly. It was a life made up of mental adventure, verbal confrontation, written murder and resurrection, and as such might have seemed idle, long-winded, and abstract. But to the people living it, it was a kind of martial art. Looking from a distance at the sort of risks they ran, you might see them as absurd samurai. But they were brave samurai if you took into account the nervous strain, material losses, and public humiliations involved. It was exhausting. Anyone whose profession it is to deal in symbols knows that these strange machines can only be fueled by an extreme of tension, an expenditure of energy, that may threaten one's vital equilibrium. It was possible, Olga found. But only if you had the comfort of Edward's protection. His letters contained scarcely any complaint, and what there was usually took the form of what looked like quotations, avoiding direct reference to himself.

"The soul chooses its company, then shuts the Door."

"I have seen it choose someone from a wider nation. Then close the Valves of its attention like a stone."

"Enclosed two sunsets. The other person's is the larger, but as I said to a friend, mine, which will fit into a hand, is more convenient."

"A strange fate, that of him who is forsaken . . ."

Such tears in free verse occurred here and there in descriptions, meant to sound impersonal and blasé, of days in New York or the chores of an international jurist. Such letters made Olga feel poetic herself, and in return she would write the kind of answers that are never sent.

Dear and incomparable friend, you have given me such pleasure and grace that my heart almost breaks—it's very fragile—in the attempt to contain both your gifts and my life here in Paris. Another present from you, together with your own faint anguish: the memory of a city at once splendid and cruel, implacable and aloof. I shall always love it, because you made it a hayloft fit for a king, a haven of undreamed-of repose. I can't choose between Paris and New York. I remain a continental, but I'm a nomad too; I intoxicate myself with words and extravagances, but I rejoice in the tact of the body I love. And yet I have chosen, for I'll always be Hervé's wife, and shall love you only now and then.

But the gift you gave me will be our heritage, one that no artist can copy, no thief can steal. Because you forged it without words. As the sea, without words, carves out the caves where the mermaids take refuge after they've wounded their feet pursuing princes over the rocks.

I can't do without either the race I have to run or the company of your mocking affection. You've given me so much peace, I have enough energy for the two of us now, if you agree to share . . . what was it? . . . this 'secret destiny.'

While you bestow yourself on me entirely, I offer you only fragments. But even though it's divided by time and space and torn by incompatible loyalties, my love is perhaps no less valuable for being fleeting. I answer your availability with my inconstancy. It may seem unworthy, but you will see that my rare passion does not contradict your serenity. I take the risk of letting you return to your own inconstancy. I don't even ask myself whether I want you to do so, though I know that when you do it will give me great pain. But after all, it will only make us even more alike, perhaps sadder and wiser and more surprising, even. Whatever happens, keep a place safe for our secret understanding, our complicity.

Olga

19

*T*he earth is brief," said Edward. "Here I am in
Paris." Yet another quotation, apparently—heaven knows
where he'd found it. By way of justification, he repeated
it: "The earth is brief, you see; the earth is brief . . ."
As a matter of fact he'd come from a NATO meeting in
Bonn to attend a legal discussion about Third World
debt that was being held in Paris.

They were both glad to have preserved the unshaka-
ble intimacy of lovers who don't lie to each other. But
Olga struck him as both more sentimental and more
careful than before: she'd lost the magnanimous abandon that had enthralled him at the Algonquin. For
Dalloway, eroticism was connected with sound: he
transformed his pleasures into aural perceptions, traveling among resonances, losing himself in the contours of
sonority, drowsing under the spell of tones. Olga, crys-

talline and precise, had now become a harpsichord—even when her body was dazed with fulfillment, there was still something lucid and lively about it. She was no longer a viola, from which a Spanish player could draw grave and dark vibrations midway between a prayer and a warrior's gallop, as at the concerts of French baroque music they'd listened to together one night at Carnegie Hall. It was a harsh and voluptuous parsimony that was a revelation to them both. Perhaps—if he stayed longer and she were less on the qui vive—the Spanish violas might come back? But Dalloway hadn't any complaints; no, no, he didn't want to be suspected of any dissatisfaction. Isn't the chord that follows a fugue on the harpsichord the very height of sophistication?

He'd been to lots of dinners, cocktail parties, and receptions, and as everyone in Paris is more or less literary—including politicians and lawyers—he hadn't been able to avoid hearing about Sinteuil. A television program here, a newspaper article there: Sinteuil has moved too far to the right; no, Sinteuil is still on the far left; no no, Sinteuil's only out for himself, why does he write for that fascist rag; oh no, my wife thought he made his position very clear in a radio broadcast, did you know he'd become a Papist? Come come, just a student hoax, what about those articles he writes about pornographic photographs? Maybe, but you can't deny he's got talent. . . . And so on. Sometimes Olga's name cropped up amid all this gossip: some people maintained she was absolutely pure, distinct from Hervé and his compromises with the media; others suspected her of some diabolical ulterior purpose. Edward felt physically nauseated. He felt like shouting out, protesting: "That's enough! I don't want to be dragged into all this! Leave me the woman I know, and whom you know nothing about, and for God's sake keep what I *don't* want to know to yourselves!" But he said nothing. Just went on smoking his cigars in silence, apparently as fascinated by the bitter smell and the swirls of smoke as a small boy might be by an electric train.

He even went and had a drink in the attic. "Hervé's always kept late in the evening by one thing or another—would you like to see my study?" So he was allowed to see Olga's life as displayed in this French interior, with its Louis Quinze desk, bronze lamp ornamented with figures of French lords and ladies, black wall-to-wall carpets, Chinese prints. When all's said and done, what people think of as a life can be reduced to a space. At least, that's what is left of a life when you take away the usual immutable egoism. The professor of government was definitely an immutable egoist, for what he saw made his eyes moist: he'd have done better not to look, and to concentrate again on his electric train or the smoke rings from his cigar.

Anyhow, that's what he did when someone pointed Hervé out to him, sitting at a neighboring table in the bar of his hotel ("The only possible one in Paris—I can have a Xerox machine in my room"). He saw a man who was exuberant, cheerful, animated; unmindful of others inside his own capsule of brilliance; surrounded by a crowd of admirers. Clearly it was from Sinteuil that Olga got the highly charged manner that, in Paris, made the mermaid of the caves exchange her former ease for the (equally attractive!) tension of a champion swimmer. As a matter of fact, Edward quite enjoyed all this literary bustle. It reminded him of his years in the Village, when he used to sit in cafés reading the beats. Of course, the great-great-grandchildren of Saint-Simon couldn't bury themselves in any 'underground.' No, they opened up chasms of mischief and provocation in the relations between politics and society; they were at a tangent to the world; but they were never out of the world or even underneath it. Dalloway was impressed by Sinteuil's stratagems: it occurred to him he need only take down from its forgotten shelf some book he'd read in his own adolescence, and he'd find himself in familiar country. But no—he soon realized that it wasn't the same book. And not only had he never read the book of the past through to the end, but the book of the present was written in a different language and a different spirit.

But I'm not as old as all that! Dalloway thought to himself, drawing on his cigar, in a last fit of what he himself called his immutable egoism. And he went and had a drink all on his own, without any jurists or Third World or Olga, on a café terrace in Saint-Germain-des-Prés. One long-legged young beauty in a miniskirt looked like just what he needed to restore a proper sense of values. She noticed him: she gave him a misty glance and let the tip of her tongue wander over her lips. The sort of mouth that knew what to do with a man's sex. Just the thing for the end of a political day. But also the sort of girl he no longer knew how to get rid of. No—what an idea! He plunged back into the amethyst afternoon light, like a spirit just out of the bottle in which it had been imprisoned for ages under the stormy sea. I'm the illusion of a solitary, looking for my own shadow, he thought, reflecting that he'd better disguise his solitude if he wanted to keep Olga. Olga and solitude—he must never mention one to the other.

Olga had the impression that Paris restored to Edward rather too much of his Reverend Mr. Bovary aspect. That was only natural, but she preferred the state of affairs in New York, when Edward's melancholy had the tart flavor of gin. She was rather disappointed to find him shyer than ever: no doubt about it, Paris inhibited him. Never mind, she'd get him to talk about politics, his work, international law: Tell me what you did yesterday, it's all Greek to me but it's very interesting, do tell me about it. Was she trying to give her fascination with the mysterious Algonquin artificial respiration?

She thought not. But Dalloway wasn't sure of anything anymore.

Peter O'Brian was one of those conscientious academics who read everything, including the left-wing papers founded in the fifties that no one else bothered with anymore—papers like the obscure *People*, edited by the once famous polemicist Nekrassov, who had made himself a reputation in the fight against the McCarthy witch-hunt. It was in *People* that O'Brian came across a second-rate but vexatious article against Olga's book on Céline, which had just come out in translation in the United States. One of Olga's former students (why? how? he'd been rather less stupid than most) went to great lengths to prove it was wrong to take an interest in a criminal like Céline: he should be erased from the memory of mankind because of his anti-Semitic pamphlets. "Mankind can do without Céline," wrote John Kramer. "Olga Montlaur tries to make a distinction between Céline the pamphleteer and Céline the stylist. What is the good of such hairsplitting? Céline's acceptance of human vileness was bound to lead him to fascism. Literature is moral or nothing."

Olga was surprised by her detractor's lack of integrity. She believed that, forty years after the war, it wasn't enough just to condemn Nazism: it was time to examine the madness of the "final solution" in detail; time to make a patient effort to analyze it; and time to point to the murky areas of the human mind to which it had once, and might still, appeal. Céline was a perfect subject for that kind of criticism: he was a master of the magic of words, a wizard of the death wish, and an abominable ideologist. There was no call to make literature—or anything else—a matter of morals. *People* took a Stalinist attitude and called for literature to be right-thinking. Hitler wanted art to be moral too: he regarded Picasso as sick and the Impressionists as mentally deficient. Using the same moralist slogans but with a so-called left-wing slant amounted to precisely the same thing: Kramer was nothing but a dogmatic Stalinist, a left-wing Hitlerite. Whereas there can be no art without a cathartic compromise. And that meant it was better to analyze than to be silent: wasn't that precisely the job of a critic, not to be confused with censorship?

Olga got passionately angry at so much naïveté and malice. O'Brian had already written a letter of protest to *People*, but as Nekrassov didn't know him, nothing had happened.

"Edward, didn't you know some of the staff on *People* when you were at San Remo?"

"That's right. I sometimes run across them still. Charming relics."

"You lived through the beat movement yourself—you know how important Céline was to the American 'underground.' It would be interesting if you'd point out why it's wrong to make a sweeping 'right or wrong' judgment on that kind of work."

"Me? But I can't write!"

"Yes, you can. And you like Céline . . . we got to know each other through him, if you remember."

"Of course I remember! But that's a private matter. And literature's a private matter. Not so important as . . . It only interests a few connoisseurs. The American public couldn't care less."

"Not so important as what?"

"As war in the Middle East, Third World debt, communism, terrorism . . ."

"The things you're concerned with . . ."

"Pure chance. Though I admit I did make a choice."

"When you left San Remo to go in for international law."

"In a way. You're not angry, I hope?"

"Me, angry? Why should I be? But you do read, and you're shocked by books that are base, and surely you don't think such things have no effect on the future of the world? At least—to speak as I imagine your colleagues do—in the long term?"

"Of course not, of course not! But I'm not an expert. If I was pushed, I'd have more to say about your book about China. I like it very much."

"That's not the point."

"But no one's interested in the other business!"

"What about me?"

"What do you mean?"

"Do *I* interest *you*?"

"That's a completely different matter."

"I don't think so. And if you do think so, you're wrong. And I'm sorry to hear it. Very sorry."

"You don't know America. No one there has ever heard of Céline. And you want me to expatiate on an academic squabble that's blown up in a publication directed at businessmen. Or rather at nobody—I shouldn't think *People* sells many copies these days . . ."

"If you want to know what I really think, I regard this as a test. How far do we agree with each other? I personally regard such 'squabbles,' as you call them, as absolutely fundamental. It's a matter of whether people are to be free to say what's compromising. To start an argument, not to have to close it. Liberty seen as a risk. A mental risk. But also as a risk in aid of what's right. Who has the right to put a stop to liberty? What law governs that right? You know all about administrative, commercial, or universal law. But is the law of art the same? Do you think that's too Western a question? Too futuristic? It's not certain. And even if it were, it would be impossible to avoid it: men cannot live by conscience alone any more than by bread."

"Now you're entering an area of turbulence. Drink your martini."

"I didn't seek the turbulence. We're in it whether we like it or not. And if you try not to think about it it'll carry you off—I don't know how, but it's inevitable, so watch out. Imagine some fanatical fundamentalist condemning a writer to death one day just for upsetting him."

"All right. I'll think about it. There's no hurry."

"There is for me."

She realized Edward didn't want to commit himself. He was minimizing the incident. Perhaps he merely wanted to avoid getting mixed up in Olga's affairs. But it was a breach. The first important breach between them. A proof that they didn't think alike on fundamental matters. Olga lived by her commitments and didn't regard them as abstractions. Edward had no idea how much he'd hurt her. Of course she still loved his metaphysical eyes, his caresses, the peacefulness of his love. But his wisdom suddenly seemed too prudent. Prudish. Pusillanimous. A wisdom that was too soft, too soothing. Stuck.

"Kramer's an unstable character, you know. Unrepresentative. Not worth getting worked up about." (O'Brian)

"I'm not a psychoanalyst. I regard stupidity as an insult." (Olga)

"I've always said there's no real culture in America. They swallow things but they don't digest them. At the least sign of emotion the facade collapses, and all that's left, at best, are moralists working at computers—sorry, Hugh, I didn't mean IBM! For them everything has to be either positive or negative. . . ." (Diana)

"I'm still enjoying your book on China. You've caught the strangeness of the place beautifully. On the one hand nothing moves—immutable eternity and Communist dogma. Take that grotesque trial. . . . I don't know who's worse, Jiang Qing or her judges! But on the other hand they're beginning to open up to Western commerce, they're more enterprising than the Russians—real businessmen. We're in for some surprises. . . ."

Hugh brought the conversation back to serious matters, though of course he was still very polite to Olga. After all, he was married to an expert on the troubadours.

The Sylvers often invited her to their house on Long Island. "Now you know New York, you don't need Edward so much. Come and have a rest at our place."

The great red ocher woods and the vastness of the space there were a great contrast to the pearly intimacy of the Montlaurs' island. But Olga was greeted by the same broad, bluish light, and by the Atlantic breeze that fills the heart with the same bracing chill on either side of the globe.

Sometimes Edward went with her. Not very often. But she spent two months in New York loving him just the same.

She had thought, in the past, of the possibility of his being unfaithful. She'd even hoped he might be, to make their relationship more equal. And now the situation had arisen, though not in the shape of a beautiful blonde. It was at once more harmless and more annoying: the two lovers were no longer on the same wavelength: had they ever been? Edward didn't share all Olga's passions, that much was clear. She quite understood he might want to assert his independence, and might even need a small revenge: if Olga insisted on her own autonomy in Paris, that sacrosanct temple of the intellect that he wasn't allowed to enter, let her get on with it on her own! All that was natural and acceptable. But still Olga felt forlorn: so Edward's protection wasn't absolute, you couldn't count on anyone, we're all extraterrestrials to one another, the Huxian syndrome reigned supreme. But she still hankered after Edward's caresses, and when he didn't make love to her she dreamed that her body had turned to water anyway, as if he really had kissed her again all over, again and again.

But it was everything about Edward and his life that Olga loved, not just what Diana called "the sensual body concealing the tiny heart of his poor depressed mother." She might never have given herself to him, perhaps, if it hadn't been for all that: for Boston, Brandeis, and the Village; Rosalind—or, rather, Ruth Goldenberg—and her flight to Jerusalem; even for the peculiar Isaac Chemtov, and Patricia and Jason; for Edward's own shyness about the family past that would always remain the great adventure of his life (together with his passion for Olga, of course); for the ultraserious summaries he gave her of his activities as an international lawyer, which sounded rather affected and not in keeping with the melancholy warmth that had finally won Olga over. (Though you might equally regard his air of respectability, and the gravity emanating from him as an eminent public figure, as a rational distillation of his delicate sensibility.)

In short, Olga was sure she loved everything about Dalloway, including the ramifications of his life story and the other characters in it, and this only rendered even more unbearable his refusal to enter into her own battles with what she called stupidity.

Her resentment didn't go away. A stiffness grew up between them and intensified. It wasn't unpleasant. The harpsichord merely ceased to sound its lucid chords. Olga was keeping her distance. Edward knew what was happening. Perhaps it was better that way. A little moderation of that childish eagerness wouldn't do any harm if she clung to her life in Paris and New York was for her merely an interlude. They must let time do its work. Love creates time, but time breaks up passions as the wind breaks up clouds: storms pass away, drawn off by an anticyclone. Yes. Avoid precipitation. Let time do its work.

20

Jessica has started studying law in New York. Arnaud wants his daughter to be a citizen of the world (no less!), and the child herself is delighted to be able to look at her family from a distance and from a height. "Do you know who I met last night at the World?—You've never heard of the World? Of course . . . It's a nightclub in the East Village, down where the streets are named after the letters of the alphabet.—Guess, then! Olga Montlaur, with our own Professor Dalloway!"

Dalloway? Where have I heard that name before? Oh yes, of course! When Arnaud decided his daughter should enter the law faculty, Dalloway was one of the attractions: "There are some very good people there. Dalloway, for example. Jessica won't be wasting her time." I see him as one of those upright types who do all they can to save respectability amid a world in chaos. Imagine Olga de

Montlaur flirting with the Established Order! Jessy sounded as if she expected me to be staggered by the news. I wonder how much she knows about Romain?

Any relationship that's conducted with good taste is pure. Preposterous, shocking, ridiculous—my pleasure with Romain is really chaste as the sea. And what is good taste? It consists in performing every action as if it were our last.

October 15, 1980

A dark-haired young woman, thin, obviously suffering, but solemn and composed. "Dr. Bresson suggested I should come—antidepressants aren't doing me any good so I'd like to try psychotherapy." *It's unusual for Romain to send me any of his patients. Carole must be pretty ill. And she must have shocked him. She talks in images, embellishing pain to make it inaccessible, but also to inspire sympathy. I find her touching, which shows I'm communicating with her sandy, sallow composure. Her bronze melancholy. I don't know how to set about loosening her armor without stirring up the death that's within, but I agreed to listen to her. Her shivering. Her lethargy. A waif from the beginning. She finds words to attract me at the same time as they keep me at a distance:* "The sky is stuck—it will never open again." "No more light: there's nothing but darkness in my brain, and when that gets less, death draws near." *If I just let her go on with her poetical pastiches, she'll commit suicide. I tried to make her tell her life story. No luck for the moment. All the stories she tells are fairy tales and erotic: nightmares or resurrections, always with projections and associations. Life's a snare—she won't have anything to do with it. Today she refused to say anything about it:* "I'm in the grave, in a nuclear particle." *I didn't press her. We'll have another try in couple of days.*

Silence.
"You haven't told me anything about your family."
"I see people dressed in tulle. My words go through them. Nobody's solid."
Silence.
"You are, in a way: you have a story inside you."
Silence.
"I'm like grass. I don't do anything. There's never been anything for me to do."
Silence.

"Like grass?"

"Grass hasn't got anything to do because it doesn't flower. It spends the day waiting for the rabbits to come and eat it, and the night collecting dew to drink."

I wait. Silence.

Who ate Carole? What does she want to drink? As for me, I like the virginity of grass and am not bothered that it doesn't bear fruit.

"Do you mean grass has no story because it doesn't have flowers or bear fruit? Like a barren woman?"

"Oh, but it was by choice! I decided it for myself. Maybe I was wrong. If I'd decided otherwise, perhaps Martin wouldn't have gone away . . ."

Her face, unstable and yellow as sand, flushes. But she goes on.

"What is a mother? The ability to abstain. Do you understand? Well, I have no mother. I wish I didn't have one."

"But you do have one, and you'd like to kill her."

Perhaps the analysis is beginning.

"Not at all! I'll kill myself first. But don't worry, there won't be a fuss, I shan't give her that satisfaction. I shall go cheerfully, like a ripe cherry falling from the tree. I'm lucky."

". . . ?"

"It's lucky to be without sorrow."

Carole puts on her bronze mask again. But we've taken one step away from her grave in the shape of a nuclear particle. I'm a bit less worried about her committing suicide.

November 1, 1980

I haven't kept this journal for years. I replaced it with records of sessions with my patients. Tried to live through their words, reading them over and over, trying to give these people another life. Not mine, theirs, but made new. I didn't put down anything about myself, except insofar as my interpretations of others are my links with them, or rather the space between me and what they think is the meaning of what they say. Probably I needed not to put into words, not to put into this book, precisely what is most personal, most sensual about myself: Romain. It's something that can't be said, unless in poetry, music, or painting. So I say nothing. I remain silent. But with a few relaxations. I do pinpoint my moments of weakness or joy. I note the flashes of light in the words of others, amid densities of meaning I wouldn't presume to violate. The subconscious fleetingly revealed in the light takes refuge in that darkness: it did show itself to me, but only as a challenge. Have I become less aggressive through contemplating the darkness of others?

November 1980

A man has just been brought into Arnaud's section: last night he strangled his wife. "He seems quite okay now," Romain tells me, "but I'd like to have your opinion." I recognize Wurst. In a state of dissociation.

He doesn't remember anything. He talks about God. Why not? He has exercised his intelligence with tyrannical rigor, but against what? What he only now dares to say shows he was fighting against his faith. I wouldn't venture to define what faith is, but I do remember what a Stoic once said about the lack of it: The absence of faith consists in thinking happiness impossible amid so many accidents. Wurst, who flaunted the fact that he was a complete unbeliever, obviously thought happiness was impossible. Any kind of happiness. Including—perhaps principally—happiness with a woman. The happiness mothers sometimes impart. The happiness Carole has never had, or only intermittently, thanks to Rosalba, Fiesole, and the Virgin Mary.

Both Carole and Wurst are suffering from depression. They are tombs containing a death that rots them from within. Wurst's suddenly exploded. In one fell swoop he sacrificed both his wife and his own philosophy. He turned dead self against impossible happiness. But his sacrifice allowed him to spare his own life. He still has some reason left. He can live. As half a robot, half a believer. Floating on a sea of oblivion that is chaos: the murder of his own identity. "Sometimes, when awareness of things ceases before life does, it seems a good idea to hasten matters."

People wonder whether Wurst alone is guilty or whether his wife wasn't partly responsible for the murder. An outrageous question. The thirst to kill arises when desire is spent, and it's very difficult for a woman to keep desire from failing. Wurst was a man who loved concepts, not women, though some women did adore him: worshipers of strangled fulfillments.

But Lauzun is silent now, and the only philosophy that holds water comes with inner demons. But Wurst fled from his. "A man is unhappy if he pays no attention to the stirrings of his soul." The psychosis of melancholy shows that a desire for God may take the place of the death wish. But who needs these cruel truths? Christians have found a compromise: theirs is a living God, their Eros is also Agape. Wurst attacked a woman's throat: he stopped her breath because there was no more breath in him. His body was disinhabited. A dead phallus. And he didn't have enough time or innocence to replace it *with faith, and simply believe in God. But he did attempt such a metamorphosis.*

I wouldn't have advised that solution, that treatment. But I don't blame anyone. I mightn't have done any better than the analysts Wurst did consult. I'm finding Carole's case difficult enough.

December 1980

The passions don't grow weaker with age, they just become clearer. They're pitiless: they sweep away all the past. But they're inevitable too, and you can direct them. I could decide tomorrow to avoid what's happening to me with Romain. But I don't want to. Age makes you able to manipulate pleasure. You can cease to suffer. But is it because of age or because of analysis?

February 1981

Every moment expands and holds an eternity. Every moment vanishes as fast as if it had never been, as if the enhanced flavor of life made it intensely short.

Phone call from Jessy: she sounds just like my mother-in-law. I remember her as a baby, and now I imagine her phoning as she does her nails before going out for the evening: a great-great-great-granddaughter of Thérésa Cabarrus will create a sensation tonight in a SoHo nightclub. And tomorrow she'll be trying to vamp Professor Dalloway.

Time goes by like a snail. Then suddenly everything vanishes. Jessy no longer exists; Thérésa and Joëlle Cabarus both disappear! All that remains, suspended like the heart of the air, is Romain's breath as he kisses me. For people in love, time is somewhere between a second and eternity. One ought to write it down in fragments. Instead of being the concentrated rhetoric of logicians, aphorisms ought to be the language of passion, which forgets nothing but has no time to lose.

March 1981

Wurst is still in our section—a harrowing presence. Sometimes he's like something prehistoric: a reptile dating from the mists of time, before mammals; an illustration from one of those books on evolution. Not dangerous; solemn and quiet, rather, but with a composure that's empty, without effort. It may be that any attempt at concentration would degenerate into fury. But no, he's no longer capable of passion: the shock has left him with the memory of a reptile—blank, empty, remote. He's bleary-eyed, like a whisky drinker trying to make his family think he's watching television. He's no more responsible for the murder than we are capable of remembering we were once reptiles too.

June 1981

Carole again:
"The outside of the within: nothing but mud. Farther in, the inside itself: rays, but only for me; rays of the desert."
Me:
"Nobody can make you think you're unhappy."
Carole:
"When I'm dead a tooth will grow out of the mud to cause a disturbance at their funerals."
Me:
"Their funerals? Are you going to kill someone?"
Carole:
"I shan't be there to feel the tooth grow, but I know it will hurt."
Me:
"A tooth against your mother,* which will hurt me too?"

Carole's voice. Under the cold beauty of her borrowed poetry, the sharp tooth of her voice. "The voice is a person's moral identity" (Epictetus). "If you take away an actor's buskins and mask and make him go on the stage like a shade, does he still exist? If he still has his voice, he still exists." Carole is preparing to die, but I can hear from her voice that she's still alive.

The ability to play many parts. Not everyone can play them all. Sinteuil seems to play more than most people. Is Olga playing a part in New York, or getting caught out at her own game? I wish I could adapt myself to any role. For even in the lowliest part an actor shows he can use his voice.

To play every part until the final one, which refuses all roles. The comparison with an actor is valid only if it includes the pantomime of suicide. Am I influenced by Caroline? Or by Marcus Aurelius? Suicide is the right to a way out. Why should we be forced to bear the unbearable?

And yet I don't agree we have a right to commit suicide, because I don't believe in a way out: my bet is on the possibility of making the unbearable bearable. I substitute caring for care. I refuse to refuse. I play the game. I sweep away the nasty "outside of the within" that is only mud. I go even

---

*In French, "to have a tooth against" someone is to bear them a grudge. Teeth are said to occur often in dreams, and to be especially sinister. *Tr.*

further: I bet that the "pure within" of death-dealing rays can be swept away too. Whereas Carole still sees her "pure within" as a sacred citadel, misunderstood and impregnable. But I go as far as complete detachment from my self. And this results in a detachment from life that has neither the fine gravitas of Stoic suicide nor the insouciance of a freethinker, who regards himself as outside the game, refuses the wager, and makes his own rules. On the contrary, caring gives back the ability to enter into it all. The simple happiness of shared facts, like the happiness of breathing. Or like the humble but vital springiness of trodden grass: ordinary, pleasant, reliable.

Happiness is a fulfilled present. No waiting. Everything here and now. A perfect circle, whether large or small, is happy because it is right, like the one Giotto drew when he was asked for supreme proof of his skill. Happiness is qualitative; I try not to restrict it to quantity. As soon as it happens, happiness is. It doesn't need to last: a perfect moment achieves eternity. But the full experience of the moment includes both love and the insignificance of love; the intensity of my pleasure with Romain and the foolishness of it. This happiness isn't a breach in time; it absorbs time and makes it present to me, but it also dismantles and obliterates it. Once—evanescently—and for all: my fleeting moment is the pinnacle of happiness. People have committed suicide for joy. I prefer to move from plenitude to nothingness, and then once again to risk losing the game. It wouldn't matter too much—almost as little as a happiness. But I would have tried everything. That's what caring is. Joëlle Cabarus: a woman who nurses those sick from the disease of life. How conceited can you get!

September 1981

Lauzun is dead. Between a father and daughter there's a solitude. A gulf. If you didn't know that, the male analyst and his female patient were invented to show you. It's the chasm that's perhaps the most painful and the most lucid of loves. You can't renounce it without killing something inside you, something intangible, a delicious suffering that enables you to live and that people call your dignity. "Joëlle Cabarus has a lot of dignity."

Lauzun has just died in the hospital, under a false name. He didn't even have the same mind anymore. But would he have wanted to lose his name, even to hide his decline? I doubt it. Let the names bury their dead. A name keeps its prestige even when mishandled by voyeurs.

For me it's a permanent sorrow, but one that's already grown duller.

Lauzun must have died when we broke off the analysis, or soon after. But real death enhances still further the dignity a daughter derives from renouncing, and yet retaining, her father's love. "Joëlle is so dignified!"

In spite of space: for I never saw him. In spite of time: for it's twenty years since I finished my analysis. A dull pain, vague but unbearable. It reminds me of a dream I had after an abortion: I'd lost my ring, a diamond ring Arnaud gave me when we got married; I searched wildly among the sheets, under the furniture, in the trash can. Nothing. But no, it isn't a ring I've lost, it's a finger. Worse: it's a whole arm that's missing—someone's cut off my arm. . . . Someone has cut off Lauzun from me. Death.

I wake up. Everything is there: my ring, Arnaud, Jessy, Romain. But not Lauzun. Silly old fool! But try as I may to make fun of his antics—I avoided the absurdity (which he loathed) of acting as his disciple—he still haunts me. A little. A lot. Perhaps because he died a slow death. Or because before dying himself he staged the death of his words. Or because he was blinded before he was extinguished. He makes me think death is omnipresent, that it lives in the place of the living and sometimes decides to throw off its disguise and hover visibly over the life we thought was separate from death. Like now, when death is carrying off so many that I too am forced to think of my own demise. But I remember that when I was in my teens I had a strange flash of inspiration telling me I was incapable of religious faith because I wasn't afraid of dying.

"It's just a matter of age. It's only natural for old fogeys of their generation to snuff it," say Arnaud and Romain, agreeing for once. Even so! There've been too many at once. And it isn't over. Death is in the air.

I'm sure all these men who are dying around me see death as part of the (to them) necessary proof that thought is not one activity among many but life itself, the end of life included. Death is thus both a fulfillment and a canceling out of all they have said. They don't tell us death will be easy because eternity awaits us (that's what a believer thinks, and I don't think Lauzun was a believer, even if he did let people think so). Nor do they say death is insignificant, because everything about us is absurd (that is the courage of Zen, and both Lauzun and Benserade took only a distant interest in that). But because they spent their lives exploring meaning—the meaning of words, of symptoms, of dreams, of texts, of crimes, of darkness with or without end—their deaths are open to interpretation. Whether challenging, absurd or stupid, their deaths are part of the meaning they constructed. Death lends drama to their work, but also, paradoxically, cancels it out, with the nonchalance of a Stoic suicide. "See how splendid what I said becomes because of my death; but also how futile. In other words, the only reason for dwelling on my death is to understand my works better."

Some ask for forgiveness, some go humbly and without question. But the men who made us think these last twenty years have managed to use the hazards of biology, or desire, or even popular movements, to persuade themselves and us that they had reached the point where one has understood everything and has no further wish to go on. They disappear in a trance of mysterious and immeasurable happiness. They want us to know that they were never bored with anything—even dying. Boredom doesn't exist when you can give meaning even to the void. Dubreuil died rationally: his philosophy provided for the absurd, and death has no meaning in the context of the absurd. Lauzun made his own death into a symptom.

Taking care of others involves a kind of undramatic suicide of oneself. Caring mustn't be confused with devotion: devotion is egoistic, and self-love has never done anything but conceal self-hate. But caring comes from an abolition of the self. The impenetrable inner rays on which Carole's depression was fixated have gone. You yourself are being transfused, and your own dissemination disperses the unhappiness of others. No content is absolute, mine any more than anyone else's. That's it: in caring I use my knowledge in order to do away with myself, but quietly. A constant transfusion of what I might have been but am not and never shall be; I leave it to others to try, in their regeneration, to become it. Caring is space, separation—the gap between symptom and projection, between a good desired and a good obtained— overcome by trust.

Carole: "I've always been very hungry. But hunger made me shrink. A bird might have taken me for a midge and eaten me. Then I was frightened and stopped being hungry, and so stopped getting smaller. I stopped, and was a frozen, withered berry. A mummified berry. I don't know why the bodies of mummies are regarded as sacred. On the contrary, they suffer the most cruel of punishments—that of never being able to disappear. For them there's neither dust nor light nor reincarnation. I can't dissolve, either."

She complains that she's a mummy. I choose to understand that she brackets the idea of that frozen corpse with the desire not to disappear. Life is putting up a resistance: life is permanent and therefore deferred dissolution.

But she has gone on.

"There are times when I'm only a shriek of horror stifled by a bandage.

You are the bandage. The loneliness of a handcuffed criminal. She can't tell anything. But there is a kind of intoxication. Why do birds sing? Out of pleasure, do you think? No—because they are asking for pleasure."

And she is asking for me.

Carole: *"Girls are often killed."* I say nothing. If someone kills them, they're not obliged to kill themselves, and it's true there are criminals around. I wait for her to tell me a story about criminals not yet handcuffed.

"I haven't told you about the Wadanis—my tribe, and Martin's too. But we've given up on them. Martin has dropped them for good. I don't know about me.

"When a hunter dies in the prime of life—eaten by a jaguar, or in an accident, or because a dead man's spirit invades him and destroys him with disease—he has to be avenged and recompensed. Do you know how? They prepare someone to be a companion for him in the other world, someone he's fond of and who will make him laugh. His daughter for preference, or goddaughter. Or simply one of the prettiest girls, who will soon be a woman and whom all the men want. She is killed at dawn to appease desire and to halt for a moment the constant ravages of death, which yesterday inflicted sickness and today may cause some jealous tribesmen to settle their scores.

"I've heard the song of the killer. Dawn was just breaking, the fire hadn't yet gone out, and the family of the victim had a good idea of her fate. But no one protested. The killer was inspired: he began with low, inaudible sounds; then the flute encouraged him, he sang more clearly, his fury mounted, the one who would try to interrupt the chain of death was inhabited by the souls of all who had died since time began. I was petrified. I had no soul left, only fear, and shame at not being able to stop anything. The girl started to run, but he must have caught her. He brought back her body. Her neck was broken.

"Of course the killer's impure. But he's going to be purified. And do you know who's going to make the murderer spew out the death wish within him? If you're a true psychoanalyst you'll have guessed: the girl's mother. 'The mother of the victim cures the killer because she is the person most alien and opposite to him,' according to Strich-Meyer, 'and so enemies are reconciled.' But that's not it! In reality the killer fulfills the mother's desire by ridding her of the young rival who reminds her she's old and must die; he leaves the matron alone, triumphant and desirable. You must have heard the story of the stepmother who kills Snow White because the mirror has told her the girl is more beautiful . . . ?"

Carole is such a black-robed vestal that Snow White has never occurred to me. And yet that jet-black hair, that soft mass inside her body . . .

"Could Martin and your mother be in league with each other?"

"How can you say such a thing! Martin would never . . . I'm afraid it may be him who's killing himself in California. Phone calls in the middle of the night—sometimes I can hardly make out what he's saying. Is he stoned, sleepy, overwrought? He's sarcastic, anyway: 'Are you still with that crazy Sinteuil?' (How ridiculous—I don't know why he's got it in for Hervé.) 'I've been thinking about you.' (That's something!) . . . Scherner's just back from Berkeley, but he didn't tell me much: just terrifying insinuations. . . . I wrote down the killer's song when it got light. The beauty of madness. Do you think it's worth going back to all that?"

I'd have liked her to go back to her own story. But after all, child murder, the attempt to kill a girl . . . Glorious mystery is song; painful mystery, poetry. It's not sufficiently realized that intellectual meditation is often a discourse on suffering.

May 1982

Carole: "The sea was freezing and it was windy, so of course we didn't go swimming. Olga spent the whole day on her mare Kissmayou, galloping like a wild thing along the sea wall. I was given Kissmayou's son, who was called Naïka and would scarcely so much as trot—he was quiet as a baby, calm and gentle and with purple eyes. . . . yes, really! Exactly what I needed: a friend who didn't mind that I wasn't much of a rider, who couldn't speak, but who let me ride him and had purple eyes. A color that's proud and sad. Almost infectious.

"I must say I find Olga almost as soothing as Naïka. She doesn't notice anything, and doesn't explain anything. She's getting ready for her next trip to New York ('I'm one of the last of the Algonquins,' she says. 'I like New York—the people there seem almost as simple as I am. But this time the trip will be much shorter—I'll only be away for six weeks.') She plays tennis with Hervé, and I think she reads letters from Edward—he writes to her often, like a lighthouse sending out its signals just in case. Olga only sends postcards. 'I'm no good at writing letters,' she says.

"Hervé shuts himself up in his mill, working away with music blaring out all the time and frightening the gulls. They've heard from a man called Zhao, who was their interpreter in China and is now some kind of big boss: he's invited them back to Peking for Hervé to give some lectures and Olga to go on with her research on Chinese women. Hervé says this makes him laugh: 'Good old Zhao!' And Olga? If I was her I'd go. Perhaps. But she looks as if she's got something else on her mind. Zhao holds no attraction for the moment. She went off for a ride on Kissmayou. Then she stayed with me, not saying anything, a ball of dark red light: trying to get me to talk, I suppose. But I prefer not to say very much; though sometimes I find myself talking to Naïka. Amazing how the silence of some women can give you peace, and even dreams, and thoughts, a kind of mental life that you thought was shut away, even dead. . . ."

The silence of some women. It makes you see the purple eyes of horses, reflecting back your own unhappiness. But your own unhappiness shifted to another place. Looking back at you. So, after all, moved slightly away from you.

"Joëlle Cabarus has a kind of dignity—she knows how to keep quiet. She's a woman of silence." Who was it who said that, now? Oh, of course— the impossible Marie-Paule Longueville. I wonder what's become of her? Running a gallery in London, I believe.

September 1982

Two trees opposite my window hold up the sky. A dazzled spider links the azure heaven to my balcony, then follows the ashen sunbeam that falls on and lights up this Journal. The same blue, the same light—but six hours back: I must call Jessica in New York, I may catch her at home, she should be just waking up. Did she come across Dalloway last night? Who was he with? I bet he was on his own, and my Jessy writes that she's feeling rather lonely just now. This would be a good time for me and Arnaud to go and see her. How long is it since we went on a trip together? I can't remember the last time we stayed at the Algonquin.

I've written down the Wadani myth that Carole found for me in her notes. A flood myth that's also a myth of rebirth:

"A sea of red water rises, swells, and swallows up the Universe. Unless it's a fire, a flame consuming every living thing. A man and a woman are clinging to the top of a pine tree to escape the red water or scarlet fire. They throw pine cones into the bloody depths; the cones disappear. The man and woman are going to fall—no, they go on throwing down the fruit of the pine tree. There's no more fire now—only the red water rising. Suddenly the pine cones hit a rock and emerge out of the red waters as little islets. The man and woman are saved. The other Wadanis are drowned, but their dead souls go on producing waves. The same waves you see when the red water rises and fire sweeps through the Universe."

I've never seen red water, and there's not much fire in my universe. But it's not certain Carole will escape the deluge. The dead keep making waves: Benserade, Edelman, the two Wursts, Bréhal's mother. But after all, other people's fires are their own affair. I'm lucky enough to be able to hold in check the pain I myself share. Therapy is space and moderation: my own reserve pitted against the deluge. "Some women's silence," Carole says. There will always be red waters and pine trees. But where shall we find the patience to transform flood into rebirth? My moments of happiness lend strength to my patience. The patience of a pine tree on a red sea full of dead souls.

I must call Jessy, and book two round-trip tickets to New York.

V. *Luxembourg*

21

T

he soil of the island was waterlogged: the sea spread in invisible layers only a few meters under the earth's sandy sun-dried crust, held in by the *bri*. This was the local name for the impermeable clay that had structured the salterns ever since Guillaume le Grand, comte de Poitou, engaged the island's first workers in the industry. The *bri* was used to shape the various basins that fed the main reservoir, and it made a checkerboard over the whole saltworks. But the partitions gradually got covered in kelp, and the clay they were made of became so hard it had to be broken up every year and replaced by new barriers. But while a whole network of reservoirs ruled the interactions of land and sea on the surface, the ocean was still at work on its clay bed below, and sometimes rose up and mixed with the water in the salterns (useful, for all its briny tang, in times of drought).

Olga's thoughts kept turning to an image: this local cemetery, so cheerfully situated in the valley below the old Romanesque church, lay above an underground salt marsh. She couldn't imagine a more lugubrious last resting place. The light was clear and sparkling this September afternoon; the bells chimed faintly in the wind, like a music box; the freshly cut flowers made you think of gardens rather than funerals; a dozen graves commemorated Australian soldiers who died on the island during the war, fighting against the Nazis. . . . It was all like a school play put on by children who saw coffins as toys and imagined death as full of angels flying hither and thither. It didn't occur to anyone that a few yards below where they stood the sea was advancing on its bed of *bri*, folding the dead in a tepid, salty embrace.

If you were an amphibian and loved water as much as earth, if you had given your heart to the island, then you'd have no hesitation. As soon as you breathed your last you'd be buried in this flower-decked cemetery, cooled by the wind and washed by the ocean. The sea wouldn't let you rot; it would salt your corpse so that you turned into crystals; its weeds would come and cover you with a green shroud. That's what Jean de Montlaur must have thought. For instead of the imposing family vault in town, he had chosen to be buried in this humble country graveyard.

"You know how modest my husband was, Olga my dear. He preferred austerity to the family," said Mathilde, not altogether covering up her disapproval.

"He wanted to cut right adrift," said Hervé, surprised and proud.

Jean de Montlaur had just passed on without bothering anyone—no fuss, no lingering, managing it all for himself. A wet road; fog; the Citroën skidded; killed instantly . . . All the Montlaur family were there, distant as well as close relatives; also friends and acquaintances. All their faces were closed up like the shutters in a fashionable residential district. No words or gestures or tears. Such total reserve made Olga feel uncomfortable. Was it due to dignity or coldness? All very different, at any

rate, from the emotions such an occasion would have evoked in
Slav souls.

Jean de Montlaur, like a Roman sage, had taken proper care
of himself, been correctly groomed, but hadn't invested himself
overmuch in life or the conventions. He never grew too close to
people, never broke off with them. He was one of those irre-
proachable beings who have no enemies, so everyone who knew
him had come to the funeral, though none had ever discovered
the secret of the man whose body would soon be engulfed in the
bri. But if Jean de Montlaur had no enemies, neither did he have
any real friends—his reserve precluded intimacy, so the living
corpses present today were silent, ashamed at never having been
able to reach the heart which from its retreat had judged them.

Unless the truth was that these society people were simply
incapable of human feeling beneath their leaden masks? An
appearance of reserve often covers real indifference—a foolishness of the senses. They were all acting the play of the funeral
just as every Sunday morning they acted the play of mass. All
except Hervé, who to everyone's astonishment was on the brink
of tears.

The body was lowered into the dry earth, soon to become a
marsh. Olga couldn't help thinking of the bed of *bri*, the caress
of the sea, bones changed into salt crystals. Then suddenly
Hervé stepped forward and, as his father reached the bottom of
the grave, took a book out of his pocket and started to read in a
voice that stifled his grief and took the onlookers aback.

" 'We say therefore that a man should be so poor that he cannot himself be "a place where God may act," nor even have God
in him. As long as a man has space within him, he also has *difference*. And that is why I pray for God to make me free of God.' "

Master Eckehart was speaking through Hervé of Jean de Montlaur: his elegant simplicity was indeed a kind of "poverty," a
poverty "free of God." Hervé thought his father had been an
atheist, but that his atheism was another kind of belief. He went
on:

" 'Because of the nature of my eternal birth, so neither can I
die: . . . I have been from all eternity, and am and shall remain

eternally! I was at once my *own* cause and the cause of *all things*. And had I wished it, neither I nor all things would have been. But if I had not been, neither would God have been. But understand that this is not necessary.' "

The humility of the man who was different, praised at the beginning of the sermon, suddenly soared into an affirmation of his infinite will. " 'And had I wished it, neither I nor all things would have been . . . if I had not been, neither would God have been . . . Now I feel I am caught up and raised above all the angels . . . But understand that this is not necessary . . .' "

In fact, nobody understood anything! They were all more shocked by Hervé's audacity than by the obscure words, which they sensed were subversive without actually realizing what they meant.

Olga gazed at him, as if trying to draw out his thoughts through that closed-up face and understand them. He had just placed his father, pragmatic and self-effacing to the point of invisibility, among the mystics. Jean de Montlaur had been "free of God," and his distance from heavenly grace was the guarantee of his humanity; but from him, in the moral peace of his own solitude, there emanated such pride that he needed no one. That was how Olga interpreted Eckehart's meditation as she stood clutching Hervé's hand, but nonetheless unable to hold back her tears. She let Hervé's painful tension pass into her own body, for though that tension had been expressed in chiseled phrases, it was still torturing his nerves.

Sinteuil didn't notice. He was somewhere else, staring into space. "As long as a man has space within him, he also has *difference* . . ." Hervé might not have God within him, but something did catch him up and raise him above the angels. A strange flash of light linked Olga's pagan sensuality to the incandescent abstractness of Hervé performing his filial duty. The new, grave face of their complicity. With and beyond death. "And had I wished it . . . if I had not been, neither would God have been . . . But understand that this is not necessary."

Mathilde walked on ahead, pale and upright, supported by François and Hervé. Olga followed, with Odile and Xavier des Réaux. But death, like love, can't be shared.

"How sad . . . A man in the prime of life . . . Accident is the most absurd kind of death, don't you agree, Olga? Unless of course . . . It's an awful thing to say. . . . Unless he was very depressed, and . . ."

Odile was trying out the theory of suicide. Olga narrowed her Chinese eyes, rejecting it.

"I never saw him in low spirits. And his business affairs were going very well, if that's what you mean. . . . But you must know more about that than I do."

"That's what people say, that's what people say, but everything's so complicated these days, my dear."

Cousin Xavier was looking like a beagle again.

François turned around. The look he gave them was withering (Upset as well, though, thought Olga), and forbade all further comment.

Olga hadn't seen much of Jean: just a few weeks during family vacations, and the Montlaurs' own occasional trips to Paris. But as soon as they'd met they'd set up a minimal code in which to communicate—a language without phrases, the body language of practical people. When Kissmayou came home riderless one day, leaving Olga lying on the cliffs with a broken shoulder and a sprained ankle, Jean had driven straight to the spot, picked her up, and without words or emotion carried her to the car as gently as if she were a baby. Then for a month he brought her flowers and cups of hot chocolate, smiling vaguely. "They say you should rest, my dear. Well, that's what you're doing. Don't think about anything." He didn't even say, "I'm here." But he was there.

Because death is unknowable, people think they themselves die when they lose someone they love: a father, mother, child— a husband or wife when they've really loved each other, as does happen sometimes. But the death of mere other people leaves us unmoved—unless of course it makes us shed selfish tears over our own mortality. And for Olga, Jean was really no more than an "other," a stranger. What was more, he himself hated bombast. Yet she was discovering in this cemetery that here in France he was her father. She had no other, in France, now that Benserade and Edelman were dead.

And the island was to her as Jean had been: out of all the

places in France, she had chosen it as a refuge. Its sunsets, from which Jean had taught her how to tell the next day's weather; the men from the saltworks, with whom Jean would walk over the marshes or have a glass of wine in a café, talking about the birds and how they were being frightened away by the noise of outboard motors; the wine growers and their gifts of local wine— "The Montlaurs are experts in the great wines of Bordeaux, but ours has a tang of the sea"—and the oyster growers, as reserved and plain and impassive as Jean himself when he thought himself unobserved.

She too would choose this graveyard when the time came. Meanwhile she would adopt his way of living with this land, this sea, these peasants.

Some people are so impenetrable they only begin to live for us after they die. Apparently the Talmud says that we ought to leave our friends with a problem unsolved, and then they will think of us for the rest of their lives. Jean de Montlaur had left Hervé and Olga without revealing the secret behind his silent abnegation. Perhaps there was no enigma. Just the purity you find in all people who are good. Was it something to make you think about him for the rest of your life? He was the kind of father you don't see anymore. "As long as a man has space within him, he also has *difference*. And that is why I pray to God to make me free of God."

Life grows more and more like television: nothing happens except scientific discoveries and accidents (in other words, death). Politics gets on with its own tedium, managing affairs, only seen in the foreground when there are wars, assassinations, riots, or hostage takings. Or when these are followed in due course by liberations, democratizations, or wage awards. The rest is left to the experts, and the general public takes the same sort of interest in it as they do in the hospital service, at once caring about and ignoring it. But Edward was completely devoted to politics and its objects. He would go from one capital to another, trying to solve some problem about hostages, living in the corridors of diplomacy, sometimes lightening and sometimes darkening the shadow on which all our fates depend. But it allowed him to disappear from sight and send cryptic but loving postcards suggesting improbable meetings in the future. The deeper his commitment became, the more utterly skeptical he himself grew. The only way to deal with the absurdity of the world was to be fair and correct and stir up as little fuss as possible. That was what Dalloway's philosophy amounted to, more or less, if you took away the legalistic refinements.

Olga saw a kind of courage in all this. But was she in love with him, or was he one of those ghosts we cling to because their ghostly endurance impresses and protects us? Are we still in love, or have we confused love with the respect that follows pain? After a few years, all that's left of fading passions is an old well covered with climbing geraniums. There's still a spring down there, and the flowers suggest life, but the level of the water doesn't rise anymore, and nobody drinks it. Many years hence the well in the garden may be covered with frozen leaves and withered flowers, the spring hidden forever from the merciless eyes of future generations.

Olga already thought of Dan as belonging to another life, looked at from beyond the grave. They'd lived together back home; loved each other, and there had been a kind of death— her going away, the break between them—and now their affair was a film she saw from its afterlife. Dan's own sudden death didn't seem normal, but absurd and pointless and so in that sense natural. This real death was only a cruel repetition of something that had already happened once. Her brave, shortsighted samurai, the inspired author of *Hagakuré, or the Art of War*, had already died one day in the metro taking them from the Bibliothèque Nationale to Montmartre.

"He spoke your name just before he died," Dan's wife wrote, with the rough honesty of the people back home, as direct in sorrow as in jealousy. For of course Dan had got married after he left the Hôtel des Grands Hommes.

His had been a strange end: a neglected lung infection, the sort of medical incompetence all too common in those parts, and he'd died before he could complete his study of Holbein's *Dead Christ*.

"It was as if he wanted his death to be a tribute to the painting, as if he was afraid his book wouldn't be worthy of such a masterpiece. I wonder, too, if he didn't deliberately leave it too late to send for the doctors. Like a lot of our friends who have killed themselves or just let themselves die, he may have been thinking of the samurais he described in the last book he wrote for you."

Rather superstitious, but straight from the shoulder.

Olga had no tears to shed. Only the mass of the memories that cut you off from the world and merge you with that part of the lost one which was a part of yourself. A part about which you wonder, does it still exist or is it already dead too? An Olga who had been Dan, and whom she had thought to be no more, started to live again, a dead person's life. Holbein's *Dead Christ*, not at all certain to be resurrected, was not only Dan, he was also Olga herself. That anguished yet tranquil desolation; that impassive nobility. A character who did not really belong to God, but to a history now made up of ineluctable deaths.

For only death was regarded as an event nowadays. Everything else was banking and jurisprudence. So Olga wrote to Edward, in a tone half didactic and half pathetic. For his part, Dalloway thought only men knew how to love; women only playact. Olga was far from being cold or superficial, but it was true—she was theatrical.

By being theatrical, playacting, he meant the way women met life in the world, experience, with rapture or despair—it came to the same thing—persuading themselves that each of their experiences contained some exceptional truth. For Edward there was only poverty, violence, and negotiation; no such thing as rapture or despair. Ruth was theatrical with her political religion. Olga was theatrical with her passionate intellectualism. It was childish to fear death, which was a fact of nature, and it was childish to hanker after events. On the contrary, he, Dalloway, did his best to de-dramatize "events," to take the hype out of them and allow people to breathe. It didn't occur to him that in depriving people of events he was turning the world gray; that without theater and color people would die of boredom. He just thought Olga's fascination with that uninteresting and inevitable phenomenon, death, together with its debased counterpart, events, only showed he no longer played the leading role in the theater of her life. Only men were capable of love. Ah well, never mind, he'd go on on his own.

"Armand . . . car crash . . . Yes, very serious . . . In intensive care . . . I'll see you at the hospital. . . ."

Hervé's anxious voice, scarcely audible.

They were all crowding around the reception area, to the annoyance of the hospital staff trying to protect the patient from distinguished visitors and clamoring media alike. The news of Bréhal's accident had stirred up everyone who used to go to his seminars.

It was easy to pick out those who'd been a success. The constipated nervousness of the ex-student become principal private secretary to a minister: Cédric. The sanctimonious conceit of the budding analyst: Frank. The expensive suits and ties of Heinz, Roberto, and a few others who'd managed to land good jobs in Paris.

Almost equally evident was the distress of a lot of fragile young men: former, present, and potential lovers; suitors—impossible, classical, romantic, or false, but all genuinely terrified, for Armand was generous, and all these people, in debt to him for what he had bestowed of his life, were caught up in his death. They were swallowed up in a humble crowd that had either preserved or betrayed the memory of May '68, or Bréhal's rhetorical adventures among the lower ranks of teachers, freelance journalists, marketing representatives, aspiring artists, and eternal thesis writers.

And of course there was Stanislas from Editions de l'Autre, and Hervé, Olga, the family. Carole hadn't been able to manage it: "Too awful, overwhelmed, perhaps tomorrow or the next day, when Bréhal's better."

"Do you believe in chance?"

"He was depressed."

"His mother's death killed him."

"Did you see the reviews of his books? He was very upset."

"The big shots at the university didn't like his teaching: 'Too fashionable, too public, too popular, too this, not enough that.' He knew and felt humiliated."

"But accidents do happen."

"Ever since he started to teach at the Collège de France the politicians have been at him, trying to exploit him for their own ends—it got him down."

People shield themselves from death by eating and drinking, and sometimes they hit on the truth. Olga remembered something Armand had said to her, sadly, a week ago: "I feel like putting my head in the plaster."

"How strange. Isn't the phrase 'in the sand'?"

"You can say whatever you like if you're Armand," Hervé had said. "But it's true he's not in very good form. He says he's going to swallow the anchor."

First there was the surgeon, his professional voice betraying the strain of the fight against death. Artificial lung, artificial kidney, a whole lot of devices to replace what had been pieces of Armand.

"It isn't the first time we've had a pneumothorax case like this. Medicine has made a lot of progress in the last few years, more than textology or sexology . . . what was your friend's subject, now? But what are all these people doing here? This isn't Saint-Germain-des-Prés!"

Then they noticed the staff's evasive eyes and blank faces: signs of what would be called panic in other professions. "How was he feeling before the accident? He's not putting up a fight. Perhaps we should call in a psychiatrist, a psychologist, a psychoanalyst, or something?"

The visits, alone with him, just one or two people at a time. The worst thing was that he couldn't speak. Science made up for missing or injured lungs by making use of the throat, ablating the voice. What had been Armand's music—subdued by chronic illness but with nothing unhealthy about it, and distinguished by its close acquaintance with books and solitude—the timbre he himself liked to call the "grain" of the voice: that was no more. Olga thought back to how attractive he'd looked in the cyclamen light of the Rosebud; asleep in the minibus near the white death of a Chinese Disneyland. . . .

"We miss you. We're waiting for you," she whispered, bending over him. But the body that had won fame by formulating philosophical sensuality no longer responded. His eyes glazed with fatigue and drugs, his face slack, he made one of those gestures of resignation and farewell that mean "Don't try to find me anymore . . . it's no use. . . . Life's a pain in the neck. . . ."

There's nothing more convincing than a refusal to go on living when it's conveyed without any hysteria: no asking for love, just a deliberate rejection, not even philosophical but animal and final, of existence. You feel like a moron for clinging, yourself, to the bustle called life that the other is relinquishing with such indifference. Olga loved Armand too much to understand what made him go with such gentle but unquestionable firmness, but she could only respect his carelessness, his last-ditch nonresistance. But just the same she told him she loved him very much, that she owed her first job in Paris to him, that it was he who had taught her to read, that they'd go on another trip together, to Japan perhaps, or India, or the Atlantic coast; the wind on the island is marvelous for the lungs, and Armand could sit in the garden with the geraniums, unless they all went out in the boat with Hervé. . . . The pale eyes filled, but Bréhal still made the same gesture of farewell.

Hervé sat silent, holding Armand's hand. What could you say to someone who didn't want to want anything?

"Armand, my friend, what it would be to write that—the melody of vanished music, lost desire. Life has no meaning, I agree, but writing isn't living!"

Armand held his old friend's fingers in an endless caress, but went on waving the same detached adieu.

"You have the right, no one can force anything on you. After all, you've taken care what you did all your life long. Just letting yourself go may seem a pleasure, like having an anaesthetic— you told me once you were afraid of that. But I don't agree with these lethal pleasures. Stay on—let's all stay on."

They thought he could hear them, even though he couldn't react. But could he understand?

"This time he's really leaving us."

Olga was weeping, out in the street.

Hervé had a strange way of consoling someone. When he was confronted with sickness, tears, or melancholy, the first weapon he turned to was aggressiveness. After all, why not? Isn't aggressiveness a form of life, the least responsible form, the one that marches against death as casually as you lean against a wall? Then he made a volte-face. A fleeting respite at last.

"I don't understand you and your worship of life," he said angrily.

Olga found herself being pilloried as the stupid representative of all who stubbornly persisted in living.

"Or rather I do understand—it's because of your progressive education with its emphasis on the will. Only everyone's going to die sometime, including you and me. If Armand prefers to choose his own time, it's up to him. All the people sniveling over it are thinking about themselves, not him. Did you see how his disciples looked at me?"

"I didn't really take much notice. . . . ."

"But how, would you say?"

"Scared. Perhaps rather hostile."

"No 'perhaps' about it! Any idea why?"

"You won't like it."

"Why not?"

"It's sociological."

"Let's hear it anyway."

"Well, you may be Sinteuil, with all that that implies, but your manner's that of a Montlaur going slumming. Your sort of people are ambassadors and presidents of banks. Just a few are writers—right-wing writers. But today's intellectuals are the sons of butchers, teachers, mailmen, and so on. Where do you fit in in all that, with your patrician ways—and left-wing ideas into the bargain!"

"That may be true. But it's too easy."

Hervé seemed a bit less tense.

"But never mind that. That's not the problem now. It's clear Armand is leaving us, and no one can do anything about it. And he'll be consigned to purgatory, his work neglected and forgotten, for a while. Do you think those new intellectuals whose origins you evoke so vividly will forgive him for taking pleasure in meanings and signs, for his cult of idleness, for the apparent flippancy of preferring the rhythms of words to the messages of ideas? Oh, and worst of all—I was forgetting: for his timidity, for being a nonconformist without a shred of militancy to his name, not even for sexual freedom!"

"I know some people who won't consign him to purgatory."

"Anyhow, they'll rediscover him. Sooner or later. And do you know why? Because he wrote as he lived: under suspended sentence. That lowers the value of things and puts music in words. Provided you have the grace that transforms a declining body into an instrument of language. A mysterious thing, but it does happen. Then a suspended sentence turns people into stylists. Even if they're professors of semantics. Armand was a delicate guy who was always within a hairbreadth of death: it restricted his pleasures, but it also gave him a slight fever that made his words different from other people's. One can only write out of death, remember—or out of loneliness, as you'll discover for yourself. Come on then, little Squirrel, come and weep in my arms if it'll make you feel better. But that's how it is, you know: 'Death, that strange voice . . .' And Armand always liked to think of you as a bulldozer—do you remember him saying that one night in the Rosebud? And a bulldozer doesn't cry, does it!"

22

While a mother is still unaware of the embryo coming to life inside her, her body already knows. It experiences a shock: the graft that is going to enlarge you starts by diminishing you. A virus clings to your entrails, a cancer grips your guts, you're attacked by dizzy spells, sudden paleness, fits of fatigue, vomiting. In some women this aggression lasts a long time. For others it's only a stage on the way to a truce.

The cells grow, divide, multiply. The breasts grow heavy, the lips swell, the belly and thighs get larger. You're not a single person anymore—you're double. There's a new world inside you—*the* World: the world outside you doesn't matter anymore, it no longer exists. You look, you listen, you touch the show going on outside; you even take part in it—it's life, obvious, shared, social. But you only seem to be part of it. In reality you're inside with your double, him or her;

there's nothing you can do together but you're inseparable, coiled up in an infinite, fervent tenderness that can't be communicated to anyone else and so has a tinge of madness. For even that part of you that's an "individual," with a name and words of its own, doesn't know what to do or say about this within. You suddenly realize that you're two: on the one hand, a bit player among other bit players; but on the other, an exorbitant nature, a mass of pulsating fiber that feels pleasure and overwhelms you. But you can't merge the two universes together: you're aware of the gulf that exists between the flimsy role you play in the drama of human relations and the great darkness that rejoices and soothes you, but that cannot be divulged, that will remain unsignifiable and thus insignificant. The other that is inside you reveals that you are an other. Not human. Minor, but supreme. Your eyes go on following the performance in which you move about, vague, visionary (getting together diapers, baby clothes, the stroller, the cot, all on top of your ordinary work), but they're not really looking at what's in front of them. They are turned inward, though they can see nothing, sight becomes hearing and touch, you're floating in a capsule of pleasure and anxiety (who knows how it will all turn out!). Pregnancy is the modern version of ecstasy. That's how it was for Olga too.

She went for a walk with Hervé in the wintry Luxembourg Gardens, bare of leaves but bracing as ever in the clear sunshine that precedes snow. No one stopped anymore by the statues of the queens of France dotted along the paths: the children didn't notice them, their parents couldn't have cared less, and there weren't any Japanese tourists at that time of year. The Little Actor of tarnished bronze, looking as though he were dressed in green velvet to take part in some royal entertainment in a mossy wood, went on juggling with his two masks, but only the row of other masks at his feet—grotesque and bearded old men—lingered to watch him. Olga too.

"Your hand's very hot. Have you got a temperature?" (Hervé)

"I've no idea. . . . I often think of Jean, you know, in his cemetery under the steeple. It was he who pointed the Little Actor out to me one day." (Olga)

"I think about him too. It's over a year now, isn't it? I didn't know he used to come here." (Hervé)

"Do you believe in reincarnation?" (Olga)

"Eh? Are you feeling all right?" (Hervé)

"Yes. . . . But in a way . . . We *are* going to have a child."
(Olga)

The light was very cold and sharp in the Luxembourg before
the first snow. It made the silence seem out of this world.

"It'll be a boy." (Hervé)

Hervé wasn't your typical family man, but the time had come
for him to be a father. Quick-thinking, decisive, faithful. He
knew, ever since the trip to China at least, that Olga wanted
this. And pregnancy is the most absolute of complicities.

The birds left the North and chose the mildness of the island to
spend the winter in. Some nested in the tundra, in Scotland or
the Netherlands, then came on to Fier, out of the frost, hidden
by the tall grasses and warmed by the ruddy ocean sun. The
young birds grew up there, took over the marshes, put on
feathers, put on weight, flew off in the fall, then came back the
next spring with families of their own. But for the time being
they were cultivating their garden—an inner section of the sal-
tern, a stretch of calm water cut off from the sea, between the
rabbits and the horses, an expanse that was resting, clarifying
itself and taking in air before, with the warmer weather, it flowed
out into the labyrinth of the saltworks again.

The shelduck was a curious bird: all black and white except
for its russet breast and red bill and feet. It fed on mollusks and
crustaceans and built its nest in the rabbit warrens, bravely
crossing the path in front of Olga and Kissmayou.

The little brent goose was less showy, with its dark plumage
and white rump, but even bolder: it had covered six thousand
kilometers to get to the island from Siberia.

The female mallards, like blue mirrors when in flight, came
there to lay their eggs early in February: with their speckled
brown bodies, white tails, and orange beaks, they merged into
the dry grass and clay as they sat on their nests.

The Finnish teal, with its russet head and white eyebrows,
seemed to be frowning doubtfully. It had just arrived, but would
soon make up its mind and fly on to the tropical warmth of
Africa.

The crested lapwing, with its lazy flight, green back, and

brick-red tail, was not conceited: as it performed its nuptial dance it tried not to think of its origins back there in Eastern Europe.

Only a few pairs of shovelers came and laid their eggs in the sweetwater marshes. Kissmayou liked to frighten them, and Olga loved watching them fly up, with their flat bills, light-blue gray-tipped wings, and the males' green heads.

But it was the gray common heron and its cousin the little egret that reigned in beauty over the fish farms. They would leave their nests perched up in the pinewoods and come and snack on shrimps and little fishes that must have shivered, even in that tepid water, at the sight of those daggerlike beaks, long necks, and towering legs. In the spring the heron acquired a beautiful white plume. How was one to tell it from the egret?

Heaven knew why nature had chosen the plumage of birds to add a wealth of color and voluptuous grace to that rather ascetic land-and-seascape. The local people scarcely noticed the flying miracles, the flashes of painting, as they bent over their labors in the saltworks or the oyster beds. Perhaps they were right, for if you looked at them closely you were dazzled by the grace of the birds, compact of nimble body and dauntless mind. If they noticed it, men might be jealous, might resent the superiority of the brent geese, mallards, shelducks, teals, lapwings, herons, and egrets—might even fear their turning into Hitchcock's fearsome flocks of killers, that image of our terrified inferiority. But as it was, pregnant Olga, walking with Kissmayou along paths giving off whiffs and wisps of ozone in the early spring sun, was the only one who watched the birds, trying to tame them with the blissful, pantheistic tenderness of a mother-to-be who has visions instead of morning sickness.

The birds were fellow creatures. When you're swept away in the flood of biology, as in illness or pregnancy, you may draw away from human beings, but your apparent solitude is full of the animal and vegetable species with which your dreams have made you identify. There are cat-women; cow-women; mare-women; squirrel-women; bee-women; crocodile-women; cactus-, seaweed-, daisy-, nettle-women; and bear-, giraffe-, and elephant-women. It must depend on the country they live in, and on whether the pregnancy is an easy or a difficult one. The

Squirrel, on that island, had joined the family of brent geese, shelducks, and, in her more coquettish moments, little egrets.

The most ardent lovers of local color aren't always stay-at-home dreamers. Migrants are often the best regionalists. It was clear that the brent goose and the crested lapwing regarded Fier as their own personal paradise. Their places of origin would call them back in due course, but for the time being they were getting more enjoyment out of the quivering of the marshes and the misty breeze than the busy housewife on her bike, hurrying to the village for a stick of bread, or the hunter aiming at a mallard, blind to the iridescent ocher of the clay-walled reservoirs.

A migrant fragments time, but when it alights somewhere, that particular bit of time is all its time, and it puts its heart in it, grows fond of it, improves it. Because it has no real home, it is at home in that land of exile and asylum. Being always on the move, instead of worrying a migrant, makes it curious, like the avocet; proud, like the male teal; coquettish, like the egret; or aristocratic, like the heron. In short, the migrant gives of its best because, despite all the tradition which we're told programs its return, this temporary home is not very certain. Who knows what will happen next year? It doesn't have any roots here—is memory a root? So the best thing is to do your best before the next departure and give the little ones all the good things possible while you're still here.

The migrant birds chirped, twittered, and chirruped in separate, scattered sounds that melted like the taste of salt into the silences of the marshes. But the gulls and cormorants felt really at home, and didn't share the nervousness of the birds of passage; they split your eardrums with loud cries or laughing shrieks, displaying crops full of gray shrimps, wings making joyful fans in the damp air, webbed feet stalking firmly over the seaweed-slippery *bri*. The visitors, impressed, fell silent, punctuating their respect for their temporary haven with only a few flutelike warbles or harplike twangs: just enough to point up the pearly sky.

Olga, on her slow ecological walks, knew people must take her for one of the brent geese from the frozen north, dark all over but for a white half-collar, who'd taken up residence on the marshes. But this flat island, battered by the winds, wasn't really hospitable. You had to have a craving for adventure to find it comfortable, this salty bit of land stretched out in the ocean like a hake, and cut in two by high tides in winter. Or else, to entrust your children to the cold and blustery storms, to regale them with sea-green oysters without lemon or other garnishes, to cradle them in the rough comfort of the wrack, you needed to be from the North Pole, the steppes, a violent climate where only wolves survive, or vultures, or a migrant with a taste for exile.

But Olga had chosen this spot because of Hervé; she was like him now. And she instinctively clung to it even more now than she had when they sailed heedlessly about on the dark *Violin,* or when she was with Jean de Montlaur, in dreams, on his subterranean bed of clay.

Of course she imagined their child riding his tricycle amid the herons, overlooked by the mountains of salt. But her relation to this part of nature was much less clear than that of other mothers who made their own shy films about the future. Olga indulged not so much in a film as in a fusion of breaths, skins, tastes, and mirages; a kind of unconscious and sensual immersion, amorous and foolish. Like a dream in which you know you're not a fish, but you can still feel your scales and fins, the fine sand under your belly, and the coral brushing against your gills; and you think you may be undergoing a terrifying but magnificent metamorphosis, while knowing all the time that you're dreaming.

The cold gray air over the marshes was her. The wisps of sun-warmed ozone wreathing heron, egret, and mallard in purple halos—they were her too. And Kissmayou, licking the salt left behind by the workmen in a little plastic-covered pyramid. And the brent geese warming up their Siberian goose pimples; the pink-breasted shelducks sleeping in the rabbit warrens after a little bath and a lunch of seaworms. And the black and white avocet with its turned-up bill poking in the mud in search of little invertebrates, proud of belonging to the largest colony of local nesters.

All these were Olga, though she no longer existed. The baby filled her now, and would soon take up all the room there was. She knew now that because of him and with him, the Olga she knew well and whom other people thought they'd met would never exist again. It was what she'd always wanted: to merge into things; to disappear into intentness on someone else who was partly her, but completely different; to let herself be invaded by her womb, her breasts, the taste of milk, the smell of stools, the caress of satin cheeks; to be just a shelduck in the pearly gray of the salt marsh, following nothing but the immemorial program of life—floating, laying eggs, growing, tending, fulfillment, satiety, decline, death.

That biological happiness for and through another was the love of pregnant women who don't yet know they love, but merge into everything that breeds, lives, and enjoys happiness and effort in the sun and wind. Such love is so cosmically real it seems unreal: a sensory hallucination. It wouldn't last, but Olga wanted it to, wanted the child to be able one day to imagine the cradle of beauty in which she'd carried and adored him. But it was incommunicable. Unless he already felt it already, in the amniotic shelter, the transparent quietness that his mother took walking, with Kissmayou, among the egrets. But she could try to capture a few snatches of this cosmos which would soon be Olga no longer, this Olga who would soon be a cosmos no longer. Photos. Photos. Photos. Photos that wouldn't be shown to anyone. Ordinary landscapes of a gestation—only the mother and father can see anything in them. Passersby couldn't care less. And the child—it will be all Greek to him.

Nothing in the world could separate Sinteuil from his Venetian pleasures: certainly not common herons, or shelducks, or the pneumatic metamorphosis of Olga carrying their baby through the migrants' aquatic resorts on the island of Fier.

In the triptychs in Santa-Maria-dei-Frari and San Zaccaria, Giovanni Bellini has depicted a Virgin in ecstasy, a sovereign creature, yet transported to a paradise that is beyond her. Her throne is part of an intricate pattern of carved and painted altars, alcoves, and vaults; the eye of the beholder is led up through them to a Mother who towers but doesn't dominate.

Sinteuil, to whom the elegance of the city of the Doges was like an elaborate symbol of his own eroticism, had long been acquainted with the Frari and San Zaccaria. And yet today

Mary's poised rapture filled him with a kind of music, that of the eighth heaven of the *Paradiso*, where the sound bursts forth after the sky becomes a pattern of brilliant rose windows. His eyes still full of the triptychs, Hervé made his way toward the Accademia.

The Madonna, Child, Six Saints, and Singing Angels. Crowd upon crowd of figures seemed to multiply the surface of the picture, the top of which curved upward into a carved dome of sparkling yellow. The skill with which the colors were folded into the spaces was enough in itself to show that motherhood was illumination.

Bellini was the painter of the Madonna's raptures, but he only managed to plunge Sinteuil into that grace by leading him first through the almost Byzantine rigidity and the reserved, even hostile placidity of the *Madonna of the Shrubs*. This Madonna troubled him. Apprehensive and humble, set stiffly there between her two pages and the two trees, she looked as if she was ashamed. If it weren't for the dense blue of her cape against the green of the panel support, and the cinematographic zoom onto two narrow landscapes painted in perspective, all you'd remember of the Mother of God would be her reticence: a modest, almost surly veil over the joy that spreads itself, full though abstract, through the caprices of the setting and the frankness of the colors. Typical Bellini, thought Hervé. The Virgin may be in ecstasy, but she doesn't show it—she's masked by her evasive eyelids. What a difference between her averted face and the baby's body, squirming with pleasure! But who knows if Mary really is joyful? Giovanni certainly is: the painter himself is certainly ecstatic. He enjoys manipulating space, calculating color, inventing architecture. He conceals the pleasure of the mother to leave room for the art of the painter. After all, the Madonna may just be angry, feeling guilty, or shy. I remember Christ is even trying to strangle her in the picture in San Paolo: a fierce baby is throttling a Madonna who's the same as the one in the *Shrubs*, only more anxious and even more rebellious. But Giovanni, who is not the Madonna, possesses and exhibits her charm. He leaves some traces of suffering on her face: her body has been run through with a sword, she will spend her time reconciling her joys and sorrows with her son. Mary's pure exultation resides only in the painter's art. Bellini couldn't have put it more plainly.

As he left the Accademia and set out for the Zattere, Sinteuil, who usually preferred to dwell on painters' techniques rather than their biographies, was nonetheless reflecting on Giovanni Bellini's strange destiny. Son of the painter Jacopo, he wasn't recognized by his father's wife: he didn't live with the family and, most surprising of all, his mother left him out of her will. Did he have another mother: a dead one, or a prostitute, or a servant who couldn't be recognized? Was he seeking her face, her disappointment, her sin, or her pleasure in his secretive Virgins, who seem to belong to some family drama rather than to a Byzantine icon? But where does the jubilation come from which the Madonnas show in the violent hues of their robes, the red heads of the angels, the curves of the landscapes, and the tottering piles of panels heaped one on top of another like crazy mandalas?

Giovanni became a father in that period, but his wife soon died, and he lost his son when he was only ten years old. Was he still influenced by the mystery of childbirth, or by a symbiosis between himself and the mother of his child, or by a symbolically maternal relationship between himself and the child after his wife's death? Or was he able, like all the great visionaries, to say, "The Madonna is me," and then, forgetting all practical worries concerning those around him, pursue a dream of ecstasy?—a dream of ecstasy the name of which was Bellini, and which made use of any and every occasion that presented itself, including even a pregnancy or a birth. For a Bellini cannot say no to pleasure: he must amplify it, glorify it in colors and volumes, make it really exist.

While boats rent the damp air of the Giudecca, Sinteuil saw again in his mind's eye the *Virgin of the Shrubs* and the triptych in the Frari. Something about that Byzantine peasant face was like the Squirrel. What was the Madonna thinking of: of her son, or of the countryside receding toward the back of the picture? Love of nature was something else the two women had in common: Olga too adored landscapes. Books and landscapes were what she lived by, and now the future baby.

Art resided chiefly in capturing the play of light. Bellini ended up undressing his Madonnas. Wasn't the last painting of this lover of Virgins a *Naked Virgin* who unashamedly shows us her behind, while we see her face only as a reflection in her mirror? The dirty old man! But had he really changed? His women's faces are always hidden in some way, or else shown merely as reflections in a glass. Only the body matters: dress it in a blue tunic and it is sacred, pregnant with promises: show it naked and it is offered up, pleasing, desacralized. "Well, I prefer the nude—I'll do without the sacred. . . . Just the same, the *Madonna of the Shrubs* does look rather like the Squirrel!"

By the way, he must call her. A wonderful invention, the telephone. People conduct their lives and their love affairs on it. Face-to-face encounters are too difficult: people can ignore or attack each other. But on the phone you can patch things up, promise, listen, not listen, dream, let your mind wander, and either it ends or it revives—life or the love affair. The telephone preserves your independence, you can do what you like, you're free, there's no other body there to cramp your style. Yet at the same time you have an umbilical cord within hand's reach: contact is soon reestablished, and in a few seconds you know all you want to know about the other person on the other side of the world—i.e., that he or she is there, that there's a link, the appearance of one, but appearances are essential, it's so much more civilized to love people by telephone, it doesn't last long but it strikes a spark, you're both delighted, then you're both separate again, autonomous, unburdened.

"Hallo . . . Olga? Everything all right? Not too uncomfortable? Not at all? I love you."

It was a vast sentence that jumped from comma to comma, exclamation to exclamation, went up, went down, got tighter, got looser from line to line, page to page, chapter to chapter, without respite, without a period, only commas and exclamations, shrill, heartrending, confused, stupefying.

It was a wave, swelling, rising to a crest, gathering strength and flinging the swimmer onto the sand with broken bones; then it started again, rose again, mustered its strength again more savagely than before, and hurled the swimmer on the clay again,

breathless, battered. . . . One, two, three . . . A small wave just
to give the big ones time to assemble their energy . . . And
again: one, two, three, it mounts, swells, crushes, you can't
breathe, hell couldn't be worse, mercy, will it ever end, you
don't exist anymore, you're an endless wave, a sentence without
an intake of breath, only cries, swellings, and shattering, splitting blows.

Pain. Give it some oxygen: get hold of the commas, make
them longer, place the cries, slide them into a slope of breathing. Introduce some time. Breath is time caressing pain, pushes
it away slightly, doesn't remove but soothes it. The wave still
whirls you about, but it's only a wave, you stifle in its fury, it
tears your belly, your back, everything, you're one huge wound,
a bloody wave throbbing and bringing flashes of pain to what is
no longer a body but a sea of pain, and yet it breathes, and so
survives, survives through air, but for how long, an air that stuns
you, empties you of thought, nothing but a chaos of flashes,
sounds, scents, a breathing dizziness.

You're falling into a black crater, or else you're rising up, what
does it matter, it's both, a stifling fleece carpets the corridor, the
mane of a lioness, a mare, a tigress, you're on it and it's stran-
gling you, red lava inside, a fall, so it's over, isn't death better,
pain has no idea, what a scouring, stunned, a clearing buzzing
with bees, smell of honey, of the daffodils on the lawn, of hot
milk and cinnamon buns, mane of a lioness, caress, oblivion, the
airy pain is bliss, a memory of a dream of paradise, Mother.

Suddenly, silence. Peace. The peridural. "Push." Blank efforts,
neutral, strong. The life that was coming agrees to come quietly.

From between the now impassive thighs the doctor extracts a
little bloodstained body. The black-haired head yells. Someone
goes off with the placenta. Pain separates the fostering waste
from the new person. An unknown person lies on Olga's now
empty womb. He fills his lungs with the air of others.

"A boy." (The midwife)
"You're beautiful, my darling." (Olga)
"It's Alex." (Hervé)

y child, my fate, what word is there for the link that binds me to you: unsuspected, delicious, desperate—the fulfillment and the loss of my every moment?

"A body? You were my body, you are so no longer—you now have the fortune and misfortune of your own chemistry.

"A love? I love your father, the flowers that grow by the Atlantic, the beach of a black Mother, New York nights, difficult books, and you. But do you see how vast the word is, and it doesn't say anything about all you've turned upside down for me.

"Time? That might be nearer to it. A time recovered. You have opened the present to me: events have no more weight since you've existed, I just let things and words and people pass me by, I give you my breast, my eyes, my nights when you cry with hunger or because you've got a temperature, my smile when you want to play, I loiter, I don't rush around anymore, I don't pursue any goal, I inhabit the space of another—yours.

"You've reminded me of the past: I'd forgotten how to be small, you find me young and fragile, I know the taste of milk in a smooth mouth again, the smell of the first strawberries on gums full of teeth just waiting to come through, the thrill of my first uncertain steps, the shock of falling over when Mother was too confident and let me run and smell the roses at the end of the path, the halos of my wondering baby eyes that could see only blue or red, and then gradually the shape of a brown face, an embroidered tablecloth, a vibrating spoon. Give me your eyes, don't gaze up at the ceiling, look at me and smile. Yes, that's right, I can see you, you yourself, you alone, don't worry. My own childhood only comes back if you give me signs of it, your reminders only revive my memory in order to please you, there are two of us in my story now, and that's the very reason it exists, and I give it to you if it can help you to come toward me, hear me, speak to me.

"And you've turned the future into a riddle: it's not a plan anymore. I leave plans and hopes to you, formulate them as best you can with your own cells, your own desires, your own words. The future curves toward and into me from your little body clinging to my shoulder, from your pink sleep, from your running soon along the street, and instead of being a program the future takes the form of a life that I accompany with trust and anguish. Yes, I know the foreseeable time that belongs to programs: as a migrant and a fighter I see it through and sometimes anticipate it. But your joys and your illnesses, your discoveries and your regressions, your wiles and your mistakes, have reconciled me to another future: to slowness, surprise, to the strange and so brief happiness that must always be paid for, to the waiting that awakens and cures.

"I'm in no hurry. I'm not going anywhere. We're going to take all the time that's necessary to solve the riddle of life together. You will continue it in your own way, neither well nor ill, as best you can, as you wish. At first you'll wait for me and I'll wait for you. Then you won't need my pacing anymore, you'll follow your own rhythm, for better or worse, and then I shall withdraw, you'll be alone in your time, my patience will have completed its own.

"But for the moment it's all yours, you are my time, my instant: present, past, and future all clutched in your fist as it clings to my thumb, in your moist lips mimicking my lullabies, in your bright eyes looking past the chestnut trees at the sound of the planes taking Father 'to work.' I myself don't move about anymore, my migration has a new meaning. Thanks to you I travel in the time of a memory looking back and forward, I'm not even sure it's mine, for your smell, your cries, your tastes graft unknown worlds on me. Through my own fantasies I guess at yours: I inhabit the fantasies of another, you reshape my memories and my words just as you reshaped my body, I'm learning now how to be different with different people, starting with you. . . ."

That's how Olga might have talked to herself, thinking she was talking to Alex asleep in his stroller, if she'd wanted to put into words the state of diaphanous suspension all mothers experience, looking at their babes. But she didn't want to put anything into words, and nor do other mothers: it's quite exhausting and important enough to dream over skins smelling of bottles, soap, and stools; over eyes that smile or weep without necessarily seeing; over cries that may be saying or rejecting something, but that certainly love and suffer already. So pleasant and exhausting to be there, just tearing oneself away to do what has to be done—feeding, smiling, rocking, looking after, washing, scolding, caressing, raising, and all the rest—that you haven't time to talk or think, and you yourself become a child in the process of being born, of growing, enjoying, enduring, sleeping, letting other people do things, but also feeding, smiling, rocking, looking after, raising, and even speaking sometimes. It's a good thing we give children names, she thought at last. "A good thing we baptize them. Otherwise what would we call all that unnamable? Don't you agree, Alex?"

When we're born we're given a name and lots of presents. Because, later on, we're always going to be asked to give, to miss out, and to make efforts, we're showered with gifts at the outset:

society feels it owes babies something. Some of the givers are trying to make up for having enjoyed some pleasure; others pay out of guilt for the restrictions and misfortunes they know will be inflicted on the poor little creatures.

In this inevitable tradition, Alex was one of the luckiest of infants. After exhausting all the most fashionable brands of baby clothes to be found in the shops, Grandmother Mathilde started knitting things herself: little jackets, little trousers, little bootees, little caps, and so on, to the astonishment of those about her and the annoyance of the mailmen who had to deliver the packages.

Diana competed from a distance, countering the French miniature-grown-up style with American robot gear. Alex came in for every gadget known to NASA: astronaut suits, helmets, boots, and gloves, all in blue and white checks, or silver, or fluorescent. Consumerism grabs us even in the cradle.

The O'Brians, grandparents themselves and experts on what pleased little children, sent an enormous seesaw like those in the Luxembourg, only more gaudy. It got shifted from the drawing room to the dining room to Alex's bedroom to the corridor: no one knew where to put the monster.

Hermine contributed a bicycle, in memory of their rides on the island: to be used in a few years' time. Sylvain Brunet, as a shy art historian, didn't come to see the baby, but got together a splendid collection of Magic Markers, also for later on.

From airports all over the earth, including the Third World, came flashy, noisy objects of varying degrees of appropriateness to Alex's age: brightly colored, complicated, electronic, with bells that rang and lights that flashed—a paradise for the parents and their guests.

"So your friend Dalloway travels all over the world and lets Master Alex de Montlaur know by sending him all manner of objects?" (Hervé)

"Edward's always been very attentive, shy, and affectionate, as you must have noticed." (Olga)

"I saw him at the Sylvers' party. We chatted a bit. Appearances!" (Hervé)

"If you like. But the Dalloway mystery's so transparent you see it all at first glance, don't you? Shy and affectionate, that's all there is." (Olga)

"Of course, of course. But not as affectionate as I am!" (Hervé)

"No doubt about that, I think. I'm here to prove it." (Olga)

"Does he still negotiate?" (Hervé)

"I suspect he's seriously afraid of another world war—the disparity between the West and the rest of the world seems insurmountable. There's an economic, legal, and moral gulf. But his attitude is that war's avoidable, and so he negotiates. And that's a form of courage, don't you think? But I haven't forgotten how he wriggled out of the Cèline business." (Olga)

"I meant does he still negotiate with you?" (Hervé)

"Don't be funny! Of course! I should hope so! But in a different way. Haven't you ever got close to someone, only to find out that you don't understand each other, but that you're fond of each other just the same?" (Olga)

". . ." (Hervé)

"Personally I like to understand, and really I only love those who understand me. You, for example. But I'm sure you know that." (Olga)

"You are a strange specimen." (Hervé)

"Specimen?" (Olga)

"But not lacking in charm, from a certain point of view." (Hervé)

"You can't help being sarcastic and seeing the opposite of the opposite in everything. Whereas *I* think about the little differences—it's not so amusing, but more soothing." (Olga)

"That's what music's for." (Hervé)

"And affection." (Olga)

"Right—the memory of pleasure. You. Where are you taking Alex?" (Hervé)

Women are queens in the Luxembourg. First, the women who push strollers, give babies bottles or even the breast sometimes, hand out cuffs and cuddles, run across the grass to fetch a lost ball or the sandbox to wipe an unwary mouth, pretend to gossip with their neighbors, but really just repeat what their mothers used to say twenty or thirty or even more years ago. And while they look rather like insects intent on their own individual tasks, they never lose track of the little footsteps, little eyes, and little woes nearby.

There are real queens too. Of stone. But since Marie de Médicis had her own palace built there in the Florentine style, the place hasn't been very propitious to the power of women. Scarcely had she got her son Louis XIII to promise to dismiss Richelieu than the cardinal, vanquished in the Luxembourg, triumphed at Versailles. And the queen mother, having enjoyed her new residence for only five years, was exiled to Cologne. Did Rubens paint her story allegorically in his magnificent pictures? What does it matter? They can be seen in the Louvre. The palace, briefly named after Marie de Médicis, resumed its original name, the Luxembourg, and Marie is now only one of the queens whose statues started to circle the inner part of the gardens under Louis-Philippe.

You can only just see them behind the green boxes containing the palms, the oleanders, and the orange trees; behind the baroque urns where ivy-leaf geraniums disport themselves; behind the chestnut trees that seem to look down more indulgently on certain saucy mythical figures than do the frigid ladies. But the queens are there all right, casting over the innocence of strollers and al fresco teas the shadow of their murky fates, which were forgotten long ago, and which no one wants to revive in this sheltered nursery.

Most pathetic is Marie of Anjou, queen of England. A young boy clings around her waist, and in a panel on her plinth she pleads: "If you do not respect a banished queen, respect an unhappy mother." Louise of Savoie, regent of France, stands grimly nearby, her right forefinger pointing downward in a gesture of defiance. Anne Marie Louise of Orléans, duchesse de Montpensier, offers up her broad countenance to sorrow, while Clémence Isaure, melancholy of eye and with a crucifix on her breast, has the ample curves of a figure on an Indian temple. A little way off Jeanne d'Albret, queen of Navarre, adds a note of severity with the chain of office of an abbess hanging from her waist; Mary Stuart still has her crown and her head, and clasps a New Testament to her heart, while beside her Saint Geneviève, patron saint of Paris, makes female students jealous with the heavy tresses snaking over her breasts. Queen Mathilde, duchess of Normandy, leans on her huge sword. The enigmatic Saint Clothilde has the face of a Madonna above her crossed wrists, and is first on the path that leads past Marguerite of Provence; Anne of Brittany; Anne of Austria, still exalted; Blanche of Castille, still authoritarian; Anne of Beaujeu, a desolate and suspicious regent; Marguerite of Angoulême, a pensive beauty with one finger on her chin; and of course Marie de Médicis, the haughtiest of all and most majestic, lost in that forest of stone princesses.

"Marie de Médicis and her Day of Dupes. Can one be a mother without being fooled? Probably not, especially if you insist on acting like a queen."

Nearby the royal series gives way to Laure de Noves, most mysterious of women, ancestress of the marquis de Sade, with the serene grace of a woman who knows she is loved, a page of Petrarch inevitably in her hand, a lyrical eye bent on the dead leaves.

Alex saw nothing of this gallery of sovereigns, which intrigued only his mother: it was the smell of the petunias—an almost imperceptible mixture of milk and honey, with an afterthought of poppy—that intoxicated and enticed him. Suddenly he let go of the stroller he was pushing along all by himself and plunged across the grass toward the flower beds to pick some of the dark pink and purple trumpets.

"Come here, Alex—it's not allowed!"

Olga tried to catch him, but her son had already managed to grab a handful of what he wanted before starting back and falling down on the gravel. His knees were scraped, but his eye was triumphant.

"He can scarcely run, he keeps falling over, but he wants everything."

"Don't keep running to help him—leave him alone and let him hurt himself. How old is he? Two?"

Carole knew better than anyone else what was good or bad for children.

"No, no—only just one and a half. You're quite right, but I can't help it—I cling to him more than he clings to me."

Olga didn't know how to stop being overpossessive; and didn't want to. Alex had got hold of the stroller again and, having given up for now on the petunias, was pushing it along in front of him—until his next tumble. Olga refrained with difficulty from running after him: of course he ought to learn by experience, but was that a reason for letting him cover himself with grazes?

"I haven't seen Hervé in ages, except on television, of course. He's very good at seeming to have the worst of the argument, but getting in some good blows and making you forget everyone else."

"Do you know what's amusing him most at the moment, apart from Alex? He's translating *Finnegans Wake* with Ron Kelley, an English friend who used to be one of Bréhal's students. The thing is to invent the richest-sounding words, containing as much meaning as possible."

"I thought he was tied up with best-sellers and ideological discussions."

"Those too, but he can do several things at once. His best-sellers are full of melody and pictures, not to mention the mixture of wit and metaphysics. But people only remember the myth, and the reviews in the papers. If that!"

"I think he's changed a lot since the *Now* period. But the other day I heard him on the radio, something about the Middle East, and I thought he sounded quite straightforward again. He wouldn't let the interviewer draw him onto his own ground—he insisted on quoting a verse from the Bible: 'Love ye therefore the stranger: for ye were strangers in the land of Egypt.' "

"Hervé's in favor of anything that puts the cat among the pigeons, and if there's nothing to hand he invents something. He's not a politician, he's a spoiler, which means as often as not he's made into a scapegoat."

"I read his last novel, *French Pleasures*. That's certainly upset plenty of people!"

"So it seems."

"Well, nothing would have surprised me. But it was quite different from his earlier books. *Exodus*, for example—I liked that a lot!"

"And yet—"

"Let me finish. It's brilliant, certain, like a musical composition. Above all I was caught up in the plot. The narrator has something of the wicked aristocrat, I grant you—aggressive, crafty, a deceiver, a practical joker, a scoundrel. But all in all, a free spirit. He's a sly fox, is Hervé, and can use the same language as everyone else just to make fun of them—but in the end you see it's with the object of liberating them. After all, there is such a thing as the French character, isn't there? Bold, ironic. Provocative and attractive nobility, at war with all the world."

Carole was letting her enthusiasm run away with her.

"You said it! Guess what his latest craze is? He's got out his great-grandfather's swords and sabers and foils, and spends his time down in the cellar, polishing them and telling Alex stories of duels."

"I gather French brilliance doesn't go down very well abroad. I don't see why that mentality should be less interesting than that of my Wadanis, for example."

"That's very kind of you."

"No, no—I'm serious."

There are real, pearly wood pigeons in the Luxembourg, fat but ravenously hungry, which descend sometimes in dozens on the lawns, among the sparrows, and gobble down the breadcrumbs thrown to them by sentimental lovers who haven't yet got any children.

"Hey, are you wearing colors now?" (Olga had suddenly noticed that Carole, instead of being all in black as usual, was wearing a blue blouse.) "So you've finally . . ."

"I got it in a sale, that's all."

"That's all? What about Saint Bernard?"

"Saint Bernard? Oh, you remember the letters I wrote to you in Peking? Yes . . . well . . . He's too complicated, and too much like me. He knows too much about the body for a saint. Between the spirit and the power of darkness our flesh is supposed to be like a cow between a farmer and a thief. You see what I mean! I don't fancy being bothered by a cow! Joëlle Cabarus is good enough for me. . . . After all, there are mountains of books on theology, and I'm not sure my method, which is based on Strich-Meyer, adds anything really amusing."

"You sound as though you've hit on something, though. . . ."

"I don't know. . . . Did you hear about Scherner?"

"Just what it said in the paper, like everyone else."

"AIDS, apparently."

"I don't go out anymore, I live for Alex, I don't see anyone. It's true Scherner used to know Hervé. But that was years ago, when he was interested in literature. Since then no news, a sort of coolness. They were suspicious of each other. Perhaps because they could each imagine only too well how far the other would go."

"Well, I'm still loyal to him, if you can use that word about him. Since you mention work, I've been going over my notes, and Martin's too. The sex life of the Wadanis, but especially the women, in relation to the history of the body that Scherner started on."

"So are you going back to see the Wadanis again?"

"I don't know yet. I think so. Not right away, but it's all that's left for me to do, isn't it? Apart from walking in the Luxembourg with you . . ."

"You're becoming aggressive—that's a good sign! Cabarus must be pleased!"

"I don't ask for her advice, but I do see her still. I shan't see her so often if I go and see the Wadanis, though I have come to rely on her. . . ."

"No one would think so."

"You don't know anything about that sort of thing. You stick to your baby's bottle! Did you know Martin's in Paris?"

" . . . "

"A ghost. Transparent. But what courage! He's dying."

"Like Scherner?"

"Apparently. He doesn't give press conferences. All he says is that he wanted to see Saint-André-des-Arts again before he died. Nothing dramatic; frighteningly calm, like a ghost. He can't stand Marie-Paule's compliments anymore: 'You're the greatest genius of your generation, but you've always been persecuted by the media.' And so on. It used to work him up in the old days, but now he only gives a horrible laugh. What's new is that I feel beyond terror: like a stone statue on a grave not yet dug."

"But you *are* upset."

"If you like. But it's something else. I'm beyond it all, but at the same time completely with him. I think he's felt it, and that's why he comes to see me: to see the stone that will still be there after he is gone, a symbol of the pain which we went through together, and which survives.

Her deliberate, colorless lucidity was intolerable. Olga would have liked to weep in her stead, and might have done so but for Alex, who had taken advantage of their conversation to smear the contents of his bottle all over himself.

"You can see him if you like. I said I'd meet him at the Puppet Theater."

"Who?"

"Martin, of course! You're not frightened of him, I hope?"

The two women and the little boy were passing by the statues of wild animals and their prey: a lion, a stag, and Baudelaire, wedged in by the greenhouse and gazing at the railings at the entrance to the garden.

In the distance they could see the gaunt figure of Martin, elegant in black leather, his hair white with weariness. Thin as a corpse. A strained smile, meant to be jaunty but seeming to come from beyond the grave.

"Hi! If anyone had told me our head nomad would ever be a mother, I wouldn't have believed them. Is Hervé still going strong? Tell him I don't bear any grudge."

"What for?"

"What for? I ought to, really. But after all, everyone has the right to do himself in if he wants to, hasn't he? Not you, though—you haven't got the right anymore. You have to look after yourself for *him*. His name's Alex, isn't it? Hello, Alex!"

Imminent death gives people an indulgent smile that is an insult.

"I'm still a nomad. There is Alex now, of course. . . . But when he's three or four years old . . ."

"New York?"

"Among other places. China too, perhaps. And don't be deceived by appearances—we're still a bit Chinese."

"How do you mean?"

"I don't know. Standardized but tough. Sensitive but hardened. Rebels underneath our conformist look."

"Don't make me laugh! A real bourgeoise! Sorry—a real noble-woman!"

She didn't want to contradict him. What could she talk to him about? His painting, his plans, his pleasures, San Francisco? A life without relief, until he died. A long look of complicity: how long had they known each other—nearly twenty years? Saint-Michel, Bréhal's lectures, Strich-Meyer's lavender-gray Institute, the move to Hervé's attic, the barricades, the Maoists, painting, all the rest.

"I haven't lost sight of you, thanks to Carole." (Olga)

"I have been constant too, in my fashion. Here I am back at my point of departure before the great journey." (Martin)

"Right—we'd better be getting on. There are lots of things to be done before this evening." (Carole)

"Goodbye, my dear. Goodbye, young man." (Martin)

"Not so fast!" (Olga kissed him.)

Alex had thrown his bottle on the ground and was crying. People turned around: the poor little boy, howling his heart out, covered with dust and milk and tears. But Olga didn't hear anything.

Lunch in the Artist's Studio was no more. Manet's fair young man, with his striped cravat and crooked gaze fixed on a drama that ended in boredom, had vanished among the leaves of the Luxembourg without a trace. Except for the aloofness that refused all ties, or broke them, and wanted only death.

"Alex, Alex, there's nothing to cry about! You've only spilled your bottle—there are plenty more where that came from! Here . . . here's one. . . . You don't want it? You want me to pick you up? You're tired? All right, we'll go home now. . . . Yes, we overdid it a bit today."

he world of a small boy is full of noises, colored smells, flights. The sounds of motors: cars, planes, motorcycles, boats, the cries of grown-ups, dogs, and birds. They're so frightening it's good to repeat them, tame them, tyrannize over them, and above all manipulate their miniature versions—toys. Alex never tired of rubbing his little Darda automobiles against their red, blue, green, and yellow plastic launching pads: they then shot off until they came to the point at which the circuit was broken, when they did a "death-defying leap" and fell down on the other side, to whiz rainbow-like around the hairpin bends, triumphant, screeching, sparkling, stunning. The planes, which included some Concordes and NASA shuttles, zoomed deafeningly, breathing fire and fury, over the lawn. They were guided by electronic remote controls, but this was beyond an impatient little boy, and the flying machines always ended up stuck in the branches of the fir trees or fell sadly on the roofs. This meant tears, so everyone would clamber up and rescue the wrecks if possible, after which the operation would be repeated, with the same result as before. Olga didn't know whether to put it down to energy or obstinacy, but it was clear that a small boy's body was itself a kind of motor, a sound of joy or fury, and that Alex had an affinity for the external equivalents of the machine inside himself.

If circumstances bring you in contact with children's games, silly as they sometimes are, and as repetitive as the rhythm of a heart or sex, something of that clear and imperious life rubs off on you. Alex could only be distracted from mechanical amuse-ments by two things: the smell of flowers, and food. Crocuses were within his reach at ground level in the flower beds around the lawn, and when he was younger he used to put in his mouth the mauve and yellow and white and striped flowers that Jean de Montlaur had planted to please the eye. He made a beeline for the hyacinths with their much stronger scent, and would have become herbivorous if Olga hadn't vigorously discouraged it. Tulips were so many different animals or people: some were peacocks proudly displaying, the white-edged red ones were Pinocchios, and all were packed into trains and trucks as passen-gers to unknown destinations. Alex, without any brothers or sisters, seemed quite content to see flowers as companions, and also, Olga suspected, to regard companions, and also, Olga suspected, to regard companions as flowers. Too bad if the game deprived them of sap; weren't they being made part of another dream?

But everyone knows that greed is a sign of life. If you're hungry you're in good form. The house on the island was full of the smell of Germaine's traditional cooking, of dishes she might take days to prepare. To the ear of the little boy, the stairs up to Father's mill crackled like a croissant. Mother was crisp and soft as an apple tart. But all these paled into insignificance and were forgotten when the smell of a quiche invaded the *mas*—that emblem of family unity, with its combination of rich pastry, melted cheese, and smoked ham, to which Germaine added slices of sausage for extra flavor. It was Alex's idea of heaven.

"He's got very masculine tastes for such a little boy," said Mathilde. "This is our home—who cares what anyone else thinks?" Hervé told Alex, thinking to sum up his son's sentiments. Alex, his mouth full of quiche, lisped his father's words again as best he could.

Simple things are never easy when you discover them late in life, or retrospectively. Suppose you've spent twenty, thirty, or forty years of your life among words and ideas, libraries and debates, books and traveling. You've become quick-thinking, lucid, decisive, disillusioned, broken and repaired, sharp, blunt, flexible but thick-skinned, sensitive but adaptable, immune from anguish and depression, yet secretly cultivating their latent, suave, and well-controlled sources. And then a little boy who was a baby but is now growing up, sometimes too slowly, sometimes too fast, starts to open your eyes, your ears, your skin. He has a character and you are part of it. He does something silly and you are part of that. He gives an innocent laugh and you are part of that too.

The waves soundlessly smooth the sand, and recede with the same joyous unobtrusiveness as butterflies wooing flowers and leaving no trace. There comes a time when you can stand and stare at that kind of thing. And at a child trembling as the butterfly wave withdraws: is it going to sweep him out to sea? But he digs his heels bravely in the sand, waiting to see what happens when the wave comes in again before he runs crying to his mother.

People find simple little things like that trivial, ridiculous, or touching. But seen from a certain angle, or in retrospect—after the blows that had undermined Carole and Martin, that had carried off Bréhal, Lauzun, Scherner, Edelman, and others, and that were always destabilizing Olga and Hervé (but such pitching and tossing is permanent, a fact of life)—touching, ridiculous, and trivial little things become full of meaning. One always tends to see them externally, and that lightens them and brings out their basic innocence. Yet one also sees them from within, from their heart, previously neglected and now suddenly revealed: and this makes them solemn and memorable. Take Alex launching his Dardas and his Concordes as he eats his hyancinths and quiches, and mustering up his courage when the cold waves threaten him. That's nothing much, perhaps. Completely ordinary. But by liberating a time hitherto left aside, it awakens a melody within you: a misty yellow mountain with a log cabin on top; Mother coming out of the forest drenched with dew and carrying mushrooms that will be cooked in butter; Father, rosy and smiling, walking up the mountainside with his backpack, bringing butter, cookies and grapes enough for a week. It's desperately ordinary and beautiful, and it doesn't mean anything, eating fried mushrooms and listening to the rain, it's only an image that makes something last, from the dew on Mother's hair to Alex's greedy mouth, something that's a personal time, a rebirth, and that puts you there on the Atlantic beach, quite wise, quite old, quite childish, but strong. . . .

But François de Montlaur didn't go in for digressions. Since Jean's death he had taken charge, run the business, and quite naturally added the role of grandfather to that of great-uncle.

"This child will be a sailor, like our ancestors. Only as a hobby, of course . . . So he must learn to swim." (François was modern and practical.) "These days they teach children to swim before they're a year old."

So there was Alex, with various inflated devices bearing him up, following his uncle, in rather cold water and out of his depth, to see who'd be first to reach the boat, anchored some distance away.

"This is crazy—you're too far out and the water's freezing!"

"Tomorrow we'll take away one of the belts and a month from now you'll be swimming properly, all on your own!"

"Not in a month—now!"

And Alex took advantage of this opportunity to slip out of the too-tight life belt Olga had made him wear.

"I love them all the same." (Mathilde was continuing her internal monologue aloud.) "All my grandchildren are exactly alike to me—I couldn't say I loved one more than another. I treat Alex and Isabelle's two little girls exactly alike, you know, Olga."

Olga knew Mathilde was trying to disguise the very difference she did make. Her daughter's children were always at the Mont-laurs—they had to be brought up in a manner that the Duval family certainly couldn't provide. And despite the distance between their mother and herself, Mathilde was really fond of the two little girls. "People say they're like me. What do you think, Olga dear? I can't tell, myself." And now she had to get used to little Alex: he was rather sweet, and he brought back memories of Hervé's childhood; it was too much, Mathilde was really very tenderhearted deep down, but she must pull herself together and not be silly. François was doing very well, but how Jean would have loved to be Alex's grandpa. Mathilde went on knitting, it calms you down, but still, why didn't she sing Alex some old songs, he learns very fast, I think he's got a gift for music.

When Alex was still an infant, Hervé—who hated babies, especially those that howled—discovered the one way to soothe him. He would pick him up and dance with him, twirling round and round, hopping about a little, then doing so more and more rhythmically, energetically, and comically. There were two tunes that seemed to do the trick best: "My heart Sighs" and "Viva le Femmine." As soon as Hervé got to the words, "if it's with love," Alex stopped crying, and by the third time he was sure to be asleep. "*Il buon vino,*" on the other hand, sung in an exaggerated bass, seemed to tickle him, and at the highest point of "*Sosten e gloria de l'umanità*" he would burst out laughing and keep asking to hear it again.

But Hervé had other things to do, so as Alex showed a penchant for repetition and you can't have too much of a good thing, Sinteul recorded on cassette his repertoire of rather unusual lullabies. Alex soon learned to press the right buttons: children are born knowing about electronics these days, and all day long you could hear the strains of *Figaro* and *Don Giovanni*, alternating with a *Magnificat, Deposuit potentes et exaltavit humilies.* Like all those with inquiring minds, Alex had a predilection for what he could't understand, and started to repeat the Latin words, hopping from syllable to syllable as spryly as a tightrope walker. "*Gloria, gloria patri et filio!*" he would chirp, singing along with the cassette, thinking about his father, whom he didn't see all that much, and meaning Olga to hear, if she was around, and be reminded that she wasn't the only one.

But that particular day Hervé had some time to spare. No
need to bother with the cassette. They were going to try something else.

"Look, Alex, We each take a stick, like this. No, not a twig,
a real stick—it's meant to be your sword. Stand firmly on your
feet, lean forward a little, and you feel all your strength concentrated and ready to spring. There under your navel is the 'sea of
breath': you dive in and stay there—it's the source of energy,
your center. So much for concentration. Now you have to let
out a yell—loud and raucous, like this: 'Aaaaaa!' Don't be frightened, it's only a game, and don't laugh either. The shout pre-
pares the way for the attack, and intimidates the enemy. The
enemy here is me, or you, depending on the point of view. You
lunge forward now, but be careful—you have to prevent my
saber from touching you, and at the same time try to hit me in a
place I've forgotten to protect. Complicated? Just you wait and
see! But that's what the game's all about: concentration, protection, and attack. Got it? Then off we go!"

For Alex the yell seemed to be the easiest part of the business.
As for attack and defense, they soon broke down into shouts of
laughter. The "swords" got broken, there were a few scratches,
but Alex took up his original position again and got ready to
give another bellow.

"You'll hurt each other with those sticks—can't you think of
something else to do?" (Olga)

"We won't use the sticks anymore. Tomorrow, when we've
got a better idea of distance, we'll play with our bare hands. Our
arms and hands will be our sabres. Okay, Alex?" (Hervé)

"Let's do it again." (Alex)

"Start slowly and calmly." (Hervé)

"I don't want to go slow." (Alex)

"You're wrong. 'All is done without doing anything.' The
winner is calm. But his calm contains all the millions of movements you have to consider before you actually make one. The
decisive one." (Hervé)

"All that's much too complicated for a child. And pointless.
Who do you want to fight, Alex?" (Olga)

"Everyone fights at kindergarten." (Alex)

"You see? You'll show 'em at break, and anyhow, you'll know

it for yourself: judge the distances and choose your moment. You get the strength you need if you concentrate and know your limits. Learn to know your own limits, and those of other people." (Hervé)

Olga was afraid Alex might get hurt, for Hervé never played, he always forgot about pretending and attacked for real. Never mind, Alex would learn by experience, and learn to play seriously too. His mother had sometimes played tennis as if it were a martial art. So teaching him *budo* fit right in. But one must find simple words, children's words, to explain to him what samurais were. Fairy stories perhaps, like "The Three Little Pigs" or "Tom Thumb," but stranger, more energetic, lighter, more violent, more soothing too. She ought to invent a story so that Alex could fit present-day words to the little drama of primitive elegance his father was teaching him, which made him laugh and hop about but which he probably didn't understand. Like a foreign word that concentrates all your dreams and energies in one place so that you can think of them when you lie awake at night, without seeing any connection between it and you and your days, your relations and your friends. But there must be a link, because of the pleasure and anguish it gives you there in the dark. I ought to make up a story to go with the game, thought Olga. She didn't like sitting down and doing nothing.

July 1988

Romain says we don't do enough things together. And he's found something we can do: flying. It's very fashionable. You fly a plane the same way you drive your car, but you take off into the air, and this liberation from weight is at once so enormous and so risky I feel as if I were going to meet the sun, and death. Something we can do together? No. Even when we fly together I'm concentrating on the plane, I'm close to the dashboard, it talks to me like a patient, but I certainly don't think of Romain for a moment, absolutely not, you need a cool head and reliable reflexes for flying. Alone with the engine, both frightened and intoxicated by its rhythm, its throbbing, its soaring. And finally, when it has carried me high enough, by the feeling that nothing is moving anymore, that I'm at the critical point where speed becomes repose. No, flying doesn't bring me close to Romain. What it gives me is the experience of being at the outer limit of existence; the experience of utmost energy on the brink of utmost danger.

"It must be like an analysis to you: close attention combined with absolute aloofness," Romain says. He thinks I reduce everything to the one subject. He's not altogether wrong.

But for once I do feel I'm doing something different. I fly as some people do yoga, nerves and muscles tensed in order to touch the void. Irrational physical fulfillment and yet total thought. Controlled acting out. And an empty voluptuousness, the solar solitude of nothing.

"Still trying to kill yourself?" Arnaud asks, with a metaphysical double-entendre meant to bring his mockery home.

"It's not a game!"

Romain becomes detached through passion. Playing at love and death, but lightly, as if it was a game. Arnaud keeps his feet on the ground, though, and is devoted to his job and to Jessica. If he so much as mentions his daughter he becomes almost ugly with anxiety and hope.

We've just landed. An intoxication infinitely more lofty than that of explorers of the sea. The ordinariness of the technique comes into it too: not really difficult, but revealing our vanity and littleness.

In a moment, happiness could turn into nothingness. So what?

Afterward, a flat, rational happiness. Enthusiasm brings disillusion.

October 1988

Jessy's going in for political journalism. Foreign politics, of course. She spends her time hanging around newspaper offices or meeting "people."

"The office is a good place for finding out you've got everything wrong, and for meeting people."

She seems very taken by some of these "people." Especially Sinteuil. Is it just a passing attraction, or more? I tease her.

"I thought you were keen on Dalloway."

"No," she says. "You don't understand. Dalloway's always thinking about his wife, who left him to go to Jerusalem, and he's in love with Olga Montlaur. But above all he's a professional—he's only interested in his international law."

"So?"

"Sinteuil's different. He's incomprehensible. He knows how to talk to women, he's in love with everything, or rather with nothing. He reads what you've written and makes weird comments on it. Irresistible, don't you think?"

What should I do? She wants to be fooled, while knowing all the time she's being taken in. I can only leave her to learn from experience. After all, her love affairs will never be anything like mine.

December 15, 1988

Everyone's busy preparing for the Bicentenary of the Revolution. And Jessy and Arnaud have suddenly remembered Thérésa Cabarrus and started taking my elucubrations seriously. Jessy's looking for the notes I took once in the enfer *at the Bibliothèque Nationale. I wonder where I put all that stuff. Some of it must have got into my Journal, but I can't let her see that. Besides, Thérésa will always be just a courtesan, no connection with the greatness they see nowadays in Olympe de Gouge's feminism or even Théroigne de Méricourt's psychosis. But she suits me well enough, our ancestress. Revolution through Eroticism, unbridled Sex versus the Reason of the goddess Terror. And, finally, reconciliation, the debased era of people who eat, drink, and are merry after other people have shed their blood and seen their ideas trodden underfoot. Thérésa, that undistinguished but successful seductress, decapitated several myths: the myth of Great Ideas, and the romantic myth of Love, though both in fact survived her.*

Is the present the age of living without myths? If so, Jessy hasn't learned the art of it. Out of her myth-less youth she creates an artificial myth. She loves and suffers, but pretends it's all a game. I don't believe her. Arrogance is the myth of people who have no more myths.

February 12, 1989

Everyone's hovering around the sacred. Some in order to believe in it, others to see what it's made of. The sacred is a myth in action. Carole is getting back in touch with it by going off to dismantle the Wadani myths. In fact, what she's going to do is feed off the illusions of others. "Tinkering" is her myth, she's not depressed anymore, but when she gets back from her explorations, we shall both go on looking for the meaning of her illusions.

Meanwhile I'm finishing Sanctuary. *Faulkner's right: the only sanctuary we have left is a word of sorrow lined with pain. The novel celebrates but also debunks this last myth by showing how stupid and mawkish it can be:*

> *Three weeks after her marriage, she had begun to ail. She was pregnant then. She did not go to a doctor, because an old negro woman told her what was wrong. Popeye was born on the Christmas day on which the*

card was received. At first they thought he was blind. Then they found that he was not blind, though he did not learn to walk and talk until he was about four years old. In the meantime, the second husband of her mother, an undersized, snuffy man with a mild, rich moustache . . . left home one afternoon with a check signed in blank to pay a twelve dollar butcher's bill. He never came back. He drew from the bank his wife's fourteen hundred dollar savings account, and disappeared.

. . . Popeye was three years old then. He looked about one, though he could eat pretty well. . . .

It gives me professional pleasure to copy this out: it's like the record card of a delinquent, the history of a borderline case.

But Popeye was gone. On the floor lay a wicker cage in which two lovebirds lived; beside it lay the birds themselves, and the bloody scissors with which he had cut them up alive.

. . . He had cut up a half-grown kitten the same way . . .

"While he was on his way home that summer they arrested him for killing a man in one town and at an hour when he was in another town killing someone else . . .

The whole story is impossible, crazy. The novel itself becomes insane so that we may share the myth of madness. The book is pitiless and debilitating, but not like analysis. It lends beauty to mental deficiency and crime by making them inspire pity and fear. The novel itself becomes a private sanctuary. So does analysis. But it doesn't beautify. It teaches me to be benevolently vigilant about my own stupid crime. Sound and fury—the heart of being is always a death-wish. Make a sanctuary out of that, if you like, but don't legalize it, and be vigilant. When a sanctuary is no longer tragically beautiful but merely childish, is it still a sanctuary?

March 6, 1989

I'm in the midst of a blue day, a blue spring, a solar year. As I went through the Luxembourg Gardens on my way to have a cup of tea in Dalloyau's, I could smell the chocolate buns the young women in T-shirts were giving their children, the scent of new-mown grass, and the almost imperceptible but intoxicating presence of the books that have been, are being, or will be read in the nearby library, or here on a green chair in the sun.

The quaint statues of the queens, with their ridiculous poses, led me to the pond, where young fathers were sailing sophisticated boats guided by remote control. The signals were getting mixed up, and so, out of reach, were the boats. To the dismay of the children, bathed at once in the peaceful afternoon light and angry tears.

Loud bangs and crashes drew me toward the bandstand, where an orchestra was giving a clumsy rendering of The Firebird. After a while I gave up trying to find a seat. With senile malice, some of the old men who share the Luxembourg with the mothers snatched a series of chairs from under my nose. Stravinsky's music, primitive and mystical, frightened the pigeons and children away, but I stood leaning against a chestnut tree, dissolved by the burning accents of the brasses, the rush of the strings, and the cruelty of winds blowing straight from the Russian steppes, where the heart of a young hero is torn out to lighten the darkness of the simple-minded. But no, it isn't a heart, it's only a feather plucked out, but the bird shrieks, I can hear it, it's on fire, it whirls around wildly until the savage strength of its dance overwhelms the grotesque and savage horde. Deliverance, jubilation from princesses submerged by cymbals and strident strings.

It was as if the blue light of day were being swamped with ocher and red; the cool of the flowering branches could not quell the furious sound of that infernal music. I looked for a quieter corner: moved by some memory of the Luxembourg from Daudet's Le Petit Chose, I think. It was my first reading book: a little boy scuffs his way obediently through the dust and faded leaves of a windy autumn day to do some work he's carrying in his satchel.

There, between a Marie de Médicis and a Laure de Noves of weathered marble, I saw two thespians: Sinteuil and his son playing at martial arts. The glints of this blue spring lent the would-be samurais a bright, exotic look. The little boy imitated the war cry of an ancient warrior, no doubt imagining himself in Japanese costume, and the father and son's strange mixture of caricature and tenderness filled me with such surprise and emotion that I stopped a moment and watched. My imagination transported them into a theater of Japanese ghosts wearing makeup, perfume, and masks of metal and leather, pathetic in their brave melancholy, fragile as women; poets and musicians as well as actors, but here and now playing and fighting fiercely under the mystical eye of Laure de Noves.

For the rest of us, dreamers in this world, the Oriental warriors regarded life as fleeting: a boat upon the waves. And in the clear light of the Luxembourg, dazzling in the morning dew but amber in the afternoon, war was only a game, and the cry of the transfixed samurai a joke that made little Alex sing with delight. The father pretended to adjust his mask, to suffer but to master his pain and return to the attack. They were playing at being tragic. The emerald reflections of the leaves and flowers made them seem strangely distant from the still lifes of the sculptured queens, lending them a kind of life, but only that of ghosts. The blue spring would not grow dark today, the peaceful sky protected the *players inside their play, ringed by light and laughter. So that's what we'd come to: civilization was a memory that could turn life and death into a game.*

April 10, 1989

"Have you seen the ad in today's Monde? Olga Montlaur's just written a children's book! What a surprise, eh?" (Jessy)

"I should think so! What's it called?" (Me)

"The Samurais. She must be kidding! Writing children's stories after all that intellectual pretentiousness!" (Jessy, jealous)

I can see her point of view. It is the limit. But of what? Perhaps, when you get right down to it, all literature is really for children. They say nearly all novels are bought by women. I'd say by child-women and child-men. It takes a talent for innocent reverie to create emotion still out of those wrinkled old signs we call words. And after all, perhaps it's only worth bothering to write in order to rewrite the game of life and death for children—the children we forget that we ourselves are. Some live, some die, and the child-adults tell one another artificial stories so as not to die while they're still alive. Telling stories for children shows enormous humility. This Journal seems intolerably narcissistic in comparison.

September 1989

A telegram to tell me of Father's sudden death. Heart attack. I was expecting it. But I also thought he would live forever. I thought I was hardened, but I'm shattered. My day is adult, but my night is a weeping child. Neither Romain's flying nor Arnaud's serenity, "reassuring" as ever, can help me. The worst is the memories. I can still see him sitting on a bench in the Luxembourg with a music box, to amuse me. He said he did it to help Mother, but in fact he loved me like a mother himself. I can still hear his voice. I can hear it all the time, denying death: rather hoarse, a little childish when he talks to me, to be on my level, but slightly stringent as well to urge me on to better things. Despite, and through, the suffering it brings, memory is a dreadful joy. It alternates with the naked, empty feeling of "never more." "Never more" is incompatible with thought, which always tries to connect, to advance. "Never more": finished, impossible. The feeling of weary anguish comes and goes. He has reached the sun, and the moment when all becomes nothing. I shan't go flying anymore. And writing seems wrong and pretentious too.

Perhaps one day I'll write a story for my father, bringing together all the fragments of my ruined memory. You never know. But not today. I must hide

this notebook. On days like this, the still blue light of the blue autumn in a
year imperturbably solar makes any personal confessions seem cruel and
stupid. Or rather, insignificant. Unless . . .

Joëlle Cabarus put her journal away in her desk, locked it, put
the key in her pocket, and went out into the dusty amber light
under the trees. The shiny dark chestnuts glowed amid the
boughs.

"Mother, where are you going? . . . Father, Joëlle's just gone
out without saying anything—she's floating along like a dead
leaf." (Jessica)

"You know your mother has her little ways. They include
appointments with time." (Arnaud)

The Luxembourg clock struck half-past four. A boat was stuck
in the middle of the pond, out of reach. Alex was pretending to
be inconsolable. But the wind soon gets up in these blue fall
days, and ships marooned are sometimes blown safely back to
those who know how to wait.